A gift of the
Eunice Gray Fund
of the
Oregon Community Foundation

JACKSON COUNTY
Library Services

deadly devotion

Center Point
Large Print

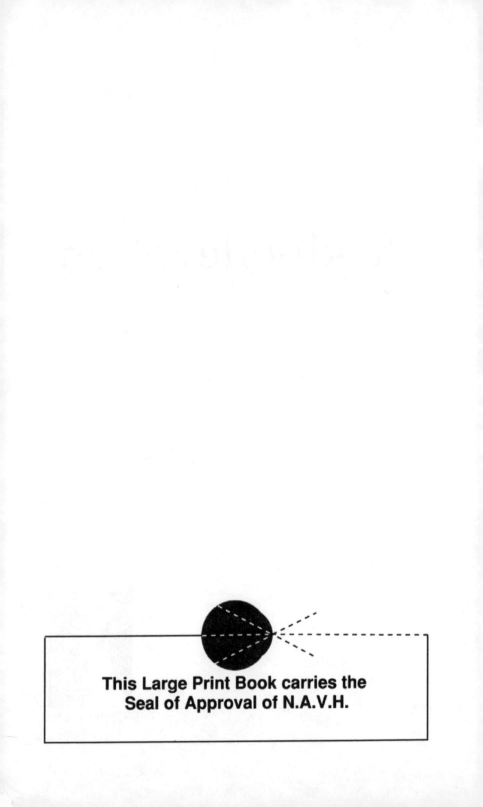

This Large Print Book carries the
Seal of Approval of N.A.V.H.

Port Aster Secrets • Book 1

deadly
devotion

SANDRA ORCHARD

CENTER POINT LARGE PRINT
THORNDIKE, MAINE

The text of this Large Print edition is unabridged. In other
aspects, this book may vary from the original edition.
Printed in the United States of America
on permanent paper.
Set in 16-point Times New Roman type.

ISBN: 978-1-61173-790-5

Library of Congress Cataloging-in-Publication Data

Orchard, Sandra.
Deadly devotion / Sandra Orchard. — Center Point Large print edition.
pages ; cm.
ISBN 978-1-61173-790-5 (library binding : alk. paper)
1. Female friendship—Fiction. 2. Herbalists—Crimes against—Fiction.
3. Suicide—Fiction. 4. Large type books. I. Title.
PR9199.4.O73D33 2013b
813'.6—dc23

2013009783

For my husband, Michael—who believes in me so much, he's not the least bit worried to find me thumbing through a *Book of Poisons* at the kitchen counter.

Acknowledgments

Writing this book has been an amazing adventure, and I have many people to thank for that. When I first met several of these people, the meetings truly felt like divine appointments, and I am so grateful to the Lord for his blessings.

I'd like to thank Beth Adams for urging me to expand my idea from a single story into a series. That process made the town and people of Port Aster come alive to me in wonderful and unanticipated ways.

Thank you to Wenda Dottridge, Laurie Benner, Vicki McCollum, and Susan May Warren for their insightful suggestions at the critiquing stage.

Thank you to the NRP officers who answered all my police questions, and some I forgot to ask.

Thank you to my daughter Christine for opening the world of horticulture to me through her expertise and experience.

Thank you to Joyce Hart for continuing to believe in this series when I was ready to leave it to warm a drawer.

Thank you to Nancy and Manuela for sharing herbal remedies that inspired fun twists in the plot.

Thank you to the awesome team at Revell, especially to my editor Vicki Crumpton for championing the story; to Vicki, Wendy Wetzel, and the proofreaders for helping me polish it until it shined; to Twila Bennett, Cheryl Van Andel, and the art department for their awesome work on the cover; to Michele Misiak for answering all my questions; and to the awesome marketing departments both at Revell and at David C. Cook here in Canada.

Thank you to my family for their incredible support.

And most of all, thank you to you, my readers. With more books than ever vying for your time these days, I feel truly honored that you chose to spend a few hours reading *Deadly Devotion*.

deadly devotion

1

Kate Adams slammed the Port Aster weekly onto Detective Parker's desk and jabbed at the headline blazed in one-inch letters: HERBAL RESEARCHER'S DEATH RULED SUICIDE.

"How could you let the editor print this?"

Parker frowned at the headline, muttered into the phone wedged between his shoulder and ear, then pressed the Hold button. "Have a seat, Miss Adams." He motioned to the chair facing his desk.

"Don't you *Miss Adams* me. There is no way Daisy killed herself." Kate drilled her finger into the newsprint. "I demand you reopen this case."

The roomful of officers fell silent. Parker, his gaze direct and unflinching, seemed to measure her resolve before gesturing to them to go about their business.

Let them gawk. She didn't care. The more people who knew about the injustice done to her friend, the better. Thanks to the cramped quarters, they'd hear what she had to say whether Parker liked it or not.

Except that when Parker returned his attention to Kate, he regarded her with such sympathy that

11

her courage faltered. She dropped into the chair and tucked her trembling hands under her legs.

Parker read the article while she chewed her bottom lip into mincemeat over her grandstanding tactics. Maybe she hadn't needed to come in with guns blazing to get someone to listen, to care enough to find Daisy's killer.

Around them, the buzz of conversations resumed as if nothing had changed.

But something *had* changed.

Her friend's good name had been smeared for the whole town to see. And the police had given up on finding the real cause of her death.

A radio crackled and Kate's insides jitter-bugged like Mexican jumping beans. She empathized with the toddler at a desk near the door, burrowing against his mother's chest. The squad room, crowded with more than a dozen desks and twice as many people, wasn't exactly a picture of the peace the police were paid to keep.

Kate drew in a wobbly breath and focused on the man she needed to win over. He didn't seem to fit with the other officers milling about the room, dressed in their dark blue uniforms, faces stern. Of course, his sympathetic expression might be a ploy to placate her. In his charcoal suit jacket and striped tie, Parker looked like he belonged in a boardroom, not a police station, although his chiseled good looks likely charmed the most resistant of suspects into cooperating.

He set the newspaper aside. "I'm sorry you had to hear the news this way."

The quiet compassion in his voice buoyed her determination. "The story's not true. You have to make the editor print a retraction."

"As the article explains, our report simply stated the poisoning was self-inflicted." Parker turned the newspaper facedown, removing the painful article from her view. "The sensationalized headline is inexcusable."

"My friend didn't kill herself," Kate repeated, hating the way her voice hitched. "Accidentally or otherwise."

"Your loyalty is admirable, but as a research scientist, you should understand better than most that we deal in facts."

Kate stared at his desktop. Memos, files, empty coffee cups, a gum wrapper, even a pair of handcuffs lay like strewn rubble. The debris of a man caught in the daily skirmishes of the war against crime. No wonder he'd written Daisy off—forgotten her.

But facts?

Kate clenched her fists. The facts didn't add up in the least. "Consider these facts, Detective. Daisy Leacock was an expert botanist. She would no more confuse a calendula with a tagete than you'd mistake a water gun for a pistol."

The muscle in Parker's stony jaw worked back and forth as if he were grinding his response between his teeth. He drew a file folder from his desk drawer. Daisy's name had been printed neatly across the tab.

The contrast to his messy desktop caught Kate by surprise. Not that neat handwriting meant Parker cared. To him, Daisy was just another case.

To think that during the interview following Daisy's death he'd been kind, even compassionate. Clearly, she'd mistaken professional interrogation techniques for genuine empathy. Anyone who would let the newspaper defame the dead like this didn't know the meaning of the word.

"I'm afraid your friend's expertise makes the evidence all the more irrefutable." Parker handed her a report. "As you can read, the coroner found no evidence of trauma to the body. Only elevated levels of this toxin." Parker pointed to a scientific name.

"Thiophene," Kate pronounced the term for him. "Found in marigolds."

"That's right. Miss Leacock's nephew said she often drank a variety of herbal teas."

"Yes, but thiophene is a phototoxic chemical, which means Daisy should have suffered nothing worse than painful skin blisters." Kate searched the report for details that might point to another cause of death. "The coroner noted the presence of hemorrhaging."

"Yes."

"But that's not a typical reaction to photo-toxins."

"Nevertheless, he is the expert."

"How'd he find the thiophene? It wouldn't be identified by a routine tox screen."

Parker tapped a pen on his ink blotter in the rapid-fire *tit-a-tat* of someone whose patience had worn thin. "We provided him a list of the dried plants stored in the house, which included a half-empty jar of dried marigolds."

"Did you identify them?" Kate doubted Parker knew the difference between a marigold and a mum, let alone between the toxic varieties and the ones used as herbs.

"Yes." Parker stabbed his pen into its holder. "Most of the flowers were calendula, the beneficial variety that perhaps Miss Leacock had intended to use. However, some tagetes were mixed in."

Kate winced. Okay, maybe he did know the difference. So if the cops could figure out the mix wasn't pure, why hadn't Daisy?

Unless someone planted the dried flowers in her kitchen—after she died. Except . . . she had the toxin in her system. "The coroner must have missed something. One or two cups of the wrong tea might make Daisy light-headed, maybe even nauseated, but the dose wouldn't kill her."

"I concede you know more about the effects of these plants than I do, but the coroner was

15

satisfied that enough toxin was present in Miss Leacock's bloodstream to suppress her breathing." Parker glanced tiredly into each of the three coffee cups sitting on his desk, stacked them, and chucked them into a wastebasket.

Kate pulled the report to her side of the desk and flipped through the pages. "You're saying the toxin paralyzed her lungs? She couldn't breathe? How do you know someone didn't hold a pillow over her face?"

"There was no evidence of a struggle, and she'd vomited. The toxin caused her death." Parker's gaze flicked to the flashing red light on his phone. "The toxin. Not suffocation."

"Daisy had access to more than half a dozen herbs that kill within minutes. Why would she poison herself with one that made her sick for hours before succumbing?"

Parker studied Kate for so long she started to feel like one of the specimens under her microscope. He took back the file. "What makes you think Daisy was murdered?"

"She. Didn't. Kill. Her. Self." Kate's voice cracked. She glanced away. "Daisy wouldn't have. God meant everything to her. She never would have taken her own life. Never."

"I understand that you want to believe that."

"It's true." Kate blinked hard to stave off tears.

Parker reached across the desk, and the warm pressure of his fingers on her arm almost undid

16

her. "I understand how you feel," he said softly. "I lost my mother not so long ago. Denial is the first natural stage of grief."

Kate's gaze snapped to his. This was not about her grief. "If your mom's name was in this headline, would you sit here and let a cop tell you the case is closed?"

"No." Parker withdrew his hand. "I suppose not."

For a moment he stared at the back page of the newspaper, and she thought she glimpsed a muscle twitch in his cheek as if her words had found a crack in his stoic demeanor.

Then he glanced past her and the moment evaporated. "I assure you, we conducted a thorough investigation."

She turned to see what had caught his attention and found the chief of police leaning against the door frame of his office, watching them. She rounded on Detective Parker. "I'm not interested in your double-talk. Are you going to find Daisy's killer or not?"

"The case has been closed."

"If you won't investigate, I will."

"I can't stop you." Parker's lips pinched tighter than her snakeskin pumps. "As long as you don't break the law."

He didn't have to say what he'd do if she broke the law. His tone made his threat abundantly clear. And affirmed every apprehension she'd

17

ever had about cops . . . since the day one stole her dad.

She tried to believe the best about everyone she met—even Parker's kind—but when he extended an open palm across his desk like a benevolent minister, she had to wonder if the gesture was another manipulative technique to gain her trust.

"We found no evidence of a struggle," he repeated, apparently still hoping to convince her to let this go. He thumbed through the pages in the file. "Daisy's nephew didn't think anything was missing from her home, which ruled out robbery."

From the doorway, the woman with the toddler blurted, "Please don't make me go out there. He'll come after me again. I know he will." Her child whimpered.

The sound twisted in Kate's chest and left a bitterness in her throat. Another victim let down by the system.

Parker, evidently as oblivious to that woman's torment as he was to her own, peeled a business card from the holder on his desk. He jotted something on the back and pressed the card into her hand. "If you can give me a reason to suspect foul play, I'll look into it. That's my cell number."

Taken aback by the gesture, for a moment Kate could only stare at the bold strokes he'd penned. So maybe he wasn't completely oblivious, but . . .

She crumpled the card in her fist. "I've given you reasons."

"If your friend was murdered"—he held up a hand—"I'm not suggesting she was. But *if* she was, why would you risk your neck to go after a killer?"

"Because she believed in me." When no one else had. Kate shoved Parker's card into her pocket. "Daisy risked her career to get me hired at the research facility. If not for her guidance and friendship, I'd still be waiting tables at the tea shop."

"But you must see that your reasons for thinking she couldn't have killed herself are based on who you thought she was. Nothing else." He bit off the words and looked away. When his eyes met hers again, they were filled with pity. "One thing you learn in my line of work is that people are rarely what they seem."

Kate sprang to her feet and braced her fingers on his desktop. "Well, in my world, Detective, people stand by their friends. I won't rest until I find out who murdered Daisy. With or without your help."

Tom Parker flicked off the recorder next to his phone and watched Kate Adams stomp away, her long red curls flouncing in her wake. If Daisy Leacock had known what a loyal friend she'd had, perhaps she wouldn't have killed herself.

He closed the case file and shoved it back

19

into the drawer. Despite Kate's anger, he'd heard the tremble in her voice, seen the red in her eyes, and almost felt sorry for her. But the last thing he needed was a maverick challenging his competency. He'd landed the coveted detective position from outside the force, so he already had enough rabble-rousers on *that* bandwagon.

Miss Adams let the door slam behind her, and two or three of the guys snickered in his direction. The chief silenced them with a glare, then, with a coffee in each hand, sauntered to Tom's desk like a cowboy who'd spent too many hours in the saddle. His gait was about the only thing that hadn't changed in the fifteen years Tom had been away from his hometown.

Tom couldn't get used to the idea of Hank Brewster being his boss. In their teen years, Hank had always looked to Tom for help out of a scrape. Now, since returning to Canada after his ill-fated stint south of the border, Tom was the one looking for favors.

Hank passed him a steaming mug. "She didn't like the coroner's report, huh?"

"I'm sure Miss Adams would have had an easier time accepting the facts if the newspaper hadn't sensationalized the story."

Hank took a long draw on his coffee. "Don't know about that."

Yeah. Tom knew firsthand how hard accepting the facts could be. Especially when the facts

20

contradicted what he'd thought to be true.

Leaving his own coffee untouched, Tom walked to the window and surveyed the parking lot. Kate climbed into a yellow VW Beetle. Five feet four inches of pure loyalty. Would she be able to handle the disillusionment when she finally faced the fact that her friend died by her own hand?

The sun glinted off Kate's fiery hair, reminding him of the spark he'd seen in her determined green eyes. She had the grit to tackle just about anything life threw her way.

When he'd interviewed her after Leacock's death, Kate had spoken of her friend in glowing terms—from her expertise in the field to her heartfelt faith. The faith part had stuck in his mind because for a moment, a look of pure joy had pushed the grief from her eyes. Or maybe because he'd recognized something he'd lost.

Joy. The reminder stung.

Given Kate's faith and unwavering belief in her friend's expertise, was it any wonder she'd refused to accept the coroner's verdict? Tom's gaze drifted skyward. Clouds floated across the blue expanse like giant puffballs. He'd forgotten how serene Port Aster's patch of sky always seemed. Unlike DC, where most of the time the gray sky had been crammed with thunderheads.

Hank clapped him on the shoulder. "She got to you, huh?"

Tom shrugged off Hank's hand. "It's been a

while since I felt as certain about anything as Miss Adams seems to be. One thing she said made a lot of sense. If Daisy wanted to kill herself, why didn't she take a faster-acting poison?"

"You think the coroner is wrong?"

A radio squawked and two officers hustled out the door. Until Kate had flinched at every sound, Tom hadn't realized how well he ignored the racket around here. What else might he have ignored?

He turned on Hank. "I think the coroner is a young hotshot trying to get his name in the paper, because I sure didn't leak this report. Did you?"

Hank squared his shoulders and dropped the jovial tone. "Watch it. I'm the boss now. PR decisions are mine to make. And you can't afford to be on my bad side."

Tom slumped into his seat. Not only had Hank stuck his neck out to get Tom this job, but Tom had pulled the lone ranger routine one too many times for the FBI to take him back into active duty anytime soon. If he burned his bridges here, he'd be walking security duty at Walmart.

Hank scooped up the newspaper and tossed it into the trash can. "Forget her. You have enough to deal with between open cases and your dad."

"Dad!" Remembering that he'd put his dad on hold, Tom grabbed the phone receiver and pressed the line button.

A dial tone droned in his ear.

"Great, he hung up. Something else to apologize for when I get home. Why do I even bother?"

Hank straddled the chair Kate had vacated and plopped his coffee mug onto Tom's desk. "Because he's family."

"Yeah." Tom scraped his fingers over his eyelids and let out a groan that had been building in his chest for weeks.

Across the room, a female cop exhaled an identical sound as a woman sporting a shiner shuffled out with the smooth-talking jerk who'd likely given her the bruise in the first place. The same scene played out too many times to count. Rarely did they make a real difference.

Tom looked from the empty spot on his desk where the newspaper had been to Hank. "Miss Adams seemed so convinced Daisy wouldn't have committed suicide."

"Could be compensating for a guilty conscience. She plays around with those herbs too, you know. Maybe she slipped the wrong one into her friend's tea."

"If you thought that," Tom shot back with more sarcasm than he'd intended, "why'd you insist I close the case?" He knew Hank was joking around, but his decision to cut short the investigation had irked Tom almost as much as Hank's unexpected appearance at Daisy's autopsy. He'd been prepared for the don't-trust-the-new-guy

23

mentality from the officers on his shift, but not from Hank.

"Lighten up, man. This is Port Aster, not DC." Hank propped a foot on his knee. "I'm just saying Adams is the only person I know who drinks flower tea."

"You're forgetting your grandma."

"Oh yeah." Hank puckered his lips like he'd sucked back a lemon. "She has a different tea for whatever ails ya."

Tom studied his buddy-turned-boss. Hank's hair had thinned on top, and he'd shaved his goatee into a mustache, but he hadn't shed his ingrained suspicion of people's motives. In the old days, Tom would've been the one telling Hank to lighten up. Although they'd grown up in the same neighborhood, they'd always seen the world from opposite sides of the street—Hank, as the son of a convict, and Tom, as the son of a cop.

Yet, for a brief moment, hadn't he too entertained the idea of Kate as a suspect?

Maybe his years in the FBI had made him more like his old buddy than he wanted to admit.

Tom replayed in his mind the exchange with Kate. Her bravado had been just that—a futile attempt to make sense of what had happened, to cling to the image she wanted to remember her friend by. He knew what that felt like.

Tom gulped the now-cold coffee and handed the empty mug to Hank. "You're right. The case is

24

closed. Let me get back to work." He snatched up the digital recorder he'd instinctively activated the moment Kate slapped the newspaper onto his desk. His years as an agent had taught him how to read people, and when he'd looked into Kate's clear green eyes and seen her heart laid bare, he knew she was as innocent as they came.

He shoved the recorder into his jacket pocket. Naïve. But innocent.

His index finger lingered on the recorder's Play button. Then again, people were rarely what they seemed.

2

Two blocks from the police station, Kate parked her car curbside. Her stomach was more scrambled than her morning eggs, and her hands hadn't stopped trembling since she marched out of Parker's office, vowing to find Daisy's killer.

Was she nuts?

What did she know about tracking down a murderer?

She could end up his next victim.

Her gaze darted from window to window. *Okay, Kate, get a grip. No one besides a roomful of cops even knows you're looking.* She pocketed her keys and stepped out of the car. A short walk might help her calm down and figure out what to do next.

Bright splotches of sunlight dappled the tree-lined street, but the scene felt wrong—as if even the sky had failed her. The weather should be cloudy, miserable, like she felt.

How could Detective Parker insinuate Daisy killed herself on purpose?

He'd acted so concerned with those soft eyes and mellow tones, and then *boom,* he delivered that "people are rarely what they seem" line. Well, she'd show him. Daisy was an open book—and more than that, a woman full of life and zest. She never would have killed herself.

And Kate would prove it.

Somehow.

She turned the corner and wandered down the cobbled main street in a daze. Everywhere she looked dredged up more memories of Daisy—the flower baskets that hung from old-fashioned lampposts, the smell of cinnamon buns wafting from the bakery, the enticing wares spilling onto the sidewalk from quaint little shops. For more than four years, she and Daisy had strolled these streets together, hashing over ideas, solving problems, sharing dreams. Dreams of discovering a miracle cure for depression. A cure they'd been on the verge of unveiling. Another reason Daisy never would have taken her own life.

Kate pushed open the door of their favorite

tea shop, and Daisy's British accent tinkled in her ears like the bell over the door. *Let's have a spot of tea. There isn't a problem that can't be solved over a good cup of tea.*

Yet as Kate walked in, the aromas of spiced teas and freshly ground coffee failed to lift her mood. She glided her fingers over the rows of glass jars lining the counter, filled with herbs of every description. In her mind she heard Daisy chatter on about the health benefit of each.

If only there was a tea that could fix a broken heart.

Blinking back a fresh sting of tears, Kate helped herself to a cup and saucer. She scooped a bit of passionflower to soothe her nerves and a bit of chamomile to help her relax, then added a pinch of ginger to chase away the acid that had begun to eat a hole in her stomach. Kate handed the blend to the new girl behind the counter. "Steep this for ten minutes, please. With a lid on."

The girl, with her straight black hair and clipped bangs reminiscent of Disney's Snow White, looked a few years younger than Kate, maybe twenty-three or twenty-four.

The mayor's wife, a chic-looking woman in three-inch heels and a pencil-straight skirt, joined Kate at the counter. "Goodness. Who has time to wait that long for a cup of tea? Molly, just give me one of those energy teas, and make it to go, will you?"

The girl handed the woman a disposable cup with a plastic cover.

Kate dug her nails into the Formica. "How can she drink a tea without knowing what's—" Kate clamped her mouth shut. Good grief, what was she doing ranting at the poor counter girl? "Um, sorry," Kate mumbled, laying a five-dollar bill on the counter. "I'll wait over there." She retreated with a muffin to her usual table in the back corner by the stone fireplace.

Nibbling on her muffin, she could almost imagine Daisy sitting across from her, telling her how dotty she'd been to yell at the detective. But Kate wouldn't let him close this case.

She wouldn't.

Daisy didn't kill herself. Kate had to make him see that. She owed Daisy that much.

If not for Daisy, she'd probably still be the server behind the counter, pouring tea like Molly back there. Kate traced her finger over the rim of her cup. She could picture the day as clear as yesterday. Daisy had marched into the shop and, instead of ordering her usual blend, demanded to know why Kate had dropped out of her class.

She'd burst into tears and Daisy had ushered her over to this very table.

"My mom died," Kate burbled, sopping the fountain works with a napkin. "I don't have enough money to, to"—she sniffed—"to pay the bills, let alone finish the program."

"Well, we can't let a little thing like money stand between you and your future." Daisy patted Kate's arm, and in a lyrical Mary Poppins voice, added, "As my research assistant."

"Your . . ." Afraid to hope, she whispered the words. "Your research assistant?"

"I do have a little pull at the university." Daisy fluffed her curly white hair. "I'm sure I can scrape up a grant to tide you over until the end of the school year."

"You . . . you'd do that for me?"

"I daresay I'd do just about anything for you. You're the brightest graduate student I've ever had the pleasure to work with. I meant what I said." Daisy's eyes, the color of perfectly brewed chai, twinkled. "I want you to be my research assistant."

Someone tapped Kate's shoulder and her arm jerked, knocking her purse to the floor.

"I'm sorry." Molly drew back, and the tea she carried sloshed into its saucer.

"No, it's my fault." Kate fluttered her hand, feeling her cheeks flush at being caught daydreaming. "My mind was . . . uh . . . somewhere else."

Molly steadied her hold on the saucer and reached for the fallen purse.

"You must be new in town," Kate said. And then, inspired by the memory of what Daisy had done for her, she added, "Welcome."

"Thank you." The girl's eyes stayed glued to the teetering cup as she rose with purse in hand.

Kate relieved her of the tea and took a sip. "I got my start here. Beth is a great boss."

"Yes, she's very kind."

"So are you interested in herbs? Working here sparked my interest."

"Yeah, I was studying pharmacology in school, but I had to drop out when my aunt got sick and needed me to take care of her. She was into homeopathy and loved teaching me about it."

"I think I heard that the research center plans to offer a course on—"

Molly set the purse on the table, and in Kate's mind she saw not her own purse but Daisy's bulging black handbag with a journal protruding from the top.

"That's it! Daisy's journal. She wrote in it as faithfully as she read her Bible."

At Kate's sudden exclamation, the poor girl startled and bumped the purse into the saucer, spilling what was left of the tea. "I'm so sorry."

Kate squeezed Molly's hand. "Don't worry about the tea. I have to run now, but I'd love to chat with you later, okay? Because if I can find the journal, I'll find the answers." And she knew just where to look.

She scooped up her purse and rushed to the door.

Kate parked in Daisy's driveway and sat staring at the brick bungalow. The masses of pansies along the front walk—yellow, violet, blue—had begun to droop in the hot sun as if they too mourned Daisy's passing. Kate opened her purse and dug out the spare key Daisy had given her for emergencies.

Glancing around to ensure no one would see her go in, Kate hurried up the porch steps. There was no question in her mind this was an emergency, but after Detective Parker's warning, she wasn't anxious to test his interpretation of the law where trespassing was concerned.

To the right of Daisy's driveway, cedar hedges blocked the neighbor's view of the house. But on the other side, a gray-haired woman stood in the middle of her yard, her gaze fixed on Kate, a pair of pruning loppers poised to trim a rosebush.

Kate slipped the house key into her pocket and started down the porch steps. Not only might this woman report Kate's appearance to the police, but she looked like the kind of neighbor who would have noticed something out of the ordinary. Something that might give Kate a clue to solving Daisy's murder.

The bone-chilling squeal of rusty hinges sounded behind her.

Kate misstepped, grabbed at the handrail, and turned to find Daisy's nephew standing in the doorway. "Edward," she gasped. "I didn't expect to find you here."

He held the door wide. "My car's in the garage. Come in. Come in."

In the three months since they'd met, Kate had only seen Edward in the suits and ties he wore for his public relations job with the research station. She almost didn't recognize him in old jeans, a flannel shirt, and three days' beard growth. She stepped inside, half expecting to hear Daisy's cheerful welcome ring from the kitchen.

And when Kate didn't hear it, the silence squeezed her heart.

Edward pushed open the living room drapes. "I came by to air out the place." The dark circles under his eyes confirmed that he too had tossed the last few nights away, grieving Daisy's death.

He lifted a watering can from the sofa table. "My aunt would be horrified if she knew I'd let her houseplants die." The tremor in his hand matched the quaver in his voice. "I still can't believe she's gone."

Covering her mouth, Kate moved farther into the room. Nothing had changed, as though the past two weeks had been only a nightmare. The old-fashioned tea cart still displayed Daisy's favorite serving set. Her sweater hung over the armrest of an upholstered rocker, and a paperback lay open on the table beside it. Kate ran her fingers over the title: *The Gardener's Daughter*, undoubtedly a romance.

Yes, at any moment, Daisy would walk into the room.

Edward watered Daisy's prized irises, which sat on the pedestals strategically placed in front of the picture window to maximize sun exposure. "To think, four months ago, I didn't know I had an aunt. Now"—his Adam's apple bobbed— "I've lost her. Sometimes I wish she'd never told me I was her nephew."

Kate touched his arm. "You don't mean that. Finding you made her so happy."

He nodded but avoided Kate's gaze. When he moved on to the next plant, she let her hand drop to her side.

"Do you intend to live here?" She scanned the room, searching for anything that might give her a clue what really happened to Daisy. "I imagine it's yours now."

"I don't want to think about that. It's too soon. I can't think straight. How can the death of someone who I knew such a short time affect me like this?"

"Daisy affected everyone she met." Kate wished Edward shared his aunt's belief in eternity and understood that her faith had inspired her goodness. Daisy had tried to explain her beliefs to Edward, but his bitterness over the circumstances surrounding his adoption had undermined any attempt to convince him of God's love, whereas Kate's certainty that Daisy now lived with her Savior was her one solace in the gloomy days since learning of her friend's death.

Daisy's desire to help Edward find faith in God was one more reason she wouldn't have taken her own life.

"My aunt was a remarkable woman," Edward mumbled.

"I know finding you after all these years meant a lot to Daisy." Kate deadheaded the potted violet on the end table. As much as she wanted to get on with her investigation, her heart ached to help Edward find some peace.

Edward moved to the opposite end of the sofa. "I wish we'd had more time."

"She would have felt the same way."

A pained look crossed his face.

Did he think Daisy actually took her own life?

Kate drew in a deep breath. "I don't believe for one second that your aunt killed herself. I intend to clear her name."

"What are you talking about? How?" Edward's voice edged higher with each question, and if the frown puckering his forehead was any indication, he didn't like her idea any more than Parker had.

She straightened her shoulders. "By figuring out what really happened."

"But the police already investigated." Edward plunked the watering can on the table, splashing water over the side. He patted his pockets and, coming up empty-handed, dried the spill with one of Daisy's crocheted doilies. "Digging around will only stir up gossip. Let the scandal die with her, and it will soon be forgotten."

"I don't want Daisy to be forgotten." Kate pointed to the newspaper he'd left lying on the sofa. "Or remembered like that."

"The police conceded her death could have been accidental."

"Daisy was an expert. She would never confuse calendula marigolds with tagetes. Calendulas don't have divided leaves and the flowers have far fewer petals."

"You think she was murdered?" He paced in front of the window, stroking his forehead with his fingertips. "But you said yourself she was a wonderful lady. She didn't have any enemies."

"No, not enemies." Kate had imagined an endless stream of possible scenarios from the moment she read the headline in the newspaper —a jealous competitor, a disgruntled student, a psychopathic drug company advocate—but working up the nerve to voice them was another thing altogether.

What if Edward thought she was as misguided as Detective Parker had?

Yet if she wanted to search Daisy's house, what choice did she have?

Kate skimmed her fingertips back and forth over the edge of the table. "I thought perhaps a disgruntled student decided to play a prank on Daisy and switched her stock of dried flowers." When Edward didn't balk at the notion, Kate rushed on. "Since Daisy would assume they were hers, she wouldn't pay attention as she scooped the petals into her infuser. Daisy kept a journal. I thought she might have written something that would tell—"

Edward stopped pacing. "I remember she'd said something about a kid." He strode to the rolltop desk in the corner of the room and yanked up the cover. Scattered papers lined the desktop. He riffled through them, then crouched and tore through the drawers. "The kid plagiarized his research report. Daisy said she'd have to inform the university." Edward slammed down a stack of files and sat back on his heels. "It's not here."

"I'm surprised she never mentioned the incident to me."

"I'm not. She wanted to convince the kid to come clean on his own." Edward stuffed the files back into the drawer and closed the desk lid. "Say you're right about the switched teas being a prank. How did the kid get the marigolds into her cupboard?"

"May I look at her kitchen?"

Edward swept his open palm toward the entrance. "Be my guest."

Sun streamed through the patio doors that opened off the breakfast nook. Philodendrons climbed from pots at the sides of the door and twined across a bar above. Two navy blue place mats decorated with white daisies—the place mats Kate had given her for Christmas—lay at either end of the table, waiting for them to sit and sample Daisy's latest blend.

Kate's throat thickened.

Edward watched her from the doorway, his expression unreadable.

She offered him a halfhearted smile and turned to the counter. She gasped at the dusty mess the police had left behind. Fingerprinting residue covered the herb-filled jars lining the granite counter and the teacup sitting at the lip of the sink, not to mention the counter itself and the dribbles across the floor to the fridge.

"I guess we should be grateful the cops saw no point in dusting the rest of the house for fingerprints," Edward said.

As much as it felt like the police had defiled Daisy's home by leaving it in such a state, Kate disagreed with Edward. If the police had investigated more thoroughly, they might not have been so quick to dismiss Daisy's death as self-inflicted. Kate opened the fridge door. A stench wafted into the room. Rotten meat. Gagging,

Kate shoved the door closed and threw open the window over the sink.

Edward reached into the cupboard above the stove and pulled out a garbage bag. "Sorry, I can take care of that. This is the first I've been back since the police released the scene."

While he disposed of the bag outside, Kate found a box of baking soda and stuck it in the fridge to absorb the odor. She shoved away the thought of how horrible the entire house would have smelled if Daisy's body hadn't been discovered so quickly, but she couldn't shake the heaviness that had settled over her.

She couldn't do this. Not here. Not now.

Edward returned to the kitchen with a cardboard box. "You might as well take the jars of herbs home with you. I won't use them."

Relief swooshed the air from her lungs. "Are you sure?"

"Trust me. Real men don't drink this stuff."

A laugh slipped out, but it felt good.

Edward loaded the jars into the box. "Is there anything else you want to see?"

Remembering the journal, Kate led the way back to the living room. A hint of jasmine veiled the stench that had crept through the kitchen. "Your aunt may have written something in her journal that will give us a clue to who would poison her."

Edward's heavy sigh rattled the jars in the box he carried. "It's almost easier to believe she killed herself than to believe someone wanted her dead."

Kate thumbed through the stack of papers on the coffee table. "She usually kept her journal with her Bible."

"I've never noticed." He set the box on the sofa. "I'll check her night table."

Kate followed him down the hallway, but at the door to Daisy's room, he stopped her.

"Wait here," he said, then plunged inside and pulled the door shut behind him.

Torn between not allowing him to face the room alone and sparing herself the sight of Daisy's deathbed, Kate hovered outside the door with her hand on the knob. By the time she pushed it open, Edward was rushing out.

"Don't go in there. I'll arrange for a guy to take the mattress to the dump. I should have done it days ago." He shut the door and handed her a stack of notebooks. "Are these what you're looking for?"

Kate fanned through the pages. "No, these are research notes."

Edward touched the small of her back and prodded her toward the living room. "Then you might as well take them. I won't read them."

She tucked the notebooks into the box next to the jars. "Was Daisy's Bible in her room?"

"I didn't see it." He scrunched his nose.

Okay, maybe she wouldn't check. When she'd

found Daisy the morning after her death, the room hadn't smelled great. But from Edward's face, it seemed the odor now rivaled that of the fridge. Funny that she hadn't picked up on it in the hall.

Edward moved toward the front door. "Can I carry the box to the car for you?"

She tilted her head. Why was he suddenly in such a hurry to see her leave?

Another possible scenario whispered through her thoughts—Daisy's long lost nephew, angry over her role in his adoption, killed her in revenge.

Kate snatched up the box. "I got it, thanks." Could he hear the strain in her too-high voice?

"I'll keep an eye out for that journal," he said, holding open the front door.

A creepy bugs-under-the-collar sensation pitter-pattered across her neck as she stepped past him. Was it her imagination, or did he seem less grief-stricken than when she first arrived? The almost imperceptible curl of his lips reminded her of a cat with a mouse by the tail.

Some sleuth she turned out to be. Of all the people who might have had a motive to kill Daisy, Edward, as her only living relative, stood to gain the most.

And she'd just told him everything.

Tom drove a different route home—one that happened to take him past the late Miss Leacock's house. From the moment Kate left his office, her demands had niggled at his mind. He trusted the coroner's report, but Kate was right. People could be bought. Tom knew that too well. And *if* the coroner falsified his report, Kate, by digging into Leacock's death, might become the murderer's next target.

Approaching Leacock's street, Tom slowed his car. He'd take a quick look around, just to check.

The street was home mostly to retired couples and devoid of the after-school ball hockey games that plugged the streets around his dad's place. Here and there a stray Tonka truck or trike, likely left behind by visiting grandkids, littered front yards. Otherwise, the area rivaled the pristine gated communities surrounding DC.

Tom parked in Leacock's driveway, and the moment he opened his car door, Mrs. C, his former eighth-grade teacher who also happened to be Leacock's neighbor, called out to him from her front yard.

"You missed them." She lopped off a shriveled lilac blossom.

The potent fragrance hung heavy in the air like cheap perfume.

Giving the house a cursory glance, Tom meandered toward her. "Who might *them* be?"

"Daisy's nephew and that friend of hers. If you ask me, they had as good an excuse as any to bump her off. Daisy's not cold in her grave yet, and the girl's already carting stuff out of the house."

"Oh?" Tom propped his foot on the short picket fence separating the yards, and rested his elbow on his knee. "What girl?"

"Daisy's research assistant. Daisy rescued her from the dregs of that old tea shop and *this* is the way she shows her thanks." Mrs. C sliced off a branch of lilacs, dispensing of the living with the dead.

Tom fought to rein in his impatience. "Are you referring to Kate Adams?" He hated to encourage Mrs. C's fondness for gossip, but it sounded like Kate had already carried her personal investigation too far.

"Kate?" Mrs. C's nose wrinkled. "Hmm, yes, that sounds right."

"How did she get into Daisy's house?"

"Daisy's nephew let her in. They were in there a long time too." Leaning toward the fence, Mrs. C dropped her voice. "You don't think they were . . . you know . . . in the middle of the day?"

The intimation knotted Tom's gut.

"Goodness." Mrs. C tossed her loppers into her wheelbarrow and scooped up the blooms condemned to the compost pile. "What's this world coming to? She'd seemed like such a nice girl too. Daisy brought her to church every Sunday, but she wasn't there last Sunday. Nope."

Tom ground his heel into the fence board.

"Perhaps Kate was too heartbroken to face everybody so soon after Daisy's death."

Mrs. C lifted her chin and sniffed. "I suppose that could be."

"You mentioned Edward was here?"

"Yes, I suppose he'll move in soon. Daisy told me that other than a few small bequests, she left everything to him and that Kate girl."

"Kate Adams?" Kate and Edward had both disclaimed any knowledge of a will. Tom tamped down a surge of resentment, loath to admit he'd let himself be duped.

"Oh my, yes. Daisy thought of her as a daughter. If not for Edward, Kate would have received the whole caboodle."

The knot in Tom's gut tightened. Since no copies of a will were found in Daisy's house, nor any indication as to who her lawyer might be, Tom had watched the newspaper for notices, when apparently all he had to do was ask Mrs. C. "When did Daisy tell you about her will?"

"Why . . ." Mrs. C rubbed her chin, her eyes drifting skyward.

He suspected she remembered the day exactly but wanted to savor the moment of knowing more than the cops.

"I believe it was three weeks ago Tuesday. She said she'd been thinking about changing her will for some time and had an appointment with her lawyer the next day."

"Did she happen to mention the name of her lawyer?"

"Oh my, yes. It's Hilda's boy. Dave McCleary. He has an office in Niagara Falls." Mrs. C removed her gardening gloves and slapped them against her hand. "I'm surprised your dad didn't tell you."

Tom's foot jerked from its perch on the fence rung. "My dad? Why would he know who Daisy's lawyer was?"

"She visited your father before she made the decision. I guess she figured with him being a retired policeman, he'd be able to give her a balanced opinion. If you know what I mean."

Tom grazed his hand across his jaw, covering a frown. He had no idea what she meant, but he intended to find out. The second he got home. If Dad withheld information pertinent to this investigation, he'd—

Tom turned toward his car. "I appreciate your time, Mrs. Crantz."

Her voice skipped after him. "So the newspaper was wrong?"

"Pardon me?"

"About Daisy's death being a suicide? You're still investigating, aren't you?" A conspiratorial glint lit her eyes. "Anyone who knew Daisy knows she'd never have killed herself. I told Hilda you planted that story in the newspaper so the murderer would think he got away with it and get cocky."

Tom muffled a groan. His sense of humor when it came to armchair detectives and their over-eager imaginations had died years ago. "I'm sorry to disappoint you, but we have no reason to doubt the coroner's findings." No reason, except that the woman who'd demanded he reopen the investigation suddenly topped his list of suspects.

Not only did the impending change to Daisy's will offer a compelling motive, but Kate had means and opportunity. So what was it about her that made him want to trust her?

Maybe it was because he couldn't get her voice out of his head. *In my world, Detective, people stand by their friends.*

He snorted. Yeah, in his world too. Until that world imploded, making it impossible to tell his friends from his enemies.

If Daisy's research proved to be as promising as Kate had suggested, with Daisy out of the way, Kate would receive the glory and an inheritance. People killed for far less.

Forty minutes later, Tom parked in his dad's driveway and grabbed the sack of groceries off the passenger seat. The grass needed cutting and flyers bulged from the mailbox. Dad probably hadn't even stepped outside today.

Tom let himself in the front door. The sun wouldn't set for three more hours, yet darkness hung over the house, broken only by the flickering light of a rerun on the TV. The canned laughter was a poor substitute for the real thing. Tom missed hearing his dad's belly-jiggling, laugh-till-you-cry kind of roar.

"I bought steaks for supper," Tom called into the living room on his way through to the kitchen. Cheering up his dad with a good meal seemed like the best way to broach the subject of Daisy. Although officially the case was closed, Tom still wanted answers.

He shoved aside the breakfast dishes to make room on the table for the sack of groceries. Closing the cereal box, he crammed it into the cupboard and took the bowls to the sink where last night's dinner plates lay crusted over with dried pork and beans.

Apparently, Dad hadn't bothered with KP duty or lunch.

Tom dropped the bowls on top of the plates and marched into the living room, where he turned off the TV and opened the curtains. "I'm trying to help you, but you have to want to help yourself."

Dad thumped the recliner's footrest to the floor and glared. For Tom, looking at his dad was like looking at an age-enhanced picture of himself, the kind the department created of missing persons. The broad shoulders, now stooped; the square chin, now marred by folds of skin beneath it; the dark hair, now salted with gray. Yep, his own physical features were all gifts from his dad.

Unfortunately, so was the mulelike stubbornness.

"I never asked you to come." Dad crossed his arms over his sleep-rumpled shirt.

"I won't let you starve yourself to death. You act like you're the only one in the world who's ever lost someone. Stop feeling sorry for yourself and start living. Do you think Mom would be proud of you like this?"

Dad shot to his feet, grabbed his coat, and slammed out the door.

Great. Why'd he have to deliver the lecture tonight, when he'd wanted to talk about Daisy? Now Dad probably wouldn't talk to him for a week.

Tom collected a dirty mug and three empty chip bags from the living room. Okay, his dad wouldn't starve, but how long could anyone survive on coffee and potato chips?

Tom put away the groceries, then filled the sink with soapy water. He inhaled the lemony scent that always roused memories of Mom. Her tulip-shaped suncatcher glittered in the window. She had loved to work at the counter and watch the colors dance across the walls. He hated to think how she would shudder at the mess her men had made of the place.

A bird flitted past the window and rose toward the heavens. Even in the darkest days of her illness, Mom had lifted her troubles to God as confidently as that tiny bird launched itself into a vast unknown. Tom wished he had a quarter of the confidence. *I don't know what I'm supposed to do here, Lord. I thought you wanted me to come home and help my dad find his footing, but I just seem to be making a mess of it. Worse than that, I have a civilian conducting her own investigation, and if her theory is right, she could put herself in danger.*

Or she was a murderer.

3

Kate lugged the box of jars to her second-floor apartment, trying to ignore the shadows skulking in the stairwell and the moans of the wind whistling through the eaves of the converted century-old house. After her roommate's wedding next month, she'd look for a new place. One with an elevator and security.

Once inside their apartment, Kate deposited the box on the table sandwiched between the galley kitchen and postage-stamp living room. Next, she stacked her roommate's scrapbook paraphernalia and moved it to the sofa. At least she'd have an hour to look through the jars before Julie got home from work. The jumbled collection of memorabilia sparked a memory of the newspaper strewn across Daisy's couch. Edward had always been a bit of a neat freak—someone who would fold the paper and set it on a table. Had he been trying to conceal something else he'd been reading?

Something like Daisy's journal.

Kate let out a huff of disgust and pressed her palm to the side of her head. Just contemplating such a far-fetched idea made her head swim. She thought she'd talked herself out of those suspicions on the drive home.

Naturally he'd hesitated to encourage her investigation. Neither of them wanted to perpetuate the scandal.

And unlike Detective Parker, Edward at least had been willing to help her. He'd given her the jars and notebooks and told her about the cheating student. Not the response she would have expected from a guilty man.

Kate pilfered a blank sheet from Julie's papers, divided it into columns, and labeled them *suspects, motives, evidence,* and *questions.* Under suspects she wrote "disgruntled student" and "Edward," then wrote possible motives for each. Under questions she wrote "Where is Daisy's journal?" She tapped the pen against her lips. Parker may have taken the journal into evidence. Or maybe Edward had . . .

No, she wouldn't jump to conclusions.

She set down the pen and one by one removed

the jars from the box. After she sifted through the items, she'd phone Detective Parker and ask him about the journal. If he hadn't taken it, maybe the fact it was missing would convince him that somebody had something to hide.

"What's all this?" Julie walked into the room, towel-drying her hair.

The jar in Kate's hand toppled to the floor, and she pressed her now empty hand to her thumping chest. "What are you doing home?"

"I got off work early." Julie rescued the dropped jar. "What is all this stuff?"

"Daisy's herbs. The police refused to reopen the investigation, so I'm going to figure out who killed her."

"You? You can't be serious. You'd mistake a purse snatcher for a Boy Scout helping an old lady carry her purse across the street."

Kate snatched the jar back from her roommate. "I would not."

"Yes, you would. And I mean that in the nicest possible way. You don't have a suspicious bone in your body."

"That's not true." For about a second and a half, Kate debated sharing her suspicions of Daisy's nephew, but she relayed her disgruntled student theory instead. "Edward told me that Daisy was about to expel one of her students. I thought if I could find—"

"You have to let this go," Julie cut in.

"No, I don't. Detective Parker said if I can give him a reason to reopen the case, he will." Her hand tingled at the memory of how he'd pressed his business card into her palm and folded her fingers over it. His gaze had been wary, but his touch . . .

She plucked his business card from her pocket, smoothed the creases, then danced it in front of Julie's eyes. "He even gave me his cell number."

Julie grabbed the card and, staring at it, sank into a chair. "You're kidding."

Kate tilted her head and imitated her mom's notorious do-I-look-like-I'm-kidding eyebrow arc.

Julie let out a good-natured snort. "Right, you never kid." She turned over the card, and her expression morphed into an eye-glowing, cheek-scrunching grin. Her tongue poked out and she caught it between her teeth as if she intended to keep Kate in suspense about what was so wonderful. "Ohhh," Julie oozed, giving the word an extra three syllables. "He must like you."

Kate's heart jogged. She laced her arms across her chest as though Julie might notice the erratic ka-thump. *Liked her?* Huh. "Why would you say that?"

"Cops don't have time to investigate non-cases." Julie scrunched her damp towel into her lap, then finger-combed her long blonde waves. "If you watched TV, you'd know that."

"This is not a non-case."

Julie read the labels on the jars. "How can any of this prove Daisy didn't kill herself?"

"I want to make sure everything in the jars is what's on the label. Parker had the gall to suggest Daisy wasn't the person I believed her to be. And I intend to prove him wrong." Kate shoved aside the notion that Edward might not be what he seemed. If Daisy knew Kate suspected her nephew, she'd have a conniption.

Daisy had loved him, trusted him, believed in him. That ought to be reason enough for Kate to trust him too.

Unless Daisy's trust had cost her *her* life.

Julie opened a jar of lavender and inhaled. "I read somewhere that statistically men are more likely to kill people by violent means, while women prefer to use pills."

"That's interesting." Kate jotted the fact in the margin of her suspect list.

Julie flipped through Daisy's notebooks. "What are these?"

"Research notes." Had Edward given them to her to distract her from the journals? Kate back-stepped into the kitchen. "I'll just grab a cookie sheet from the cupboard. To empty those jars onto." Out of Julie's sight, Kate drew in a deep breath to try to calm the latest attack of jitters.

Julie's voice cut through the clatter of metal

pans. "Uh, Kate, I think Parker might have a point."

Kate poked her head around the doorway.

Julie held up a dried palmate leaf with sharply toothed, narrow leaflets. "Do you know what this is?"

"Cannabis. Where'd—?"

"Are you kidding me? It's marijuana. *Marijuana,* as in totally illegal. I'm getting married in three weeks. No way am I going to let you get us arrested for possession."

Kate set a cookie sheet on the table and took the leaf from Julie. "Stop overreacting. I know it's marijuana. Cannabis is its proper name. Was this in one of Daisy's notebooks?"

"Yes, and I don't care what its proper name is." Julie snatched up Parker's business card. "I love you like a sister, Kate, but if you don't call the detective, I will."

Kate looked from the marijuana to Julie. "And tell him what?"

"I don't know, but I want that . . . that thing out of here."

"You're right, this might be the evidence I need to convince Parker to reopen Daisy's case. If Daisy stumbled onto an illegal grow-op and the growers found out, that's a motive for murder. Don't you think?"

"Yes, they shoot people who stumble upon their little gardens of pot out in the woods." Julie held out the card. "Now, call the police and let them handle it."

"Not yet. It's still just a theory." Kate took the card and placed it on the table. "Until I find out where Daisy found the marijuana, I have nothing."

Julie flagged her arms back and forth. "No way. Uh-uh. I'm not going to let you nose around looking for drug dealers." She grabbed the card and marched out of the room. "I'm calling the cops."

Kate chased her down the hall. "Wait a minute. Let's talk about this."

"No." Julie slammed her bedroom door, and the lock clicked.

Rattling the knob with one hand, Kate slapped the wood with her other. "Don't do this. You'll ruin my investigation. What if Parker confiscates everything?" She curled her fingers into a fist and pounded harder. "The cops had their chance."

When Julie didn't come out, Kate grabbed the notebooks and combed through them as fast as she could, looking for anything out of the ordinary that might indicate where Daisy had been or who she'd talked to.

Less than ten minutes later, the doorbell rang.

Kate stuffed the notebooks under a pile of magazines on the bookshelf and fluffed the throw pillows at either end of the sofa.

An impatient *tap, tap, tap* came from the door.

Kate pushed back her hair and peered through

the peephole. Parker had lost the tie and suit jacket and looked a whole lot more tired than he had a few hours ago. With any luck, he'd be in such a hurry to get home that he wouldn't question how she happened to have all Daisy's herbs sitting on her table. Kate unlatched the deadbolt and opened the door. "Thanks for coming," she said with about as much enthusiasm as she'd welcome her dentist.

Parker stepped inside and seemed to take in her, her re-emerged roommate, and their miniscule apartment in one all-consuming glance. "I hate to tell you, but your find proves my point. People aren't what they seem."

Kate scowled as she handed him the single leaf, which proved absolutely nothing, except that Parker had a tendency to jump to conclusions about people. "Daisy didn't use this stuff."

"Lots of people use marijuana. She was probably one of those hippies in the sixties." His voice gentled, as though he might have a heart buried under all that cynicism. "She had arthritis. Could have been medicinal."

"Right. That's why there was only a single leaf in her entire house." Parker seemed to consider her words, so Kate pressed her advantage. "I think Daisy found a grow-op. If drug dealers caught her snooping, that would be a motive for murder."

Parker's gaze swept over the jars lining the

table. "An honest person would report their find to the police."

"Maybe they killed her before she had a chance."

"Oh?" Humor lit his baby blues. "She invited them over for tea to chat about their indiscretions and they just happened to spike hers?"

Julie chuckled.

Kate silenced her roommate with a glare, then planted her hands on her hips and turned that glare on Parker. "Maybe the coroner is in on the operation. I hear there are lots of drug dealers high up."

"Trust me. The charge for getting caught running a grow-op is a slap on the wrist compared to murder. No criminal in his right mind would take the risk."

"Have you ever known a criminal in his right mind, Detective? Maybe someone didn't want to lose their job."

Julie slouched onto the sofa. "If you don't look into this, Detective, she's going to scour the countryside looking for grow-ops just to prove her point."

Parker shook his head, but a small smile wrestled the scowl off his lips. "Okay, give me a paper bag for the evidence and I'll see what I can uncover."

Julie jumped to her feet and bounded to the kitchen. "Good, because I can't afford to lose my maid of honor."

Kate called after her. "He's just saying this to stop me from looking."

Parker stepped closer. He was half a foot taller than her, and his nearness seemed to swallow the air, but his gaze telegraphed more concern than she expected. "I promise I'll look into this."

Julie's teasing "he must like you" remark flickered through Kate's thoughts, bringing with it a whole different kind of jittery feeling. She shook out her arms the way a boxer shakes off his tension before starting the next round. Nothing could dissuade her from her mission. Least of all a smooth-talking cop who was too handsome for his own good.

"Promise me," Parker added, his voice low and sort of protective. "Promise me you won't go looking for grow-ops."

At seven the next morning, after tossing half the night away mulling over her suspicions and denying her silly burst of attraction to Mr. Promise-Me, Kate cruised into the deserted parking lot of the Agricultural Research Center. Detective Parker may have wheedled a promise out of her not to look for grow-ops, but he hadn't said anything about not looking for Daisy's journal. If Edward was on the up-and-up about not knowing its whereabouts, here was the next most logical place to search.

Climbing from her car, Kate inhaled the fragrance-laden air. The peach and cherry blossoms were at their peak—a stunning array of pinks and creams. She picked up a fallen blossom and traced its delicate petals, trying to ignore the weight pressing on her chest.

Were there flowers in heaven?

Daisy had often talked about heaven and how she looked forward to worshiping her King face-to-face. Kate pictured her friend there now. Singing to her King. Maybe even in tune. The thought made her smile, but her heart still ached for answers. She hurried to the front of the building. If she didn't want her search interrupted, she didn't have time to waste feeling sorry for herself. She swiped her card through the card lock and tugged open the door.

Her footsteps echoed in the empty halls, yet another grim reminder of how empty her days would be without Daisy. The demand for natural medicines, coupled with a generous research grant from the Foundation for Herbal Studies, had detoured the research she and Daisy had been doing from the facility's stated mandate into the realm of herbal remedies.

Would the foundation pull their funding now that Daisy was gone? When they were on the verge of a breakthrough that could revolutionize the treatment of depression?

If the board believed Daisy killed herself, they might.

Kate unlocked her lab, and the sight of the microscopes, test tubes, and Bunsen burners they'd shared steeled her resolve to restore Daisy's untarnished reputation and bring her killer to justice. She tossed her keys and purse onto the workbench and rummaged through the drawers.

A shadow slid over the cupboards.

Kate spun around, but no one stood at the window. She edged closer and peered outside.

The grounds were empty.

Must've been a cloud shadow. She squinted up at a lone cloud in the clear blue sky. Reining in her overactive imagination, she moved to the storage cupboard and checked each shelf.

A brusque voice sounded behind her. "What are you looking for?"

The files Kate held spilled from her hand. She scrambled to reorder the documents. "Darryl, don't sneak up on me like that."

Her supervisor reached under the cabinet for a page she'd missed. "I didn't realize you didn't hear me come in. Why are you here so early?"

"Uh . . ." She'd already told one too many people about the journal. "I'm looking for one of Daisy's notebooks."

Darryl handed her the page he'd retrieved. At six foot four, he stood a foot taller than her, but while most people found him intimidating, she knew he was a teddy bear. "Is the notebook part of your research?"

"Uh, yeah. That's right." Kate stepped back and tapped the pages on the counter. "Um, Darryl, do you really think Daisy killed herself?"

He shrugged out of his jacket and hung it behind the door. "Not on purpose."

"Well, you can't believe she'd brew herself a cup of toxic tea by accident."

Darryl tapped Kate's medic alert bracelet. "I seem to recall a cup of vanilla hazelnut tea almost did you in."

"That's different and you know it. I'm allergic to hazelnuts. Besides, one cup of the wrong marigold tea wouldn't kill someone."

Darryl picked up the electric kettle and filled it at the lab sink. "One cup might trigger a blood pressure spike."

Kate slapped her stack of papers onto the counter. "Enough to kill her?"

"They don't call high blood pressure the silent killer for nothing. What else could it have been? There was no sign of trauma on the body."

"How do you know?" Kate injected just enough suspicion into the question to suggest he'd seen Daisy's dead body, but his change in expression told her how utterly ridiculous the accusation sounded.

"I read the newspaper like everyone else." He plugged in the kettle, then snapped open his briefcase. "I know you miss her, but she'd want us to carry on." With a sympathetic smile, he handed Kate a piece of paper.

"What's this?"

"A list of all those infernal interns Daisy took under her wing. You get to follow up on them."

A new smidgen of hope took root in her heart as she scanned the list. Daisy had started her first round of visits the day before she died. Following her steps was exactly what Kate needed to do.

She grabbed her purse and keys. "Good idea, Darryl. I'll start right away."

He staggered backward in mock disbelief.

She grinned. "Hey, I don't always disagree with you."

Ten minutes later, Kate squeezed her VW into the last parking spot at Landavars Greenhouses and reported to the owner.

"Please accept my condolences," he said in a thick Dutch accent and pointed down the main aisle of the greenhouse to a door at the other end. "The intern's in the cold frame."

Kate strolled through the greenhouse, taking time to scan the benches for anything suspicious. Not that she expected to find marijuana plants in the open where anyone could walk by them, but a leaf or two might have fallen when plants were moved in and out.

By the time she reached the cold frame, sweat beaded her forehead, and despite its name, the cold frame's air wasn't much cooler.

"Hey, Miss Adams. I wondered if you'd be our new supervisor."

Kate recognized the plump, dark-haired girl from the night class she'd helped Daisy teach last semester. "Had Daisy been in to see you since you started?"

"No, I saw her nephew, though." Patti's hands fluttered as she talked, her eyes gleaming with the light of a teenage crush. "He was delivering something to Harm."

"Probably more of his promotional freebies. They must work. Donations have been way up since he took over our PR department."

"It's his Clive Owen good looks raking in the donations, don't you think?"

Kate gave a little shrug and made a mental note to ask Julie who Clive Owen was. Some heartthrob actor, she imagined.

"I guess you want to know what I'm doing." Patti banged a plant out of a four-inch pot into a wheelbarrow. "We start seed trials tomorrow, but today, I'm on grunt work. Aren't I lucky?"

"Ah, yes. I remember those days well." Kate peeked over her shoulder to make sure no one was eavesdropping. "Did the police happen to interview you after Daisy's death?"

"Sure, for a few minutes. They talked a lot

longer with the interns Miss Leacock visited the day she died."

Kate's hopes surged. Knowing which interns Daisy had visited would save Kate a lot of time. She showed Patti the list. "Could you tell me who they are?"

"Sure. Carol, Ned." Patti tapped her finger on the name Gordon Laslo. "He's not around anymore."

"Why not?" She managed to ask with a nonchalant tone even though her imagination went wild at the news. Gord might be the student Daisy caught plagiarizing a report. A retaliatory prank turned deadly would explain his sudden disappearance.

Patti shrugged. "He just up and left a couple of weeks ago."

"Are you sure? A full two weeks ago?"

"At least, yeah. I remember because Ned had to borrow money from me to make their rent payment."

"Do you know where Gord is now?"

"No. No one's heard from him. He's not answering his cell phone."

Kate returned to her car and pinpointed the location of Gord's work placement on her road map. Daisy died fifteen days ago, which meant Gord had left around the time she'd succumbed. That either made him innocent or made him guilty of premeditated murder.

Maybe his boss knew where Kate could find the young man and get some answers.

Unfamiliar with this part of the Niagara region, she drove slowly on the hilly roads, watching for farm numbers. Jersey cows dotted the land-scape, and the smell of manure scented the air. Whenever a white clapboard farmhouse came into view, a farm dog inevitably appeared and raced her car, barking until she'd driven past.

Soon pastures gave way to bush. She double-checked the address. No, she had it right. Another mile down the road, a faded lot marker dangled from one corner—1250. She braked and peered through the trees. No greenhouse was visible from the road, and no sign advertised its presence. She checked her list again.

The numbers matched.

She flipped on her turn signal and entered the drive. Naked locust branches loomed overhead, casting mottled shadows on the winding lane. Deep potholes yanked at her steering wheel, and the farther she rattled along the driveway, the darker it became—not exactly a typical setting for a greenhouse operation. Delivery trucks must hate coming here.

Four hundred yards in, the driveway widened to a parking lot—empty, except for an old school bus. On the far side sat one long cement building flanked by rows of white plastic-covered greenhouses. The whirr of a generator assured Kate the place wasn't abandoned.

Clipboard in hand, she headed for the open bay door. At the entrance, she inhaled deeply. The air was a culinary feast. Endless rows of potted herbs filled the place. Daisy must have been flabbergasted by Gord's decision to quit such a plum job—if he told her.

"May I help you?"

Kate jumped. Why did everyone keep sneaking up on her? She turned and extended her hand to a squat, bearded, dark-eyed man who assessed her with a frown. "I'm Kate Adams from the research center."

The man wiped his dirty hands on the rag hanging from his belt loop but made no move to shake her hand. "I told the last lady who came here that we don't want no more interns."

So Daisy had come here. Kate glanced at the floors under the benches. "May I ask why?"

"They're lazy. Migrant workers cost less, work harder, and don't come with paperwork."

"Are you managing the operation for Mr. Groen, Mr. . . . ?"

"The name's Al. Groen sold the property to Herbs Are Us. I work for them."

"Oh, I hadn't realized . . ."

A teenaged Mexican boy came through the bay with a bag of fertilizer slung over his shoulder.

Al jabbed a finger toward a storage area. "Over there."

The boy slid his gaze down Kate, then deposited his load in the designated area.

Al motioned Kate toward the door. "If there's nothing else, I need to get back to work."

"Yes, of course. I'm so sorry to keep you, but I was hoping . . ." She shot a quick look around the place.

The boy leaned against a pillar and watched her as he rolled a cigarette.

"Pedro, *vuelva para trabajar*," Al said, snatching the cigarette out of the boy's hand.

The boy snickered and stalked out of the building.

Al shook his head. "Your intern was a bad influence on that boy. I was glad to see the last of him."

Kate couldn't think of an appropriate reply, given that she hadn't really known Gord. "Did he happen to leave a forwarding address?"

"If he did, I wouldn't give it out. What with privacy laws the way they are."

She started to protest, but one look at the man's hardened jaw told her protesting would be a waste of breath. "Thank you for your time," she said instead, and strode toward her car. The prickle on the back of her neck told her his steely gaze tracked her exit. She climbed into her car and shifted into reverse. Out the rear window to the left of the rows of greenhouses, she noticed two narrow swaths rutted through the trees—tire tracks on an abandoned laneway, overgrown with two-foot-high weeds and brambles.

Interesting.

Resisting the temptation to linger, she turned her attention back to the parking lot. A shadow detached from the corner of the main building. Pedro. His gaze drifted from her to the laneway behind her. He flicked his cigarette to the ground and crushed it with his heel.

Heart pounding, Kate stepped on the gas, certain she'd stumbled onto something significant. Back on the main road, she turned right at the first crossroad and pulled onto the shoulder about four hundred yards down.

Her stomach felt like an invasion of gypsy moths had laid siege. But she wouldn't let that stop her. Everything about this place felt suspicious.

Given how Al felt about their intern, she hadn't dared ask him for a tour . . . Okay, maybe not asking had more to do with Daisy's death.

Kate stared into the trees, her hand frozen on the car door handle. Was she crazy to risk sneaking through the woods to see where those tracks led?

Parker's harsh assessment—*people are rarely what they seem*—replayed through her mind for the umpteenth time. She'd prove him wrong, at least as far as Daisy was concerned.

Kate opened the door and plunged into the woods before she could talk herself out of looking. It wasn't as if she was looking for a grow-op, exactly. She estimated the tire tracks would be about three hundred yards east of the side road.

The tightly spaced trees choked out undergrowth, which made walking less treacherous. However, the light filtering through the thick branches cast eerie shadows on the rotted leaves layering the ground.

She counted paces, willing her heart to stop galloping. Two hundred forty-eight. Two hundred forty-nine.

Two hundred and fifty paces in, she spotted a tin roof through the trees. She slowed, straining to step soundlessly. The roof belonged to a dilapidated potting shed with cracked windows, rotted wood cladding, and a shiny new padlock on the door.

Her pulse quickened all over again. She could think of two or three reasons why someone might lock a rotted old shed—none of them good.

She hid behind the trunk of an enormous maple tree and surveyed the building. The ground around the door was well-trampled, and faint indentations led toward the tire tracks she'd spotted earlier. Indentations that could only have been made by exceptionally large boots. She squinted through the trees for any sign that

Bigfoot might still be around. As if to assure her that the coast was clear, a chipmunk hopped from a branch onto one of the window ledges, disappeared through a hole in the glass, and a moment later scurried out with its cheeks stuffed.

Kate crept to the shed and peered through the dirty window. The room appeared empty. Although from the slick streak across the dusty table, something had recently been removed.

She edged toward the next window.

Behind her, a twig snapped.

She froze. The sound could have been a squirrel, a deer, any number of—

Leaves crunched.

Not daring to move, she slid her eyes in the direction of the sound.

A tall, dark figure rushed toward her.

She screamed as a hand clamped over her mouth.

4

All set to assure Kate he'd followed up on her marijuana find, Tom tapped on the door of her research lab. The woman had too much moxie for her own good, and he hoped the personal appearance would convince her to let go of the notion that Leacock had stumbled onto a drug ring. Because if Kate wasn't convinced, he had no doubt she'd do exactly what her roommate had said and scour the countryside for proof.

For all his FBI training, he hadn't known what to make of the speechless look Kate gave him when he'd asked for her promise not to look for grow-ops on her own. And her hesitant nod when he repeated the request hadn't given him the warm fuzzies that she'd heed.

If only he could keep her distracted with a more innocuous theory. Problem was, not a single plausible idea came to mind, except for the obvious ones. The nephew killed her for her money, or Kate had.

He tried the doorknob. Locked.

"She's not here." The supervisor he'd interviewed during the initial investigation, Darryl Kish, stepped out of the office next door, brown lunch bag in hand. The man was an oddity. With the height of a basketball player and the build of a football player, he looked more like a mafia hit man than a lab geek.

"Has Miss Adams gone out for lunch?"

"No, she's checking on Daisy's interns."

Tom stifled a groan. Despite the brief time he'd known Kate, he was fairly certain that *check on* was code for *interrogate*. He'd interviewed all of Leacock's interns following her death. Kate wouldn't find any leads there.

Kish locked his office door and shoved the key into his pants pocket. "I should say *her* interns, now."

"Oh?"

"This morning the board voted unanimously to promote Kate to Daisy's former position." His gaze drifted down the long, empty hallway. "Of course, the appointment won't be a surprise. Daisy groomed Kate for the job from day one."

"You don't think she's up to the job," Tom ventured, noting the cynicism in Kish's voice.

"She's young, unproven. She's got ambition. I'll give her credit for that, but ambition only carries you so far."

"Ambitious in a climb-the-ladder kind of way, or a save-the-world kind of way?" Tom asked, not wanting another reason to suspect Kate of murder.

"Oh, she's definitely a save-the-world gal. Probably why Daisy took such a shine to her. Depression robbed Kate's mom of a lot of years, which is what made their newest discovery all the more important to Kate."

Yes, Tom recalled how Kate's eyes had lit up when she explained the unprecedented calming effect of the herbal combination she and Daisy had created. If she had a personal stake in the research's success, she certainly wouldn't want to bump off her colleague.

"Daisy tried to bring Kate back to terra firma.

One set of positive lab results does not a cure-all make."

Hmm. Tom didn't like where that kind of disagreement might have led. "How long ago did Miss Adams leave?"

"A couple of hours ago." Kish glanced at his watch. "Maybe more. Why? Are you here about Daisy's case?"

"No. The case is closed." Tom cringed. His tone came off sounding as harsh as the chief's had when he'd caught Tom skimming the grow-op files this morning. Tom handed Kish a business card. "If you see Kate, please ask her to give me a call."

Satisfied Kate's fruitless interrogations would keep her too preoccupied to get herself into trouble, Tom returned to his car and headed to the station.

Miles of flowering fruit trees lined the road. The contrast of their bright colors to the greening grass was a welcome change from the dreariness of winter. He loved this time of year—a promise of new beginnings. Just what he needed.

Rounding a bend in the road, his attention strayed to a plastic-covered greenhouse tucked behind a copse of trees. Tom slammed on the brakes and pulled to the side of the road. A person's determination was like a river. You could only keep it dammed up for so long. If Kate used the excuse of checking on her interns to do more serious sleuthing, she could wind up in serious trouble.

He dug out the list he'd compiled of suspected grow-op sites under surveillance by the department. A couple of the locations were near the placements of two of the interns he'd interviewed, and Kate was probably foolish enough to waltz into a suspicious-looking greenhouse and start asking questions.

Tom drummed his thumbs on the steering wheel. Hank had warned him to steer clear of the drug task force's territory . . . but it hadn't been an order, exactly. More like friendly advice. Besides, if Tom intended to reassure Kate that he'd investigated her theory, the least he should do was drive by the locations Daisy might have discovered.

Hank need never know.

Tom pulled back onto the road and took the next left. Cruising along Turnbull toward the first location, a splash of yellow on a side road caught his eye. He slowed at the crest of the hill. The yellow belonged to a VW Bug parked on the shoulder. A VW like Kate's. He turned onto the side road and parked behind the car. A quick search on the license plate confirmed his suspicions.

What did the woman think she'd find in the middle of the woods?

Tom checked her car. Nothing seemed amiss.

No houses were in view, only trees. Aside from the warble of birds and the distant rumble of what sounded like a generator, the area was quiet. He scoured both sides of the road for signs of which way Kate might have gone and found a faint trail leading into the bush.

A cut-short scream broke the calm.

Tom's heart climbed to his throat. He grabbed his radio and called for backup, then sprinted toward the sound of the scream—certain it had been Kate's. He prayed that she'd merely been frightened by a wild animal.

Tree branches slapped his face. He hurdled a log, laser focused on the direction of the scream. Why hadn't she just trusted him to look into this?

A small shed came into view thirty yards ahead of him.

He shoved away the image of what he'd found the last time he came across an abandoned shed in the woods. Slowing his pace, he strained to hear over the roar of his pulse thrumming in his ears.

A thud. A grunt. A whimper. Then the scrape of something—or someone—being dragged across the ground.

Tom reached under his suit jacket and drew his weapon. "Stop! Police. Come out with your hands up."

Sounds of a scuffle erupted from behind the building.

"Let go of me," Kate yelled, but Tom still couldn't see her.

He stepped closer. His grip, slick with sweat, tightened as his index finger skimmed the trigger guard. "I said, come out with your hands up."

For one long second, the smell of dank earth pressed at his throat.

Then Hank stepped into view.

"Hank?" Tom's gaze cut to the shed. "What are you—?"

Hank yanked an enraged Kate to his side, her cheeks dented with finger impressions, her hair knotted with rotted leaves.

Tom eased his grip on his gun, but he wasn't ready to holster it. He didn't even want to think about what this looked like. "What's going on here?"

"I caught her sneaking around," Hank said from between clenched teeth, his fingers clamped around Kate's arm.

Kate shoved Hank away and wrapped trembling arms around her waist. "You didn't have to cover my mouth or drag me behind the shed."

"I was trying to keep you safe. Tom could have been anyone. Like one of those drug dealers you're bent on finding." Hank clenched and unclenched his hands. "If you don't want to end up like your friend, you'd better stop playing Nancy Drew."

Kate gasped. "So you admit someone killed her?"

"I didn't say that."

Kate's gaze sought Tom's, and he fought the sudden urge to pop his boss in the chops. From the look of Hank's fat lip, Kate hadn't hesitated. Good for her. Tom pinned Hank with a fierce look and pitched his voice low and menacing. "How'd you know she was here?"

Hank wiped his hand across his swollen lip. "How did you?"

"I saw her car. When I got out to investigate, I heard a scream."

Hank's eyes narrowed as if he expected an explanation as to why Tom happened to be in the neighborhood.

Tom drilled back with a look that asked the same question. The chief belonged behind a desk, not out here chasing innocent—if somewhat reckless—women through the woods.

Kate edged closer to Tom, and the movement drew his attention to the rundown shed.

A shiny padlock hung on the door. Interesting.

"I stopped by the greenhouse to drop something off for my dad and spotted Miss Adams sneaking around. I figured I'd better find out what she was up to since we've busted grow-ops around here before."

"I was right," Kate blurted. "I told you Daisy wouldn't kill herself. She must have seen where they were growing marijuana and—"

Tom shoved his gun into its holster. "And it

didn't occur to you that you could've put yourself in the exact same danger you seem to think your friend stumbled into?"

Kate's eyes grew as round as her open mouth.

Good, maybe they'd finally frightened some sense into her. Tom returned his attention to Hank. "I called this in. You'd better radio headquarters and call off the cavalry," Tom ordered, realizing too late he'd spoken in a tone best reserved for subordinates.

Hank's return glare could've ignited a raging forest fire, but he made the call. Then he stuck his face close to Kate's. "Remember what I said, young lady." He cocked his head, waiting for a response.

Kate remained mute.

Hank straightened and jabbed a finger into Tom's shoulder. "I want you on real cases. This one is closed. Got it?"

Tom bit back a smart remark. As much as he wanted to rip into Hank for how he'd treated Kate, he couldn't afford to sabotage his job. "I'll escort Miss Adams to her car and see she gets safely to work."

"Then I want to see you in my office." Hank disappeared into the trees without waiting for a reply.

Tom gave Kate a stern look. "Do you know how much danger you could've put yourself in?"

Shafts of sunlight speared through the trees,

striking a fire in her eyes. "You said growers wouldn't kill over a little weed."

Tom blew out a breath. *Not weed, no.* He slipped his hand through a broken pane on the shed, wiped his finger through the dust on the counter, rubbed it between his fingers, then sniffed it. Explosives.

He could hardly believe his nose, but he'd recognize that acrid smell anywhere. Port Aster was the last place he expected to run across a bomb-making operation. Tom scanned the perimeter, noting the footprints, the tire tracks. Kate had no idea what she'd stumbled onto.

Did Hank?

Not likely—he'd been too irritated over being caught intimidating an overzealous civilian to see what was really going on in these woods.

Tom cupped Kate's elbow and steered her away from the building.

"Why did you smear your finger through the dust inside that shed?"

He shrugged off the question as if the action had been no big deal.

"It was dust. Wasn't it?"

"Fertilizer."

"That's weird. Why would someone store fertilizer in the middle of the woods?" Kate retraced the path she'd trampled from the road. "You'll want to make sure you wash that stuff off your hands before you touch your laptop. A few weeks ago, Darryl was supposed to fly to Denver for a symposium and missed the plane when security swabbed his keyboard and the detector lit up like a Christmas tree. The guards thought he was a terrorist. Can you believe that?"

Unfortunately, he could.

Kate didn't seem to expect an answer and continued her nervous chatter. "Did you know explosives have some of the same compounds as fertilizers? Security wouldn't release him until the research center confirmed that Darryl regularly handled fertilizers in his job. I can't believe how paranoid we are nowadays."

"You can never be too careful." Swatting branches out of their path, Tom kept pace at her side. "Like your promise not to look for grow-ops."

"I wasn't. I was visiting interns."

"I visited the interns during my investigation. These woods weren't on the list."

She stopped and extracted a paper from her pocket. "It's on mine." She pointed to 1250 Turnbull.

"This is Turret Street. Turnbull is around the corner." Tom made a face he usually reserved for his mischief-making nephews. "Normal people go to the front entrance."

"I did," Kate snapped, but she couldn't mask the way her hand trembled. She stuffed the paper back into her pocket. "I noticed tire tracks heading into the woods and thought I should find out where they led."

He checked the urge to launch into another lecture on the importance of putting her safety first. Somehow, after this fright, he didn't think he'd have to worry about her doing something so foolish again.

"Your chief blew my being here way out of proportion." Kate resumed walking, faster this time, apparently her irritation with Hank fueling her steps. "If he hadn't snuck up on me, I wouldn't have screamed."

Tom whacked a branch out of his way. "What did Hank say?"

"Nothing. Not until after he clamped his hand over my mouth. Which any sane man would realize is going to terrify a person even more."

Tom struggled to keep his tone even as he conjured that image. "Maybe Hank wanted to show you that amateur sleuths can get themselves into trouble if they're not careful."

Kate let out a huff that rivaled Mount St. Helens. "You told me I could investigate."

"If you didn't break the law."

Her cheeks flamed. "I didn't go into that shed, so I didn't break and enter." Her tone turned icy. "And I certainly didn't steal anything."

"Ever heard of trespassing?"

Kate's head jerked back as if she'd been slapped. "But Daisy was here." Desperation crept into Kate's voice. "She saw something she shouldn't have, and now she's dead."

Yeah, and Daisy wasn't the only one who saw something she shouldn't have. The sooner he got Kate away from here, the safer she'd be. He prodded her forward.

Kate's hands clenched at her sides, but she kept walking. "Your chief said there have been grow-ops around here."

"If drug dealers wanted to bump somebody off, they wouldn't go to the trouble to make the death look self-inflicted."

"Well, if they wouldn't kill to protect their operation, why was your chief so desperate to keep me quiet?"

Good question. One he wanted answered too. Tom chose not to point out that he hadn't said the growers wouldn't kill, only that they wouldn't go to any trouble. At the edge of the woods, he caught Kate's arm. "Our department routinely keeps suspected grow-ops under surveillance, to uncover all the players ahead of a raid. If they suspect we're onto them, they could ship out and destroy evidence before we make the arrests."

Clearing the trees, Kate jumped over the ditch between them and their cars. "That doesn't excuse your chief's behavior."

"You gotta understand he's under a lot of pressure to prove himself." Tom stepped across the ditch, his words tasting as unpalatable as the stagnant water beneath his feet. Hank had worked hard to get out from under the shadow of his father's past, but . . . "Some people in this town don't think he deserves to be chief." And Hank was paranoid enough to think an amateur sleuth questioning his judgment would tip the balance of public opinion against him. It was the only explanation for his behavior that made sense.

Kate stroked her jaw where a faint impression of Hank's thumb was still evident. "I can see why."

At least she'd calmed down enough to be able to joke about the incident. Whereas his annoyance with her for putting herself in danger, and his annoyance with Hank for being Hank, were still duking it out inside his chest. "We are thorough in our investigations."

Kate leaned against her car door and plucked burrs off her slacks. "If that were true, you'd have Daisy's killer behind bars."

"I promised I'd investigate your grow-op theory. Now"—he rested his hand on the roof of her car—"can I trust you to go back to work and stay out of trouble?" He reached down and pulled a leaf from her hair—soft, silky hair.

"I can't. I have more interns to visit."

He blew out an exasperated breath. "Then do me a favor and stick to the parking lots and main doors."

She gave him a smart-alecky salute, then hopped into her car.

Climbing into his own car, he watched her drive off. Why couldn't this woman appreciate how much danger she could get into if she stuck her nose into the wrong people's business?

He still wasn't convinced that someone murdered Daisy, but he didn't like what he saw out in those woods. Somehow, Kate had gotten herself into a hornet's nest, and he intended to make sure she didn't get stung.

Kate glanced at Tom in her rearview mirror and mulled over his cryptic statement about the police chief. If the chief had something to prove, he might have something to hide too. Something connected to Daisy's death.

Kate signaled right and drove toward town. Intern assessments could wait. This development was too hot a lead to put off chasing.

From the way Brewster had clamped his sweaty palm over her mouth and hissed warnings in her ear—warnings that sounded a whole lot like veiled threats—she'd guess he knew exactly who killed Daisy. And would stop at nothing to make sure Kate didn't figure it out.

Kate rubbed her leg where his holstered pistol had jabbed her when she'd struggled against his hold. She shuddered to think what he might have done if Tom hadn't shown up.

An image rose in her mind of her dad being shoved into a police car. "Remember, I love you, Kate. I will always love you," he'd shouted.

She'd broken free of Mom's embrace, but a burly cop slammed the door before Kate reached the car.

Dad pressed his forehead to the window and with tears streaming down his cheeks said again, "I love you, Kate. Don't ever forget."

The driver had looked at her with sadness in his eyes, but he still drove away.

Tom's unmarked black sedan loomed in her rearview mirror. Tom looked a lot like the cop with the sad eyes—a trick of her memory, no doubt. She'd never been so happy to hear the words, "Stop! Police."

Except . . .

She swallowed the emotions wadded in her throat. She couldn't trust Parker any more than the cops that railroaded her dad. Brewster was his boss, after all—the top lawman in the county— which made him that much more dangerous.

She parked outside the town library. The tired brick building housed little more than children's picture books and a mishmash of outdated nonfiction books, but Julie had access to just about anything from the library's computer.

Kate's car door swung open without her touching it. Her heart jolted.

A shadow towered over her. Tom, with one hand on the top of the door, the other on the door frame. "Since when do you have interns at the library?"

She snatched her key from the ignition and dropped it into her purse. "What business is that of yours?"

He stepped back with a frown, and her conscience pricked.

"I'm sorry. Your chief put me on edge. I'm here to meet my roommate. She's the librarian."

Tom scrutinized her a moment longer, then nodded. "Stay out of trouble."

The concern that rippled beneath his words softened her opinion of him—a little. Maybe not all cops were heartless.

The library door creaked open, and Julie stuck out her head. "What are you doing here?"

Kate hurried up the steps before Tom heard enough to start wondering why Julie was surprised to see her.

Stepping outside, Julie raked her fingers through Kate's hair and presented her with a couple of dead leaves. "What happened? You and Detective Parker been scouring the woods for clues?" She waggled her eyebrows in that googly way of hers, slanting her head so Parker couldn't help but see too.

Kate grabbed Julie's arm, twirled her around, dragged her back into the library, and shoved the door closed with her foot. "Parker rescued me from the police chief who caught me sneaking around looking for clues—apparently where I didn't belong."

Julie's mouth gaped. "He arrested you?"

"Worse—he threatened me."

"The chief?"

"Yup."

Julie scrunched her nose. "You sure you didn't imagine it? All this sleuthing has you . . . kind of . . . keyed up."

"You don't believe me?"

"Shh." Old Mrs. Peabody, her finger glued to her lip, glared at them from behind an ancient edition of *National Geographic*.

Julie maneuvered Kate past the stacks of books to the back of the library. "You're accusing the chief of police of what?" Julie's hands swept through the air. "Uttering death threats?" The swoops widened with each question. "You think he killed Daisy and now he's after you? What possible motive could he have?"

Kate opened her mouth, but she didn't have an answer. Not yet, anyway.

"If you ask me, Edward or that student you mentioned are far more likely suspects. At least they have motives."

"I think I have a name on the student. Gord Laslo. One of Daisy's interns. He skipped town a couple weeks ago."

"Did you tell Parker?"

"No." Kate spied a couple of blue-haired ladies lounging nearby, pretending to read, with their ears cocked in Kate's direction. They might have fooled her too, if one of them weren't holding her book the wrong end up. Kate steered Julie to another corner. "I'm here because I want to know more about Brewster. Tom said that some people in town don't think he deserves to be chief."

"Oh, I don't think anyone really holds his dad's past against him."

"Past? What past?"

"Shh. Do you want to get thrown out of here?" Julie glanced at the convex mirror mounted above their heads. A mirror that allowed them to see half of the main floor *and* allowed its occupants to see them.

Old Mrs. Peabody had left her post by the front desk, but the two blue-haired ladies' eyes were glued to the mirror, along with those of a young man. Kate hadn't noticed him before. A baseball cap shadowed his face, making it impossible to identify him from the tiny reflection.

"Come on." Julie grabbed Kate's hand just as she was trying to sidle down the aisle for a closer look. After all, Brewster might have sent a young rookie in to spy on her.

Julie led Kate up the back stairs into a small room. A microfiche reader sat along the far wall, flanked on either side by filing cabinets. "Here's where we'll get your answers. I don't think I ever knew what Hank's dad did, but I remember he went to jail. Hank was a few years ahead of me in school, but that kind of news gets around, if you know what I mean."

Jeers of the schoolkids after her dad's arrest echoed in Kate's mind. She knew firsthand how fast news like that got around and how hurtful the kids' taunting felt. But she wasn't ready to share that particular secret with Julie, let alone feel a smidgen of empathy for Chief Grab-First-Ask-Questions-Later Brewster.

"I do know Hank's uncle has a reputation for walking on the edge of the law. He owns the garage across the street, and the rumor is that it's a place where you can buy more than auto parts, if you know what I mean." Julie fed a film into the microfiche machine. "One thing is for certain. Port Aster's weekly would have devoted an entire front page to his dad's arrest. If news of Mr. Halloran losing his false teeth down the storm drain can earn front page status, an arrest would have been a publishing coup." An image of a twenty-year-old edition of the *Port Aster Press* flashed onto the screen. Julie wound through page after page. "Here it is. 'Brewster Brothers Arrested in Drug Bust.' "

Kate stared at the photo of a squat, dark-haired man. "That's Al from Herbs Are Us greenhouses. He's much older now, but I'm positive it's the same guy."

"You know him?"

Kate pulled out her suspect list and feverishly

jotted down notes. "I just met him. The intern I was telling you about worked for this guy until he quit around the time of Daisy's death." Goose bumps erupted on Kate's arms. "No one has seen him since."

Julie's face paled. "You think Al got rid of the intern because the kid saw something he shouldn't have?"

Kate covered her mouth at the sound of her suspicions voiced aloud. She closed her eyes to orient her thoughts, then slowly lowered her hand to her pounding chest and released the breath she'd been holding. "I'm afraid that's a real possibility." She scanned the article. Al Brewster and his brother Cal had been sentenced to two years in prison for growing marijuana. "If Daisy got too inquisitive about what happened to Gord, Al might have decided he needed to get rid of her too."

Julie pushed her chair away from the desk. "But Daisy died from a toxin in her tea. How could Al have poisoned her tea?"

"I don't know." Kate stared at the screen. Al didn't seem like the kind of guy who would have invited Daisy into his office to share a cup of anything. Kate squinted at the grainy negative image of Al and his brother being carted off by police—or more precisely, at the woman standing in the background. "Is that Grandma Brewster?"

Julie leaned closer, tilted her head from side to

side, her expression uncertain. "Probably. She's Al's mom. Why?"

"Grandma Brewster gave Daisy elixirs to sample all the time. Al—or his son—could have easily spiked one. How better to get away with something illegal than to have a son as the chief of police? It makes perfect sense. If Daisy found the marijuana at Herbs Are Us, she would have reported it directly to Hank to protect him from a scandal, believing he would handle the matter quietly."

Julie nodded, her whole body swaying in agreement. "Instead, he filed the report in the trash and disposed of the only witness—to protect his dad and his precious reputation."

"It explains why he came after me in the woods. I wondered how he had spotted me from the greenhouse. His father must've warned him someone else had been nosing around."

"But if that's true, what can you do? Hank Brewster is the chief of police!"

5

At police headquarters, Tom marched straight to Hank's office. Questioning the chief's actions was never a good way to stay under the radar, and that's where Tom needed to be if he intended to find out who was responsible for the explosives residue in the shed. The sooner he got the reaming out finished with, the sooner he could get on the blower to someone at the National Security Agency and find out what was really going on in this town.

Hank's secretary dipped her chin and looked over her glasses at Tom. "The chief's gone for coffee." She scrutinized him like he was an uncooperative suspect she wanted to break. "You're supposed to wait in the conference room." Carla had been sweet on Hank in high school, running interference for him like anallstar. Apparently, that hadn't changed.

Tom felt the stares of half a dozen cops bore into the back of his neck as he slipped into the empty conference room. He shut the door and closed the blinds, then scrolled through the numbers on his cell, found Zeb's name, and hit Connect.

His NSA buddy picked up on the second ring. "Hey, Tom. Rural life getting to you already?"

Zeb bellowed like he was still every inch the burly quarterback he'd once been. "Craving some excitement?"

Tom snorted. "You're the adrenaline junkie, not me. But I have run across something you might consider exciting."

"What? A trip over Niagara Falls in a barrel?" Zeb guffawed, and Tom could picture him rolling back in his chair, slapping his thigh.

"Yeah, it's great fun. You should try it some-time. Now, seriously, any chatter at NSA about an impending threat?"

"Why? You planning an invasion?"

"Are you going to tell me what I want to know, or do I go over your head?"

"You check your sense of humor at the border?"

Prying apart the blinds, Tom peered out the window. "Is Cliff still your boss?"

"Okay. Okay. Yeah, there's chatter. There's always chatter. We stopped some arms coming across the forty-eighth parallel into Minnesota last week."

"What about from Niagara?"

"What're you sitting on?"

Tom let the blinds fall back into place and paced the room. "I may have found the remains of a manufacturing operation. Could be old, but seems like they cleared out in a hurry."

Zeb whistled. "What makes you think the stuff is coming our way?"

"Memorial Day weekend's coming up." Tom plowed his fingers through his hair, wishing he could scrape away the image seared on his brain of last year's Memorial Day picnic.

This was Port Aster. Things like that didn't happen here. That's why he'd all but renounced his US citizenship and returned to the quiet Canadian town where he'd been raised.

"How big an operation are we talking?"

"All I've seen so far is a shed in the middle of the woods."

"Oh, good one. You had me going there for a second." Zeb laughed—no, howled—but when Tom didn't join in, Zeb abruptly stopped. "You're serious?"

"Think about it." Tom stopped pacing and stared at the map pinned to the wall. "Port Aster is a stone's throw from the border. The Niagara region is a perfect launchpad for smuggling explosives into the States."

"Yeah, tell me something I don't know. I'll put a couple of guys on it. But listen, Tom, this isn't your problem anymore."

A child's face flashed across his memory— a girl of about six, blonde pigtails, front tooth missing, screaming for her mother.

"Tom? You hear me?"

"Yeah, I hear you, but you're wrong. I'm still a police officer."

"Okay, but all I'm saying is—"

"I know what you're saying. Just give intel a heads-up, will you?"

"Of course, we'll take it from here . . . unless you happen to uncover something we can use, like shipment destinations, dates, transportation methods. *Names*."

The doorknob turned.

Tom drew in a breath. "Okay, I'll get back to you on that."

"You do that." Zeb left the *I won't hold my breath* unsaid, but his tone said it all. The rumors floating around the FBI had evidently found their way to NSA.

Tom shoved his phone into his pocket and jerked open the door.

Hank tumbled in carrying a wad of files.

"Sorry about that," Tom said. "You wanted to see me?"

Regaining his composure, Hank glowered. "What were you trying to pull by undermining my authority out there today?"

Tom held up his hands and backed up a step. "Hey, I heard a scream. I investigated. End of story. Why were you so desperate to keep Miss Adams quiet?"

"I told you. I thought you might be a drug dealer."

"So are you willing to admit there might be something to Kate's theory?"

"Kate, is it now?"

"Come on. What's really eating you?"

Hank glanced toward the window overlooking the squad room and lowered his voice. The shadows under his eyes had darkened over the past week or two, and the craters etched in his forehead verged on canyons. "I got a call from the mayor this morning. Seems Miss Adams complained about our handling of the Leacock case. With tourist season around the corner, the mayor doesn't want rumors of unsolved murders tarnishing the town's reputation. He told me to handle it."

"Great, all we need is a politician telling us how to do our job."

Hank shrugged. "Get used to it."

"The day I stop doing my job because some suit at town hall tells me to look the other way is the day I hand in my badge for good."

"Well, I guess I won't have to worry about you eyeing my job then."

"I'm the least of your problems. Did you notice the padlock on that shed in the woods?"

"Lot of good it did them with a broken window."

"Them?" Tom zeroed his attention on Hank. "You know who's been using the place?"

"Sure. Bert and Clarence use it to assemble fireworks for the fair. They've been making them for years."

"Fireworks?"

"Yeah, they like to assemble the stuff well away

from nosy kids. But not far enough away from nosy women, apparently. What did you think it was used for?"

The tension that had been building since lunchtime finally loosened its grip. "Something like that." Tom laughed. "I wasn't sure." He turned to leave.

Hank caught his shoulder. "Not so fast. What you were doing out on Turnbull Road this afternoon?"

Tom silently counted to five. "Kate's boss told me she was visiting interns, and I was afraid she'd do exactly what she ended up doing."

"And I told you that case was closed." Hank's tone lightened as he waved his hand dismissively. "No matter, after today's adventure, I doubt Miss Adams will give us any more trouble."

"Don't you think there might be something to this drug connection? You must, to have followed her." Afraid he'd already pushed too hard, Tom stopped short of criticizing Hank's treatment of Kate.

"No, I was afraid her snooping would get her into trouble," Hank said without a moment's hesitation, or rise in pitch, or blink of the eyes to suggest he'd lied.

Okay, so maybe concern had prompted Hank to follow Kate into the woods.

"I'd still like to look into it," Tom pressed.

Hank's fingers turned white where they curled

around the files. "The Leacock case is closed." Hank slapped the stack of papers onto the conference table. "These are real cases—unsolved cases—that need your attention. Don't let our friendship make you forget who's in charge. If you cause trouble here, you'll be blacklisted in every county from Niagara to Nunavut," he said, his tone as cold and merciless as the ice-crusted territory.

Tom blinked. He'd known the other guys resented him. But not Hank. They'd been best buddies since grade school. Tom had stood by Hank when he didn't have another friend in the world.

Hank grinned and gave Tom's shoulder a good-natured jab. "You should see your face, man. Glad to see I finally got your attention. Now, get to work."

"Yes, boss." Tom picked up the stack of files and carried them to his desk. *Got my attention. Right.* The man was on a serious power trip. Tom flipped through the file folders—minor stuff like stolen bicycles and graffiti on the bank's new brick facade. Hank's resentment clearly ran deeper than Tom had supposed. For all he knew, Hank had resented him since their youth and this was payback.

Tom shuffled over to the break room and drained the last of the coffee from the pot. The thick sludge was as black as his future if Hank caught him digging any deeper into the Leacock case. Not that *that* would stop him. He'd made Kate a promise.

Even if his terrorist theory was a bust, too many things about this case didn't add up, and the fact that Kate's sleuthing infuriated Hank only heightened Tom's curiosity.

"What will you do, now?" Julie grabbed her purse and hurried after Kate.

"Whatever I have to do to prove Hank's guilty." Kate stopped on the steps outside the library door and scanned the vicinity for eavesdroppers. "Except, if the chief is involved in a cover-up, who can I trust?"

Julie cupped Kate's elbow and steered her toward the crosswalk. "What about Tom?"

Kate shivered at the memory of his drawn gun. "I don't know. Tom saw how Hank manhandled me in the woods and practically defended his actions."

By unspoken agreement, or maybe habit, Kate and Julie crossed the street and headed for A Cup or Two.

"You *were* on private property."

Kate stopped in the middle of the sidewalk. "Whose side are you on?"

Julie hiked her purse strap up her shoulder and tugged Kate forward. "Yours, of course. But somebody has to be your voice of reason."

Kate huffed. Okay, she'd admit she had a tendency to overreact whenever someone in a uniform got within twenty yards of her. Watching one's dad get carted off by the police did that to a person. But if she'd learned one thing from the aftermath of losing Dad while he was in police custody, it was that cops protected their own. "The chief clamped a hand over my mouth. A dirty, clammy hand at that. And okay, maybe I was trespassing, but really . . . who needs the reality check? There wasn't another soul out in those woods, except Quick Draw McGraw."

"And lucky for you he was." The bell over the shop door tinkled as Julie pushed it open.

Kate closed her eyes and inhaled. "Mmm, smell that coffee." The delicious aroma of dark roasted coffee instantly calmed her frayed nerves.

"You're a nut." Julie slapped a teacup into Kate's hand. "You never drink coffee. Yet every time you smell it, you get this giddy 'my seeds sprouted' smile."

Kate's gaze skittered over the handful of people seated about the shop. "My seeds sprouted?"

"Sure. You know . . . Every spring you start trays and trays of seeds in the south window, and when they start sprouting, you get all giddy and walk around the apartment with this silly grin on your face." Julie paused, a strange expression on her face. She tapped her finger to her chin, her lips widening with each tap into a grin of their own.

"Kind of like how you looked last night after your detective paid us a visit."

"I did not." Kate turned her attention to the canisters of herbs lining the side counter, her insides as jittery as the teacup on her saucer.

"Whatever." Julie spooned green tea leaves into her cup. "So what are you going to do about the chief?"

Kate's heart hiccuped at the too-loud question. She swept her gaze over the chattering customers sitting at the tables. Satisfied that no one seemed interested in her conversation, she whispered, "I plan to keep an eye on him and his dad."

"Are you sure it's not his uniform that makes you suspicious? Let's face it. From the way you rant about their speed traps, cops are about the only people in this town you *would* suspect of a crime."

"That's not true. There was Daisy's intern, and like you said, Edward might have had a motive, if he knew Daisy wrote him into her will."

"If that's a motive, then you'd be the police's prime suspect."

Kate's spoon clattered to the counter, sending raspberry leaves flying. "I'd never kill Daisy for money."

The hum of conversation in the shop stopped.

Kate's face heated under the glare of eyes.

"I know you wouldn't. And *you* know you wouldn't," Julie hissed, brushing the scattered leaves into her hand, then dumping them into the trash. "But the police don't know that. They would suspect you as quick as Edward."

Kate offered the rubberneckers in the room a reassuring smile and focused on adding herbs to her cup while ignoring the sudden flurry of whispers.

Molly wandered over, looking a little wary. "Are you finding everything okay?"

"Oh, sure," Julie said. "We come here all the time."

"Hi, Molly." Kate injected extra cheer into her greeting to put the girl at ease after yesterday's spilled tea incident. "The university just announced the dates for that homeopathy class I told you about. Do you think you might be interested?"

Molly's cheeks colored. "Uh, actually, I'm not sure I'll be able to—"

"Don't worry about the cost," Kate interjected, anticipating her explanation. "There are funds available to help needy students."

Molly's eyes widened. "I don't need anybody's"—her forehead puckered—"charity."

"No, I didn't mean . . ."

The doorbell tinkled, and Molly used the excuse to hurry back to the cash register.

Julie nudged Kate's arm and pointed to the door, or more precisely, to Edward swaggering through it. "Speak of the devil."

"What an awful thing to say."

"I don't trust him. He's too slick. Have you seen the car he drives?"

Kate doubled the dose of lavender in her tea. She needed all the help she could get to relax. Sniffing coffee wasn't going to work today. "So he drives a Porsche. What's the big deal?"

Edward bypassed the tea counter, seemingly oblivious to their presence, and honed in on Molly behind the cash register at the back of the shop.

Julie elbowed Kate in the side. "He seems chummy with Molly."

"He charms all the girls. It's probably why donations to the research station are up forty percent since he took over. Do you think I offended Molly by suggesting she needed financial help?"

"Oh yeah."

Kate's heart fell. "I just wanted to encourage her the way Daisy did for me. I called Beth last night and she said Molly has no one."

Julie tilted her head in the girl's direction. "Could have fooled me."

Kate let out a sigh. Given Edward's playboy reputation, the relationship wouldn't last. She carried her cup to the back counter and quietly cleared her throat.

Edward stepped aside. "Sorry, I didn't mean to monopolize the counter. Oh, Kate, it's you." He leaned close and lowered his voice. "Come up with any clues?"

"One or two."

Molly's giddy smile disappeared as her gaze flicked from Edward to Kate, and the puckered brow made a reappearance.

Edward grinned, but Kate wasn't sure what he thought was funny—the idea of her sleuthing, or Molly's frown at his arm draped over Kate's shoulder. "Molly, have you met my aunt's assistant, Kate?"

Molly's polite acknowledgment was noticeably cooler than their earlier conversation.

Kate pretended not to notice as she handed over the money for her brew. "So, Edward, did you find Daisy's journal?"

"I found a few, actually. Why don't you come by her house later and I'll show you?"

Kate shot Julie a victorious look. "I can come right now if you like."

"Sure." He picked up his cup of coffee and winked at Molly. "Drink your tea first. Then we'll go."

Julie slapped money on the counter and, without bothering to wait for change, dragged Kate to a corner booth. "You can't go see Edward alone. You just told me he was a suspect."

"He wants to help me." Kate glanced to where Edward was now leaning over the counter, twirling Molly's hair around his finger. "If he was a murderer, he wouldn't hand over Daisy's journal."

"He could be luring you to her house to do away with you."

Kate burst into laughter, sloshing tea across the tablecloth. She grabbed a wad of napkins and sopped up the mess. "Invite me over in front of a coffee shop full of witnesses? You've been watching too many movies."

"Well, if you watched more you might not do something so stupid."

"If you're worried, come with me." Between the marijuana leaf in Daisy's notebook and Hank's suspicious behavior, coupled with his dad's history, Kate's suspicions of Edward had vanished, especially since he seemed eager to share the journals he'd found. "Because I'm going. If Daisy learned something that jeopardized Hank's career, he would've had a strong motive to silence her, and her journal probably has that something spelled out in black-and-white. Think about it. Hank had means and opportunity. As the chief of police, Daisy would have trusted him, invited him in for tea. He could have slipped anything into it, then bribed or blackmailed the coroner to declare her death to be from natural causes."

"Hello?" Julie glanced over her shoulder at Edward, then leaned across the table and spoke in a hushed voice. "If you really believe that, aren't you paranoid enough to realize you could be next?"

"No, I'm not."

Edward set his mug on the counter and caught Kate's attention with a wave.

Kate lifted a finger to indicate she'd be another minute and added for Julie's ears only, "Because, unlike Daisy, I don't trust Hank. If I find anything incriminating, I'll take it to another police station where the cops don't answer to him."

"Girl, you're high on this marijuana theory, and I'm just praying you don't come crashing down."

6

After spending several fruitless hours trying to track down leads under the guise of researching the cold cases Hank had handed him, Tom headed home, hopeful a chat with his dad about Daisy's will would yield better results. Tom bypassed the living room, stopping in his bedroom to remove his coat and secure his gun and take a moment to pray for wisdom first. If he'd taken the time yesterday, he might not have botched last night's attempt.

Dad must've bought a new air freshener when he was out because the house smelled of freshly baked apple pie. Unfortunately, the uplifting aroma hadn't altered the status quo. As usual, Dad sat in his recliner, TV blaring.

Tom glanced at the family photos lining the shelves and prayed again for patience.

When had the skin on Dad's neck begun to hang like ripples on the shore? If he kept on like this, he'd be following Mom to an early grave. How had his sister not seen the signs? "Dad, can we talk?"

Dad pushed up his sleeves and waved Tom off. The veins bulging from Dad's thin arms cast a bluish tinge to his skin that betrayed a frailty he'd rather die from than acknowledge. "If you're going to lecture me about how I should live, save your breath. You've never loved a woman. You can't possibly understand what it feels like to lose the best part of yourself, let alone know what I should do about it."

Unwilling to reveal how deep Dad's words cut, Tom moved to the window. "This isn't about Mom. It's about a case."

Dad sat up. The recliner's footrest clomped closed with a thud. "Well, why didn't you say so?"

Pleased by the sudden enthusiasm in Dad's voice, Tom took a seat across from him. "You remember Daisy Leacock?"

"Sure. Five foot four, medium build, early sixties, curly white hair, always smiling, what about her?"

Tom closed his eyes. The police report–like description didn't surprise him. After all, Dad had been a cop for over thirty years. It was the fact he didn't seem to realize she was dead that made Tom cringe. Whether Dad agreed or not, he had cut himself off from the world. Only this wasn't the way Tom wanted to point that out.

Tom shifted in his seat, uncertain how to continue. His palm crunched stray potato chips. Stalling for time in the vain hope that another option would miraculously present itself, Tom knocked the chips off the couch. When no lightning bolt speared through the ceiling, Tom took a deep breath and leaned toward his dad. "Do you remember the last time you spoke with Daisy?"

Dad's eyes sparked. "I may have lost my wife. I haven't lost my memory. She came here about a month ago on a personal matter."

"About her will?"

"That's none of your business." The scowl on his face matched the one he wore whenever Tom broached the subject of Mom, and Tom's patience careened out the window.

"Dad, if you're withholding key evidence in a murder investigation, it is my business."

"Crump's dead?"

"Crump? Who's Crump?"

Dad looked at him as if he were a few bullets short of a magazine. "Daisy's nephew."

Tom shook his head. His dad's memory obviously wasn't as good as he thought. "No, Dad, Edward Smythe is Daisy's nephew."

"No, son," Dad shot back in the same patronizing tone Tom had used. "Smythe was an alias."

Tom winced at how disrespectful he'd sounded. A microsecond later Dad's words sunk in, and Tom's apology balled in his throat. "Wait a minute. You're telling me Smythe is a fraud?"

"Yup. A two-bit con artist who preyed on little old ladies by pretending to be a long-lost nephew. Didn't Daisy tell you? The silly woman, she was determined to keep his secret." Dad scrubbed his palm over his whiskers. "This'll break her heart."

Tom swallowed hard, unable to force out the words Dad needed to hear.

"I tried to warn her that his past would catch up to him," Dad continued, "but once Daisy gets an idea into her head, it's next to impossible to change her mind. She thought that if she put 'Jim Crump' in her will, instead of 'Edward,' then after her death he'd realize she'd known the truth all along and had loved and accepted him as her own anyway. How'd he die?"

Tom felt sick. He averted his eyes and found himself staring at Dad's outstanding service plaque for thirty-five years on the force. Dad had loved being a cop. The enthusiasm in his voice at the prospect of discussing a case with Tom had proclaimed the fact loud and clear. A fact Tom had overlooked in all these months of trying to reconnect. If only the breakthrough weren't the result of yet another death. "Dad," Tom said, the word scraping his throat raw. "Crump didn't die. Daisy did."

The color drained from Dad's face, leaving him as chalky as the outline of a murder victim. "Daisy? How? When?"

"I'm sorry, Dad. I didn't know you two were friends or I would've told you sooner. She died two weeks ago." Tom suppressed a fleeting urge to add, *If you went out once in a while you'd hear these things.* He'd learned his lesson.

Dad's lips pressed into a tight line. He closed his eyes, took a deep breath, and then slowly let it release. "Daisy had this Pollyanna idea that her unconditional love would soften Crump's attitude toward God."

"Her death was self-inflicted—a poisoning."

Dad lifted his head. His composed cop mask was firmly fitted in place, his emotions compartmentalized to deal with later . . . or not. "You don't sound convinced."

"Daisy's co-worker thinks she was murdered."

"And you think Crump did it for her money." Dad rose and paced the room. "He's never killed before."

"How can you be sure?"

"I had a buddy check his record, but I suppose that only proves he's never been caught."

"Why did Daisy come to you about her will?"

Dad opened the curtains and beams of sunlight chased the shadows from the room. "She wanted to know what I thought about the idea of including Crump. I told her it was her money, but that if I were her, I wouldn't tell him—just in case. I guess she didn't listen. Unless . . ."

"Unless what?"

"Unless she told the person who stood to inherit the bulk of her estate before Crump came into the picture."

Tom's chest tightened. *Kate Adams.* At least, according to Mrs. Crantz. Daisy's lawyer had refused to divulge any information without a court order.

"You look like you don't believe it. The top two motives for murder are always passion and money. Didn't they teach you that in the FBI?"

Tom chose to ignore the criticism in Dad's tone. He'd never approved of Tom "renouncing" his country to work in the States, simply because a quirk of circumstances had led to him being born south of the border instead of in Canada. But this time, Tom suspected Dad's rant was a displacement of his own frustration over his role in this unhappy drama.

"I only just learned about the will. There was no paperwork in Daisy's house naming a lawyer

110

or mentioning the existence of a will, and Edward claimed not to know about such things."

"Well, he wouldn't. Would he? But now that you know, find out who didn't want Daisy to change her will."

Kate. But despite all his *people are rarely what they seem* tirades, Tom couldn't picture Kate spiking her best friend's tea. Crump, on the other hand, sounded exactly like the kind of slime who would stoop to such a plan. "Getting answers won't be that easy. The case is closed. And Daisy's lawyer isn't talking."

"Well, in my day, I investigated a case or two behind the captain's back." Dad picked up a photo of Mom from the end table. His finger trembled as he touched the image, his lips curving into a smile. The kind of smile that hinted at a special memory they alone had shared. He set the photo down and turned that smile to Tom. "Yup, more than a case or two, and my defiance usually landed me in a heap of trouble. But I don't answer to the department anymore." He rubbed his palms together. "Tell me what I can do."

Kate coasted into Daisy's driveway behind Edward's late-model, mint-condition Porsche Boxster and tried to forget Julie's intimation that someone with such expensive taste in cars might need all the money he could get his hands on. Kate shook the ridiculous thought from her head. He'd had the car before he'd ever wheeled into Port Aster.

The curtain in the neighbor's front window shifted, and Kate made a mental note to have a chat with the woman. She could stop in after she collected Daisy's journal. Kate climbed out of her car and followed Edward to the front door.

The pansies along the pathway were perkier today. Edward must have watered the flower bed. More evidence of his innocence. Someone who took time to water flowers wouldn't stoop to murder to make a few bucks.

A sudden wave of melancholy swamped Kate as she stepped into the house. Never again would Daisy bustle out of the kitchen with a tray of tea and biscuits. Kate's gaze skittered over the room in search of a safe place to land, a place that wouldn't fracture her tenuous hold on her emotions.

"So," Edward asked as he shut the door, "what clues have you uncovered about my aunt's death?"

Kate stopped at the end table a few feet into the front room and fiddled with the petals of an African violet. "I'd rather not say just yet." If her roommate thought her theories were far-fetched, she'd rather not know what Edward thought of them until she had the proof to back one up.

"Oh?" The deadbolt clicked. From the shadowy

entranceway, Edward's eyes speared her. "Why's that?"

Kate edged around the table, putting it between them, even as she reasoned that he'd locked the door out of habit, nothing more. "I wouldn't want to falsely accuse someone."

Edward took a step toward her, and she scrabbled for some tidbit of information that would appease him. "I . . . I think I've figured out which student Daisy confronted about the plagiarism. Does the name Gordon Laslo sound familiar?"

Edward's gaze lifted to the ceiling and his lips moved as though he was repeating the name to himself. "Gord, yes, I think that might have been the guy."

"Good. Well . . ." Kate sidled toward the window as Edward rounded the sofa. "Uh, I still haven't tracked Gord down, but that shouldn't be too difficult." If the nosy neighbor was still watching the house, she might—

Kate's leg bumped a wicker plant holder. The schefflera plant teetered.

"Grab it." Edward lunged, hand outstretched, but Kate caught the plant a second before it would've smacked the floor.

"I'm sorry. I don't know why I'm so jittery."

Edward took the plant from her with a sympathetic smile. "No apology needed. Daisy's death has us both upset." He placed the plant back in its stand and studied her for a long, uncomfortable moment. "I'll get those journals for you now," he finally said before disappearing down the hall.

"Yes, thank you." Kate pressed her hand to her chest and willed her heart to slow.

Within moments Edward reappeared with a stack of floral-covered books.

"That's them!" Kate clutched the books to her heart. "Thank you, Edward. This means so much to me." A wealth of wisdom graced these pages.

A twinge of guilt pinched her stomach. Daisy might not like anyone reading her most private thoughts. But how else would Kate learn what danger Daisy had gotten into and who might have wanted her silenced?

"I'm not sure if you'll find anything in them," Edward said. "But I'm glad to help. I found something else downstairs I think Daisy would want you to have."

"Oh?"

"Wait here. I'll go get it." Before Kate could argue, Edward trotted down the basement stairs.

Her trepidation forgotten, Kate walked over to the fireplace and smiled at the photo on the mantel of her and Daisy celebrating graduation. Daisy had filled the void left by Mom's passing. With Daisy gone, Kate truly felt like an orphan.

Her legs grew warm. Why would Edward light the fire on such a beautiful day?

Kate opened the fire screen. A few half-burned pages lay among the smoldering embers. The handwritten pages were lined like the pages of a notebook.

A swirl of smoke reached into Kate's throat and cut off her airway. She snatched a scrap of paper from the edge of the firebox—the same floral paper that covered Daisy's journal.

Edward.

Kate slapped the fire screen closed and whirled toward the door. In her hurry, she knocked over the poker stand. The brass implements clattered onto the brick hearth.

"What happened?" Edward shouted up the stairs. "Are you okay?"

"Yes, yes. I'm fine. I . . . I just remembered I have a meeting and I'm late."

Footfalls bounded up the stairs. "Wait!"

Kate fumbled with the deadbolt. She just bet he wanted her to wait. Clutching the journals under her arm, she used both hands to twist the latch. *Come on. Open.* She glanced over her shoulder as Edward hit the main floor at a run.

His gaze skittered over the toppled fire poker and skewered into her.

With Julie's you-could-be-next warning blasting in her ears, Kate wrenched on the door with one last heave.

7

"I think Kate's in danger," the woman on the other end of the phone blurted before Tom had a chance to say hello.

Pressing the phone to his ear, he strode to the bedroom to grab his car keys and gun. "Danger, how? Where is she?"

"She followed Edward to Daisy's place."

The news coupled with the warble in Julie's voice breached the barrier between his job and his emotions—the barrier he prided himself on, the barrier he needed to maintain if he wanted to be an effective cop. He fumbled with the lock on his gun locker.

"You've got to find her. Edward claimed he found Daisy's journal, but I don't trust him, and Kate's not answering her cell phone."

The lock released and Tom snatched out his gun. "Okay, I'm on my way. Let me know if you hear from her." He pocketed his phone, strapped on his shoulder holster, and headed for the door.

Dad had taken over Tom's spot in front of the laptop at the dining room table and was typing in search parameters from the reams of notes they'd compiled on Jim Crump, aka Edward Smythe.

"I've got to go. Jim's got Kate."

Dad's sharp inhalation bumped up his fears that Jim had raised the stakes on his little con game. Dad caught the door as Tom rushed out. "Be careful."

"I will. Find me something I can stick to this guy."

"I'm on it."

Tom sped out of the driveway, wheels squealing.

Dark clouds bruised the sky. Houses passed in a blur, but not fast enough to spare him from imagining horrible possibilities. No, he refused to let his thoughts go there. If Edward killed Daisy, he couldn't have known his real name was in her will, because the inclusion guaranteed he'd be the prime suspect in the event of a suspicious death.

Except . . . if he found out that Leacock knew about his cons, he had to be worried that it was only a matter of time before Kate stumbled onto the truth with her relentless digging.

In his mind, she'd have to be silenced.

Not tonight, though. Not when her roommate knew of his invitation to meet at Daisy's house. Too big a risk.

Tom mentally scrolled through a contingency plan in the event he was wrong, and this call went south. He veered his car onto Leacock's street and slowed to a crawl.

Edward's Boxster sat in the driveway, but not

Kate's VW Bug. Relief flooded Tom's chest, swamped promptly by alarm. Edward might've taken Kate for a drive in her car to make her death look like a traffic accident.

Tom parked on the street, blocking the end of the driveway, and reached for the radio to request a BOLO—Be On Look Out—for Kate's yellow VW.

Edward appeared at the garage door, lugging a body bag–sized duffle.

Tom forced down a rise of bile as his finger hovered over the call button.

Edward heaved the bag over the lip of his trunk.

Hand itching to grab his gun, Tom stepped out of his car as casually as his racing heart permitted. "Planning a trip?"

Edward's arms jerked at the sound of Tom's voice, but he immediately resumed what he was doing. "No, this stuff is for Kate," he said, seemingly unfazed by Tom's arrival. Edward's smudged polo shirt told another story.

"Are you all right?" Tom asked, his hands poised at his side, ready to draw his gun if necessary.

"Sure, why wouldn't I be?"

Tom motioned to his chest. "You have blood on your shirt."

Without so much as glancing toward his shirt, Edward reached into his pocket.

Tom went for his gun.

Edward pulled a paper towel from his pocket and pressed it against his palm. "I cut my hand on a broken mirror in the basement."

Tom let his gun settle back into its holster and cautiously made his way toward Edward's car. "Let me give you a hand with that bag." Tom helped Edward stuff the bag into the trunk, all the while feeling along its sides. Whatever was in the bag, it wasn't a body.

"What're you doing here?"

"Looking for Kate. Do you know where she is? Her roommate told me I'd find her here."

"You just missed her. Said she was late for a meeting."

"At the research station?"

Perspiration beaded Edward's upper lip. Whether from nerves or exertion, Tom couldn't be sure.

"Don't know." Edward wheezed as he struggled to wedge the duffle deeper into his miniscule trunk. "She ran out of here like a bat out of you-know-where."

Tom schooled his reaction. He knew better than to ask questions that might prompt the man to demand his lawyer, but neither was he ready to take Jim—aka Edward—at his word. The man's act was slicker than his car.

"Why?" Edward gave the bag one last shove. "Has Kate convinced you to reopen the case?"

"Not officially, no. Unofficially, there are a few loose ends I'd like to see tied up."

Edward slammed the trunk closed and fingered his keys with a little too much interest.

Oh yes, this man knew exactly what some of those loose ends might be.

When Edward spoke again, the bravado in his voice sounded forced. "Glad to hear it. Because my aunt was too smart to drink the wrong tea."

Nope, Edward wasn't as cool as he'd like Tom to believe. Of course, now wasn't the time for Tom to tip his hand. Not with one suspicious death, and Kate, still unaccounted for. One mention of Edward's true identity and he'd be lawyered up before nightfall.

Mrs. C tootled her fingers from her vantage point on the other side of the picket fence. From the look of the pile of weeds in her bucket, she'd been on patrol for a while, which boded well for Kate's safety. Julie's overactive imagination had gotten them both a little too keyed up.

Tom's cell phone rang. That was probably her now. "Excuse me, I need to take this." Confident Edward wouldn't try to leave while Tom's car blocked the drive, he put some distance between them before answering.

"Edward killed Daisy," the panicked voice on the other end of the phone shrilled.

"Kate?" Tom pinned his gaze on Crump, who'd gone back into the garage and started rummaging through a box along the wall. "Are you okay?"

"Yes. No. I don't know. Listen to me."

Her rattled response had Tom on the verge of ripping into Crump, demanding to know what he'd done to her.

"Edward burned Daisy's journal. It must've had something incriminating. You have to arrest him."

Tom could just imagine the incriminating details Daisy might have written about Crump in her diary, but without the evidence he had no grounds for an arrest. "Where are you?"

"I can't believe we trusted him." Tires squealed and Kate's next words sounded breathless. "Daisy loved him like her own son."

Tom's chest tightened at the sound of Kate careening through traffic. "Where are you?" he all but shouted, digging his keys from his pocket as he jogged toward the car.

"I got out of there as fast as I could. I was so scared. What if he finds out I know?"

"Know what?"

"Aren't you listening? He killed Daisy."

Edward's gaze snapped to Tom's.

Tom covered the mouthpiece. "Sorry, I've got to go." He climbed into his car and closed the door. "Tell me where you are."

"On Chestnut, coming up to Oakland Avenue."

"Okay, go on home. I'll meet you there, and you can show me what you've found."

"But I think someone's following me. They'll find out where I live."

"Someone who?" If she was right and Edward

killed Daisy, the tail was likely a product of her overactive imagination.

Or Edward had alerted a fellow conspirator.

"I don't know. Someone!" she screamed, bypassing panic and taking the one-way straight to hysteria.

"Okay," he said calmly. "Here's what I want you to do. Turn left, then right, and tell me if the car follows." He pulled onto the street and headed toward Oakland.

For a moment the phone remained silent, then Kate's thin voice crackled over the airwaves. "Yes. The car's still behind me."

Tom turned the corner in time to see a red LeSabre slow behind Kate's car. The driver glanced Tom's way, then sped past. *Not her imagination.* "Kate, I'm coming toward you. Pull over."

Tom drove past, did a U-turn, and parked behind her car. He let his head drop back against the seat and took a moment to steady his breathing.

After a quick call to her roommate to let her know Kate was safe, he approached Kate's car. "Was the LeSabre the vehicle you saw following you?" he asked through her open window.

"Yes." White-fingered, Kate clamped the steering wheel as if she were mere seconds away from careening over a cliff.

Alarmed by how her fear dug into all his raw places, Tom dropped his gaze to the pavement.

He cleared his throat. "The license plate was distinctive—*T42*. I won't have any trouble tracking down the owner."

"Tea for two?" Surprise and a hint of relief replaced the wild look in Kate's eyes. "That's Beth's car."

"Who's Beth?"

"My supervisor's wife. She owns A Cup or Two."

"Shoulder-length hair? Dark? Straight?"

"Yes, that's her."

"Why would she follow you?"

Kate ducked her head. "I must've been mistaken. Edward had me pretty rattled."

Tom wasn't convinced. The driver had seemed pretty intent on Kate until she caught sight of him rounding the corner. And as Tom recalled, Kate's supervisor had been less than enthusiastic about the news that Kate would take over for Daisy.

What if they had it wrong? What if Darryl—not Edward—killed Daisy?

With a wife in the herbal tea business, Darryl had access to every imaginable brew he'd care to concoct to dispose of someone, and as Daisy's boss, he had plenty of opportunity. But why would he kill her?

Tom plowed his hand through his hair. Oh, man. He was jumping from theory to theory like a rookie, or worse, like a man thinking with his emotions instead of his brain. He should've known from the way he'd pounced on Julie's call that he'd lost his perspective on this one.

Kate peered at Tom through her open car window, wondering what he must think of her.

"Follow me," he said, his brow creased in concern.

Or was that annoyance?

"Where?" Fear might have driven her to call him about Edward, but that didn't mean she could trust him any more than she trusted Hank Brewster, even if Brewster didn't kill Daisy. Except . . . given the way she ran out of Daisy's house, leaving the fire poker strewn on the floor, Edward had to know she'd seen what was left of the journal he'd burned. So until she convinced Tom to arrest Edward, she wouldn't be safe.

A car turned onto the street and Tom faced the driver, shielding Kate with his body. Not that there'd ever been a drive-by shooting in Port Aster. Of course, until Daisy's death, there hadn't been a murder in as long as Kate could remember either. Clearly, Tom wasn't taking any chances.

The car sped by without slowing.

Kate let out a breath. Maybe she could trust Tom. Anyone who'd stand in the line of fire for her deserved a second chance, even if he was a cop. Not to mention she was fresh out of options.

Edward knew where she lived.

Tom rested his hand on the door frame and hunkered down to her eye level. If she didn't know better, she might have mistaken the concern —definitely concern—in his eyes for something more than duty. "I want to introduce you to my dad. He's a retired police officer and might see something we're missing. You can tell us what you've found, and we can decide what to do from there."

"You're going to reopen the case?" she practically squealed.

A muscle in Tom's jaw flinched. "We'll see."

His lukewarm response cooled her hopes, but she followed Tom to his dad's house. Edward wouldn't come after her as long as Tom was close by.

His dad lived in a cheery, yellow-sided bungalow on a tree-lined street. The masses of purple phlox, hyacinths, and forget-me-nots amid a variety of other yet-to-bloom perennials suggested he shared her love of gardening, although the bed was in need of some serious weeding.

Tom opened her car door. "Please excuse the mess when we get inside. My dad hasn't been the same since Mom died."

"Of course, I understand." Too well.

Tom's gentle touch at the small of her back plucked her from the edge of an emotional cliff. He steered her toward the front door, and she reminded herself that he too was grieving.

The strong perfume of the hyacinths whisked her back to the many happy hours she'd spent with Gramps weeding flower beds. Her friends had thought she was crazy, but she'd loved to linger over the chore, talking with Gramps. He'd given her a love of flowers—especially perennials, something that could be depended on to come back year after year.

A slightly gray-haired version of Tom, bearing the same distinctive blue eyes and chiseled chin, opened the screen door. "You must be Kate."

"Yes." She smiled, pleased that Tom had talked about her with his dad. Perhaps Tom hadn't completely dropped Daisy's case.

"Call me Keith," Tom's dad said, pushing the door wide so she could walk past him.

The aroma of baked apple pie greeted her. "Mmm, it smells like Saturday afternoons at my grandparents' in here."

"Don't let your mouth water," Tom said, stepping in behind her. "The smell is from an air freshener."

Keith let the screen door bang shut. "Always a critic in every crowd."

The hall opened into a bright sitting room that by the looks of the worn leather recliner served mainly as a TV room. Family photos graced every shelf and tabletop to the point of looking cluttered, but not messy. "You have a beautiful home, Keith. I love your flower bed by the front porch."

"Gardening was my wife's passion." He motioned for Kate to take a seat in the TV room. "I'm afraid I haven't given the garden the attention it deserves since she passed on."

The affection in his mellow bass voice made Kate miss not only Daisy but Mom and Gran and Gramps too. "I was so sorry to hear of your loss."

He gave her a vacant nod. A nod she understood all too well. The kind of nod she'd been guilty of dispensing herself when on the receiving end of too many empty condolences.

"I'd love to help you with the garden," she said, "if you like."

His eyes brightened. "Thank you. I'd appreciate that."

She sat on the sofa and found herself relaxing. The quiet tick of a miniature grandfather clock made of foam puzzle pieces reminded her of quiet afternoons reading in Gran's living room. How strange that she should feel so at home here.

She shook the notion from her head and frowned at the potted dracaena in the middle of the coffee table. The tips of its leaves had turned brown, a symptom of salt damage. She rotated the pot and found the culprits—fertilizer sticks. Plucking them out, she said, "You don't want to use fertilizer sticks. They're notorious for burning the roots."

"Didn't I tell you?" Keith said to Tom.

Tom lifted his hands and shrugged. "The plant looked like it was dying, and that's what the lady at the store told me to use."

Kate let out a frustrated sigh. "Obviously not someone who knows anything about plants. The pot is too crowded. All you need to do is flush the soil and give the poor thing a bigger pot."

Keith laughed, a roaring belly laugh. "I guess she put you in your place, son."

Rather than look annoyed by his dad's burst of laughter at his own expense, Tom smiled as if he relished the sound.

One of Kate's co-workers had said that he moved back to town to keep his dad company following his mom's death. Seeing Tom's eyes crinkle with pleasure at the sound of his dad's laughter confirmed how deeply Tom cared for him—the kind of selfless affection she'd cherish in a relationship.

Whoa. Where had that thought come from?

Julie's silly romantic notions must have found a patch of fertile ground in her heart, and Kate needed to weed them out. Now. Before she made a fool of herself. Never mind that Tom's muscular shoulders were broad enough to handle her worries. Dad's fateful scrape with the law had long ago squelched any childish fantasies of finding her happily ever after with a man in uniform.

"Kate?"

Kate looked from Keith to Tom. "I'm sorry. My mind went somewhere else for a minute. What did you ask?"

Tom drew his chair closer, which didn't help her concentration one bit. "Did Edward threaten you?"

Edward, right. Maybe her mind had wandered into daydreams about Detective Parker because daydreaming beat thinking about the danger she'd gotten herself into. "No. Edward gave me a stack of Daisy's journals. I'm sure he thought I wouldn't realize one was missing. But after the way I ran out of there, he's got to know I figured it out. He wouldn't burn her books unless he had something to hide."

Tom caught her hands and held them still. "Most people do." A tremor rippled his jaw as if perhaps he too harbored such a secret. "That doesn't make them killers. I can't arrest Edward without proof."

"When Daisy's sister gave birth to Edward out of wedlock, Daisy's parents compelled her to give him up for adoption. Even all these years later, with Daisy trying to make amends, he never tried to mask his bitterness over being rejected by his biological mother and grandparents. Isn't revenge a prime motive for murder?"

"Motive is not proof."

Kate yanked her hands from Tom's hold. "What does he have to do for you to act? Come after me?"

"Absolutely not. But we have to be discreet. The chief told me in no uncertain terms that this case is closed."

The chief. She fought to suppress the throb of raw uncertainty. If she shared her suspicions about Brewster on top of her accusations against Edward, Tom might accuse her of crying wolf about every person who had the remotest connection to Daisy.

Keith cleared his throat. "What Tom is trying to say is that you can't do anything that will draw attention to the fact that he's still treating your friend's death as a possible homicide."

"Possible?" Kate seethed, squaring her shoulders.

"Yes." Keith's tone brooked no argument.

Kate let her shoulders droop. The last thing she wanted to do was alienate the only two people, besides Julie, who believed there might be something to her theories.

"You've presented us with probable cause," Keith continued, "but we can't alert Edward or the department to our suspicions before we have enough evidence to haul him in. Guilty suspects are set free every day because the court disallows the use of improperly obtained evidence."

"But I didn't take the stuff out of the fireplace." She gasped. "Edward has probably destroyed it by now." Kate gripped the edge of the sofa cushion to keep her hands from fluttering in her frustration.

"It'll be okay," Tom said, his voice soothing. "If Edward's guilty, we'll get the evidence somehow. For now, if you run into him, it's imperative you treat him exactly the same as you have in the past. Pretend you are following up on some other lead, if you must. Whatever it takes so he won't think you suspect him."

Just the thought of being anywhere near Edward made her insides shake. "I . . . I don't think I can."

Tom squeezed her hand. "You can do this."

She wanted to believe him, but she couldn't escape the horrible scenarios looming in her mind. "What if he comes to my apartment or . . . or . . . ?"

"You have to trust us." Keith's no-nonsense tone reminded her of Gramps—a man she'd trusted implicitly. "We won't let Edward hurt you. But . . . trust no one else. Don't share your suspicions about Edward with another soul. Otherwise, he may hear about them. Do you understand?"

Now she knew where Tom came by his *people are rarely what they seem* attitude. Trouble was, she'd started to agree. "I understand, yes."

Except if Julie was right and Kate couldn't tell a Boy Scout from a purse snatcher, how could she be sure Tom and Keith weren't part of an elaborate cover-up?

After all, a few hours ago she'd been certain Chief Brewster was behind Daisy's death. What if Tom's help turned out to be like the apple pie baking in his dad's kitchen?

An illusion.

8

A *scratch, scratch, thunk* jolted Kate awake. Okay, not really awake since one had to actually fall asleep to be awakened, and her visions of Edward trolling around outside pretty much guaranteed that sleep wasn't in her near future.

The *scratch, scratch, thunk* sounded again.

Kate scooted up against her headboard, dragging the blankets with her, and switched on the bedside lamp. Between the bats in the attic and the mice in the walls, the place was one giant hotel for homeless critters, so she didn't usually get spooked by the odd scratch or thunk in the middle of the night. After Dad died, she and Mom had moved in with Gran and Gramps into their big old farmhouse, a veritable critter haven, so this converted century-old mansion had always felt like home.

The floor creaked.

Heart pounding, Kate grabbed her pet rock paperweight and slipped out of bed on the side farthest from the door. Outside, the blackness held more boogeymen. She imagined Edward spidering up the oak tree and peering through her window. She stuck her nose to the glass and cupped her hand around her eyes to block out the light.

Another pair of eyes lasered in on her.

She jumped back, stumbling over a pile of books.

Her peeping tom meowed.

She pressed her hand to her chest and laughed. At least it would've been a laugh if she'd been able to gulp enough air to emit the sound.

The floor creaked again. The same creak it made when someone stepped on the left edge of the hall five feet from the living room, give or take an inch. She fished through the pockets of the clothes she'd dumped in the corner and yanked out her cell phone.

It blipped on just long enough to show one microscopic green bar, then promptly went black. Dead battery. *Perfect.* And of course, Julie had to pick tonight of all nights to stay at her mom's.

Hinges squeaked. The door slowly swung into the room.

Kate pressed her back to the wall and this time eyeballed the tree outside her window for an entirely different reason. But the closest branch was at least three feet away, and she'd flunked long jump in school.

"Oh good, you're still up," Julie chirped.

The air left Kate's chest in a whoosh. She lowered the rock she couldn't remember raising over her head. "I thought you were staying at your mom's tonight."

"And wait until tomorrow to get all the juicy details on how Tom came to your rescue?"

"How did you know?"

"Because I called him when you didn't answer your cell phone."

"What made you think I needed rescuing?"

Julie looked pointedly at the rock still clutched in Kate's hand.

"I thought you were an intruder!"

"Admit it. You thought I was Edward."

Kate plopped the rock on her night table and plugged in her cell phone. "What if I did?"

"You want to watch a movie with me?"

"Is that a new version of 'I told you so'?"

Julie laughed. "Come on, a good movie always takes my mind off my troubles."

Kate grabbed her pillow and blanket. Watching a movie wasn't such a bad idea. Anything was better than the images that had been reeling through her mind for the past hour. "You do realize that normal people just eat ice cream when they're upset."

"Well, you're in luck. I think there's still a carton of chocolate fudge buried in the bottom of the freezer for just such an emergency."

They dug out the ice cream, slipped *Australia* into the DVD player, and rehashed the evening's events during the slow scenes. By the time Kate climbed into bed three hours later, she fell asleep the moment her head touched the pillow and was visited by dreams, not of Edward stalking her with a fire poker, but of Hugh Jackman sweeping her onto his horse and riding off into the Australian sunset. The scariest thing in her dream was that Jackman looked an awful lot like Tom Parker.

The next morning, Julie stubbornly ignored Kate's protests and dragged her to A Cup or Two for breakfast. Kate didn't want to face Edward without thick metal bars between them, and from the way he'd flirted with Molly yesterday, chances were too good that he'd show up at the tea shop again. So when Kate and Julie arrived, Kate refused to pick up a tray until she'd meticulously scanned the room and assured herself that he was nowhere in sight.

Temporarily appeased, she scooped her tea in record time, grabbed a muffin, and headed for the cash register. A special one-page Friday edition of Port Aster's so-called weekly newspaper sat on the counter.

"Port Aster High must've won a ribbon at track and field yesterday," Kate muttered to Julie, praying the news-challenged editor hadn't considered Daisy's apparent suicide worthy of a follow-up. Kate handed Molly a five-dollar bill for the tea and muffin while voices in her head argued over whether or not she should warn Molly to stay away from Edward.

This wasn't the time or place to inform Molly that her choice of boyfriends stunk. Besides, Kate was pretty sure Molly would think Kate was sucking sour grapes. And if Molly divulged Kate's concerns to Edward, that would only make matters worse.

Without waiting for the change, Kate scurried through the crowded dining area to the last available table, smack in the middle of the room.

Julie plopped her tray on the table and poked at the headline on the paper she'd picked up. "Look at this."

"Buying those extras only encourages Harold to print more, you know."

"Ooh, someone got up on the wrong side of the bed this morning."

Kate poked out her tongue as she dragged the news page to her side of the table. "Pharmaceutical company looks to Port Aster for new home," she read aloud. "What's the big deal? The mayor's been wooing businesses to the area from the day he took office. It'd only be news if the reporter uncovered proof that the mayor scored kick-backs for his efforts."

Julie rolled her eyes. "Honest Abe probably doesn't know what a kickback is. But I think he's hit the big league this time. It says here that the development will bring hundreds of new jobs to the area."

"New jobs mean more people."

Julie's eyes brightened. "Yeah, hungry people. What better time for me to open my chocolate shop?"

"Lack of clients is not what's stopped you so far. Call me backward, but I like our small town the way it is. Small. I already have a hard enough time finding a table in here."

The tea shop attracted a surprisingly diverse clientele, from men in business suits grabbing a quick bite before their morning commute to the contingent of senior ladies who tended to jib-jab over their cups of tea for a good two hours before starting their day. When Kate used to work here, she heard more about the goings-on in town than the local hairdresser and barber combined.

That reminded her of someone. Kate pulled out her suspect list and jotted a reminder to talk to Daisy's neighbor.

A silver-haired businessman stopped beside the table. "Pardon me for interrupting. You wouldn't happen to be any relation to Gwen Baxter, would you?"

Kate spluttered into her tea. She hadn't heard that name in over twenty-five years, not since Mom reverted to her maiden name after Daddy's death. "Yes, Gwen was my mother."

Julie's brow scrunched in understandable confusion, but thankfully, for once, she didn't blurt out the questions that had to be racing through her head, starting with, *Why did your mother change her name?*

If this guy knew about Dad's arrest and Kate didn't cut him off, everyone in the tea shop would learn her dirty little secret, which meant everyone in town would hear the rumor by nightfall. And wouldn't that go over well with the powers who held the purse strings on her research project?

There *were* a few disadvantages to living in a small town.

The bell over the door jingled, and in walked none other than Herbert Harold III, the illustrious owner and editor of the *Port Aster Press.*

Terrific. If he caught wind of the juicy gossip, she'd be tomorrow's extra-special edition head-line. If only she'd snuck off to work this morning like she'd intended and laid low until Tom arrested Edward, none of this would have happened.

"You're the spitting image of Gwen," the gentleman gushed. An observation Kate had heard many times over the years. "Your mom living around here now?"

"No, she died."

"Oh, I'm sorry. I hadn't heard. After your dad—"

"I'm sorry, Mr. . . . ?"

"Call me Peter."

"Nice to meet you, Peter, but I'm afraid I'm already late for work." Kate swallowed her tea in one gulp, tucked her muffin into her purse, and threw Julie an apologetic glance.

"Yes, of course, sorry to keep you. Perhaps I'll see you again sometime."

The suggestion sent an icy chill through her despite the hot tea burning her throat. If he talked to others about her family's skeletons, she'd be served up as the special of the day for a solid month. Longer if no better news cropped up. "Are you in town for long?"

"Not this time. On my way out now, as a matter of fact, but if everything goes according to plan, I'm sure I'll be back."

Wonderful. She couldn't wait. Not.

After pacing the floor half the night, thinking about where he might uncover a telltale slipup that would give him the ammunition he needed to take Crump down, Tom decided that the coroner's office was the logical place to start. Early in the morning, he followed the maze of corridors through the hospital's basement to the cramped quarters of the county's forensics team.

The clerk at the front window, who had the unsavory job of logging all the bodies, sent Tom to the supervisor's office in the back. The office was miniscule and doorless—an ego-deflating blow to a guy who'd spent half a decade in medical school to get here. The kind of demoralization that might justify accepting a little palm greasing if the opportunity arose.

Tom rubbed his nose in a vain attempt to get rid of the stomach-curdling smells swirling up his nostrils.

The slight thirty-something doctor looked up from the report he was scrawling. His milky coloring suggested he rarely ventured outside. "May I help you, Detective?"

"Yes, I have a few questions regarding your report on Leacock, Daisy—apparent poisoning."

"Well, I'd offer you a seat, but as you can see, we're a little short on space here."

Tom looked around the eight-by-eight room for a place to park himself, but the boxes occupying every square inch of available floor space didn't look strong enough to support his weight. He leaned on the door frame instead. "You stated in your report that Daisy died from thiophene poisoning."

"That's correct. According to her medical records, she had high blood pressure and arthritis but was otherwise in good health. No evidence of trauma to the body. The information's all in my report."

"Isn't thiophene a phototoxic chemical, not one that you'd expect to cause death?"

The coroner tilted his head from side to side, his lips a tight line, as if he was reluctant to agree. "Generally speaking, yes. However, you wouldn't expect peanuts to kill people, yet every year hundreds of people die from eating them."

"So you're saying Miss Leacock had an allergic reaction to the poison?"

"No, I merely cite that as an example of how we can each have a different response to the same stimulus. Forensics is a science, Detective. I stand by my conclusions."

"In your report, you noted the presence of hemolysis. What is that?"

The coroner tossed his pen on the desk and kneaded the muscles in the back of his neck. "Simply put, it means the red blood cells were breaking up. You don't need to understand the process. That's what they pay me for."

"But there are other poisons that weren't tested for?"

"Of course. The department can't afford to test for a fraction of the possible poisons. As it was, we tested for some fairly obscure ones based on the herbs you found in the victim's home. And, I might add, we got the results back to you in record time."

"Yes, we appreciate that."

"Well, let's hope the mayor shows his appreciation with an increase in funding." The coroner's tone suggested that there was an *or else* behind his words. "In a strange twist of fate, Leacock may have done her community a greater service than if she'd lived to develop her newest herbal remedy."

"How so?"

"By reminding the public that negative reactions to herbal mixtures are not uncommon. Sometimes they are downright deadly."

Tom propped his elbows on his desk and rubbed his fingers over his forehead in slow circles. His chat with the coroner had raised more questions than answers, and after hours of poring over police reports from four counties, he still wasn't convinced Edward was guilty of anything more than trying to swindle the old woman and then covering up the evidence. Except since Daisy had known Edward wasn't really her nephew, charges of swindling would never stick.

A rush of greetings hailed the chief's late arrival.

Tom shoved the reports on Edward into a folder and slipped it beneath the robbery file he was supposed to be working on.

Hank detoured off the direct route to his office and zeroed in on Tom. "Afternoon." Hank glanced at the open file. "Made any headway on those cases?"

Tom leaned back in his chair and pasted on a confident expression. "Some."

Hank hovered over the desk.

"Was there anything else?" Tom asked in his best impression of wide-eyed and innocent.

Hank's grunt suggested he wasn't buying the act. His gaze slid to the open file a second time before he stalked to his office.

So much for having an ally on the force. Around the squad room, clusters of officers downed their afternoon coffees while swapping stories. At least with the collective cold shoulder Tom had gotten from everyone else in the department since his arrival, he didn't have to worry about anyone other than Hank scrutinizing his actions too closely.

Tom stuffed the Leacock file back into his drawer. He knew the contents by heart anyway. Not a shred of evidence connected Daisy to a grow-op. Edward burning one of her journals made him look guilty, but of what? Murder? Or simply of wanting to keep his con a secret? And how did Darryl Kish's wife fit into the picture?

If the fear in Kate's eyes hadn't gripped Tom's heart as fiercely as her white-knuckled fingers had gripped her steering wheel, he might've written off the apparent tail on her car last night as a coincidence. It hadn't helped that he'd wanted to tug Kate into his arms and assure her everything would be okay. Not exactly the feelings of an impartial detective.

Although he hadn't missed how her eyes had

continually strayed to his as if she too felt an attraction. Years of police work should've inoculated him to the effect of what probably amounted to nothing more than a short-lived case of hero worship.

If not for the fact the case was supposed to be closed, he'd pull himself off the investigation. Gaining a clear perspective of whether or not the marijuana leaf in Daisy's notebook, Edward's con game, and Daisy's death were related was difficult enough without throwing a volatile mix of chemistry into the investigation.

At least his concern that explosives might be headed for a Memorial Day event in less than two weeks had been unfounded.

Tom reached for the phone to check in with his dad. The internal line buzzed. Tom connected and Hank's voice resonated over the line.

"Get into my office. Now."

Tom groaned. He didn't have time to deal with whatever had tied Hank's boxers in a knot this time. Tom stepped into Hank's office and closed the door.

Hank stood behind his scarred wooden desk, staring out the window toward the clock tower across the street.

The tower bells pealed their rendition of the Westminster chimes, and then a mournful gong counted off the hour.

"I told you the Leacock case was closed."

Hank's fist tightened around a slip of paper curled in his hand.

"Yes."

"Then why are you harassing her lawyer for details about her will?"

Tom pressed his lips together. He should have known the lawyer would snitch.

The veins in Hank's neck bulged. "Well?"

"Since we last spoke, I've learned that Edward is an heir to Daisy's estate. Kate expressed concern about his trustworthiness, given the time line between his arrival in town and Daisy's death. I simply wanted to set her mind at ease."

"Yesterday Miss Adams thought Leacock stumbled onto a grow-op. Today she thinks Edward killed the woman for her money. What will it be tomorrow? Her boss killed her because she caught him dipping into the coffee fund?"

Hank's wisecrack hit too close to the niggling concern Tom had so far ignored. "I know it seems like Kate is going off on a hundred different wild goose chases, but we do the same—gather evidence against a few possible suspects until we narrow in on one. And you've got to admit Edward's sudden stake in Daisy's estate looks suspicious." Tom didn't mention what else he'd learned about Edward. Hank didn't need any more fuel with which to burn Tom for disobeying orders.

"I told that woman to stay out of trouble. The

last thing I need is a civilian questioning the competency of my department."

"Perhaps if you allowed me to sift through the evidence she's foun—"

"You have been doing that. Without my permission. Against my orders, in fact. You're on thin ice here, Parker. Just because we're old friends doesn't mean I won't fire you for insubordination."

"Understood," Tom said with a healthy dose of boot kissing in his tone. Clearly, Hank felt threatened by more than Kate's investigation. From the way he was throwing his weight around, he seemed worried Tom would steal his job.

Hank strode across the room and held open the door. "I want you on those other cases. Now get out of here."

Outside Hank's office, Carla actually gave Tom a sympathetic look. "Your dad called. Said it was urgent."

Tom's thoughts flashed to Kate. If Edward had slipped past Dad's surveillance . . . Tom rushed to his desk and punched in Dad's number.

Dad picked up on the first ring.

"What's wrong?"

"I'm not sure Kate's as safe in that lab of hers as you'd like to believe."

"Is Edward on his way there?"

"No, Edward's still over an hour away."

"How do you know?"

"If I told you, you'd have to arrest me."

Tom pictured his dad slipping a GPS locator into Edward's pocket or affixing it to his car. "Okay, never mind. I don't need to know."

"I called in a few favors and got the scoop on the lady who tailed Kate last night."

"And?"

"It seems the Kishes have some cash flow problems. Last year, Darryl lost a research grant for his project to Leacock's. Another application is coming up for consideration, one that wouldn't have had a chance if not for her death."

"You think Darryl killed Daisy to clear the way for his grant?"

"Money is the most common motive for murder. Darryl pulls in a decent salary, but his personal account is overdrawn, and despite the steady stream of customers into A Cup or Two, the store's credit rating is in the toilet."

Tom shuffled around the files on his desk, searching for his car keys. How could he have ignored his niggling suspicion of Darryl and let Kate walk right into his lair? "We've got to get her out of there."

"If Kish is our man, yanking Kate will only alert him to our suspicions. Kate thinks Edward killed Daisy. As long as Kish knows that, he has no reason to silence her."

"But he won't know that, because we told her not to tell anyone."

9

With the curtains drawn, the research lab felt like a tomb. The polished marble floors and stainless steel counters only added to the chilly feel of the place. Kate buttoned her lab coat and turned up the heat. One glimpse of her pasty reflection in the metal vent hood and a sour taste slid down her throat. She looked like a walking zombie.

A little sunshine might make her feel better, but until Tom arrested Edward, the curtains would stay closed and the lab door locked. With any luck, Edward wouldn't spot her VW parked behind the implement shed. Not that she believed in luck. She closed her eyes and winged a prayer heavenward for the hundredth time today, painfully aware that she was just plain ignoring the elephant in the room.

Oh, who was she kidding? It was a great big woolly mammoth. A mammoth that had been around since the day Dad was ripped from her life. A mammoth she'd just as soon usher straight back into its cage rather than let snort about lancing open scabbed-over wounds.

And that was exactly what she intended to do.

She grabbed a test tube and concentrated on the

task at hand. Without the distraction of passersby outside the windows or colleagues sticking their heads in the door, she might actually get the gene she needed isolated by the end of the day. Her grant sponsors wanted results, not excuses. If the whispered rumors that Daisy's death was the result of an experiment gone wrong reached the higher-ups before Kate could prove otherwise, they wouldn't hesitate to nix her funding. After all, as Darryl had so tactlessly pointed out, a breakthrough in herbal research wasn't worth risking the foundation's spotless reputation.

She plodded through the required protocol with meticulous accuracy, doing her best to confine her thoughts to her work.

Four hours later, her cell phone rang for the sixteenth time. Kate glanced at the incoming number and let out a sigh. "This better be important, Jules."

"Why are you ignoring my calls?"

"I'm working."

"That's never stopped you from answering before. What if I'd had an emergency?"

"You would have left a more detailed message than 'we need to talk.' "

"Well, we do, starting with why you have a different last name than your parents."

On the plus side of this oh so not-positive day, Kate's inability to constrain her thoughts to her work had given her plenty of time to rehearse answers to the questions she knew were coming. "After Dad died, Mom reverted to her maiden name and changed mine too."

"Why?"

"I don't know. I was young. I scarcely remember being a Baxter." Kate hooked her Bluetooth receiver over her ear so she could set down her phone and continue working.

"You never asked your mom?"

"Sure I did, but I never got a reasonable explanation." Wasn't that the truth? Mom gave lots of explanations, but none of them were ever reasonable. A man who did nothing wrong didn't get carted off in a paddy wagon.

"From the way you brushed off that guy in the café, I got the impression your old name made you uncomfortable, scared even."

"You're reading way too much into this. I'm tired. I'm behind on my work. I'm preoccupied with the murder investigation. I just didn't feel like rehashing stories about my parents, okay?" Kate stared at the beaker in her hand and couldn't remember what she'd been about to do with it.

"I'm sorry," Julie said, sounding a little more empathetic than the *National Enquirer* reporter she'd been imitating a minute ago. "I should have realized. You know that if you ever want to talk about . . . anything, I'm here for you."

"Thanks, Julie." Not going to happen. Some secrets were better left buried.

"Will you let me in?"

Kate steeled herself against the tug of Julie's heartfelt offer. "I don't need to talk, honest." A knock sounded at the door. "Listen, I've got to go. Someone's at the lab door." Kate clicked off her phone and waited quietly, hoping whoever was in the hall would give up and leave.

The knock sounded again. Louder. "I know you're in there and I'm not going anywhere until you talk to me."

Julie? Kate yanked open the door and Julie held up a tub of ice cream and two spoons. "Therapy time," she sing-songed.

Kate left the door standing open and retreated to her workbench. "You do realize that if you keep up this kind of therapy, you won't fit into your wedding gown."

"Oh, I just pretend to eat it. It's all part of my top secret plan to fatten you up so I'll look that much better on my wedding day."

"Very funny. I really do have work to do."

"Why do you have the room so dark? No wonder you're down." Julie plopped the tub of ice cream onto the workbench and tugged open the curtains. "That's better."

At the sudden brightness, Kate's head pinged in protest.

Julie dragged a stool over to Kate's workbench, dug her elbows into the counter, and rested her chin on her hands. "Okay, I'm all ears."

Kate shuffled the test tubes she'd been in the middle of filling. "There's nothing to talk about."

"Don't lie to me, Kate Adams. Around about the fourteenth time you let my call go to voice mail, I finally realized what a pitiful friend I've been, skipping from cloud to cloud preparing for my wedding, oblivious to how hard Daisy's death has hit you."

"I'm fine, really."

"See, that's where you're wrong. You stuff your feelings into a little box and hide them away so the rest of us are fooled into believing you're okay."

"I am okay."

"See, you've even got yourself fooled."

Kate's breathing turned quick and shallow. The woolly mammoth had sharpened his tusks on the metal bars of his cage and was preparing to make a break for it. And she was pretty sure she wouldn't survive the stampede. Not in one piece. "Julie, I really do not want to talk about this."

"I am not going to let you hide away in your lab, pretending everything is hunky-dory when I know darn well it's not."

"I'm pretending no such thing. Daisy was murdered and the police aren't doing anything about it. I can hardly be accused of keeping how I feel about that to myself."

"True." Julie licked a dollop of ice cream off

her spoon and then pointed the spoon at Kate. "But have you considered that the investigation is an excuse to avoid facing your hurt over losing Daisy?"

"That's ridiculous." Kate snatched up the other spoon and dug into the tub of ice cream.

"Think about it. You lost your dad when you were way too young. In your head, you knew he didn't choose to die, but in your heart you must have felt abandoned. I know I would have. Now you've lost Daisy, and deep down you must feel abandoned all over again."

"Daisy did *not* abandon me." Kate gulped down a gob of ice cream, but the icy milk didn't cool the burn in her throat.

"No, she didn't abandon you. Even if she committed suicide."

"That's not why I'm—"

Julie held up her hands. "Okay, okay. I'm just saying that maybe your compulsion to prove the police wrong is rooted in something deeper than you realize."

Kate dropped her spoon into the ice cream tub, wondering how they'd jumped from a name change to her supposed abandonment issues. "I've got to get back to work."

"See, this is what I'm talking about. You refuse to face your feelings."

Kate wished she could curl into a ball and hide until the pain in her chest eased. She knew that if she waited it out, the ache would eventually become bearable. Just like it had when she was a little girl.

Okay, so maybe she did have issues.

"What are you afraid of?"

"Nothing."

"Hogwash. A look of pure panic crossed your face when that Peter guy mentioned your folks."

Kate reshuffled the test tubes as she struggled to snuff out the mutiny her emotions were waging in her chest. "Maybe I didn't want memories conjured up when I'm already frazzled by Daisy's death. As you so aptly pointed out, I don't like to wear my emotions on my sleeve."

"Uh-huh. Now tell me what you're really afraid of."

Kate looked her friend in the eye. Instead of accusations, she saw compassion.

The crust around her heart began to crack. For years she'd wished for a friend like Julie, someone who would see the hurt she'd hidden away from the world like the good little girl she was supposed to be, and just understand.

Tears pressed at Kate's eyes. By the time Daisy had come along, Kate had gotten so good at the hiding that she hadn't realized how much she'd held back. "I'm afraid of becoming the town's latest gossip," she admitted.

"Because of something your folks did?"

"My dad, yes, and please don't ask me what."

To Kate's surprise, this time Julie didn't press for details. "The people who genuinely care about you won't love you any less because of something your parents did."

"That hasn't been my experience."

Julie reached across the bench and squeezed Kate's hand. "I'm sorry, Kate. I truly am."

Afraid that she'd break down if she said any more, Kate merely nodded.

"I'll let you get back to work."

After Julie left, Kate locked the door and went to draw the curtains. Drawn by the warmth of the sun on her face, she lingered. As she stared at the sky, God whispered to her heart. *Tell me what you're really afraid of.*

Kate swiped her sleeve across her eyes and swung her head from side to side, but the urging didn't relent.

I'm afraid that the stories Mom told me about my dad aren't true and that maybe what I believe about Daisy isn't true either. And that knowing the truth will hurt more than I can bear.

The tight band crushing her chest eased its grip, and in its place she felt Jesus wrap his loving arms around her. A Bible verse whispered through her thoughts: *Then you will know the truth, and the truth will set you free.*

Leaving the curtains open, she returned to her work.

Kate pipetted five hundred microliters of extraction buffer into micro tubes of lyophilized calendula leaves.

A movement at the window startled her into dispensing too many drops from the strawlike tube. She glowered at the curtains rippling under the force of air rising from the heat vents and let out a frustrated groan. If she didn't get a grip, she'd never finish this experiment.

She grabbed a clean test tube and started again.

The doorknob rattled, but this time she managed not to jump at the disturbance. She carefully finished adding the drops to the tube and ignored whoever stood outside. Ignored, that was, unless she counted the way her pulse sped up and her hands trembled.

A key scratched the lock.

Edward doesn't have a key, she told herself, but she jabbed the test tube into its holder and edged toward the side door anyway.

The hall door burst open and Darryl strode in. "You are here." He stopped short. "What happened? You look terrible."

"Why, thanks. So nice of you to notice." She finger-combed her hair, wishing she'd taken Julie up on her offer of drops for her bloodshot eyes. Not that she could blame their present redness on staring into Daisy's journals at four in the morning.

Darryl frowned. "Please tell me you aren't still trying to convince the police Daisy was murdered."

"Well, she sure didn't commit suicide. You know as well as I do that even if she'd been dying of some incurable disease, Daisy would never have gone against everything she believed and taken her own life."

Darryl opened his mouth as if he might rebut, but Kate stopped him.

"Don't say it. Daisy was too smart to make such a critical mistake. In fact, based on other symptoms the coroner noted in his report, I'm not convinced Daisy died from thiophene at all."

Darryl stared at her for a full minute, his expression unreadable. "You have to let this go."

"I won't. I—" Kate clamped her mouth shut. Keith and Tom had told her to keep a low profile and trust no one, and here she'd just about spouted her theory to Darryl. But she had to be right about Edward. What other reason could he have had for burning Daisy's journal?

Not that she had a good explanation for why Hank had ambushed her in the woods, or why he was so adamant that the case not be reopened.

Then there was the missing intern. She'd forgotten to tell Tom about him. When she'd thought Brewster was behind Daisy's murder, Gordon's disappearance had seemed connected, but not if Edward was the murderer.

157

As casually as her jittery nerves allowed, Kate lifted a rack of test tubes to the bench. "Did Daisy happen to mention to you that one of her interns quit?"

"You're blaming her death on a student now?"

"No." Kate squared her shoulders and repeated more firmly. "No, I'm responsible for them. Remember? I was just wondering if you were aware one had quit."

"Sure, Gord . . ." Darryl looked at the ceiling as if the name might be etched in the tiles. "Sorry, I can't remember his last name."

"Laslo."

"That's it. Bright kid, but he was more interested in his gadgets than botany."

"Gadgets?"

"He invented stuff. Usually things that minimized how much work he'd have to do. Nothing that ever worked too great. Although he once came up with a moisture meter that wasn't half bad."

"I checked with the registrar at the university. They have no record of him quitting."

Darryl pulled a box of beakers down from a shelf. "You know how kids are. They just leave. They don't think about who they're supposed to tell. Do you mind if I borrow a couple of these beakers?"

She waved off the question as if he didn't need to ask. "So you think Gord quit because he didn't want to do the work?"

"Could be. Daisy probably told me, but you know how it is." Darryl removed two beakers, returned the box to the shelf, looked at the two he'd removed, pulled the box down again, and took out two more.

"Everything okay?" Kate asked, noting how preoccupied he'd been lately.

"Fine. Everything's fine." He stuffed the box back on the shelf. "Could soon be great, actually. Did you see the article in the paper about the pharmaceutical company that wants to build here?"

"I saw the headline."

"Well, one of their reps, a guy by the name of Peter, was talking to the director yesterday."

Peter. That had to be the same guy who talked to her in the tea shop. The guy who knew her parents. The guy who could blow her secret.

"The company wants to partner with us on some research. It'll mean a nice cash injection for our department."

"A drug company wants to partner with *us?* They're our worst critics."

"Yeah, but they have deep pockets, and they won't be so critical if they want to stay on our good side."

"I don't like it."

"You might have to lump it, whether you like it or not. Two more donors revoked their funding to your project since news of Daisy's cause of death broke."

"I don't believe this."

"Believe it."

"I don't get your attitude. You should be as anxious as I am to prove Daisy didn't kill herself by drinking marigold tea."

"I have enough on my mind worrying about what folks are drinking at my wife's shop." Darryl paused at the door. "She's been too sick to work, and I've had to take up the slack."

"She's sick? I thought I saw her out driving last night."

"No, she's been in bed for days."

Kate hesitated. "I'm sorry to hear that. What's wrong? Is there anything I can do to help?"

"No," he said abruptly, his hand on the doorknob. "I've got it under control. Thanks." He left without telling Kate what was wrong with Beth, and Kate had a sinking feeling the lapse wasn't just an oversight.

She *had* seen Beth's car last night. Tom had confirmed the plates. Why would Darryl lie about her going out? What was he trying to hide?

Kate sank onto a stool and laid her head on her arms.

What's happening to me, Lord? I used to trust everyone, believe the best about people, no matter how things looked. Now I'm becoming like Tom—suspicious of everyone. I don't want to be like that, Lord.

Except Tom wasn't suspicious of *her,* even

though she stood to gain from Daisy's death too. No, Tom had seemed genuinely worried about her. Willing to risk his job to find the truth. And here she sat squirreled away in her lab, taking nada risks, while he and his dad tried to solve her friend's murder. The least she could do was track down the missing intern and then pay Beth a surprise visit. Find out if she really was sick.

Reenergized by the decision to take action, Kate finished her experiment and then phoned the registrar's office for Gord's home address.

"I can't give out private information. You should know that," the receptionist said.

"It's information I could get out of any phone book or online directory."

"Then go ahead."

"Do you know how many G. Laslos there are in the region? And I don't even know if he's from this area."

"I'm sorry. I can't help you."

Kate could picture the smirk on Lana's face—a woman who loved power way too much. Kate would love to be a spider on the wall when she sicced Tom on her and he marched in flashing his badge, demanding information or else. Of course, knowing Lana, all Tom would have to do was flash his pearly whites to get the information.

Kate's mouth soured. Maybe she'd find another way.

She gathered her purse and headed toward the

rear exit. First she'd check out Beth's alibi for last night. Kate phoned Tom's cell and left a voice mail detailing where she was heading, then slipped outside. Despite Keith's promise to phone the minute Edward's car came within an hour of Port Aster, she slinked toward her parking spot in the shadow of the building, scanning the lot for a green Porsche.

Once safely locked inside her car, Kate let herself breathe again. Maybe paying Beth a surprise visit wasn't such a smart idea. Kate's heart could take only so much racing in one day. Besides, Darryl hadn't seemed too pleased by her offer to help.

Men. If Beth had been stuck in bed for a few days, she must be desperate for company. Of course, she hadn't been in bed last night.

But her following Kate had to be a weird coincidence.

And the only way to find out was to ask.

Kate parked in front of the bakery. A half-dozen warm-from-the-oven apple fritters were just what she needed to get Beth talking. The door to the shop opened and Kate's stomach gurgled at the delicious smell of sweet pastries that wafted out.

Molly walked out in a stunning black sheath, dripping with diamonds—well, cubic zirconium, more likely. Convincing, though.

A light blend of floral scents—rose, iris, orange

blossom—enveloped her like a fine silk wrap. Kate inhaled. Wow, the fragrance didn't smell like any department store perfume she'd ever tried. More like something only the rich and famous wore. She'd have to ask Molly where she found such a great knockoff.

Absorbed in a phone call, Molly almost plowed straight into Kate. "Yes, Daddy, everything worked out perfectly. I love you too. Bye."

Kate whistled. "Hot date?"

"Yes." Molly beamed. "Edward's taking me to the theater."

"Oh." Kate choked down her surprise. "That's great. How long have you two been dating?" And why hadn't Keith called to warn her that Edward was back in town?

"We're engaged."

"Engaged?" Kate squeaked. "Really?" Suddenly more worried about poor Molly than where Edward happened to be at the moment, Kate debated how to respond. How could Edward drag such an impressionable young woman into his sordid schemes? If only she hadn't been so busy with the investigation, she might have gotten to know Molly well enough to warn her.

Curiosity tugged Kate's gaze to Molly's left hand, and the girl obliged by fluttering her mustard seed–sized diamond under Kate's nose. "Gorgeous, don't you think?"

"Wow. Congratulations. I can't believe Edward

didn't tell Daisy that he planned to ask you. She would've been thrilled."

"Yes, he misses her terribly. Her death hit him so hard." Molly cupped her hands over her heart as if she shared his heartache. "But it's made him realize how very lonely he's been without me."

"You knew each other before moving here?" Kate couldn't keep the surprise from her voice.

"Yes." Molly's lips curved into a satisfied smirk, no doubt savoring her victory over a would-be rival. "He had a brief bout of cold feet after my aunt died but has come to his senses now." She glanced at her watch. "Oh, look at the time. I've got to run or I'll be late."

Elsie Wagner, strands of gray hair dribbling from her bun, opened the bakery door. "Are you buying? We close soon. *Ja*?"

Kate followed her inside and let the yeasty, cinnamony smell transplant her concern for Molly. Rows of pastries, squares, and old-fashioned donuts lined the shelves behind the glass. "I'll have six apple fritters, please."

Elsie wiped her floury hands on her apron, then took up the tongs and boxed the decadent delights. If these couldn't coax the truth out of Beth, Kate didn't know what would.

Confident Edward would be more than preoccupied with his fiancée for the next couple of hours, Kate left her car parked in front of the bakery, walked the half block to A Cup or Two, and slipped down the side alley to the back stairs that led to Darryl and Beth's second-floor apartment.

A scuffling erupted behind her. Flattening her back to the wall, she knifed her keys between her fingers. What had she been thinking, trapping herself in an alley with no other exit?

A rat scurried out from under a jumble of boxes and disappeared through a hole in the back fence.

Kate cringed and ran up the metal stairs before any other creatures appeared. She half expected the clatter would draw Beth to the door, but it remained firmly shut.

At the top of the stairs, Kate smoothed her hair, held up the box of fritters, took a deep breath, plastered on a smile, and knocked.

The deadbolt scraped open, then the chain latch rattled against the door at the same time that her cell phone rang. She couldn't very well juggle the fritter box and dig her phone out of her purse, let alone be rudely talking on it when Beth opened the door. Whoever was calling would just have to wait. The worn brass knob seemed to turn in slow motion. Then as the door opened, Kate pulled her gaze from the knob to—

Her breath caught. "Darryl?"

10

How could Kate think he wouldn't mind her visiting the woman who'd tailed her car last night? Halfway through Kate's phone message, Tom grabbed his coat and raced out of police headquarters.

The clock tower clanged out the time. Each gong lobbed Tom's chest with the force of a billy club. Five. Forty minutes since Kate left the message on his cell. Hours since the call from his dad.

In the parking lot, Tom darted around two officers. He never should've let Dad talk him out of pulling Kate from the lab. Tom punched her number into his cell phone. It rang five times, then cut to voice mail. He tried again. *Come on, Kate. Pick up.*

Daisy's charcoaled journal should have proven to Kate that no one could be trusted. What did he have to do to get that fact through her brain? Spell it out with tulips in a giant flower bed?

He sped out of the parking lot and headed for A Cup or Two. The Kishes lived above the store, so with any luck they wouldn't draw attention to themselves by threatening Kate where a shop full of patrons might overhear.

Have you ever known a criminal in his right mind, Detective?

The recollection of Kate's flippant remark doused his wishful thinking like a splash of icy water.

As he turned onto Main Street, he slowed his car. The warm spring evening had drawn people out in droves, Friday night revelers celebrating the start of the weekend.

Crowds were good. Darryl wouldn't try anything with this many witnesses around. Then again, a scream above a noisy street might scarcely be noticed.

Tom spotted Kate's empty VW Bug outside the bakery, and his emotions seesawed between relief and worry. He parked across the street and jogged over to check it out.

Elsie Wagner bustled through the front door of the bakery trailed by a yeasty aroma. "*Ach,* Tommy. Look at you." She smushed his cheeks in her doughy fingers. "You need to eat more. Come. I give you schnitzels to take home to your dad."

"I can't now. Thank you. I'm looking for Kate Adams. Have you seen her?"

Elsie's eyes twinkled with the same matchmaker's gleam she'd sported the night he'd escorted her daughter to the high school prom. Except tonight his heart was pounding a hundred beats a second for an entirely different reason.

167

"*Ja*, she was here. Half an hour ago, maybe."

"Thank you." He sprinted the half block to the front door of A Cup or Two and scanned the shop through the front window. A teenager was wiping down tables. A couple of booths had patrons, but no sign of Kate. Taking a deep breath, he plunged down the side alley.

A cat screeched and streaked past him.

He gripped the metal handrail and mounted the stairs two at a time. Rust crumbled beneath his palm. The trash-tainted air tasted foul. Tom didn't want to think about what other foul-smelling secrets they might be hiding behind their fancy storefront.

At the top of the stairs, he willed his heart to slow. How would he explain his sudden appearance on their doorstep without making Darryl suspicious?

Tom recalled the twinkle in Elsie's eye. Yes, a ruse could work, if necessary. He tapped on the door.

Darryl, his shirt rumpled and hair a mess, as if he'd been wrestling something or someone, frowned. "Detective? May I help you?"

Tom looked past Darryl's shoulder as discreetly as possible but couldn't see beyond the narrow hallway. "I'm looking for Kate. I saw her car down the street, and she'd mentioned she might drop by to visit your wife."

Darryl's taut stance relaxed a fraction. "Kate,"

he shouted down the hall. "You have company."

Kate appeared in the hallway, eyes wide with surprise.

At the sight of her unharmed, Tom's concern melted. "There you are, sweetie," he crooned, stepping forward to catch her hands in his. "You had me worried."

An adorable flush washed over her cheeks. "Tom?" The inflection she added to his name asked, *Why are you here, acting like my boyfriend?*

"I made our reservations at the Wildflower for five." Tom shifted his gaze sideways to indicate the ruse was for Darryl's benefit. "You must've lost track of time." Tom showed her his watch.

Kate blinked, looking a little stunned. "Oh. Is it that late already? I'm sorry." She grabbed her purse from the kitchen counter.

He took the opportunity to survey the room. Aside from her purse, the counters and table were empty. A tropical tree with a spiny greenish-purple fruit stood next to the tiny window overlooking the side alley. He stepped back to let Kate go in front of him and scanned the tiny living room off the other side of the hall. A ratty sofa, two chairs, and a TV were the sole contents. The couple was definitely cash-strapped.

Kate hitched her purse strap over her shoulder. "Was that you on the phone earlier? I had my hands . . . oh, never mind. Let me say good-bye to Beth and then we can go."

For Darryl's benefit, Tom flashed her a grin that said, "I can't wait."

The color in her cheeks deepened. Kate was a natural. She couldn't have acted the part of besotted girlfriend better if they'd planned it. The gentle sway of her hair as she flitted down the hall awakened a yearning to run his fingers through her curls to see if they were as silky as they seemed. Maybe stopping by the Wildflower for dinner wasn't such a bad idea. For appearances' sake. After all, they had to eat, and he wouldn't want Darryl to catch on that this had been a ruse.

"I'm surprised Kate never mentioned you two were dating," Darryl said a little too offhandedly for Tom's peace of mind, especially since his latest suspect in Daisy's murder investigation now stood between him and the door.

If Kate's safety didn't hang in the balance, Tom would've liked nothing more than to interrogate Darryl right then. Instead, Tom rubbed his jaw and said, "Well, you know how it is. Until I closed the Leacock investigation, I wasn't at liberty to make my feelings known. But . . ." He lifted his palms in an exaggerated shrug, letting his gaze drift down the hall in the direction Kate had disappeared, wishing he'd trailed her in order to catch a glimpse of the bedroom.

He forced his attention back to Darryl. "I think the attraction is mutual."

"Huh," Darryl grunted. "I'd kind of gotten the impression she despised cops."

The revelation jabbed Tom square in the chest. Being despised was part of the job description, but Kate didn't seem like the type who would share the revulsion. "Really? Why's that?"

"I don't know. Just this attitude she gets when anyone talks about being caught speeding, that sort of thing." Darryl elbowed Tom's side and gave a couple of exaggerated winks. "Maybe she thinks getting in good with someone on the inside will get her out of a ticket."

Kate flounced toward them, wearing a sassy grin. "I do believe Darryl's jealous." She breezed past Tom and tapped Darryl's chest. "And no, I won't ask Tom to fix *your* speeding tickets."

Tom laughed. Ah, he could love this woman. "Sorry, Kish. Do the crime. Pay the time."

Darryl snickered, but with just enough edge to suggest a guilty conscience.

Tom rested his palm at the small of Kate's back and urged her toward the door. "We'll see ya."

Kate fluttered her fingers at Darryl as she stepped onto the outside landing. She continued to play the part of love-struck date until her feet hit the ground and the click of a deadbolt echoed in the narrow alley. "Now, do you mind telling me what that was all about?"

Uncertain whether Kish might be listening through an open window or watching for them from the front of their apartment, Tom hurried Kate forward, still touching her waist. "The show's not over yet. I'll walk you to your car. We'll talk at the Wildflower."

She stopped and gawked at him. "You really have a reservation?"

He winked.

A jumble of emotions, from surprise to befuddlement, paraded across her face. The fact she didn't seem at all displeased by the idea of joining him for dinner prompted him to silently pray that a table would be available at the busiest restaurant in town.

As they emerged from the alley, Tom glanced up at the Kish apartment and glimpsed movement behind the window. Tom dipped his head and whispered in Kate's ear. "We're being watched." Her fragrance—lavender, if he wasn't mistaken —teased his senses, and he let his gaze linger on her profile. Her creamy complexion radiated a natural beauty he had no business noticing when he should be focusing on the case, but he couldn't resist. Surprisingly, for the first time since his partner's death, Tom didn't want to resist.

To Kate's credit, she kept walking down the sidewalk toward her car and surprised him by entwining her arm around his. "Honestly, Tom. If you wanted to go out with me, all you had to do was ask." The teasing smile on her lips made his heart do a tiny flip. She slipped her arm free and tapped the unlock button on her key remote.

At the beep, he opened the driver's door and met her gaze. "All right then, will you join me for dinner?"

"I'd love to. Thank you."

The mischief in her eyes made his legs buckle. *Oh, boy.* How was he supposed to ensure *she* stayed out of danger when she had enough firepower in one glance to do serious damage to his common sense?

He hurried across the street to his own car. Once inside, he dug the business card for the Wildflower restaurant out of his wallet and dialed the number. If there hadn't been a hit-and-run in the restaurant's parking lot his first week on the job, he probably wouldn't have known much about the town's hottest new establishment, let alone had its phone number.

The hostess answered on the first ring. Tom gave his name and asked for a reservation for two as soon as possible.

"Oh, I remember you," the hostess squealed. "You're that nice detective who tracked down the guy who hit Sally. Just a minute, I'll see what I can do."

Tom set his cell in its holder and pulled onto the street behind Kate's car. Good thing for him he'd solved the hit-and-run case, or the hostess might have told him to eat somewhere else . . . like Mike's Truck Stop on the edge of town. He might never have had a steady girl, but Tom was smart enough to know that you didn't take your date to a restaurant where all the clientele wore plaid shirts and baseball caps, or where the tables had laminated place mats with ads for the local septic tank cleaning company, or where dollar-store plastic vines were wrapped around an indoor arbor spiked with artificial flowers covered in more dust than last winter's snowfall.

"Detective," the young woman came back on the line. "You're in luck. I have a table for two that will be available in about ten minutes."

"Perfect. Thank you." Now all he had to do was figure out what reason he'd give Kate for cutting short her visit with Beth. A reason that would make her cautious around Darryl without divulging her boss's possible link to Daisy's murder.

The hostess led them to a small table tucked into the corner, perfect for a private conversation.

Out of habit, Tom took the chair that backed to the wall so he could watch the room. The place was packed with casually attired couples in their mid-thirties to fifties—not a plaid shirt in sight. No one showed any special interest in him or Kate. Soft music played in the background, and flickering candles added to the romantic atmosphere.

After the hostess left them with their menus,

Kate looked at him with a mix of curiosity and delight. "I can't believe you brought me here. I thought for sure you were just worried about my visiting Beth and made up the dinner plans so Darryl wouldn't know you were still working the case."

Tom rubbed the back of his neck and lifted one side of his lips in a sheepish grin. "I *was* worried. And I *did* make up the story, but after you accepted my invitation, I couldn't resist following through. It's been a long time since I've had the pleasure of taking a beautiful woman to dinner."

The color that rushed to her cheeks reassured him that Kate, loyal Kate, was the sweet, innocent, hometown girl she seemed. Nothing like the woman who'd hijacked his partner's heart and cost him his life. Maybe when this case was over they could enjoy a real date.

"You know . . . you don't have to flatter me to get the information you're after."

"Trust me. That was not flattery."

"*That* coming from the man who told me to trust no one?" she teased, ducking behind her menu.

He tipped the laminated page forward. "I believe those were my dad's instructions. I'm the one who launched the recovery effort after you marched into Kish's apartment despite Dad's warning."

Kate's eyes rounded, the mischievous twinkle

supplanted by apprehension. "You thought Darryl or Beth would hurt me? They're colleagues, friends. You're supposed to be getting the evidence to lock up Edward."

"Beth followed you last night and then sped away. I think that's suspicious."

"You think everything is suspicious. Is there no one you trust?"

"Yes." He leaned toward her, lowering his voice in the hope she would do the same. "I'm trusting *you* to stay out of trouble."

"Well, all you have to do is arrest Edward."

Tom held in a sigh. If only the solution were that simple. "How did Beth explain her actions last night? I assume that's why you dropped in on her."

Kate laid her menu on the table and realigned the salt and pepper shakers. "The person following me couldn't have been Beth. She's too sick to go anywhere." Kate met his gaze for only an instant, then fussed with the pansies on the center of the table.

He picked up the vase and moved it out of her reach. "What aren't you telling me?"

Kate's shrug, a clear sign that she intended to deny the obvious, dampened his appetite.

"If you want me to help you, I need all the facts," he said.

"Has anyone ever told you you're moody? Because I could recommend a tea for that."

"Yeah? Do you have one that will get uncooperative witnesses to talk?" That earned him a smile.

"Okay, Beth mentioned that she lets Molly borrow her car. Molly's been helping her out by running errands for her. Last night she used the car to pick up groceries for both of them." The shift in Kate's gaze suggested she'd been selective in which facts she shared.

"Who's Molly?"

"The counter girl at A Cup or Two."

"Really?" Maybe Darryl had given the girl some extra work trailing Kate.

"She's also Edward's fiancée. They got engaged last night." Kate's gaze dropped to the fork she was fiddling with. "Molly seemed kind of . . . insecure . . . when Edward ran into me at the shop yesterday. I think maybe she followed us." Kate stopped fingering the cutlery and met Tom's gaze. "But now that Edward has asked her to marry him, I'm sure she won't worry anymore."

"In my experience, jealous lovers are exactly the kind of people one should worry about."

Kate frowned and then gnawed on her bottom lip. "I don't think she's jealous, exactly. No, definitely not. I spoke to her outside the bakery and she was positively twitterpated. I just hope she doesn't blame me when you arrest Edward."

"I'd be doing her a favor." Tom let out a

frustrated sigh. He'd hit nothing but dead ends tracing Crump's history in search of outstanding arrest warrants. "It could be some time before I have enough evidence to make an arrest. You need to be on your guard."

"Me? What about Molly?"

"She's a waitress. Edward isn't going to kill her for her money."

"No, but the longer this goes on, the more devastated she'll be. What more do you need? Edward did it."

"We don't know that."

Uncertainty crept into her gaze. "You still think Daisy killed herself, don't you?" Kate said in scarcely more than a whisper.

He stroked his thumb over the back of her hand. "No, I believe you." But divulging his reasons was too risky. He'd have to figure out some other way to convince Kate to lie low and let him handle everything. He dropped his gaze to their hands and traced the edge of her bracelet. "What's this for?"

"It's a medic alert bracelet. I'm allergic to hazelnuts."

Reflexively, he squeezed her fingers. Life was way too fragile. "I promise you, I will get whoever is responsible for your friend's death."

Dutiful maid of honor that she was, Kate felt too guilty not to spend Saturday morning helping

Julie take care of wedding details. She sucked in her stomach as the seamstress zipped up the back of the satin bridesmaid gown.

"I should probably let it out on the side," the woman mumbled around a mouthful of pins.

Kate barely took a second to admire the drape of the gown or how well the emerald green suited her complexion. "It's perfect as is," she said on what little air she could breathe in. The sooner she got through Julie's to-do list, the sooner she could check into the newest theory tangling her thoughts like vines of creeping Charlie.

Julie frowned. "Are you sure the waist isn't too tight?"

"It's fine." Kate wiggled to prove she wouldn't pop a seam and made a mental note to cut out the corn chips for a couple of weeks. In the floor-to-ceiling mirrors lining the enormous octagonal fitting room, her multiple fidgeting reflections looked like a crowd of bridesmaids with gnats in their knickers.

She motioned to the seamstress to unzip her.

Julie didn't look convinced. "You're mad at me, aren't you?"

"Why would I be mad at you?" Kate lifted the dress over her head. They still had the caterer and florist to visit before she could get away. Not that she was complaining. The errands had been a perfect excuse to pass on Edward's invitation to go through Daisy's belongings. Of course, Julie needn't know that Kate was being unselfish for selfish reasons.

"You've been kind of distant since I force-fed you a carton of ice cream." Translation: since I held you at spoon-point while you bared your soul. "And you weren't too thrilled this morning when I told Edward you couldn't help him today."

"Trust me. Edward is the last person I wanted to spend the day with." Kate hated keeping her suspicions about Edward a secret, but Tom and his dad had been insistent that no one be trusted.

And Julie did love to talk.

After the seamstress carried Kate's dress out of the dressing room, Julie whispered, "Do you think Edward poisoned Daisy?"

As Kate pulled on her slacks and T-shirt, she debated how to answer the question without answering it. "Let's just say I share your uneasiness about him." As soon as she finished her maid of honor duties this morning, she intended to unearth the proof she needed to bury him. A notation she'd found in one of Daisy's journals suggested the proof might be on the research lab's computer.

"You should leave this to the police. I don't want you being next. And I'm not just saying that because I'd have to find a new maid of honor." Julie made a quirky face, but the tremor of her chin suggested she was far more concerned than her teasing indicated.

"Don't worry about me. Parker's making sure I stay out of trouble."

The seamstress returned with Julie's wedding gown draped over her arm. "Tom Parker?"

"You know him?" Kate asked, not surprised that the woman would jump into the conversation. Conversation jumping was one of Port Aster's most popular pastimes. One that, if handled right, might prove informative.

The seamstress's professional smile turned dreamy. "I had a major crush on him in high school. I saw him at the Wildflower restaurant last night, but I couldn't place the face until you mentioned his name just now. Was that you he was with?"

Julie's jaw dropped, but only for the second it took for her voice to rise to Mount Everest altitudes. "You went to dinner with him and you didn't tell me?"

Kate tugged at the collar of her cotton tee. Wow, was it hot in this room or what? She edged to the farthest corner, half afraid that any second daggers might shoot from Julie's eyes and ricochet off the mirrors. "It's no big deal. It's not like it was a date or anything."

Although more than once Tom had intimated that it was, and despite her issues with his line of work, she'd enjoyed spending time with him, and okay, maybe she wanted to see him again. But first they needed to prove Edward killed Daisy.

"Besides, you weren't home until late last night, so I didn't have a chance to tell you."

Julie planted her hands on her hips and looked at Kate as if she were a rabbit that had eaten her wedding bouquet. "In case you haven't noticed, we've been together more than two hours. Plenty of time to tell me all about your date."

"This is your day. The evening was no big deal."

The seamstress helped Julie into the gown, apparently missing Kate's can-we-drop-this tone because the woman chattered on for a good five minutes about how good-looking Tom had been in high school.

Suddenly, her face flushed. She stopped fastening the buttons on the back of Julie's dress and glanced at Kate. "Oh my, if you're worried about me, don't be. My husband and I were at the restaurant to celebrate our tenth anniversary."

"Congratulations," Kate said, ignoring the woman's inconsequential assurance that she wasn't a rival for Tom's affections. Kate straightened Julie's train, which prompted the seamstress to finish fastening the row of buttons.

Thirty-seven buttons later, the woman stepped back and surveyed the fit.

The dress, with its sweetheart neckline, basque waist, and A-line cut, was exactly the style Kate might choose for herself. One day. "It's perfect. I wouldn't change a thing."

Julie grinned at Kate's reflection. "A dress like

this could be in your future sooner than you think."

Concealing the zing prompted by the comment, Kate rolled her eyes. "Tom and I shared one dinner. That's all."

"Tom, now, is it?" Julie teased.

Kate's pulse skittered the same way it had when Tom appeared on Darryl and Beth's doorstep, looking all worried. Hypnotized by the protective glimmer in his eyes, she'd slipped into the role of girlfriend with scarcely a moment's hesitation. Having someone worried about her had felt surprisingly wonderful. But she couldn't let wistful thinking undermine her good sense. Tom seemed like the kind of guy who would be equally worried about any man, woman, or child. Or a cat caught in a tree, for that matter. She shouldn't read more into their time together than there was—no matter how tempting.

Kate looked at Julie in the mirror. "I'd rather not talk about this right now." She slanted her head toward the seamstress. "Okay?"

The seamstress took the hint and made quick work of pinning the places on the dress that needed altering.

As Kate watched, her thoughts drifted back to her conversation with Tom. Although she'd known him only a short time, she could tell by the way he'd intently studied her face in the restaurant that he hadn't believed she was telling him everything. Beth had made her promise not to tell anyone she was pregnant. Two previous miscarriages had shattered her confidence that she'd be able to carry the baby to term, and Kate hadn't felt right about betraying her promise to satisfy Tom's curiosity.

Since he'd warned Kate not to talk about the case with anyone, she couldn't very well tell him about the other possible poisons she and Beth had discussed. Poisons whose effects better matched the symptoms recorded in the autopsy report. Poisons anyone could've slipped into Daisy's food or beverages. Poisons that were virtually undetectable.

At least not until she had some proof.

The seamstress left the room, and Julie waited only a millisecond before launching back into her quest for information. "How did you and Tom *happen* to meet up for dinner? I thought you said the local police couldn't be trusted."

"Uh, we were both following the same lead and sort of ran into each other. I'm telling you, the date meant nothing. We were simply comparing notes."

"But you admit it was a date." Julie smirked.

Kate threw up her hands. "You win. It was a date. Tom's madly in love with me and can't bear the thought that I'm putting my life in danger by hunting down a killer."

Julie yanked up her jeans. "For crying out loud,

Kate, if you don't want to talk about him, just say so."

"Wha-a-a-t?" Kate splayed her hand on her chest and feigned a hurt expression. "You don't believe he could be madly in love with me?"

"No, I believe that part."

Julie's matter-of-fact statement gave Kate's heart a jolt.

"It's the putting your life in danger part that better not be true."

Kate's momentary happy bubble burst with an ear-thudding pop. In a couple of weeks, Julie would be on her honeymoon and no one would be at home, waiting for Kate, ready to call in the cavalry if she was late. Or missing. Or dead.

Maybe she was crazy to try to solve Daisy's murder on her own. Certifiable, even.

Daisy's favorite maxim whispered through Kate's mind. *We're never alone.*

But if that was true, where was God when Daisy drank that tea?

Kate shoved away the thought. Just this morning she'd found a passage in the Bible that said, "The righteous are taken away to be spared from evil."

If God took Daisy to spare her from something worse, the least Kate could do was ensure Daisy's reputation wasn't sullied by unfounded allegations.

"You worry me," Julie said. "Two days ago,

you were certain Brewster was connected to Daisy's death. You insisted the local police couldn't be trusted. What if you were right? Tom and Hank go way back. What if Hank asked Tom to cozy up to you to figure out what you know?"

"I thought you liked Tom. You were the one who called him to my rescue the other night."

"I do like him. He seems nice. I just think you need to be careful."

"You're making a bur oak out of a bonsai," Kate quipped, trying to lighten the mood.

Julie scrunched her eyebrows in incomprehension.

"Big tree out of a little tree. Big deal out of nothing."

"Oooh, I get it." Julie laughed. "Let's hope so." She looped her arm through Kate's and towed her toward the door. "I know you miss Daisy, and I understand how important finding out what really happened is to you. I just worry."

"I know you do. I promise I'll be careful." How dangerous could searching the lab computer be?

On a Saturday afternoon, the building would be deserted.

Kate swung the shop door wide and headed down the street. "Come on, no more dillydallying. We have a cake to pick out."

An hour later they stepped out of the bakery, and a sudden chill that had nothing to do with the change in temperature slid through Kate's veins.

Gripped by an uneasy sense they were being watched, she scanned the windows above the shop, thinking Edward might be spying down on them from Molly's apartment. The blinds were closed.

Kate squinted toward the Kish apartment up the street, but it was too far away to tell if anyone stood at the windows.

Julie nudged Kate's arm and jutted her chin toward the hardware store. "Do you know that man over there?"

A group of gray-haired men were congregated around the barrels set up in front of the store for games of checkers.

"See him?" Julie pointed, cupping her hand over her pointer finger to disguise the action. "The man in the blue shirt. He's staring at you."

Their eyes met and Keith tipped his ball cap.

The chill melted from her veins. "That's Tom's dad." Tom must have asked him to keep an eye on her, be her bodyguard. The thought warmed her more than she liked to admit. After all, Tom was a police officer—one of the very people she'd spent most of her life distrusting. Although unlike the men who arrested her father, Tom was willing to admit he'd made a mistake by closing Daisy's case. A mistake he seemed determined to remedy.

Of course, he wouldn't be too happy when his dad reported that she'd returned to the lab after hours. But she couldn't just sit around twiddling her thumbs while Edward got away with murder.

11

Tom accepted a delicate teacup teetering on an equally dainty saucer, and sunk into Nora Hopkins's poufy floral sofa. His hostess had refused to answer a single question about the robberies she'd reported—robberies from the research station—until she'd served tea. Her cozy living room with its comfortable chairs, collection of lighthouse replicas, and bright bay windows was as different from Kate's cluttered apartment as the plump, white-haired woman was from Kate.

He groaned. There he went again, letting his thoughts stray where they didn't belong. It was bad enough that Dad thought he had a thing for her.

Tom cringed at the memory.

At breakfast this morning, without warning, his dad had said, "Have you told Kate how you feel about her?"

Of course, Tom did what any red-blooded male would do. Deny. Deny. Deny.

But apparently he hadn't tamed the goofy grin that had been smiling back at him from the bathroom mirror a few minutes earlier because his dad just said, "Uh-huh," and launched into a story about the day he'd met Mom after clocking her going fifty-five in a fifty zone.

Halfway through the story—a story Tom had heard a hundred times—Tom finally blurted the truth. "Okay, I like her." A lot. But if he didn't stop thinking about her and start making some progress on the other cases Hank had dumped on him, he'd be out of a job.

Following up on suspects in the Leacock case would have to wait until the end of his shift. Figuring out what to do about his feelings for Kate would have to wait a whole lot longer.

Regardless of how much he'd enjoyed sharing dinner with her, Kate had withheld information, of that he was certain, and after the number Zoe pulled on his FBI partner, Tom was in no hurry to play Russian roulette with his heart.

He returned his attention to Nora Hopkins, the research station's janitor.

The woman had long since settled into her chair and now looked at him with a peculiar expres-sion, as if she knew his mind had been a million miles away—or more precisely, six blocks.

He downed his tea in one long gulp and unburdened himself of the cup and saucer. "So, when did you first notice the items missing?" he asked, extracting his notebook and pen.

Nora set her teacup onto the end table and her hands flew into action as she talked. "Miss Leacock was the first to notice. Since I clean all

189

the labs, she'd thought I put the missing items away in a cupboard."

"What items exactly?"

"That's what's so strange. They were little things like spools of wire, beakers, half empty jars of chemicals. Pilfering, really."

"What kind of chemicals?"

"Fertilizers, mostly." She twisted her fingers together and pressed her hands into her lap. "When other researchers started noticing things missing from their labs and storage closets too, enough to prompt them to ask me if I knew anything about them, I wondered if they thought I took the stuff." A blush crept up her neck and into her cheeks. "That's why I filed the report. Maybe it was silly to bother the police with such a small matter."

"Not at all." Boy, Hank must have scraped the bottom of the barrel to pull out this complaint. "Can you tell me when the thefts began?"

"Oh my. A month and a half ago now. At least that's when people started noticing. Things went missing for a few weeks and then the thefts stopped around the time Miss Leacock died."

The coincidental timing piqued Tom's interest.

He reviewed the list of stolen items. Wires. Chemicals. The kinds of things that could be used to build bombs.

His grip on his pen tightened. In his experience, coincidences were few and far between, which meant his terrorist theory might not have been the dead end he'd been led to believe. If Leacock snooped where she didn't belong, she might have paid for her curiosity with her life.

Mrs. Hopkins's eyes shimmered with unshed tears. "When the police didn't follow up on my complaint . . . well, I understood how busy you were. It's not as though anything of much value was stolen."

"Who has access to the labs?"

"The researchers, their supervisors, and security personnel all have keys. During the day, student interns are often in and out too. And that new PR fellow was in a lot, visiting his aunt."

"Edward Smythe?"

"Could be. I don't know his name. I remember him because he always left a trail of dirt in the hall I'd have to mop up." Nora wrinkled her nose. "If not for the fancy suit, you'd think he spent his days tromping around the orchards."

Or woods.

Tom punched his pen against his notepad. He needed to go back to the shed and verify Hank's claim that it was used for building firecrackers . . . not bombs. Tom's gaze strayed to the window and the bright blue sky. He could just imagine what Dad would say about this theory.

Tom's phone beeped and Dad's name flashed on the display.

Tom closed his notebook. "Excuse me, I need to take this."

"Son." The urgency in Dad's voice yanked Tom to his feet. "You need to get to the research station, pronto."

"What's wrong? Wait. Hold on a minute." Tom pressed a business card into Mrs. Hopkins's hand and moved toward the door. "Thank you for your time. If you notice anything else peculiar, please don't hesitate to call."

Her eyes widened. "Really?"

"Yes, we can never be too careful."

Hurrying to his car, Tom strained to rein in his overactive imagination. "The research station is supposed to be closed on Saturdays."

"It is. Locked tight. But Kate's in there. Somewhere. And Edward just let himself in."

"What?" Tom cranked the ignition and gunned his car onto the street. "She promised she'd be careful."

The woman obviously didn't know the meaning of the word.

Empty. Kate shoved her palms against the edge of the lab desk, and her chair skated backward. Who would've deleted Daisy's internet browsing history?

Edward grinned at Kate from the gilt-framed photo on Daisy's desk.

Of course. After he found something incriminating in Daisy's journal, he'd probably worried there'd be more of the same on her computer. Kate dug through the desk drawer. When her fingers touched the cool metal of a portable hard drive, she let out a whoop. Every Friday without fail, Daisy had backed up the entire computer, including all the temporary internet files.

I bet you didn't know about this when you sabotaged Daisy's computer, did you, Mr. Smythe?

Kate's fingers tingled with anticipation as she plugged the USB into the computer port. If Edward had gone to so much trouble to conceal the internet surfing Daisy had been doing, it had to reveal something incriminating.

Kate clicked on one file after another. Pages and pages held profiles of the various herbs they were researching. Applications for research grants. A news report on some guy who'd swindled an old lady out of half of her fortune.

What?

Kate hit the back arrow and stared at the article until her head pounded from forgetting to breathe. The description of how the guy gained the victim's trust held eerie similarities to how Edward ingratiated himself into their lives. Had Daisy suspected Edward of running a con?

No, she would have said something, and she wouldn't have named him in her will.

In the list of websites Daisy had visited in the past couple of months, Kate spotted an adoption registry site. *Bingo.*

She clicked on the site, but the page had expired.

She worked through the layers of information to try to find data on Edward's adoption, but without specifics on his birth mother and date of birth, she couldn't get the system to spit out the answers she wanted.

Kate pulled up Daisy's email and searched the inbox for correspondence from the adoption registry. A message from the Werland Detective Agency caught her attention.

As requested, we are writing to confirm that your nephew Leonard Leacock was adopted by the Smythe family of Pinehurst, Ontario, and given the name Edward. The adoptive family . . .

Something clunked out in the hall.

Kate jumped. The noise had sounded like the security door being pushed shut. She froze and strained to listen for the slightest noise. Nothing.

No, wait. Were those footsteps?

The rhythmic squeak of shoes grew louder.

Heart racing, she shut down the lab computer, pocketed the backup hard drive, stuffed her notes into her purse, and scanned the room for something she could use to defend herself.

The door inched open.

Spotting a myrtle spurge plant, Kate eased toward it, not daring to take her eyes off the door.

Long fingers, manicured yet masculine, curled

around its edge. One foot—one very large foot—stepped into view.

"Who's there?" she called.

The door burst open.

"What—" Kate swallowed hard, struggling to pull her voice down a couple of octaves. "What are you doing here?"

Edward, dressed in dark clothes and sunglasses, swaggered into the room. "I was driving by and noticed your car out front." The door clicked shut behind him.

Trapped. What was wrong with her? She should have parked around back like she did yesterday. And she should have told someone where she'd be. If only she hadn't lost sight of Tom's dad somewhere between the florist and the caterer.

Edward sauntered along the wall in her general direction.

With Tom's warning not to betray her suspicions blaring in her head, Kate pasted on a *how nice* smile and discreetly reached behind her, searching by touch for the plant.

"Your roommate told me the two of you were doing wedding stuff all day. Yet here you are." Edward stopped at the computer and rested his palm on the hard drive as if he knew exactly what she'd been up to.

"We finished early." Kate walked her fingers along the counter until they bumped into the myrtle spurge. Without looking, she snapped off a runner and prayed the toxic juice wouldn't spurt onto her own hands.

Edward tilted his head to one side. "What's the matter? You look nervous."

"What do you expect?" She waggled the plant runner at him. "You scared the bejeebies out of me. I thought you were an intruder."

He chuckled. "And what did you plan to do? Whack me with that weed?"

She jabbed the air with it, trying to act playful. "You bet. This baby works way better than pepper spray. Not only will the sap make your eyes and skin sting horribly, it'll make your face swell fatter than roadkill on a hot summer day."

"Ni-i-ice." He shuddered exaggeratedly. "Lucky for me I'm your friend."

If only she could believe that. She lowered her arm. "What are you doing here?"

"Like I said"—he hitched his thumb over his shoulder—"I saw your car outside, and since I have that stuff from Daisy in my trunk, I figured this was as good a time as any to give it to you." Edward took a step toward her, looked at the weed in her hand, and seemed to have second thoughts. "If you want to give me your keys, I can throw the stuff into your car."

She grabbed her purse from the end of the counter. "That's okay. I'll go out with you." When she didn't release the myrtle spurge, Edward gave her a funny look.

What was worse, escalating his suspicions or giving up her weapon?

She opted to drop the plant into the trash and poked her keys between her fingers instead. "I'm sorry I didn't return your call," she said, striding past him and out the lab door. "With everything that's been happening, I've gotten behind on my work here."

"No problem. Did you find anything helpful in the journals?" His tone, if it could be believed, held friendly curiosity.

Was he being nice to lure her into a false sense of security? He had to know she'd seen the remnants of the journal he'd burned.

Kate tried to swallow the sudden clog in her throat. Shouldn't she be able to see evil in a person's eyes?

Glancing away, she said, "No, I haven't found anything yet."

Edward squeezed her shoulder. "I'm sorry."

She shrank from his touch, barely stopping herself from bolting out of the building.

He let his hand drop. "Are you upset with me?"

"Upset? Why would I be upset with you?" Her voice sounded unnaturally high even to her own ears. The long hall to the main door felt like a dark tunnel. And in the silence, the echo of their footfalls sounded downright terrifying.

"If I hadn't turned up in Aunt Daisy's life

when I did, you would've gotten her whole estate, I'm sure."

Kate gasped. "I've never even considered the idea. Until Daisy died, I had no clue I was even named in her will. I don't begrudge you a penny. Believe me. If anything, as her only blood relative, you should get it all." *If you didn't kill her.*

Kate pushed through the main door. At the sight of people strolling through the grounds, she was finally able to take a full breath. Surely Edward wouldn't threaten her in a public place.

He laid his arm across her shoulder and squeezed her to his side. "You were like a daughter to Daisy."

If Edward was aware of how she stiffened in his embrace, he didn't show it.

He grinned down at her. "That makes us kind of like cousins." Halting, he curled his arm toward his chest bringing them face-to-face.

She froze under his intense gaze. Edward had always been a flirt, but never like this. Interest simmered in his eyes. Interest, and something more. Something like surprise, as though he were seeing her—really seeing her—for the first time.

He skimmed his thumb over her lips. "Or maybe not cousins."

She pushed her palm against his chest, breaking his hold. "You're supposed to be engaged. Remember?"

He blinked, grinned. "Yes. Molly's the best thing that's ever happened to me."

The roar of an engine split the air, startling them both. A red car sped out of the parking lot.

"Was that Molly?"

Edward stared after the disappearing car, his unwelcome flirtation thankfully forgotten.

Kate's car sat in the shadow of a nearby copse of oaks—perfect for staying cool, not so good for staying in view of the afternoon visitors to the grounds. But the sooner she got what he came to deliver, the sooner he'd be on his way. "Were you going to get me that stuff or not?"

"Right." He popped his trunk and wrestled out a duffle bag.

"What's in it?" And did she really want it in her trunk? For all she knew, he'd buried a bomb inside. After all, only she stood between him and *all* of Daisy's money.

"Uh, ladies' stuff. You may not want any of it. We'll have to plan a time to go through the rest of my aunt's belongings together."

Kate left her trunk closed. She had no intention of going through anything with Edward. Not alone anyway. But reminding herself of Tom's instructions not to reveal her suspicions, she said, "Sure," in as cheerful a voice as she could muster.

Edward rested the oversized duffle bag on her car bumper. "Are you going to open the trunk?"

"That's okay, just set the bag over here on the grass." She moved to the front of her car. The sun slipped behind a cloud, and the long afternoon shadows faded. "I'll, um, go through the items before I leave, in case there's, um, anything I want to drop off at the thrift store."

Edward set the bag where she'd directed but didn't release the handle. "It's heavy. Are you sure you can manage? I'd be happy to follow you home."

"No. Thanks. I'll be fine." She eyed the bag suspiciously. If it held a bomb, he wouldn't let her rummage through the contents on the research station's lawn. Would he?

Edward released his hold and skimmed his fingers over the bag. Backing away, he glanced at his watch. "Well, if you're sure you'll be all right, then"—he hitched his thumb toward his car—"I'll get going."

His gaze dropped to the bag one last time, and he gave her a tight smile.

Her heart kicked, but before she could find her voice, Edward ripped out of the parking lot in a spray of gravel.

12

Everything and everyone, from the birds chirping in the trees to the dozen or so people wandering the grounds, stopped at the sound of Edward careening out of the parking lot in his flashy Porsche.

Warn them, Kate's mind screamed, but like a quivering reed, she stood transfixed by the bag he'd left at her feet. From the way he'd glanced at his watch and then hightailed it out of there, she knew she should run. Run before this bag blew her to smithereens.

But her legs refused to cooperate.

A hand touched her shoulder.

She whirled around, keys clawed between her fingers, and missed a nose by inches.

Tom grabbed her wrist. "Whoa, there! I'm on your side."

Jolted out of her trance, Kate screamed, "Bomb! Get everyone away!" She swept her arms through the air and ran toward the research building. "Everyone stay back. Stay back. I think there's a bomb."

Keith appeared and joined her and Tom in urging people to move back. Dog walkers wrangled in their pooches and dragged them well away, while those who'd been out of ear-shot jogged over to see what the commotion was about.

Tom formed a barrier with his arms and raised his voice above the murmur. "Please, everyone stay back. I'm Detective Parker. We have a suspicious package. Until we're sure it's safe, we need you to stay back."

"What makes you think there's a bomb in the bag?" Keith whispered in Kate's ear.

"Edward was acting so strange, and he wanted to put the bag into my trunk, and when I wouldn't let him, I thought I saw him fiddle with something in the bag. The news reporters talk about car bombs all the time. I just thought . . ."

Keith met Tom's gaze, and without a word being spoken, Keith nodded and then moved toward the bag.

"What are you doing?" Kate tried to grab his arm, but Tom yanked her back. She pummeled his chest. "You have to stop him. We need to call the bomb squad."

"Dad used to be in bomb disposal," Tom said quietly, crushing her clenched fists against him. "He knows what to do."

At the feel of Tom's protective arms around her, she stopped fighting him. "I . . . I was so scared," Kate mumbled against his shirt.

"You did great."

Keith knelt next to the duffel bag and muttered something she couldn't make out.

She eased herself from Tom's arms. "Shouldn't he be wearing protective gear? What if the bomb goes off when he opens the bag?"

"Trust me. Dad knows what he's doing. Tell me again why you think there's a bomb in the bag. What did Edward say to you?"

"I . . . I don't remember. But he was acting so strange and—" A sob cut off the rest of her explanation. Putting her reasons into words made them sound embarrassingly far-fetched.

"It's okay. You did the right thing." Tom's grave tone made her fears seem absolutely legitimate. He drew her farther away from the bag and then gently lifted her chin. "Are *you* okay?"

She sniffed. "I'm sorry. I don't know what came over me. It's just that Edward showed up at my lab and all I could think of was how you'd warned me to be careful. But I didn't know what to do." She hugged her arms around her waist and focused on Keith.

He pulled out a long yellow rope attached to pulleys and gingerly set it on the ground.

A man in the group whispered to his wife, "That looks like that thingamabob you exercise with."

The woman jabbed him with her elbow. "Shh."

Next Keith pulled out a black rubber ring, about a foot in diameter, with red sponge handholds on either side.

More whispers swished through the crowd and Kate's heart sledge-hammered her ribs with bone-crushing thumps.

Slowly Keith pulled out a pair of turquoise, gelatinous-looking balls. His head tilted as he studied the one in his right hand, pressing his fingers one after the other into the semisolid material.

Kate held her breath, every muscle taut, as she watched his examination.

A moment later, he tossed the balls onto the grass. The group gasped.

Kate ducked, certain the gelatinous masses would explode on impact.

They didn't.

And maybe Keith hadn't exactly tossed them, but he could have moved them with a lot more caution.

"That stuff is just exercise equipment," a woman in the group said, waving a hand at the collection on the ground and then walking away.

Kate glanced from the seemingly innocuous items to the skeptical faces in the crowd, but her own pounding heart wouldn't let up. Not until . . .

Keith pulled the next item from the bag—a pair of thick purple spirals, joined in the middle by a black plastic, sausagelike thing—and Tom actually laughed.

"Isn't that one of those thigh beaters?"

"Oh yeah." Keith chuckled. "Your mom went through a couple of these puppies. Swore they shaved inches off her thighs."

Kate cringed at how ridiculous her fears looked in light of what was really in the bag.

Keith sat back on his heels. "Nothing suspicious here." He grinned. "Unless you count the—ahem—torture gadgets."

The spectators laughed and broke into applause.

"Okay, folks," Tom announced. "It's safe to go."

As Keith tossed the items back into the bag, Tom returned his attention to Kate. Oh, joy. This was not the kind of attention she'd wanted.

"Why did Edward come here?"

"To give me the bag. He said he saw my car. He wants me to go through Daisy's belongings with him, but I don't think I can do that. I can't bear the thought of him pawing through Daisy's things. Why haven't you arrested him?"

"I can't arrest him without evidence," Tom said, all traces of humor gone.

"Well, he wiped the browsing history and emails from Daisy's lab computer. An innocent man wouldn't do that. And—" Kate told Tom about the backup disk and the detective agency and the article on the swindler. "I think Daisy was suspicious of Edward and he knew it."

Tom cupped Kate's elbow and steered her toward the research building. "Okay, I want you to show me what you've found."

Kate swiped her ID through the exterior electronic lock and led the way to her lab.

"How would Edward have accessed Daisy's computer?" Tom asked.

"She kept her pass card and keys in her purse. Security probably never thought to ask for them back."

"What about her password?"

"That would've been tougher. Daisy changed it every week. She'd go through the alphabet using Latin plant names." Kate unlocked the lab door and switched on the lights. "If Edward knew what letter she was on, he could have guessed the password. That's how I got in. Or maybe he watched over her shoulder as she entered it."

Tom nodded, but his furrowed brow suggested he was dubious about her theory. "Your boss accessed Daisy's computer for me after her death."

"He has administrative privileges. They probably allow him to override passwords. I'm not sure."

"So he might've cleaned the personal stuff from Daisy's computer."

"Darryl? I can't think of any reason why he would. It's got to be Edward." Kate powered up the computer and pulled the portable hard drive from her pocket.

"Did Daisy mention anything to you about someone pilfering from the labs?"

"No." Kate's gaze strayed to the bare spot she'd

noticed on the shelf over her workbench. When Tom's followed, she backpedaled, self-conscious about the apparent discrepancy. "I don't know. Maybe. What's that got to do with anything?"

"It's another case I'm working on. Daisy's name came up."

"You think the thefts had something to do with Daisy's death?" Kate recalled Darryl mentioning that the missing intern used to invent stuff.

"The timing is suspicious."

"We had an intern named Gord Laslo quit around the time Daisy died. Apparently, he used to tinker. He could have taken the stuff for his inventions."

"Why didn't you tell me about this guy sooner?" Tom practically growled.

"I found out about him the day your boss accosted me in the woods. Can you blame me for forgetting?"

"Any other potential suspects you've forgotten to tell me about?"

She chewed on her bottom lip. If she revealed her suspicions of Brewster after imagining Edward planned to put a bomb in her car, Tom might lock *her* up. Better to stick to one suspect at a time. "No, just Gordon. Daisy had threatened to have him expelled for plagiarism."

"You think this kid committed murder to get out of an expulsion?" Tom pulled a notepad from the inside pocket of his jacket and started writing.

"No." Kate sunk into the computer chair. "I *had* thought that he might have switched Daisy's tea as a prank and then skipped town when the prank went bad."

"Wait a minute. You're saying Gordon left town?"

"Yes."

"And you didn't think this was important enough to tell me?"

"Edward is the one who told me about Gord. He probably wanted to keep me busy chasing ghosts."

"If you're going to be a detective, you can't ignore half of your clues because they don't fit your suspect. This student had a motive and he had the knowledge and means to substitute the marigolds. How about opportunity? There was no sign of forced entry at any of Leacock's doors or windows. Would she have allowed Gordon into her house?"

"Daisy welcomed everyone into her home. But I don't think Gord's our killer. If Edward hadn't been the one to point me toward him, I'd be more worried the kid was another victim."

"Victim?" Tom's raised voice rattled the test tubes.

"Yes, a victim." To avoid Tom's scowl, Kate punched in Daisy's password and navigated through the computer pages. "Gord worked at the greenhouse near where your chief grabbed me in the woods. I thought Gord might have seen something he shouldn't have." The horrible scenario unfolded in Kate's mind, and for a moment, she forgot about Edward. "If he'd mentioned *that something* to Daisy before going missing, Daisy might have asked the wrong people questions."

"What wrong people?"

"Drug dealers, of course." The news article about a swindler loaded onto the computer screen, reminding her where they needed to focus. She tilted the screen toward Tom. "Never mind about that. It was just a theory. I know you think I'm letting my imagination get carried away, but take a look at this."

"No," Tom said, blowing out air like a dying balloon. "I think you're right that Daisy stumbled onto something that got her killed." He skimmed the article, showing no sign of surprise at its content. "Figuring out what she stumbled onto and proving it is a different matter."

"We can't give up."

"We won't. I'll see if I can track down this Gordon Laslo, but I don't want you putting yourself in any more danger."

"But—"

Tom stopped her words with a fingertip to her lips. His touch made her shiver in a whole different way than Edward's had. "Please, don't argue. I promise I will do everything I can to get to the bottom of this, but I won't risk your safety."

"You're the most stubborn woman I know," Tom said with a mock glare, a half hour later, as they stood side by side on the front porch of Gordon Laslo's family home.

Unable to think of a snappy comeback, Kate just poked out her tongue.

"Oh, and mature too." Tom's voice held censure, but his eyes twinkled.

She gave him a toothy grin. She wasn't the kind of woman who flirted with any single guy who came along, especially not law enforcement types, but the little zaps that kept knocking her heart out of rhythm every time Tom smiled at her made her want to flirt with him. Later. After Daisy's murderer was safely behind bars.

If she hadn't waited so long to divulge the rest of her suspicions to Tom, they might already have the proof they needed. He'd plugged Gord's name into the driver's license database and within seconds the computer spit out addresses for five Gordon Laslos in the region. Only one was Gord's age, and voilà! They had their match. The best part was, Kate hadn't had to expose Tom to Lana with the long eyelashes to get the address.

Tom pushed the doorbell for the third time. "Looks like we'll have to come back later."

A kid delivering newspapers popped a wheelie on the sidewalk in front of the Laslo house. "They ain't home."

"Cool bike," Tom said and joined the boy at the curb. He admired the long handlebars and banana seat, making an instant friend. "You know the Laslos?"

The boy shrugged the shoulder not weighed down by a bagful of newspapers. "I'm their paperboy."

"We're looking for their son, Gordon. Have you seen him around?"

"He's away at college."

"Does he come home for visits?"

"Sure, I guess, but Mr. and Mrs. Laslo went to Europe for a month."

"Without their kids?"

"I dunno. All they told me was to stop delivering their paper until the middle of June."

The boy popped another wheelie and swerved into the next driveway.

"Now what?" Kate said. "We don't know if Gord's missing or gallivanting through Europe with his folks."

"Shouldn't be too hard to figure out what airline they flew with, and then it's just a matter of looking at the passenger manifest." Tom held open the passenger door of his car for her.

"Won't your boss give you a hard time if you start flashing your badge on a case he's told you to stay away from?"

"Laslo's a robbery suspect. Asking about him won't rouse suspicions." Tom rounded the car and climbed into the driver's seat. "Of course, having you join me at the police station might raise some eyebrows."

"All right, I get the message. You can take me home now."

For a few blocks, Tom said nothing, and the silence gave her too much time to think about the research she'd fallen sorely behind on. About the rumors that could jeopardize her funding. About Edward, and what he might do next.

"Is your roommate expecting you?" Tom asked.

Considering how pathetic it was that she had no plans for a Saturday night, Kate let out a laugh that sounded too much like a snort. "You're kidding, right? What kind of fiancée chooses her roommate over her groom-to-be?"

"How about I drop you off at my dad's then?"

She crinkled her nose. "So he can protect me from roving exercise equipment?"

"That"—Tom grinned—"and so you can give him the gardening help you promised. I'll pick up a pizza for us when I finish my shift."

"You don't have to babysit me. I'm sure Edward will spend the evening with Molly. Not plot ways to sneak into my house."

"The fact that you're even thinking about the possibility is reason enough not to send you home alone. Besides, you'd be doing me a favor by keeping my dad company."

"Well . . ." Kate injected an enthusiastic lilt into

her voice. "If you put it that way, how can I refuse?"

Tom was pretty sure that leaving Kate and Dad alone for a couple of hours was a colossal mistake. No telling what Dad might say about him. But leaving her with Dad beat the alternative—leaving her unprotected.

Tom waited until they disappeared into the house, then backed out of the driveway. When he'd arrived at the research station, he would've liked nothing better than to put the fear of God into Edward, but alerting him to their suspicions could've backfired big-time. As it was, when Edward wrapped an arm around Kate's shoulder, he'd had to dig his fingers into a tree to stop himself from tearing the scumbag away from her. And any illusions that he would've felt the same surge of protection toward any woman were swept away when Kate burrowed into his chest and dampened his shirt with her tears.

The last time his chest had hurt that much, he'd been lying flat on his back after going five rounds with a semiautomatic. Thankfully, those assailants —unlike Kate—hadn't had armor-piercing ammunition.

Instead of turning toward the police station, Tom headed out of town. He still needed to take another look at that shed in the woods. Between Kate's car bomb speculation, the petty thefts from the research lab, and a missing intern, his terrorist theory wouldn't stop gnawing at him. Before he admitted to Zeb at NSA that his concerns were groundless, he needed to verify Hank's fireworks claim.

Tom drove to the general area of the shed and parked behind a farmer's hedgerow, out of sight of passersby. He checked the batteries on his flashlight, jogged across the road to the bush, and slipped into the trees.

The sun wouldn't set for another couple of hours, but in the dense trees darkness had already closed in. He jogged along the faint trail they'd trampled a few days earlier, but without fear for Kate's safety driving him forward, the shed seemed a lot deeper into the bush than he remembered. About to turn around, thinking he'd gone too far, he spotted the roof to his left.

Tom skulked closer. The padlock still hung on the door. He shone his flashlight through the window. Aside from a dusting of residue on the bench, the place was empty. He skimmed the light over the walls. To the side of the bench, a cardboard chart hung from a nail. Chemicals and amounts were listed under names such as Roman candle, glitter palm, dahlia, and crackle—fire-cracker names.

So much for his bomb-making theory.

He should be relieved. He was relieved, except . . . the theory had neatly connected the missing intern, Leacock, and her muddy-shoed nephew who'd stoop to anything to make a buck. Tom trudged back to the road. Now all he had left was the grow-op angle and the con angle.

If Gord knew about a grow-op and divulged the information to Leacock, or if she suspected foul play in his disappearance and got caught snooping around, the perpetrators might have taken her out. It was just unlikely they'd do it with a cup of tea. And with no proof, the theory was nothing but pure speculation.

The con angle was the most credible scenario. A scenario that, in the absence of further evidence, relegated the research station thefts and Gord's unexplained disappearance to mere coincidence.

Tom hated coincidences. There had to be a link.

Back at the police station, Tom quickly realized that on a Saturday night, without a departure date and destination, he wouldn't get anywhere in his search for information on the Laslos' trip.

Tom finished his shift and then headed for the Pizza Shack.

The second he stepped through the door, a familiar female voice called out, "Tommy Boy, look how you've grown."

"Hey, Lorna. Go easy on the baby names, okay. How am I supposed to intimidate bad guys if they hear you calling me Tommy?"

Widowed at a young age, Lorna had been

the honorary auntie to half the kids in town. Nowadays, pushing sixty and the spitting image of Mrs. Claus, she was probably considered honorary grandma to the next generation of rug rats. She reached across the counter and pinched Tom's cheeks. "You'll always be Tommy to me. You were my favorite boy to babysit."

"Uh-huh. I bet you say that to all the guys." He gave her a peck on the cheek. "Just remember, I never ratted you out when I caught you necking with your boyfriend on the couch."

She laughed. "Just remember, I changed your diapers."

So much for his tough cop image. Tom shook his head, 99 percent certain his cheeks—the ones on his face—were flaming red. The anonymity of DC definitely had its advantages.

His mouth watered at the yeasty smell of baked dough and the spicy aroma of Italian sausages. "The travel agency so slow that you have to moonlight selling pizza now, Lorna?"

"I'll have you know my travel business is booming. I'm filling in here for Greg. His Grandma Verna's cat ate one of her houseplants. The poor thing's deathly sick."

"Has she taken it to the vet?"

"Vet's out of town, but Grandma Brewster made the poor thing an infusion that seems to be helping. That woman's a genius when it comes to herbs."

Tom chuckled, recalling Hank's take on his grandma's concoctions. Tom had always thought their success had more to do with the power of the placebo, but if she could help a cat, maybe it wasn't all snake oil.

Marvin pushed Tom's pizza through the takeout window and then came around from the kitchen. He dried his hands on his white apron—white, that was, if you ignored the tomato sauce smeared across his spare tire. "After what happened to Daisy messing around with that herbal stuff, I'm surprised you'd go in for that rubbish, Lorna." Marvin snagged a can of pop from the display fridge next to the counter and popped the tab. "If you ask me, all that eye of newt stuff is just another way to part a fool from his money."

"No one's asking you, Marvin." Lorna elbowed him out of her way.

Marvin winked at Tom.

Not about to step into that minefield, Tom took out his wallet and handed over the cash for the pizza.

Lorna twirled her finger in the air and hit a key on the old-fashioned cash register. A bell dinged and the drawer popped open. She grinned. "I get a kick out of that every time. Gotta get me one of these." She counted out Tom's change. "Pay no mind to Marvin. Grandma Brewster has helped lots of people around here. If that new drug company that's moving to town wanted to make

217

a fortune, they'd figure out Grandma Brewster's secrets."

"A drug company's moving to town?"

Lorna's hands stopped midair, and she gave Tom a you're-not-from-around-here look.

"What? Am I expected to know every rumor in town just because I'm a detective?"

She slid her hand down the counter, caught the edge of a very thin newspaper, and slid it toward him. "I know the *Port Aster Press* is no *Washington Post*, but every once in a while old Harold actually digs up a decent story. Sounds like the mayor's been working overtime trying to woo this baby. Between the research station and this new company, the mayor predicts we'll become the Silicon Valley of pharmaceutical and herbal research. Can you imagine?"

"No. That's like putting the wolves in the sheep pen." Tom fished a couple of quarters from his pocket for the newspaper and picked it up with his box of pizza. His stomach gurgled at the aroma.

"If you ask me . . ."

Tom set the pizza box back down on the counter. Whenever Lorna started a sentence with "If you ask me," it was time to get comfortable.

"The only reason a drug company would want to ally with our researchers is to get an inside scoop on new developments."

"Could be." As an FBI agent he'd been weaned

on industrial espionage cases. Nothing would surprise him.

The door opened, letting in a waft of cool night air and the counter girl from A Cup or Two.

"Hey, Molly," Marvin said. "Your pizza'll be another five minutes." He polished off his can of pop and disappeared into the kitchen.

Molly, still dressed in her green-and-white smock from the store, dropped tiredly into the nearest chair.

The sight of her reminded Tom that he had his own tea girl waiting for him at his dad's—well, sort of waiting for him. "I need to get going." He grabbed up his pizza box again. "Dad can't stand his pizza cold."

"Say hi to your dad for me, and tell him I've got some great deals on cruises," Lorna said.

"That'll be the day."

"Just you wait. He'll come around."

"Hey." Tom stopped halfway to the door. "Did you happen to sell plane tickets to a couple named Laslo? To Europe."

"I didn't. Most people book their own flights these days. This for a case?"

"I'm trying to locate their son."

"The last time I flew to Europe I flew out of Buffalo," Molly spoke up.

The *last* time?

Molly must've socked her tips away for months to afford more than one trip to Europe. Once upon a time, he'd traipsed across Europe with nothing but a backpack, riding the trains and sleeping in hostels, but in his day, those were once in a lifetime trips. *In his day?* He groaned. He was starting to sound like his father.

"You should check with the border guards at the Peace Bridge," Molly suggested.

"Not a bad idea. Thanks." Tom waved good-bye to Lorna and Marv and made a beeline for the door. For the first time in months, he couldn't wait to get home, and it wasn't for the pizza.

13

Kate sat back on her heels and dusted the dirt from her hands. "That takes care of this flower bed. What do you think?"

Keith handed her a glass of lemonade. "Looks a hundred percent better. Thank you."

"It was my pleasure. I love getting my hands dirty." Kate pushed to her feet and brushed the dirt off her knees. "Of all the jobs I've done at the research station over the years, tending the herb garden was my favorite."

Keith led her to a couple of lawn chairs and picnic table in the shade of a large oak tree to the side of the house.

From there she caught a peek of the back of the property. An ancient swing set sat next to a sandbox, bittersweet reminders of the march of time. The forgotten vegetable garden carved out a third of the yard, while here and there along the weatherworn wooden fence a daisy offered a splash of sunshine.

"Oh, wow," Kate said, settling into the lawn chair. "We could have a lot of fun with those gardens." Nothing like a beautiful display of flowers or a hearty garden of vegetables to lift a person's spirits.

"I've never been much of a gardener. That was always my wife's domain."

"Gardening is in my genes. My grandfather was an avid gardener, and my gran was our hometown's version of Grandma Brewster. Helping Gran was how I got interested in herbal remedies."

"Like Grandma Brewster, huh? Without the wart on the nose and a straw broom in the corner, I trust."

Kate swatted his arm. "You're as bad as the kids."

"Ah, I'm just teasing you. When I was a tyke, we went to a doctor if we were sick. There weren't a dozen"—Keith made quotation marks in the air with his fingers—"alternative specialists hanging out their shingle. Just the kooky lady down the street who still swore by mustard plasters on the chest."

"Oh, I see . . . you're one of those people who prefer to smell like menthol instead of mustard?"

"That's me." His eyes twinkled. "No-fuss medicine."

"Well, thanks to people like me, the squeamish can now get all those old-fashioned treatments in neat and tidy capsules. Myself, I still prefer tinctures and teas."

"Blech!" Keith stuck out his tongue and shuddered. "I can still taste the cod liver oil my mom used to force down me."

"I have a tea for that," she teased. "To help with the aftertaste problem, I mean."

Keith leaned back in his chair and roared.

Tom came out the patio door, pizza box and a stack of paper plates in hand. "Sounds like you two are enjoying yourselves."

His dad opened a lawn chair for him. "Kate was just telling me about her herbal remedies. I think she has a tea for just about anything."

"Well, let's hope she has one for heartburn, because I had them put Italian sausage on the pizza."

"A spoonful of honey will do the trick," Kate said.

"Mmm, I like the sound of that," Keith drawled. "You might make an herbal guru out of me yet."

Tom set the pizza box on the picnic table, slid a couple of slices onto a plate, and handed it to his dad. "I'll believe the cure when I see it."

Kate hopped up from her chair and rinsed her hands under the garden hose. "I can see I have my work cut out for me trying to convert you two skeptics."

"Nope, Grandma Brewster might beat you to it. I heard Verna's cat got sick from eating a poisonous houseplant and Grandma Brewster's given the animal a concoction. I figure if she can cure a cat, there's probably something to these herbal remedies."

"She's probably given the poor thing a purgative to rid the body of poison as quickly as possible. Most people don't realize how toxic even some common foods can be to their pets. When I was a kid, we had a dog that got violently ill after wolfing down a bunch of cooked onions with the roast drippings."

A car door slammed shut, followed by a second and third. Moments later, two tawny-haired boys, their grins as wide as their faces, tore around the corner of the house and launched themselves at Keith. "Grandpa!" they squealed in unison. "We brought pizza."

Keith hooked a boy under each arm and spun them around. "Yum, my favorite. How'd ya know?" His fingers played the piano on their bellies and sent them into a fit of giggles.

A tall, dark-haired woman appeared in their wake. In her casual attire of mint green capri pants and a floral tank top, she looked remarkably elegant, despite having two preschoolers in tow. Even if her munchkins hadn't rounded the corner yelling for their grandpa, Kate would have instantly pegged the woman as Tom's sister. Vivid blue eyes obviously ran in their family.

The woman slid a pizza box on the table beside Tom's. "I see great minds think alike."

"Hey, sis." Tom gave her a hug. "I'd like you to meet Kate Adams."

"Hi Kate, I'm Tess." She offered a firm, I'm-so-happy-to-meet-you kind of handshake. "You must be the mystery woman who's keeping the dynamic duo here on their toes."

Kate laughed. "Yeah, I guess I am."

"Good for you. These donut-eating cops need the exercise." Tess snagged Tom's lawn chair and made a show of getting comfortable as she flashed Tom a teasing grin.

Kate adored Tess already.

Keith plopped his twin grandsons back onto their feet and restrained them with a palm on each head. "This is Timmy." Keith patted the boy on his left. "And this is Terry," he said, patting the boy on his right.

Kate hunkered down to their eye level. "Well, hi there. I'm happy to meet you. I'm Kate."

The boys pulled away from their grandpa and tackled her. "Hi, Auntie Kate," they squealed.

She swallowed them in her arms, thrilled by the greeting. She'd always wanted to be an auntie.

Tom plucked each boy off by the collar. "Hey, guys, let her breathe."

Their mother handed them each a plate of pizza at the picnic table. "I hope you don't mind if they call you auntie. We like them to use a formal title when they address adults."

"I don't mind at all. It's sweet."

"Guess what their father's name is," Keith said with a glint in his eye.

"Ted?"

"Not even close." Tom plopped onto the end of the picnic bench without offering so much as a hint.

"You two." Tess gave Tom a swat. "My husband is Xavier. He's French. But since Tom and I both had T names, we decided to continue the tradition with the twins."

"Is your husband coming tonight?"

"No, he's away on business—a buying trip. We own the antique store on Third Street."

"Oh, I've been in there. You have some beautiful pieces. I'm partial to the old books myself. I don't think I've ever seen you there. I always talked with an older woman. Norma, I think her name was."

"That was my mom."

Kate felt the blood drain from her face. "I'm so sorry. I didn't realize." She glanced from Tom to Keith. She was supposed to be helping take Keith's mind off his wife, not heaping on more reminders of what he'd lost. Yet neither man appeared disturbed by her faux pas. They actually seemed pleased that she'd known Norma. "I thought your wife looked familiar when I saw her photo," Kate said to Keith, "but I couldn't place where we'd met."

"She lost a lot of weight after those photos were taken." Tess's gaze drifted, and a fleeting smile touched her lips. "After I had these two hooligans, Mom almost singlehandedly ran the store and kept me sane. We have a new girl working for us now, although I'm always around somewhere. Our house is attached to the back of the store."

"Oh my. Living beside an antique store adds a whole new meaning to the term 'baby proofing.' "

"You can say that again." Tess's laugh came easily. "What do you do for a living?"

"I'm an herbal researcher."

"That's right. Tom mentioned that to me."

Kate's heart shimmied around her chest in a delighted fit. She snuck a peek in Tom's direction and he winked. A wink that said, "Yep, my talking about you means exactly what you think it means."

Kate took another bite of pizza and savored how wonderful this new discovery felt.

His nephews practically swallowed their slices whole, downed their glasses of lemonade in one long gulp, then raced to the swing set, escaping their mother's attempt to swipe their faces clean.

Tess fell back into her chair with an exhausted but amused sigh. "So how do you feel about a pharmaceutical company setting up in town, Kate? It's all everybody who came into the shop talked about today."

Remembering the Peter guy who'd recognized her resemblance to Mom, Kate squirmed. If that Peter was the same Peter that Darryl met from the pharmaceutical company, the company's move could impact her work in more ways than she wanted to think about.

Tom picked up the copy of the *Port Aster Press* he'd brought out with him. "Yeah, I saw the headline in the paper." He skimmed his finger over the opening paragraph. "Have you heard of the company? It's called GPC."

Kate choked on a chunk of pizza. Coughed it loose. Sipped her lemonade.

Tom patted her back. "You okay?"

"Yes, fine, thank you." Avoiding eye contact, she took another sip of lemonade. *GPC.* She hadn't heard that name in twenty years. She closed her eyes and drew in a deep breath. Oh, this was so much worse than she'd thought. Peter didn't just *know* her parents. He'd probably worked with Dad.

Tom nudged Kate's chin. "Are you sure you're okay? You've gone white as a ghost."

Ghost was right. The ghosts Mom had done her best to guard Kate from all these years, going so far as to move halfway across the country, far from their reach, but apparently not far enough. And the worst thing was, Kate still didn't know what Dad had done that was so bad, or why Mom had adamantly insisted that Kate never mention to anyone where Dad had worked.

"Kate?" Tom echoed, concern pinching his voice.

Kate took another sip of lemonade. "I'm fine, really."

Keith grabbed the pitcher from the table and emptied it into her glass. "I'll get us some more."

After Keith disappeared into the house, Tom turned his attention to Tess. "Are you coming for lunch tomorrow?"

"Sure, we'll be here. The kids just couldn't wait that long to see their grandpa."

"Your dad seems like a terrific grandpa," Kate chimed in. Until Gran and Gramps died, their home had been a place she could drop by anytime, unannounced. She missed that.

"Yeah, Dad's great with the boys. We all really miss Mom. Tom came home so Dad wouldn't be alone, but when the kids are around it's hard to stay sad for long."

"Where did you work?" Kate asked Tom.

"I was with the FBI in DC."

"But you're Canadian, aren't you?"

Tess laughed. "Technically, not. Mom said that he was born wanting to be an FBI agent. Mom and Dad were happily enjoying their second honeymoon in the Poconos when he stormed into their lives, not about to wait until they got back to Canadian soil. For years after Tom left for DC, Dad would brag about him working for the FBI and no one believed him."

"Dad bragged about me?" Tom sounded shocked. "I thought he resented my decision to move to the States."

Tess looked at Tom like he'd turned green and sprouted leaves.

"I acted like that," Keith said, meandering toward them with a full pitcher of lemonade, "so you wouldn't get too big for your britches."

Tom's jaw dropped, and for a moment he just stared at his dad.

"What?" Keith swiped at his mouth, his cheeks, his chin. "Do I have food on my face?"

"No." Tom's voice cracked. He cleared his throat. "No. I just had no idea you felt that way."

This time, Tess winked at Kate. She wasn't sure what it meant, but she was certain she was going to have a lot of fun getting to know Tom's sister better.

For the next couple of hours, in between roughhousing with the twins, Keith and Tom one-upped each other with humorous cop tales. Hearing Tom and Keith talk about their jobs like two regular guys showed her how silly her "us and them" mentality about cops had been. It was fun hearing them laugh about their gaffs and spend an evening not thinking about murder suspects. Best of all, the conversation never circled back around to the topic of the drug company eyeing their town.

"I'll walk you to your apartment." Tom slid out of the driver's side of the car, walked around to her side, and opened the door.

"Thank you," Kate said, certain she should protest that such precautions weren't necessary but afraid she might be wrong. "I had a wonderful time this evening. I think hanging out with your family did more to lift my spirits than I helped lift your dad's."

"That's where you'd be wrong. I can't remember the last time we enjoyed each other's company so much." Tom's hand skimmed the small of her back and her skin tingled.

Kate gulped. *Oh, boy.*

They climbed the stairs to her apartment, making small talk as if neither of them wanted to mention the elephant in the stairwell— actually two—the reason Tom felt compelled to escort her to her door, and the attraction that seemed to be blooming between them. For tonight, that suited her just fine. Never mind that she could open her own zoo with the elephants she'd collected of late. She was happy to forget about Edward for one night and dream about spending more time with Tom and his family.

When they reached the second floor, Tom took the key from her hand and unlocked the apartment door.

"Hi . . ." Julie said, adding six extra syllables to the word. "I wondered where you were."

Tom reached for Kate's hand, cupped his palm overtop, and surrendered her keys. "Looks like you're in good hands. I'll pick you up tomorrow at ten."

"I'll be ready." Kate tootled her fingertips like a giddy schoolgirl and closed the door.

"*Not* dating him, huh?" Julie hopped onto the couch and hugged her knees to her chest. "Spill."

Kate brushed off the suggestion with a flick of her wrist. "I spent the evening with his dad and sister and two adorable little nephews."

"Oooh, you met his family already! This *is* serious."

Kate didn't hide the smile that snuck onto her lips. "Maybe," she said with just enough tease to drive Julie's matchmaking mind crazy. She pressed the button on the answering machine.

"You have one missed call," the automated voice droned. "First message."

A male voice came on. "This message is for Kate Baxter."

Kate froze at the sound of her former name.

"I think you'll want to talk to me. I'll be in touch."

14

Kate had a sweetness about her that could make a man dream. And dreaming was dangerous. Except . . .

Tom propped a foot on his desk and sipped his coffee as the Tuesday morning shift trickled in. His dreams the past few nights—filled with images of strolling through the park with Kate, sharing meals, laughing, teasing—hadn't felt dangerous.

Nothing like the nightmares he'd been facing down since his partner's death. Kate made him believe that he could still make a difference working in law enforcement.

She probably didn't have a clue about the feelings she'd sowed in his heart with that green thumb of hers, especially since he'd implied more than once over the weekend that his motive for spending so much time with her was to keep her out of trouble.

So far nothing about coming home had worked out the way he'd expected. For more than two months, he'd tried to convince Dad to attend church again. Yet Dad had accepted Kate's invitation without a second's hesitation.

Tom closed his eyes and revisited the memory. Kate's sweet singing voice and the radiance on her face during the worship service had reawakened his own yearning to draw nearer to God—some-thing he'd hoped leaving the FBI and returning home would make easy for him. But Kate's joy and the exuberance with which she'd discussed the pastor's message had underscored just how far off course he'd wandered.

The computer beeped, prompting him for his password.

Giving his head a little shake, Tom opened his eyes. Yup, dreaming was dangerous business. He'd begun to think that he and Kate could have a future. That she might be someone he could believe in.

After his partner's betrayal, that wasn't some-thing he'd ever thought he'd do again.

"Tom." Officer Hutchinson, the youngest rookie on the force—a lanky kid who looked like he'd started shaving last week—planted himself in front of Tom's desk. "The chief wants to see you in his office."

Not good. In the past week, Hank had gone from bringing him coffee and resting his feet on the corner of Tom's desk while they rehashed old times to sending rookies to summon him to the office. Tom grabbed the three files he'd been working on since Hank's ultimatum, in case he expected proof.

When Tom stepped into the office, Hank's scowl warned him that this week wouldn't be an improvement on the last. "Shut the door." Hank twisted the window blinds closed, cutting off the one source of brightness in the room. "I just got off the phone with Dave McCleary."

Hank's pronouncement mimicked the rapid-fire staccato of an automatic assault rifle, and Tom knew better than to return fire. He searched Hank's face. Maybe the man hadn't completely dropped the case. If he was calling Leacock's lawyer, he must harbor at least some suspicions. "That so?"

"Yup. Little Miss Loyal Friend is getting greedy."

"Excuse me?"

"Kate Adams. She's blinded you with a few flutters of her eyelashes."

Tom folded his arms over his chest as if Hank might notice the way his heart kicked at the suggestion. "What are you talking about?"

"Don't deny it. I saw the two of you at dinner together Friday night."

"Why would I deny that I went out with her? Since when is it a crime to take an attractive woman to dinner?"

Hank rested his hip on the edge of his desk and crossed his arms. "The two of you looked pretty chummy as you came out of church Sunday morning too."

"You were at church?"

"I happened to drive by when it let out."

What was Hank doing? Spying on them?

Tom fisted his hands under the cover of his armpits. "What does this have to do with McCleary?"

"Your new girlfriend went by to see him yesterday afternoon. She's questioning Edward's claim to Daisy's estate."

"So? Maybe she has a valid concern." Tom clamped his mouth shut and weighed the collateral damage that revealing what he knew about the "nephew" might incur. If Tom lost his job, the investigation was over for good.

Hoping to pacify Hank by appearing to capitulate, Tom dropped his defensive stance and sank into the chair opposite Hank's desk. "Edward's real name is Jim Crump. He's a swindler, not Daisy's nephew."

Looking angrier than before, Hank rose and moved behind his desk. He braced his fingertips on the desktop and leaned toward Tom. "How long have you known this?"

"I found out last week."

"Does Miss Adams know?"

"No, I didn't want to encourage her sleuthing."

"Her sleuthing?" Hank's voice rose skeptically, before lowering to a growl. "Or her ploy so we wouldn't suspect her?"

"Suspect her of what?"

"Leacock's murder, of course."

"Kate?" Tom sprang to his feet and planted his own fingers tip to tip with Hank's. "You closed the case. Said Leacock's death was self-inflicted. Now you want to pin it on Kate?"

"Crump's not the only one who changed his name. Or did Miss Adams neglect to tell you that she was once a Baxter?"

Tom's sharp inhalation gave away the answer.

"I didn't think so." Hank straightened and looked almost sorry that he'd been the one to tell him. "I saw how Adams played on your sympathies. I'm surprised you allowed her to draw you into her web. After what happened to your partner, you should know love is a trap."

Hank's comment sparked a slow burn in Tom's chest. Kate wasn't anything like . . .

An image of the spy who lured Ian to his death flashed through Tom's mind. No, he wouldn't believe it. Not of Kate. "You've got the wrong Kate Adams. She would have told me if she'd changed her name."

Her boss's quip slid through Tom's thoughts. *Maybe she thinks getting in good with someone on the inside will get her out of a ticket.*

No, not Kate. The logistics didn't add up. "We closed the case before Kate set foot in this office. If she killed Leacock, why would she storm in here demanding the case be reopened?"

"Because we blamed the death on herbs, which cast a big shadow on her research. Far better to hang Leacock's death on some conspiracy. I'm surprised she didn't go after the big drug companies she'll be competing with."

"I don't believe this. You think Kate killed her mentor for a piece of her estate. She doesn't care that much about money."

"That's what she'd like you to believe. She's using you the same way that broad used your partner. That's why I ordered you off the case."

Tom sucked in a breath, but the air didn't seem to reach his lungs. How dare Hank compare Kate to that woman? They were nothing alike.

"Think about it," Hank continued, as if a couple more blows might convince Tom of Hank's version of the truth. "Motive—get all the glory for their research and all the financial reward, including Daisy's estate. Means—the herbs they use every day. Opportunity—by Adams's own admission, we know the women drank tea together on a regular basis. And what the coroner didn't put in his report was that the toxin that killed Leacock likely accumulated in her system over several weeks. Unfortunately for Miss Adams, Leacock added her nephew to her will before the toxin did its job."

"That's pure speculation," Tom growled, even as his mind revisited the suspicions he'd harbored after Mrs. C told him of Kate's stake in the Leacock estate.

"Is it? Adams is the one challenging the will, not Edward."

"Of course he's not, because he knows he has no legal leg to stand on."

"And you think Adams does? She's the one who was intimately familiar with Leacock's tastes and habits, had access to the toxic ingredients, and had the opportunity to slip them into Leacock's tea."

"The same could be said of Edward, or of Darryl Kish, or of the waitress at A Cup or Two, for that matter. You have no proof."

"That's where you're wrong. I have a sworn affidavit by Gordon Laslo, one of Leacock's interns. He claims Miss Adams has a stash of dried tagete leaves and that he saw her brew tea for Leacock on more than one occasion."

"Laslo came here? When?"

"Yesterday afternoon. Hutchinson took his statement."

Tom paced the room. Kate couldn't have known Gord planned to come in. The fact she'd suddenly named him as a possible suspect was merely a coincidence. More than likely Laslo had heard the police were looking for him. "Did the kid also mention that Miss Leacock planned to expel him for plagiarizing a research paper?"

"Where'd you hear that?"

"Kate told me."

"Kate told you . . . How convenient."

"Well, if this kid saw her brewing toxic tea, why didn't he stop her?"

"He didn't know the tea was toxic until he read the newspaper account of Daisy's death."

"How convenient," Tom shot back, mimicking Hank's sarcasm.

Officer Hutchinson appeared at the door and Hank waved him in. "I've got that search warrant you requested, sir."

"Give it to Parker. I want you to go with him."

Tom snatched the paper out of Hutchinson's hand. "What's this about?"

Hank motioned the rookie to wait outside. "A warrant to search Adams's lab. If you find any tagete, I want her arrested. I won't tolerate a detective on my force who's willing to turn a blind eye because he finds a suspect attractive. Face it, Parker. She played you."

Tom fought the urge to crush the page in his fist. "After we turn her place upside down and find nothing, I'll expect an apology." Tom stalked out. How dare Hank suggest he fixed a case, let alone demand he make an arrest on such flimsy evidence? Even if he found tagete, it proved nothing. Gordon's testimony would never stand up in court.

Then again . . . Tom could just imagine the prosecutor twisting the reason for the kid's sudden disappearance into threats from Kate, especially if her name change turned out to be true.

Annoyed that he hadn't insisted on interrogating Laslo before executing the warrant, Tom climbed into the passenger side of Hutchinson's cruiser.

The rookie started the car and sped out of the lot without comment. But from the way he kept glancing sideways, Tom knew Hutchinson itched to talk.

"The chief said you took Laslo's statement," Tom said.

"Yeah, that's right."

"Did he seem nervous?"

Hutchinson tilted his head from side to side. "Sure. A little, I guess."

"How long did you question him?"

"I just asked him for his contact information. He had a statement already typed out, so I attached it to one of our forms and had him sign it."

Tom scratched his forehead. "And that didn't seem strange to you?"

"The chief didn't have a problem with it. You think this warrant is a waste of time?"

No, I think Hank's pushing my buttons because he likes the sense of power a little too much. Or maybe this was some elaborate get-the-rookie gag. It would make a whole lot more sense than Hank's irrational behavior.

Not to mention that after Tom served Kate with a search warrant, he could kiss good-bye any hope of convincing her to go out with him again.

And the fact that this bothered him more than the time wasted serving a warrant—time better spent tracking down suspects—should be sounding all sorts of alarms in his head.

"So the chief didn't tell you what I turned up on Adams?"

"You?" Rookies were supposed to be out on the street writing up traffic violations, not investigating non-suspects in a non-investigation.

Hutchinson filled Tom in on the lead that prompted him to check into Kate's background. "It turns out her old man used to work for GPC."

"Should that mean something to me?"

"GPC is the pharmaceutical company that plans to move to town. Kate's dad was arrested for stealing company secrets."

"That's hardly relevant. Her parents are dead." The cynicism Tom managed to inject into his voice belied the way his heart had lodged in his throat.

"I'm just telling you what I know." Hutchinson pulled into a visitor's parking spot in front of the main entrance to the research station.

Dark clouds loomed overhead and thunder rumbled in the distance. The fruit trees that two days ago had been bursting with colorful blossoms now stood ravaged by the gusty winds.

Tom had no doubt that Kate would feel equally violated if he didn't handle this search just right.

He led the way inside, but before he could

intervene, the overeager rookie jockeyed past and reported their business to the receptionist behind the security glass in the lobby. The first time Tom came here, the same receptionist had happily escorted him to Kate's lab. This time she took one look at Hutchinson in his uniform and buzzed security to do the honors.

The security guard swiped his card across the sensor that unlocked the hall door and escorted them to the lab. With a brisk tap on Kate's door, he opened it and said, "The police have a warrant to search your lab." Then he left, as if this kind of thing were a routine occurrence.

Kate's welcoming smile turned to a frown the moment Hutchinson stepped into the lab behind Tom. Kate held a trembling hand to her throat. "What's going on?"

"Nothing to worry about." He closed the distance between them, hoping to speak to her without being overheard by the overzealous kid in a cop uniform. "The chief has reopened Daisy's case."

Hope lit Kate's eyes, and her hand dropped to her side. "That's wonderful news."

Hutchinson meandered toward them, scoping out jars along the way.

Kate edged along the table, keeping Tom between them, and jutted her chin in Hutchinson's direction. "Why's he here?"

Tom handed her the search warrant. "I'm afraid

the police chief has evidence to suggest we might find tagetes in your possession. This grants us permission to search."

"Of course I have tagetes." She reached to the shelf above her head and took down a glass jar filled with dried petals. "I experiment with plants." She handed him the jar. "I have hundreds of samples in the lab."

Her innocent expression, and the whole exchange, reminded him of how well she'd played the part of his forgetful date when he arrived at Kish's Friday night. A natural, he'd thought at the time. Couldn't have acted the part better if they'd planned it. The burn in the pit of his stomach festered.

What if Hank was right? What if Tom was blind to Kate's true personality just like his partner had been to Zoe's?

Hutchinson snapped on a latex glove and lifted the jar from Tom's palm.

Kate's face paled.

Tom steeled himself against a rush of empathy and took out his notebook and pen. "Why would you use a flower that contains a known toxin?"

She backed away, her gaze flicking from Hutchinson to him. "Lots of toxic substances are beneficial in small amounts. Digitalis, warfarin —aka rat poison—to name a couple."

"Why didn't you tell me you had this bottle during my initial investigation?"

"You never asked."

The hurt in her eyes, whether genuine or meant to gain his sympathy, only fueled his smoldering resentment.

Kate pushed a hank of hair behind her ear. "How could you think I'd hurt Daisy after everything that's happened? You know me. You saw the car following me. You saw how freaked out I was when Edward showed up here."

Yeah, he'd seen her fear. Had believed it . . . at the time. If he hadn't been so relieved that she was all right, he might have remembered to be spitting mad that she'd disregarded his instructions by going alone to the deserted research lab in the first place.

Hank's accusations—*she played you*—screamed through Tom's mind. For all he knew, Kate lured Edward to the research station, knowing Dad was watching. Tom only had her word that Edward had burned one of Daisy's journals and that Beth's car had been following her for blocks. Now that he thought about it, once he identified the car, she'd seemed intent on forgetting the whole thing.

"Is your real name Kate Baxter?"

Her mouth formed a small "oh."

The disappointment that at first had merely pinged his chest like a stone chip in the windshield now streaked through him, shattering what was left of his trust.

"My mom reverted to her maiden name after my dad died."

"Why didn't you tell me?"

Kate shrugged. She didn't say "It never occurred to me" or "Why would I?" She shrugged, like she'd deliberately *not* told him and wasn't about to tell him why.

Tom searched her eyes, hoping to find a truth he could believe in, because he didn't want to believe she was connected in any way to Daisy's death, let alone responsible for it.

Yet Hank's tone had been clear: *If you don't arrest her, I will. And if I have to, you'll be out of a job.*

From the way Hutchinson continuously fingered his handcuffs, Tom knew if he didn't convince Kate to accompany them quietly, Hutchinson would haul her out with her hands shackled behind her back.

"Am I under arrest?" she whispered.

Tom shot Hutchinson a back-off scowl.

"I'm sorry. My orders were to bring you in if we found evidence on-site."

The day Kate stormed into the police station and demanded he reopen the case, Tom had accused her of wanting to believe in Daisy because of the person she thought her friend was. The irony that he now felt the same way about Kate left a bitter taste in his mouth.

15

"You can't think that I—" Kate must've been staring at Tom with her jaw hanging open because suddenly her mouth felt so dry she couldn't finish the sentence. She moistened her lips and swallowed hard.

"The chief wants to ask you some questions," Tom said by way of explanation.

The lab around Kate blurred. She braced her hand on the bench. Tom had believed in her, befriended her. He couldn't think that she'd . . .

I think you'll want to talk to me.

The cryptic message left on her answering machine replayed in her mind. Had the caller known someone intended to implicate her in Daisy's death?

Or had the caller gone to the chief with his incriminating fairy tale because she refused to play his little blackmail game?

Clearly, ignoring the message had been a mistake. And from the icy expression on Tom's face, an explanation about her name change at this point would be too little, too late.

The stormy gray in Tom's eyes blotted all traces

of the faith she'd thought he had in her. "If you're willing to come to the police station voluntarily, I won't need to arrest you." His gaze flicked to the uniformed officer holding the jar of marigold petals—their evidence.

"I never made tea for Daisy or anyone else with those petals."

"I have my orders," Tom said, his tone as unyielding as rock-strewn clay. "We can do this the easy way or the hard way."

Kate frowned at the name printed on the jar's label. She never would have mistaken tagete petals for calendula. If only she were as adept at spotting the imposters amid people. "If I had something to hide, don't you think I would have gotten rid of that jar?"

"Criminals rarely act sensibly," Tom said in a backhanded reference to the time she'd asked him if he knew of any criminal in his right mind.

The other officer reached for his belt, and she heard the clink of metal.

Handcuffs?

Tom wouldn't slap her in handcuffs and lead her out like a criminal just to answer a few questions. Would he?

Sweat slicked her palms. She skimmed them down her lab coat. Desperate to rein in her racing heart, she moved automatically, clinging to the normalcy of routine. She turned off the Bunsen burner, returned the leaf samples to the freezer, powered down the centrifuge.

The other officer stepped toward her, but Tom halted him with a raised hand.

"I'll be happy to answer all your questions." Her words came out in a rush that sounded as jittery as she felt. "Anything that will help track down Daisy's *real* killer."

The corner of Tom's lips tipped up at her emphasis on the word *real,* but he made no comment.

Kate removed her lab coat, hung it on the hook by the door, and grabbed her purse.

Tom and the officer waited for her to lock the lab door, then flanked her as they walked to the main entrance. Curious colleagues gathered in their respective doorways. The officers said nothing. Not even their shoes on the tiled floor made a sound. All she could hear was the thump of her heart. How ironic that with the building full of people, she felt more scared and alone than she had on Saturday while walking this same hall with Edward.

Once outside she motioned toward the side lot. "I'm parked over there."

Overhead, thick gray skies threatened rain.

Tom cupped her elbow, but unlike on the day he'd escorted her from Beth's apartment, his touch felt far from protective. "We'll drive."

"Is that really necessary?"

He looked at her with eyes as flat as his voice. "It's preferred."

Tom opened the rear door of the cruiser and placed his hand on her head as she ducked into the backseat. When he closed the door, she thought she might be sick. The interior stank of heated vinyl and stale beer tinged with body odor, no doubt left behind by the last person they'd arrested.

Not that she was under arrest. It just felt like it.

She tried to open the window, but it wouldn't budge. A heavy screen separated her from the front of the car where the uniformed officer now sat in the driver's seat and Tom in the passenger seat. A few of her colleagues stared at them from the lawn.

Her chin trembled. She wanted to yell, "This isn't what it looks like!" Instead, as the car drove out of the parking lot, she pressed her forehead to the window much like her dad had done the day the police took him away. He hadn't been under arrest either. No handcuffs, anyway. But he never came back.

He never came back.

A metallic taste coated her tongue. She cupped her hand over her mouth to cover a whimper and realized she'd chewed her lip raw. Last week it had taken more guts than she'd thought she had to march into the police station and demand they reopen the case. But to be escorted inside like this—under a cloud of suspicion for the very crime she'd demanded they investigate—she didn't think her legs would hold her.

What if they arrested her?

Julie would kill her. She'd warned her that being named in Daisy's will made her a prime suspect and had begged her not to investigate.

Kate squeezed her eyes shut. After what happened to her dad in police custody, how had she thought she could trust the police to uncover the truth?

Now she'd rot in jail and her best friend would have to find a new maid of honor.

Kate shook her head. No, she couldn't let her fears get the better of her. This was a terrible mistake, a misunderstanding that would be cleared up in no time. No time at all. It had to be. She tapped on the screen behind Tom's head. "Um, how will I get my car later? I'm supposed to be at a bridal shower tonight."

His expression grim, Tom glanced over his shoulder but didn't meet her eyes. "Someone will drive you back."

Someone. As in, not him. She crossed her arms over her chest and rubbed away a sudden chill. She wanted to run and hide, to escape the cage he'd thrust her in, before the tears pricking at her eyes broke loose and betrayed her wounded heart.

Of course they'd assume she killed Daisy.

Edward, as Daisy's blood relative—if he really was—had more right to the estate, which made Kate look like the desperate interloper afraid she'd lose her stake to him.

The cruiser slid to a stop outside police headquarters. "You go ahead and deliver the evidence," Tom told the driver. "I'll escort Miss Adams inside."

Not *I'll escort Kate*. But *Miss Adams*. Crisp and professional.

Tom waited for the officer to climb out and shut the door, then turned to her. "You should know that you are under no obligation to answer any questions."

"Why would I withhold information that might help you find Daisy's killer?"

A muscle in Tom's cheek flinched, and he seemed to mentally wrestle with what to say next.

Maybe his earlier brusque treatment had been for the benefit of the other officer. Maybe he was finally going to explain why he was treating her like a criminal.

"Before we go in there, I want you to understand that unless the chief files charges, you are free to leave at any time. You can refuse to answer any questions. You can ask for a lawyer."

Charges? Charges! How could Tom do this to her? Just the day before yesterday, they'd gone to church together, shared Sunday dinner, even flirted a little. She searched his eyes, but a stranger looked back at her.

Scraping up her pride, she squared her shoulders. "I have nothing to hide."

He sucked in a breath and held it a moment, as if he might argue.

But he didn't need to say what was on his mind. She could read it in his eyes—he didn't believe her. How many times had he warned her that people are rarely what they seem?

She just hadn't believed he meant himself.

He held open the car door and then accompanied her inside the station. No light touch at the back to guide her. No reassuring words. No indication that she was anything more to him than a witness, or worse, a suspect.

The air inside the station tasted stale. Radios crackled. Tinny voices talked in choppy sentences, punctuated by codes she didn't understand. Tom steered her around a corner, and two uniformed police officers bore down on them.

Her throat closed. Squeezing her eyes shut, she whispered a breathless prayer. *Please, Lord, don't abandon me. Not here. Not now.*

"Kate?" Tom's voice sounded thready, and when she opened her eyes, he was studying her intently.

She blinked back a rush of tears. Her search for Daisy's killer had kept her from dwelling on how alone she was—no family, no mentor, and a best friend who'd soon be preoccupied with her new husband.

Bible verse after Bible verse flooded her mind. *I am with you always, to the very end of the age. I will not leave you as orphans. I will come to you.* She took a deep breath and managed a wobbly smile. "I'm fine," she whispered, swiping at a tear that had somehow leaked out.

One of the other officers took her by the arm and turned her away from Tom. "The chief wants you in here," he said, prodding her toward a barren room.

She glanced over her shoulder.

The other officer said something to Tom, and Tom stormed off in the opposite direction.

The officer holding her arm pushed her into the room.

Dread clamped her throat. She slumped into a cold plastic chair and stared at the wall-sized mirror. To her dismay, her ashen complexion betrayed her fear. *Lord, why is this happening to me?*

The chief appeared at the doorway behind her and smiled—no, smirked—at her reflection.

Suddenly Tom's warnings about answering questions made sense. Hank had set her up to take the fall, or at the very least was attempting to scare her into dropping her investigation.

She must have gotten too close to the truth.

A truth that would ruin him.

Since discovering scraps of Daisy's journal in the fireplace, she'd been so convinced of Edward's guilt that she'd let her suspicions of Brewster fall by the wayside.

Clearly, that had been a mistake.

16

Duped.

Tom carried his coffee to a table near the front of A Cup or Two and surveyed the street. Nothing was what it seemed. Not even the buildings. In the fifteen years he'd been away from his hometown, carpenters had concealed half of Main Street's crumbling brick buildings behind brightly colored facades reminiscent of a bygone era. Coupled with the recently cobbled street and Victorian lamp stands, the place looked straight out of nineteenth-century England—quaint, friendly, trustworthy. Kind of like what he'd mistaken Kate for.

He gulped his coffee, letting the bitter taste strip away his ambivalent feelings for the woman he'd left at the police station. When he'd tried to warn her to be cautious and she'd squared her shoulders, claiming she had nothing to hide, all he could see were Zoe's lying eyes. If only he'd remembered his own motto that people are rarely what they seem. Watching his partner's car blow up should have seared that fact into his brain for life.

Dad yanked out a chair and planted himself across the table from Tom. "You mind telling me what's going on? I just got a call from Lorna, who got a call from Marjorie down at the research lab, telling me my son just arrested Kate Adams."

Tom twisted his coffee mug between his hands. "Your grapevine's not quite accurate. I brought her in for questioning."

"Then what are you doing sitting here?"

"What do you think?"

"Did Hank fire you?" Dad's blunt question hit too close for comfort.

"Not yet."

Dad's grim frown reinforced Tom's fears. "What does Hank think he's got?"

"New information."

"Are you going to make me pry it out of you?"

Tom leaned across the table and spoke in a low voice. "That Laslo kid I've been trying to track down, the one I thought might be connected to the case. He showed up yesterday."

"Dead?"

"No. He came into the police station and claimed he'd witnessed Kate serve tagete tea to Leacock."

Dad nodded. That was it. No reaction. As if the

revelation was inconsequential. "What did the kid say when you talked to him?"

"I didn't."

"Well, don't you think you should?"

"Sure, if I want to be fired." Not that that would stop him. He just needed a few minutes to stew first. "That's not all Hank found out."

"Oh?"

"Kate Adams is really Kate Baxter."

"So? It's not a crime to change your name. Maybe she's widowed."

"Never been married and her father worked for GPC until he was arrested for stealing company secrets."

"How does that give her a motive to hurt Daisy?"

Tom swirled the coffee in his mug. "Maybe it doesn't, but it's one more thing Kate's been hiding from us."

"Like how you didn't tell her Edward is Jim Crump?" Dad's biting sarcasm could've stripped the varnish off the table.

"That's different. I was trying to protect her. The less she knows the safer she'll be."

"Fair enough, but why would she even think to mention that she used to be a Baxter?"

Tom slapped his mug onto the table. "She was thinking about it all right. Saturday night. Didn't you notice how she clammed up when we started talking about the drug company coming to town?"

"What of it? If I'd been arrested, would you share that fact the first time a girl had you over to her parents' house for dinner?"

"That's hardly a valid comparison."

"Isn't it? Seems to me she didn't want to sully your opinion of her by parading out the skeletons in her closet. Any fool with two eyes can see she likes you."

"Yeah, well, not anymore."

"I'm sorry, son." Dad's gaze drifted to nowhere in particular as his fingers drummed on the tabletop. A moment later, he tapped all his fingers together in one brisk tap and refocused on Tom. "How'd Hank figure out Kate's history if you missed it?"

"Hutchinson overheard some guy ask Kate about her mother. Kate seemed bothered that the guy had made the connection and the difference in last names tweaked Hutchinson's curiosity."

Dad shook his head. "He must've searched all four million hits on Google to dig this stuff up." His expression morphed into a look Tom hadn't seen since the time he forgot to call Mom on her birthday. "Don't tell me you think Kate's guilty?"

The bell above the shop door jangled, and Tom grabbed hold of the opportunity to duck the question by glancing toward the entrance. An elderly couple ambled in. The woman held a pie box from Wagner's bakery. The aroma of apple and cinnamon entwined itself around Tom's thoughts, fingering other memories of Kate. Sunday's dinner, with roast beef and apple pie, had been—thanks to Kate's presence—the first meal since Mom's death that he and Dad had sat through like a real family. If not for Kate, Tom might still be collecting empty chip bags and coffee mugs from the living room instead of sitting here defending his conduct to a father very much engaged with what was going on around him.

Tom wanted to believe her actions last week weren't an elaborate scheme to convince him to arrest Edward. He'd stopped short of actually arresting Kate, hadn't he?

But he'd brought her in. And then left—as per Hank's orders.

The pie couple deliberated over the array of specialty teas and then methodically scooped their choice of herbs from the containers lining the countertop. Did Tom really believe Kate could heartlessly watch her friend sip poison day after day?

An image of Zoe with her arms draped around his partner flashed through Tom's mind. Some women were capable of anything.

He returned his attention to Dad. "Doesn't matter whether or not I think Kate's guilty. After today, she won't want my help, and Hank would likely have my badge if I offered."

"I thought Hank was supposed to be your friend. Why's he gunning for you?"

"The mayor's pressuring him to make this murder case go away. I think Hank's afraid I'm going to show him up."

"Are you sure that's all he's afraid of?"

Like the glare of oncoming headlights, the question momentarily blinded him. "What do you mean?"

"You've been away a long time. People change. Maybe Hank's the one with something to hide. You said yourself he's been acting strange."

Tom pinched the bridge of his nose. After all his rants about people rarely being what they seem, he had dismissed Hank's behavior too easily. "Okay, I'll have a talk with him."

"And with Kate. You owe her an apology." Dad splayed his hands on the table and pushed to his feet. "Don't mess this up, or your sister and I might have to disown you."

"Promises, promises."

"I'm serious, son. You're looking at this all wrong."

Someone tapped on the café window.

Dad waved to Lorna. "I gotta go. She talked me into taking her to lunch."

Tom did a double take. Lorna and Dad? Tom was missing way more than he'd realized.

Molly cleared the cups from the next table and swiped away the crumbs. The sun glittered off her diamond ring, splashing a rainbow of colors across the chair backs.

Tom set down his mug. "When's the big day?"

The dark-haired girl gave him a confused look. He pointed to her engagement ring.

As if the sun rose inside her at the mere thought of her groom-to-be, Molly's face lit up. "Oh, we haven't set a date."

"That's good."

"Pardon me?"

"I mean, I think it's good to take time to *really* get to know a person before you marry them." With any luck he could spare her from making a huge mistake. She seemed like such a sweet girl. He hated to have to tell her she was engaged to a con artist. Too bad too, because Edward must love her. Wooing cash-strapped waitresses wasn't his usual modus operandi. Tom finished off his coffee.

Molly nodded toward the empty mug. "Can I give you a refill?"

Tom covered the top with his palm. "No, I've gotta get back to work. Thanks."

Hank's dad sauntered into the shop, carrying a bloated paper lunch bag. He'd grayed in the past decade and a half and had added another twenty pounds to his waistline, but he still looked as disheveled as ever.

Beth Kish met him at the back counter.

Tom hadn't even noticed her come downstairs. His observational skills had gone down the tubes right along with his FBI job.

Beth opened the cash drawer, and in exchange for the paper sack, she handed Brewster a wad of bills. He stuffed the money into his wallet, tipped his hat, and sauntered out of the shop.

Molly reached for Tom's empty cup.

"Brewster delivering lunches now, is he?" Tom motioned to Brewster as he passed by the window.

"No." Molly shot a nervous glance to the back counter. "Beth sometimes buys special herbs from him. Excuse me. I have more tables to clear."

Suspicion coiled in Tom's gut. The last time Brewster was caught selling herbs, they were of the illegal variety. Beth Kish clearly bought pounds of herbs every week to stock this place, and if not for Brewster's history, Tom would have no reason to think the exchange he'd just witnessed wasn't a legal business transaction.

Except that a businesswoman wouldn't pay cash out of her till for stock she put through her books. Surely Brewster wouldn't be stupid enough to sell his produce in broad daylight in the middle of a crowded coffee shop. Then again, who would suspect the police chief's father of being so brazen?

Tom jerked to his feet. Was Hank's warrant a cover-up?

Hank had been peculiarly aware of Kate's whereabouts all weekend, including their dinner at the Wildflower and attendance at church. What if those had been more than casual observations? Maybe Kate's crazy grow-op theory had been right all along.

Tom slipped out of the shop and scanned the street.

Brewster, whistling as if he didn't have a care in the world, headed into the hardware store.

Tom climbed into his car. He wouldn't put it past Hank to follow Kate to make sure she didn't uncover anything that might expose him to public scrutiny. If the newspaper found out Hank's dad was growing again, it'd destroy Hank's career. That was a powerful motive for alienating an old friend and trumping up charges to scare an innocent woman out of her sleuthing.

Recalling Kate's watery eyes, trembling chin, and ashen face, Tom felt sick. He'd steeled his emotions against her distress and convinced himself that she'd used him the same way Zoe had used his partner.

Not only had he failed to protect her, but he might have just delivered her into her enemy's hands. From day one, Hank had taken an unusual interest in Daisy's case, overly eager to dismiss her death as a suicide or accidental poisoning, then later frantic to squash Kate's investigation. Pressure from the mayor?

Yeah, a convenient excuse.

Tom pulled his car onto the street. If his hunch proved right, the real question was, how far would Hank go to cover for his dad and protect his job?

He'd have to work fast to unframe Kate and figure out what was really going on, before Hank railroaded him off the force, or worse, trumped up charges against him too. How could he have let their friendship blind him to Hank's deceptions?

The streets blew by in a blur. Within minutes, Tom reached the station. *Lord, whatever it takes, help me make this right. I was so quick to believe the worst about Kate that I probably obliterated our relationship. Please, help her be willing to trust me one more time.*

A ray of sunlight pierced through the clouds.

Hank nabbed Tom the minute he walked in the door. "Where were you?"

Tom shrugged off Hank's hold and kept walking toward the interrogation room. In his current state of mind, if Tom so much as looked at Hank, he might confront him. And without any solid proof to back up his suspicions, that would be a colossal mistake. "Taking my lunch break. Why?"

"I thought you'd like to know I released Miss Adams."

Tom about-faced. "What happened to your rock-solid evidence?"

"Never would've held up in court. You know that as well as I do. But I thought we might crack her if she believed we'd figured out the truth."

"Whose truth might that be?"

Hank laughed. "You've really got the hots for this woman, don't you?"

"She doesn't deserve to be treated like a prime suspect on a case you adamantly refused to reopen."

The chatter in the vicinity ceased.

Hank steered Tom into his office and shut the door. "Despite what you think, I didn't have Adams brought in to mess with you, or her. I had new information. Information I needed confirmed or refuted. Your attachment to her was an unfortunate complication."

"So why'd you send me to the research facility to haul her in?"

"I needed to prove to myself, and your colleagues, that you could act impartially despite your feelings."

"Oh, and why's that?"

"If the rumor gets around that the FBI let you go because your relationship with a woman compromised an operation, no one will trust you to have their back."

"You know that was my partner, not me."

"I also know that a couple of my men are still ticked that I hired you as detective ahead of them. But just so *you* know, I won't bother Adams anymore. Laslo's affidavit was a forgery. Adams asked what the kid looked like, and when her description didn't fit the complainant's, we checked his school records. The signatures didn't match."

"So you're telling me someone tried to frame Kate?" *Somebody besides you.* "What are you doing to find this kid?"

"Not much we can do. All we have is a vague description and a contact number that's been disconnected."

Tom had the sudden urge to punch his fist through something. "So you're going to drop it?" He didn't buy Hank's story, but a fine line stood between rattling his cage enough to trip him up and revealing too much before Tom had the evidence to make an arrest. "Aren't you the least bit curious why someone would try to frame Miss Adams for a homicide that the police were no longer investigating?"

"She seemed happy to drop the whole thing."

Yeah, Hank had probably scared her off good. "You must have a theory. Who do you think sent this kid here?" Aside from the obvious—*someone* who wanted to divert attention from his father's illegal activities.

Hank shrugged. "Someone who wants her out of the way, I suppose."

"But why?"

"Maybe to sideline her research. Drug companies can be cutthroat."

Tom picked up a photo of Hank shaking hands with the mayor. "That's the second time you've said that about drug companies. A drug company wouldn't happen to be thumbscrewing the mayor, threatening not to expand into our community unless the competition is eliminated?"

Hank's face reddened. "How would I know?"

Tom slapped the photo onto the top of the filing cabinet. "You're the chief of police. It's your job to know. Clearly someone framed Kate because she was too close to the truth."

"What truth? She's found squat. You said she suspected Leacock's nephew, but she sure didn't act like it. Smythe charged in here, demanding her release, and she seemed more than willing to accept his offer of a lift."

"What?" Tom felt like he'd been sucker punched.

"Yep. I told her one of my men would be happy to drive her, but she declined the offer."

"I don't doubt that. But no way would she accept a ride with the man she's convinced killed Daisy. What are you playing at?"

"Nothing. Look, I'm sorry I messed things up between you and the woman. I thought I was doing you a favor."

Tom drew in a breath and held it. Hank had always been a lousy liar, which from the look on his face meant either he'd learned to lie really well in the last decade or Tom had turned into the paranoid cop the FBI psychologist—the one who'd insisted on an indefinite vacation—said he was.

Three things he knew for certain. Someone killed Daisy. Someone framed Kate for the murder. And the real Gordon Laslo was still unaccounted for. After that, things got a lot grayer.

Edward and Darryl both had motives to kill Daisy. Whereas, if Hank was worried Kate would expose his father, he wouldn't let her go.

With Edward of all people.

"I've got to find her." Tom flung open the office door and strode down the hall. He never should have left her alone here. She'd probably been so distraught over being questioned by the police that she'd clung to the first person who appeared to be on her side.

Edward Smythe, the man who had the most to gain if she was incarcerated.

Or dead.

17

Kate relaxed into the baby-soft leather of Edward's Porsche and let out a sigh. After more than an hour of the chief's incessant questions—the same questions, over and over, phrased a hundred different ways—Kate had been certain he intended to bury her.

Bury her the same way the cops had buried her dad. Or at least that's what she'd once overheard one of her grandma's friends say. Her dad had known things he shouldn't have, and people of power had wanted him silenced.

Just like the chief seemed to want her silenced.

Maybe she should have insisted on a lawyer like Tom had advised, but that felt too much like an admission of guilt.

Exactly what they'd been fishing for.

But they wouldn't break her. Or stop her. If anything, their veiled threats that *if* Daisy had been murdered, Kate was the most likely suspect only galvanized her resolve to dig out the truth. Even if she had to fight the entire police force to do it.

She lowered her window and breathed in the air of freedom. "Thanks for getting me out of there."

Edward gave her the kind of conspiratorial smile Kate and Gramps had shared after a successful raid on Gran's cookie jar. "Hey, family has to stick together. Right?"

Family. She'd started to feel like a part of Tom's family.

When Tess told her how Tom had given up his career with the FBI to return home after their mom died, Kate had started to believe he could be a man she might be able to love. A man who would put family first.

Clearly, she'd been wrong.

As for Edward, theirs was a peculiar kinship— two orphans connected by their mutual love of

Daisy. Kate smoothed her hair. In her distress, the way he'd charged to her rescue at the police station had taken on fairy-tale proportions, but she knew his heart belonged to Molly.

In fact, just because the chief had catapulted to the top of Kate's suspect list didn't mean she was ready to trust Edward again.

She stiffened. So what was she doing in his car? The last time she'd seen him, she'd been certain he was delivering a bomb.

The chief's questions had gotten her so frazzled she hadn't stopped to question Edward's motives for springing her. She gripped the door handle and shifted to face him. "Uh, how did you know where I was?"

He flashed a *GQ* smile. With his wind-tousled hair and shadow of a beard, he looked like a movie star behind the wheel—not the image of a man who needed Daisy's money. Kate could almost taste the wealth he exuded. "I stopped by the research station, and the place was buzzing with how you'd been arrested."

Kate muffled a groan. Once that rumor made the rounds, she could kiss her grant money good-bye. Maybe even her position. How many more ways could she fail Daisy?

"I'm glad it wasn't true. I know you didn't kill Daisy. Any more than I did."

Guilt squeezed Kate's chest. Edward had rescued her from her darkest nightmare, while she'd done nothing but think the worst of him. When had she become as cynical about people as Tom?

She laid her cheek against the seat and watched grassy fields dotted with yellow dandelions swim past. The purr of the supercharged engine might have lulled her into a sense of security, if the scent of leather didn't remind her of Tom.

Or more precisely, how safe she'd felt encircled in Tom's arms after the last time Edward had come to see her—the time she'd been convinced he was Daisy's murderer and Tom was the one she thought she could trust.

If the chief went to so much trouble to coerce her to drop her private investigation, surely Edward couldn't be involved too. She should just ask him about the scraps of paper she'd noticed in Daisy's fireplace. He probably had a perfectly logical explanation for burning one of Daisy's books.

Far more logical than any explanation Tom might conjure up to justify handing her over to the police chief. How could she ever have imagined he might care for her?

She glanced at Edward. He seemed to be smiling to himself, humming quietly, his attention fixed on the road.

He gave her a funny look. "Aren't you going to answer that?"

"Huh?"

"Your phone."

The ring tone cut through her foggy brain. "Oh." She snatched the phone from her purse and snapped it open. "Hello."

"This is Mr. Werland's receptionist returning your call."

"Who?"

"The Werland Detective Agency. Mr. Werland asked me to respond to your inquiry about the Smythes. They died in a car crash when Edward was three."

Kate cupped her hand around the phone and turned toward the window. "Where'd he go after that?"

"No, you misunderstand. The boy died too."

Edward died? She shot a glance across the car. Her chest tightened.

"Mr. Werland repor—" The phone cut out.

Blackness swept over Kate's vision. Her head pounded. Her lungs screamed for air. She clutched the dashboard and sucked in a breath. The air seared her throat going down. She inhaled again, fighting to pull herself together. Slowly, the blackness receded.

Edward slowed the car. "Are you okay? Who were you talking to?"

Kate faced him, her head swimming at the movement.

Outside, the fields had given way to forest. *Forest!* There weren't any forests between town and the research station.

Her heart jackhammered itself into her throat. If Edward overheard her conversation . . . She gulped. "Uh, I was talking to a colleague who's been doing some research for me." She gripped the lip of the window and craned her neck to peer behind them. Nothing looked familiar.

What if he planned to kill her and dump her body somewhere, to somehow make it look like she'd fled the country so the police would be convinced they'd had the right murderer, but she'd gotten away?

No, a roomful of cops saw Edward escort her from the station. He wouldn't try anything.

Would he?

He'd be the first person they'd suspect of foul play . . . if they suspected foul play.

How could she not have noticed that he'd changed routes? She dropped her hands into her lap and frantically typed a text message to Julie, all the while scanning the horizon for signs that might tell her where they were. *Please, Lord, let me catch a signal.* "Where are you taking me?"

"You're so jittery," Edward said in his butter-smooth voice. "I thought we'd stop for a cup of tea."

She sucked in a breath. *Tea.* That's how he murdered Daisy. Kate's thumb slipped and the text message she'd been typing disappeared.

No!

•••

Outside the police station, the forecasted storm had blown over, but Tom couldn't shake the fear that something worse was brewing. He jumped into his car and headed for the research station. If he had the time, he would plaster a police sketch of Gordon's imposter all over the news. Because if he found the kid, he'd find the guy who hired him to frame Kate. But his gut told him there wasn't enough time.

Lord, please let my gut be wrong about Smythe. Let me find Kate safe and sound in her lab.

Tom had no illusions she'd ever trust him again. But he hoped that after he offered a heartfelt apology, she'd forgive him enough to listen to his concerns.

Once he'd cleared the town, Tom floored the gas pedal. Two miles out, the stench of a dead skunk seeped into the car. He almost hoped his old buddy—Chief Hank Brewster—was as dirty as that skunk, because Edward's twenty-minute head start offered Tom little hope of stopping him.

He tried Kate's cell again. When voice mail kicked in for the third time, Tom punched in Dad's cell number.

He cut off the automated voice with a jab of his thumb and tried their home number next. He was 99 percent certain Dad had attached a GPS locator to Edward's Porsche. If Tom could get a hold of Dad, he might be able to give Tom a location.

The phone rang and rang. Tom hit End and punched in the station number. "Carla, it's Tom. Can you call Lorna's Travel Agency for me? Tell her that if she knows where my dad is, to have him call me on my cell. It's urgent."

"Sure. Right away."

Tom swerved into the research station's parking lot just as Darryl Kish hurried out the side door. Darryl. Another man with motive, means, and opportunity. A man who also knew about Gordon Laslo's connection to Daisy and Kate. Tom zipped across the half-empty lot and screeched to a stop behind Darryl's hybrid Fusion, blocking his exit.

Darryl stalked toward him. "What do you want now, Parker? Haven't you done enough damage for one day?"

From Darryl's ragged appearance and glazed look, anyone would think he'd been the one who spent the last couple of hours under interrogation. Or was all the bluster to mask his fear that *he'd* been found out?

"I'm looking for Kate. Have you seen her?"

"How should I know where she is? You're the one who hustled her out of here in a police cruiser. Are you trying to ruin us?"

"I don't see how—"

Darryl's face turned redder than an overripe tomato. "The rumor that she was arrested spread like wildfire. I spent the last two hours on the phone with our financial supporters doing damage control. Now, if you'll excuse me, I need to get home to my wife."

"Not so fast." Tom stepped out of his car and slammed the door. "When's the last time you saw Gordon Laslo?"

Darryl glared, making no attempt to hide his irritation. "I already told the chief."

"Now I'm asking."

"Daisy wanted to give the kid one more chance to prove himself. That was four"—Darryl's eyes shifted, referencing an invisible calendar—"no, it was almost five weeks ago now. Anyway, I refused." Darryl opened his car door. "The way I see it, the kid was smart and dropped out before we charged him with plagiarism."

Tom scrutinized Darryl a moment longer. No pursed lips as if he might keep the truth from slipping out. No liar's lean as if to convince Tom of his sincerity. No stumbling over words as if he was uncertain. From all appearances, the man was telling the truth.

And Tom was wasting precious time.

If Kish had hired an imposter to rat out Kate, he'd be sweating bullets over being asked Gordon's whereabouts. "Okay, if you see Kate, tell her I need to talk to her."

Darryl snorted. "Fat chance she'll want to talk to you after today."

Yeah, that was exactly what Tom was afraid of. He returned to his car and pulled ahead so Darryl

275

could leave. Whether Kate liked it or not, Tom intended to do whatever it took to clear her name and keep her safe. But first he had to find her.

A quick check at the reception desk confirmed Kate hadn't returned. He tried her cell phone again.

"Hello—"

"Kate? Kate, where are you?"

Dead silence answered.

Dropped call, or had Edward . . . ?

No! Tom redialed, but Kate didn't pick up. This was worse. Much worse.

He scrolled through his old calls and found Julie's number. She answered on the first ring. "Julie, this is Detective Parker. Have you heard from Kate?"

"No, I'm at work. Did you try her cell?"

"There's no answer, and I need to find her."

"Hold on a sec." The rattle of computer keys sounded in the background. "I know the password for the GPS cell phone tracker app she uses. If her phone's in the network's area, I can pinpoint its coordinates."

Tom prayed that last dropped call was a temporary blip.

"Oh, won't Kate be surprised?" Julie added.

Oh yeah, she'd be surprised all right, but not in the happy way Julie seemed to think.

"I need to put you on hold for a minute. A patron needs my help."

Waiting a minute felt more like waiting an hour as Tom imagined every possible scenario of where Kate could be. He checked her car and scanned the grounds. One minute forty-five seconds later, he debated disconnecting in favor of ordering a BOLO for Edward's Porsche.

A few seconds later, Julie came back on. "I'm tracking Kate on my computer now. She's at Sumpner's Falls on Seventeenth Street."

Tom blasted out of the parking lot toward the conservation area. "Is she moving?"

"Very slowly. Let me zoom in . . . She's off-road. She must be walking one of the tr—" A call-waiting blip momentarily cut off her words. "Hold on a sec."

Tom tried to get ahold of his breath, but the report swiped the air from his chest. Images of the remains of other women who'd been dragged into the woods piled into his mind.

"Oh no!" Julie cried out.

"What?" Tom hammered his escalating urgency into the question, hoping against hope that he was wrong about Edward.

"I just got a text message from Kate. It says, 'Help. Trapped in ES car near—' That's all." Julie's voice cracked. "She never finished."

Tom tamped down the white-hot rage blazing through his veins. "Okay. Stay on the phone. Let me know if there's any change."

"ES, that's got to be Edward. I knew he couldn't

be trusted. The fact she's still moving is a good sign, though, right? She must've typed this earlier, and it only just got through, because she can't still be trapped in a car if she's on a trail."

Tom sped past a slow-moving truck. All they knew for certain was that her *cell phone* was moving off-road. What if Edward intended to toss it—with Kate—over the falls?

The driver of an oncoming pickup laid on his horn and swerved onto the shoulder as Tom swung back into his own lane.

"Uh, Tom?"

The anxiety in Julie's voice yanked his taut nerves to the breaking point. "What?" He careened onto Seventeenth Street, fishtailing wildly. Two more minutes and he'd be there.

Julie gulped so loud, Tom could hear the sound over the phone. "She's stopped."

"Where?"

"It looks like she's at the top of the ravine."

Tom's heart climbed to his throat. He blew past the main gate and veered to a stop behind Edward's Porsche. Grabbing his cell, Tom jumped out of his car, gave the Porsche a quick once-over, then booted up the trail toward the falls. *Please, Lord, don't let me be too late. Not again.*

18

Kate stared at the water roaring over the cliff and dropping to a churning pool eighty feet below. "I really do need to get back to work, Edward. My colleagues will be worried about me."

He steered her toward a large, flat rock. "Let's sit over here. What I have to say won't take long."

His grim tone made her wonder for the hundredth time what foolish notion had possessed her to walk to the top of a cliff with this imposter instead of screaming for help the second she stepped out of his car. She hadn't thought she secretly had a death wish, but maybe the voice nudging her to trust Edward wasn't God's voice at all.

As if to confirm it, the foliage at her feet rustled, and a snake slithered onto the sun-baked rock.

She bit hard on her lip to hold in a squeal.

Edward broke a branch off a wild plum tree and flicked the snake away. "All clear."

Her insides squirmed as she backed away from him. "Uh, I'll stand. Thanks."

Edward tossed the stick into the river. It careened down the rapids, bouncing from rock to rock until it disappeared over the cliff.

Edward slumped onto the rock. "Daisy showed

me this place. Said she liked to come here when she and God had some serious talking to do."

"That sounds like Daisy. She always felt closer to God when she was out in his creation." Kate hugged her waist and took another step back.

A hawk screeched overhead, then dove for the earth.

Edward pointed to the raptor swooping away with a mouse in its beak. "That's how I see God—waiting up there to catch me where I shouldn't be."

"No, God's not like that. The Bible does say God pursues us, but that's because he longs to love us."

"I wish I'd asked Daisy more about her faith. She always seemed so . . . content."

Sensing from Edward's tormented expression that he battled unwelcome emotions, Kate remained silent, praying for wisdom, praying Edward wasn't merely lulling her into a false sense of security. Praying she wasn't an idiot to walk to the top of a cliff with him.

"I have everything I thought I wanted. A home, a great job, a woman who loves me." He snapped off a violet and plucked its petals one by one. "But I feel so empty."

A breeze ruffled the grasses, revealing not just violets but orange dogtooth lilies and other wildflowers she hadn't noticed at first glance. Sensing that God was revealing his presence, his unseen protection, Kate felt her apprehension leach away. "Daisy used to say God put a God-sized hole in each one of us that only he could fill."

Edward bolted to his feet. "I'm sorry, this was a mistake."

"Wait." Water thundered over the cliff, mimicking Kate's runaway emotions. "You said you wanted to tell me something." When Edward didn't respond, she said in a tremulous voice, "Was it about the journal you burned?"

He slumped back onto the rock. "I was wondering when you'd get around to asking me about that." He rubbed his palm over his forehead. "The truth is, I'm a fraud. I'm not Daisy's nephew."

Although the announcement wasn't news to her, she couldn't stop the way her body trembled and her feet edged farther away.

Edward lunged forward and gripped her forearms. "You have to believe me. I would never hurt Daisy."

"Why . . . why are you telling me this?"

"Because if the police reopen her case, they're bound to find out about my past, who I am. They won't care that Daisy loved me anyway."

"Past? You've done this before?" The pieces clicked together in Kate's mind—the article about the con artist, the fact that Daisy's real nephew was long gone. "You make a living out of conning little old ladies out of their estates?"

"It was never like that. I was more like the son they never had. But yes, Daisy knew. Only I didn't know she knew. Not until I read her journal. She wrote about how she hoped that by adopting me into her family I'd finally understand God's love." Edward's grip on Kate's arms tightened. He shook her. "Don't you see? I had to burn the journal. If you'd read that, you would've gone to the police. They never would have believed I didn't kill her."

Kate struggled against his hold. "Did you?"

"No!" His shout echoed off the rocks of the cliff face. "I could never have hurt Daisy. I've never hurt anyone."

"You're hurting me."

His grip instantly relaxed, but he didn't let go. "Promise me you won't tell the police. Next to Molly, you're the closest thing I have to a friend. And if the truth about me comes out, the police will lock me up and throw away the key. I'll lose her for good."

The anguish in his voice cracked the revulsion that had balled in Kate's chest. She shook off his hold and put more ground between her and the cliff edge. "Does Molly know what you are?"

"What I *was*. Yes." Edward pushed his fingers through his hair. "I never came to Port Aster intending to swindle Daisy or anyone. I swear it was just dumb luck that my newest alias matched Daisy's nephew."

"You expect me to believe that?"

"I know it looks bad, but I swear that I came here to start a new life."

"Then why didn't you tell Daisy she was mistaken?"

Edward shifted awkwardly. "I tried, but she wanted to believe I was her nephew, have a chance to make amends for forcing her sister to give up her child for adoption." Edward shook his head. "She pursued me, and I played along. Habit, I suppose. I don't know."

"How gullible do you think I am? Not only do you show up in Port Aster to start this new life bearing the name of Daisy's nephew, but you land a job at the very place she works."

"It was Molly's dad's idea. He saw the ad for the public relations job. A job in a town hundreds of miles away from his daughter. He said that given my gift for exaggeration, PR was the perfect job for me."

"Molly's dad?"

"Molly's parents refused to consent to our marriage and sent me packing."

"Because you're a criminal."

"No, because they're Gilmores and I'm a nobody."

The image of Molly in her black sheath flashed through Kate's mind. The expensive-smelling fragrance. The glittering . . . "Gilmore, as in the Gilmore Diamonds Gilmores?"

"Among a gazillion other enterprises, yeah."

"If Molly's rich, why's she working at A Cup or Two and living above the bakery in a rinky-dink apartment?"

Edward's eyes brightened and his lips spread into a cheek-splitting grin. The kind of grin she'd only seen three or four times in her life, always on the face of a groom as he watched his bride glide down the aisle toward him. The kind of grin that said, "I am the luckiest man alive."

"She says she's proving to me that she doesn't care about her parents' wealth. All she wants is me."

"You drive a Porsche. You can't be that bad off."

"It was a gift . . . of sorts."

"Oh?" This sounded worse than Kate had feared. Had Edward helped himself to the "gift"? Or blackmailed someone?

"Molly's dad bribed me to disappear."

Kate's breath escaped in a rush. "Does Molly know?"

"I'm sure her dad threw my shallowness in her face the second I drove away. He was always telling her that she had to marry someone with money, otherwise she'd never know whether the guy was marrying her for her, or for her money."

"Are you marrying her for her money?"

Edward ducked his head. "At first. But not anymore." He pressed his hand to his chest.

"Molly loves me. Me. She loves me enough to defy her parents and fight for my love. Her parents never spent any time with her. They gave her everything she could possibly want except themselves. She doesn't want to be tied to a rich guy who will always be off working his next deal. So she broke all ties with her parents and set out to find me."

Kate lifted an eyebrow.

"Believe me, if her father knew she was in Port Aster, I'd be working in Moose Jaw and wearing a Rolex." He shook his head. "No. That's not true. I don't care if Gilmore is the richest man in the country. I won't be bought off again like some corporate merger. I won't lose Molly again. No one has ever loved me like she does." He lifted his gaze to Kate's. "No one except Daisy."

Kate nodded. Maybe she was as naïve as Julie kept telling her, but Kate believed him. "I need to know one more thing. Did you frame me for Daisy's murder? To get me to stop looking?"

"No. Don't you see? I don't want the police to take more interest in this case. The more they dig, the more likely they'll pin the murder on me. They closed the case. Why can't you just leave it alone?"

"Because someone killed her. No one would go to the trouble of framing me if it wasn't true."

"Aren't you afraid you'll wind up the same way if you push this?"

Her pulse jumped. "Is that a threat?"

"No." He grabbed her arms, digging in his fingers. "Stop twisting my words."

Kate cried out.

"I'm sorry." His grip eased. "I'm sorry." His eyes pleaded for absolution. "Please, you've got to believe me. I just want to start over with a clean slate. You're my only hope."

Tom drew his gun and sprinted full-out the last five hundred yards to the top of the falls. The sight of Kate teetering at the edge, face white, Edward's fingers clamped around her arms, ripped Tom to shreds. He leveled his gun at the man's chest. "Let her go. Now."

Edward's gaze snapped to his, a crazed glint in his eye. Tom's throat turned to sandpaper. He tried to swallow, but the torrent of water plummeting over the cliff couldn't have touched the dryness.

Kate flung her arms and broke Edward's hold, but instead of running for safety, she stepped in front of him and deliberately obstructed Tom's line of sight.

Stunned that Crump didn't immediately clamp his arm around her to protect himself, Tom spoke low and insistent. "Kate, step away from him. Now."

"Not until you put that gun away." She lifted her chin, but he didn't miss how it trembled.

"This man is not who he seems."

Her eyes narrowed. "There's a lot of that going around."

Tom clenched his jaw as her words found their mark. "He's not your aunt's nephew. His name is Jim Crump. He's a con artist who preys on rich old ladies."

Edward sucked in a breath and took a step backward, dangerously close to the edge of the cliff.

Kate glanced over her shoulder at his stricken face, then turned on Tom with fight in her eyes. "Edward didn't kill Daisy. He didn't even con her. Daisy knew who he was."

"Is that what he told you?"

"Yes."

"And you believe him?"

"Yes." She spat the word. "It's a bad habit, I know, believing in people."

Ouch. She sure knew how to deliver the blind-side punch. So much for thinking storming to her rescue would make her forget how he'd let her down this afternoon. "It doesn't matter whether or not he conned Daisy. I'm sure I can dig up a trail of arrest warrants on him," Tom said, even though he'd spent hours tracking Edward's history, trying, without success, to find an excuse to arrest him. But he had him now.

Edward held up his hands and stepped around Kate. "There are no outstanding arrest warrants on me. And for the record, I brought Kate here to talk. Nothing more."

"That's not what her text message implied." Tom motioned toward the dirt with the muzzle of his gun. "Down on the ground. You're under arrest for kidnapping."

Without a word, Edward dropped to his knees and then laid facedown on the ground.

Not trusting his quick compliance, Tom kept his gun trained on him. "Move away, Kate."

"You can't do this. I was upset. I didn't know what I was saying when I texted Julie."

"The man had you by the arms at the edge of a cliff when I showed up. Wait for me in the parking lot. We'll talk about what happened back at the station."

"No, I won't go back there. If you expect me to set foot in that police station again, you'll have to arrest me too."

The tortured dread rippling beneath her words undermined his resolve. Tom motioned toward the trail, darkened by lengthening shadows as the sun slid toward evening. "Start walking."

Her watery eyes held his for a moment longer, then she dropped her gaze and shuffled down the trail. No matter what she claimed happened here, the wobble in her legs proved she'd been frightened.

With Kate out of harm's way, Tom holstered

his gun and slapped handcuffs onto Edward. "Okay, let's go."

"The charges against me in King City were dropped. I haven't done anything wrong." He slowed his step and sent Tom a pleading look. "You've got to believe me. I changed my name legally. I came here to make a fresh start."

"Convenient how those charges happened to be dropped. Almost as though someone paid off the complainant."

The twitch in Edward's cheek told Tom his guess had been right.

Tom shoved him forward. "Get moving."

"Please, I'm telling you the truth. I just brought Kate here to talk."

Kate walked ten paces ahead of them, her back stiff. How had he ever thought she was loyal? The woman traded allegiances more readily than his most unreliable informants. Without her cooperation, he had nothing to hold Edward on.

Tom could just imagine what Hank would say if Tom brought Edward in with Kate nipping at their heels, protesting that she wasn't kidnapped.

The one consolation was, Tom's instincts told him Edward had only brought Kate here to convince her to stop investigating before his past caught up to him. Because the real murderer would have stopped at nothing to ensure her silence.

How ironic that she finally had the power to get

what she'd wanted—Edward's arrest—and she was thwarting their prime opportunity by refusing to cooperate.

Tom sent a text message to Julie to let her know Kate was safe. Then he tried again to catch Edward in a lie. "Who did you hire to impersonate Laslo?"

"Impersonate?"

"Why did you tell Kate that Laslo was Daisy's killer?"

"I didn't. I couldn't even remember the kid's name. I told Kate that Daisy had threatened to expel one of her interns. Kate figured out it was Laslo."

"Why'd you pick her up at the police station?"

"Because I knew from personal experience how grueling an experience being arrested could be."

"Where is Laslo now?"

"How should I know? I've never met the kid."

"Isn't it true that you visited the local greenhouses in your capacity as the PR rep?"

"To meet with owners, not interns."

"Isn't it true that you visited Landavars Greenhouses on the day before Laslo disappeared?"

"I don't know when he disappeared. I was at Landavars a few weeks ago."

Nothing in Edward's body language suggested he was trying to hide anything—namely, that Laslo didn't work at Landavars but at Herbs Are

Us. "Okay, Crump. Here's the deal," Tom said quietly so Kate wouldn't overhear. "I'll let you go, but I don't want to see you anywhere near her. Do we understand each other?"

"Perfectly."

When they reached the parking lot, Kate stationed herself next to the Porsche, arms crossed over her chest.

Tom unlocked Edward's cuffs, and Edward immediately strode to the driver's side.

"The detective will give you a ride home, Kate."

Her eyes widened in a look Tom could only describe as mortified. "I'd prefer if you'd give me a lift back to my car."

Edward slanted a helpless glance Tom's way before answering. "Sorry, I can't."

Kate turned on Tom. "So you plan to kidnap me now. Is that it?"

As Edward peeled out of the parking lot, Tom's relief that Kate was safe—and as feisty as ever—made him smile, which only made her scowl darken. "I'll drive you wherever you'd like. Despite what you may think, I came here because I thought you were in danger. I want to help you find Daisy's killer."

"Four hours ago, you treated me as if I'd killed her!"

"I had my orders. I'm sorry I doubted you. Clearly, someone tried to frame you and—"

"Someone?" she blurted. "Your boss, you mean. The one giving those orders you're so quick to obey."

Whoa, she suspected Hank too? "If Hank is behind this, we'll figure out a way to prove it."

"We?" Her snarky voice, so out of character, betrayed how deeply he'd hurt her.

"Yes, *we*. I made a mistake, and I'm asking you to forgive me." He lifted his hand to touch her cheek, but she shied away. Reluctantly, he opened the passenger door and waited for her to climb in. "I want to help you."

"It's not that easy," she muttered, dropping into the seat.

"You forgave Edward easily enough, and he lied about his identity from the day you met."

"That's different."

Tom shut the door, walked to the driver's side, and slid into the car. "Different how?"

Kate wrapped her arms around her middle and faced the window. "He never pretended to be something he wasn't."

"What are you talking about? That's exactly what he did."

"That's not what I mean and you know it. You acted like you cared about me and then turned around and handed me over to the police."

"I wasn't acting. I *do* care about you."

"If you cared, you would have stuck by me. Edward may have lied about who he was, but when I was in trouble, he was the one who came to my rescue. Not you."

"What do you call what I just did?"

She stared out the window without answering. Apparently those rose-colored glasses she saw Edward through didn't work on him. Tom started the car and pulled onto the road.

After a couple minutes of stony silence, Kate spoke. "Why didn't you tell me sooner what you knew about Edward? What else are you hiding?"

"What am *I* hiding? You're the one with an assumed name. And when did Chief Brewster become your number one suspect? 'Cause I missed the memo."

"How did you even find me way out here?" A wild-eyed expression swept over her face, and she picked frantically at her clothes. "What did Hank do? Slip a tracking device into one of my pockets?"

Stunned that she could think he'd conspire with Hank against her, Tom could only gape. "Julie told me where you were by using your cell phone tracker app."

Kate whipped out her cell phone and started pushing buttons.

"What are you doing?"

"Changing my password."

"Kate, I brought you in for questioning this afternoon because I was ordered to," Tom explained. "But you're right, I could've stuck around. I was upset, and yes, for a while I did doubt you. I'm sorry.

"As for Edward, I didn't tell you what I knew because I didn't want to upset you more. You believe in people, and as naïve as I think that is—proven, you'd have to agree, by what you've now learned about him—I saw no reason to rub your nose in the fact, when you'd already decided he was guilty. What I don't get is why you've changed your mind about him."

"You'd probably think I was worse than naïve if I told you."

"Try me."

She curled her fingers into her lap, hesitating. "I think God prodded me. As Edward talked, I remembered how alone in the world I felt after I lost my mom until Daisy pointed me to God. That's when I knew I had to show Edward that I believed in him. The way Daisy had. He wants to change, and I think he's starting to figure out that he needs God's help to do it."

Kate's eyes shimmered with a faith so pure and a concern for Edward so genuine that Tom felt utterly humbled. "You are one special person. Edward's lucky to have you on his side."

Kate's cheeks flamed. She turned her attention to the passing scenery.

"But please remember that until we have definitive proof, Edward is still a suspect." As the forest gave way to orchards, Tom eased his foot off the gas. In a few minutes they'd be at the research station, and he needed every available second to ensure she cooperated, or before he knew it, she'd run headlong into more trouble.

"I told you he—"

"Save your breath," Tom ordered. "You won't change my mind. Now, our best hope of identifying Daisy's killer is by finding the kid who masqueraded as Gordon."

"He's probably some delinquent Hank caught spray painting the back of the bank and offered to let off with a warning in return for a favor."

"Whoa, if you're not careful, you're going to ruin that Pollyanna reputation of yours," he teased.

"Very funny. Hank has to be the one who hired the kid. Otherwise why would he refuse to investigate when I'd obviously been set up?"

As tempted as Tom was to agree with her, his seesawing suspicions afforded him a measure of perspective he hadn't managed to scrape up an hour ago. "Hank could be afraid of what we'd discover. Or he might be afraid of the bad PR if reporters linked the false allegations to an unsolved murder he'd claimed wasn't murder."

"At least you agree with me on that point."

"How would Hank have known about your connection with Gord?"

"I wasn't connected with him." Her voice rose

defensively. "He came to our lab now and again. Lots of interns did."

"Then who knew he'd been in your lab?"

"I don't know. Other interns, maybe. Darryl."

Darryl. Tom wrung his hands over the steering wheel. His prime suspects were switching up faster than ducks in a shooting gallery. "Whoever sent our Gordon impersonator to the police might've known you were suspicious of him and decided to turn the tables. Who knew that you'd taken an interest in Gord's whereabouts?"

Kate slammed her foot into the floorboard as if she had a brake. "Al Brewster did. Gord was an intern at Herbs Are Us. Brewster must have told Hank I'd been asking questions. Did you know that he was once arrested for growing marijuana?"

"Yes, I did." Tom hated how everything seemed to point back to Hank and his dad. "Anybody else?"

"Why won't you face the truth? The police chief's corrupt. You said yourself that lots of the town's citizens were wary about his appointment to chief."

"A few days ago you were dead certain Edward was our man. So let's not jump to any more conclusions." Tom signaled a lane change. He'd done enough conclusion-jumping for both of them.

"I asked Darryl about Gord," Kate said, her tone

more subdued, "and I think I might've mentioned him to Edward too."

"Of Darryl, Edward, and Brewster, was Darryl the only one who knew you kept tagetes in the lab?"

"Anyone who'd been through my lab or who was familiar with my research would know I have jars of dozens of different herbs. Someone only had to plant suspicion that tagete was one of them, because if the police failed to find it, they'd just claim I'd disposed of the evidence."

Her unemotional assessment of the scenario sparked an unwelcome thought. If she hadn't *happened* to ask the chief what the complainant looked like, the fact he was an imposter wouldn't have been discovered so soon.

Tom slanted a glance at Kate. What was he thinking? That she planned the ruse to force the department into reopening the case?

An attempted frame-up certainly merited the consideration.

No, she wouldn't. With the help he'd been giving her, she'd had no reason to stoop to such deceptions. He couldn't even imagine her capable of them. Not really. Besides, until he'd gotten sidetracked by Edward's interference, he'd been certain that Hank and his dad were behind everything.

As if she'd read his thoughts, Kate said, "I think Hank is covering for his dad, which means he'll thwart any attempt we make to prove Daisy was murdered unless . . . we expose him publicly."

"*We* will do no such thing."

"But it's simple. We ask him to meet us at A Cup or Two, and then—"

"Leave this to me."

Kate frowned at his clipped response.

Tom let out a sigh. "This isn't an Agatha Christie mystery. Telling the probable killer you know he's guilty is not the way to flush him out, unless you want to be his next victim."

"How'd you know that's what I was going to suggest?"

"Because I know you. If you want to help, go home. Forget about the investigation. I will find Daisy's killer."

"You don't believe me. You can't believe your boss would do such a thing. Can you? But you thought I could."

He braked and faced her. "That's not it at all."

Skepticism lined her face.

"I need you to trust me."

"This from the man who says 'people are rarely what they seem.' How do I know Hank didn't send you to deal with me?"

The accusation flattened Tom with the force of a battering ram to the chest. "You know me." He sucked in a breath. "How could you think I'd—?"

"I don't know you. The man I thought I knew

never would have dumped me at the police station."

He punched the gas and ate the remaining couple of miles to her work in about as many seconds. He swerved into the lot and pulled into an empty spot a stone's throw from her yellow Bug. "I said I'm sorry. What more can I do?"

"You've done enough. You've proven people aren't what they seem. That's what you wanted. Wasn't it? Well, I was happier believing in people. You should try it sometime." Kate sprang from the car and slammed the door.

Tom ground his teeth so hard his jaw hurt. Okay, so he had a lousy opinion about the character of people. And okay, he'd let Kate down this afternoon. Maybe he even had some serious trust issues. But he had his reasons. Good reasons. Reasons he might tell her about if she'd stop long enough to listen.

She pushed the remote on her key chain and the car beeped.

The sound triggered a flash of memory: A ground-shaking explosion. Glass ripping through the air in every direction. Black smoke spewing from what was left of his partner's car.

"No!" Tom burst out the door and tore after Kate. "Stop!"

19

Kate cupped her hands around her mug of hot cocoa and snuggled into the corner of the sofa. "I'm telling you, Julie, the man will stop at nothing to convince me to stop investigating. Tom scoured every inch of my car. He even crawled underneath. He swears I'm putting myself in danger."

"So why aren't you freaking out? I'm freaking out and I just live with you. What if he's right and whoever killed Daisy comes after you next?"

Kate rubbed her arm where Edward's fingers had dug into her flesh. She shivered at how her near-hysteria over being arrested had caused her to accept a lift from Edward without hesitation. What if it was another lapse in judgment that compelled her to take his side on top of the cliff?

Shoving away the memory of Tom's ashen face when she stepped in front of Edward, she forced out a laugh. "If Tom believed I was in danger, do you think he would have left here after following me home?"

Julie edged the curtain aside and peeked down at the street. "Um, I hate to tell you this, but he's still out there."

"You're kidding me." Kate jumped from the sofa, spilling hot cocoa over her fingers. "Ouch, ouch, ouch." She set the mug on the table and rushed to the window.

"I'm kidding." Julie laughed. "Look at your face. I think you're disappointed."

Kate licked cocoa off her fingers. "Don't be ridiculous." She plopped onto the sofa and snagged her mug. "Do you think I want a killer to come after me?"

"Nope. I think you want Tom to be that worried." Julie waggled her eyebrows.

"Oh, please." Kate grabbed a throw pillow and tossed it at Julie's head. "You make me sound desperate." She refused to be desperate. No matter how much Tom's terror-stricken expression outside her car had burrowed under her defenses, she wouldn't let him back into her heart. If he'd cared about her at all, he wouldn't have been so easily duped by the *evidence.*

Julie stuffed the pillow behind her back and hugged her knees. "If you ask me, you should have let Tom haul Edward off to jail. You would've been doing Molly a favor."

"I get the impression Molly can take care of herself." Kate knew being miffed about Molly's charade was petty. But the woman owned a diamond necklace that could pay Kate's salary for two years and then some. "She probably laughed out loud when I suggested a scholarship." Kate snorted. "She needs my help like she needs more diamonds."

"Hey, I'm supposed to be the skeptic, not you. I kind of feel sorry for her. I mean, sure, she brought some valuable stuff from home, but she's essentially still alone with only Edward as a friend."

Kate's conscience pricked. "You're right. Edward said she never knows whether people befriend her for her, or for her money. Just because Molly can take care of herself doesn't mean she doesn't need friends."

"And what about you? Everyone in town is talking about your quote–unquote arrest. I had three people stop me in the grocery store and ask me if the rumor was true. It's a wonder Harold's not camped out on our doorstep, waiting to get the scoop. There hasn't been this much excitement in town since Joe Metler's mare gave birth to the colt with a fifth hoof."

"So glad to hear I rank right up there with a mutated quarter horse."

"Come on, I'm serious. What are you going to do? I don't want to sound self-centered, but my wedding is in less than two weeks and . . . I need you . . . alive."

Kate sprang to her feet. "Oh no, Julie, I completely forgot."

"Forgot what?"

Kate yanked out her hair elastic, fluffed her

hair, and smoothed her blouse. "We have to go."

"Go where?"

"Barbara's. No, wait." Kate dug through her purse and pulled out the shower invitation for the surprise party she was supposed to have had Julie at—Kate glanced at her watch—ten minutes ago. "Betty's."

Julie rose with a knowing laugh. "The B and B. How did you plan on getting me there without tipping me off?"

"I didn't. Just act surprised, okay? It's bad enough I'm getting you there late. Serena will never let me live it down if she finds out you knew about the party too."

"Yeah, I can see her revenge now. She'll cut your hair two inches shorter on one side than the other."

"Hey, don't laugh. She would. Did you see the dye job she gave her ex-boyfriend's mom? If she weren't the only hairdresser in town, she'd be losing clients in droves. Come on. We need to hurry."

They jogged down the stairs and along the street. The smell of freshly mown grass scented the air. Hopscotch games drawn in brightly colored chalk decorated the sidewalks. Seniors reclining on their front porches, enjoying the cool evening air, waved as Kate and Julie passed by. Murders weren't supposed to happen in places like this.

Half a block from the B and B, Kate caught Julie's arm, and they slowed to a stroll. "Remember what I said. Act surprised."

Julie's eyes bubbled with amusement. If Kate didn't know better, she might think Julie enjoyed seeing her tormented.

Before they reached the front door, Serena slipped out the French doors at the far end of the rambling porch. At 162 years old, the B and B, originally the mansion home of the town's first mayor, was the oldest Victorian in town. In her hip-hugging skirt and moussed-up hair, Serena didn't fit the ambience. "It's about time you two showed up. Clara was about to call our men in blue to haul you all in."

"Ooh, that would've been fun," Julie said. "How about we wander down the street a while longer and Clara can send Detective Parker out to look for us?"

Kate pushed Julie toward the door. "Very funny. Can we please go inside?" Kate followed Julie through the doors to a chorus of "Surprise!" Streamers crisscrossed the ceiling, gussied up here and there by brightly colored balloons—not the pastel pinks typical of bridal showers. Leave it to Serena to shake things up a little.

Julie laid her arm across Kate's shoulder and squeezed. "Happy birthday, roomie."

"Huh?"

Julie turned Kate toward the banner hanging

over the stone fireplace. It said, "Happy 30th Birthday."

"Surprise," Julie squealed into Kate's ear.

"Ahh! I can't believe this. I totally forgot."

Serena handed Kate a glass of punch. "Shut the date out of your mind more likely. But don't worry. Being thirty is not so bad. Trust me, I've had a couple years' experience." She grinned.

Every woman in town Kate knew was here, plus more than a few she didn't. "How'd you get all these people to come to a party for me?" Kate whispered to Julie.

"Easy. Notoriety brings out the glamour seekers."

"Ha ha."

Before Kate knew what was happening, she was being passed around the room like a Hug-Me-Suzie doll. Marjorie, the receptionist from the research station, tugged Kate into a bear hug. "I've been so worried about you, dear. Did the police fingerprint you?"

"No, the police only wanted to ask me some questions."

"Oh, what a relief. Darryl was pulling his hair out trying to handle the flood of calls after word got out that the police had come for you."

Kate tried to smile but didn't quite manage to pull it off. Marjorie meant well, but she was born with notoriously loose lips. Poor Darryl. It sounded like he'd borne the brunt of the damage this time.

"Oh, I do hope Harold gets the real story before he goes to press," Marjorie went on. "You know how that man is when he latches onto a headline."

"I'm hardly headline worthy."

"Oh dear, you're too modest. Everyone knows the only reason we even have a police station in our tiny town is because we're smack-dab in the center of the region and the officers can get every-where else quickly. Nothing ever happens here."

"Maybe that's just what they want you to believe."

Marjorie shivered, but the smirk that accom-panied it suggested the idea of a cover-up was more intriguing than worrisome. "Ooh, Mrs. C and Hilda said the same thing. They said the police want to lull Daisy's killer into a false sense of security so he'll get careless and reveal himself. Mrs. C said Detective Parker practically confirmed it."

"Really? Now that is interesting."

"She taught those boys in school and can read them like a book. She says Hank and Tom were always thick as thieves. They're cooking up something. You can be sure of that."

Kate's heart dipped. That's what she was afraid of.

"Oh my, yes, Mrs. C can always tell." Marjorie patted Kate's arm. "Don't you fret. We all know Daisy wouldn't kill herself."

Kate wished she could be equally as certain

that Tom wouldn't cover up a crime for his boss.

Julie sidled over to them. "Look who else is here."

Tom's sister peeked her head out from behind Julie.

"Tess! Wow, it's great to see you."

Julie hugged Kate's shoulder. "After hearing how well the two of you hit it off this past weekend, I hunted Tess down at the antique shop and invited her to the party."

"And I'm so glad she did. You should have told us it was your birthday." Tess held out a floral-wrapped gift. "This is for you."

They exchanged you-shouldn't-haves and I-wanted-tos until Julie blurted, "Open it, already."

Kate tore into the package. "Oh wow, oh wow, oh wow," she whispered at the sight of an ancient book—*Culpeper's Complete Herbal.* Originally published in 1653, it was the first herbal medicine book written in English instead of Latin. In utter disbelief, she traced the embossed lettering on the front cover, then opened it with trembling fingers. According to the date inside, this edition was over 150 years old.

"Oh," she said again, too overwhelmed to string together a coherent sentence. She carefully turned the ragged-edged pages, brittle from age. At the page on chamomile, she gasped again. The former owner of the book had added handwritten notes in a calligraphic-like script. "Tess, this is amazing. I can't believe you found this, or that you'd give it to me."

"You're the only person I know who would truly appreciate it."

Tears sprang to Kate's eyes. She closed the book and gave Tess a long hug. Kate hadn't thought she'd find another friend like Daisy, one who she not only felt an immediate kindred spirit with but who also understood her passion for herbs. "Thank you," she whispered, squeezing Tess harder. "You can't imagine how precious this gift is to me."

"I'm so glad you like it. Finding it was God's doing. That woman from the tea shop—"

"Beth?"

"No, not the owner. The cashier. I think she said her name was Molly. Anyway, she was in the store looking for a gift for her dad and spotted the book in one of the boxes my husband was unpacking. Said her dad is really interested in herbal folklore." Tess touched the book, her lips curving into a pleased smile. "Of course, the minute I saw the title I thought of you. Molly was all set to buy it, but when she saw the writing inside, she changed her mind."

"Lucky for me!" Kate opened the book to one of the pages that had a note added. "I think the handwritten annotations make the book all the more special."

Beth, looking much better than she had a few days ago, joined Kate and Tess and Julie. "Did I hear my name?"

"Oh, Beth"—Kate turned the book toward her —"you've got to see some of these entries. You could glean interesting quotes for your tea shop."

"I'm not sure how much of the book you should believe," Tess cautioned. "I looked up marigolds, and Culpeper touts them as being good for the heart. But aren't marigolds what the coroner said—"

Julie grabbed Tess's arm. "Please don't get Kate started on the differences between edible and inedible marigolds."

"Oh, I don't know," Julie's aunt Betty—owner of the B and B—chimed in. "After what happened to Verna's cat, I think people need to be made more aware of the dangers, especially those with youngsters."

"Thankfully most toxic plants are so bitter that children spit them out before any harm is done," Kate said. "The plants you need to be diligent about are the ones with sweet-tasting berries. I had a professor whose child almost died from eating the bright red berries of the yew tree in their front yard. The flesh is sweet and safe to eat, but the tiny seeds inside are deadly."

As the women launched into a litany of similar near-miss stories, Beth leaned over to Kate. "I guess I'd better do something about that tree in my kitchen before long."

Kate gave Beth a side hug. "It's so good to see you well enough to come tonight."

"I told Darryl that I'm going stir-crazy cooped up in our apartment. He's been working such long hours that I'm bored to tears on my own all day."

"Couldn't you go down to the shop and keep him company while he closes up?"

"Most nights Molly has it taken care of before he gets home."

"But—" Kate caught herself before saying something that might upset Beth. Most days Darryl came in late and left the research station early. Kate had assumed he was helping in the shop.

"You must have told him about Verna's cat, huh?" Beth said. "I noticed that he'd picked the pods off my castor tree."

The hairs on the back of Kate's neck prickled. Three well-chewed—or ground—castor beans could kill a person. "Uh, Marjorie probably mentioned it."

"Right." Beth chuckled. "Nothing gets past her. Well, I'd better let you mingle."

"Don't overtire yourself. I don't want to end up in my boss's bad books." Especially if he was harvesting castor beans.

Tess touched Kate's arm. "Are you okay? You're white as a ghost."

Kate glanced around to ensure no one was listening, then whispered, "I think I might have figured out who murdered Daisy."

Tess pulled her into a corner. "Who?"

"I'd better not say here."

"Do you want me to call Tom?"

"No. He's the last person I want to talk to."

"He feels horrible for letting you down."

"Letting me down?" Kate said, her voice rising in disbelief. "He all but arrested me and then abandoned me at the police station."

"You need to give him another chance. He's usually not such a jerk."

"I'd just as soon work solo. Thanks."

"What do you intend to do?"

"Get proof."

"You can't hunt down a killer on your own. At least let me call my dad." Tess's blue eyes, too much like Tom's, begged Kate to be reasonable.

Kate nibbled on her thumbnail. If she followed Darryl in her yellow Bug, he would spot her for sure. "All right. Tell Keith to pick me up at six tomorrow morning. I have a plan."

Trusting Tess to keep an eye on Kate, Tom headed for Herbs Are Us. He wasn't sure if Tess befriending Kate would help or hinder his chances of undoing the damage he'd done by practically arresting her. He'd made a fool of himself searching for a bomb in her car. Although from the slight softening he'd seen in her stance, maybe his concern had won him back a yard or two in the trust department.

He shook his head. *Focus on the priority here, Parker. Find the killer and Kate will be safe.* Tonight that meant establishing Hank and Al's innocence or guilt once and for all. Hank's behavior this afternoon coupled with Al's exchange at the tea shop was too suspicious to ignore. Tom upped his speed. Not suspicious enough to get a warrant, of course. And without a warrant, nothing he saw at Herbs Are Us would be admissible in court. Anyhow, the last thing he wanted to do was broadcast his suspicion that the chief's dad was a drug dealer by showing up on Brewster's doorstep with a search warrant. Far better to happen by on the pretense of wanting to question him about his former employee Gordon Laslo.

If Brewster hired the Laslo imposter to testify against Kate, his reaction was bound to give him away. Hank might soon regret tossing the pilfering case onto Tom's desk.

Tom swerved onto the long driveway that led to the greenhouse. Gnarled branches cloaked the rutted lane. No wonder Kate had been suspicious of this place. It felt like something straight out of a horror flick.

The driveway opened into a large clearing occupied by rows of interconnected greenhouses.

A group of Mexican men, ranging in age from late teens to midforties, sat on picnic benches next to the parking lot, eating their supper and chatting in Spanish.

Tom parked his car and approached the group. The spicy aroma of refried beans and hot sauce made his stomach growl. "Excuse me. I'm looking for Mr. Brewster."

The group fell silent. Tom was mentally working out how to say the same thing in Spanish when the eldest-looking man spoke around a bite of his tortilla. "I think he go out."

"I'll check to be sure. Thanks." Tom headed for the bay door of the main building.

"Wait. Boss don't like gringos looking around."

That fact made Tom all the more eager to do so, but, reluctant to rouse suspicions, he stopped and turned to the man at the table. "It's important that I find Mr. Brewster. Would you mind checking for me?"

The man looked from Tom to his tortilla and frowned. "You go ahead."

Satisfied that he couldn't be accused of illegal entry, Tom strode through the rows of domed greenhouses and, under the pretense of looking for Brewster, scanned for telltale signs of marijuana. If Tom *happened* to notice anything suspicious, he'd get a search warrant.

He moved into the glass-enclosed houses. The late evening sun on the glass-paneled roof cast long shadows over benches filled with every imaginable type of herb from anise to yarrow—every one except cannabis.

The farthest greenhouse was different. It housed a variety of annual flowers. Six-inch pots of dahlias sat loaded on racks ready for transport. With the long weekend approaching, everyone would be anxious to get into their gardens and plant their flowers. Maybe he should buy a few trays for Dad to rejuvenate Mom's other flower beds. Tom stepped forward to take a closer look at the dahlias.

"May I help you?" Brewster's gruff voice rattled the glass walls.

Tom jerked back his hand. "Yes. Hello. I'm Detective Parker."

Brewster betrayed no recognition of the name.

"I'm wondering what you can tell me about Gordon Laslo."

If Brewster was bothered by the question, he didn't show it. "The kid worked here as an intern for a few weeks, then up and quit."

"Did he give a reason?"

Brewster shrugged. "Didn't like the work, I guess. What'd he do?"

"I'm not at liberty to say. During the time he was in your employ, did you notice any items go missing?"

Brewster rubbed a hand over his whiskered jaw and seemed to give the question serious thought

—the picture of a cooperative witness. "Can't say as I did, no."

"Do you know where I might find Mr. Laslo now?"

"No clue. If there's nothing else, I need to drive my workers home." Brewster turned with an air of expectation that Tom would follow.

"There is one more thing. I'd like to buy a tray of those potted dahlias."

Glancing over his shoulder, Brewster narrowed his eyes as if the idea of selling a plant was more bothersome than answering questions about Laslo. "We're the middlemen on those flowers. I brought them in to fill an order. There's none to spare. Sorry."

"Where are they going?"

"Why?" His gaze flicked from Tom's notebook to the rack of pots.

"If they're going to a store nearby, I can purchase them there."

"That order's heading stateside." Brewster's fingers flapped nervously against his palm as he led the way back to the main building.

Hmm, so he'd struck a nerve after all. "Thanks for your time. I'll see myself out." Tom walked sedately across the parking lot, pretending to admire the scenery as he scanned the surrounding forest for evidence of a grow-op. He didn't spot anything suspicious, but Hank had said there'd been several in the area. When Tom reached his car, he glanced back at the door to the main building and waved.

Brewster retreated inside without responding.

Tom flipped through his notebook pages until he found the list of suspected grow-ops under surveillance in the region. No site remotely close to this area was on the list—a serious slip on Hank's part.

Tom cleared the driveway and stepped on the gas. He was through pussyfooting around Hank. The only way to get to the truth was to confront him. Make him see that covering up for his dad was ten times worse than mopping up any public relations fallout from arresting him. Hank had to suspect his dad was up to something. Otherwise he wouldn't have been so worried about Kate out in the woods, and he wouldn't have warned Tom off of stepping on the drug task force's toes, when the only toes in the vicinity were Hank's dad's.

Ten minutes later Tom pulled into Hank's driveway. He lived in a log cabin squirreled away in the middle of three acres of bush on the outskirts of town. The kind of place where you go to escape.

Tom rolled down his window and inhaled. Pine scented the air, and beyond the trees, the setting sun streaked the sky in purples and reds. A raccoon—also uninvited—scurried around the cabin. The windows glowed orange from the sun's reflection, and a wisp of smoke swirled from the stone chimney. Tom parked behind Hank's SUV.

Crickets chirruped a welcome song, interrupted by the occasional *thunk*.

Tom skirted the building in search of the source of the sound.

In the clearing behind the cabin, Hank stood next to a woodpile, shirt off, ax in hand. He propped up a log and swung the ax. With one blow, the wood split in two.

Tom gave the swinging ax head a wide berth as he moved toward Hank.

Hank split two more pieces of wood before stopping, then leaned on his ax handle and gave Tom his full attention. "Problem?"

"Yeah, I want to know why you claimed there'd been grow-ops near where we found Kate in the woods."

Hank swiped at the sweat dripping down the side of his face. "To scare some sense into her."

"I'm not buying it. You were edgy about Kate being out in those woods. Too edgy. What didn't you want her to see?"

Hank's head jerked as if he were taken aback by the question, but was it because he was affronted or afraid?

"What's your dad selling in brown paper sacks to Beth Kish?"

"Huh?" Confusion furrowed Hank's brow. Then

the question's implication seemed to settle in, and he squared his jaw. "He sells herbs for her teas like half the local growers around here."

"For cash?"

"What are you getting at?"

Tom gave him a you-tell-me look.

"I don't believe this." Hank slapped his ax into a stump and clenched his fists. "You think my dad's dealing again? I thought I could count on you, of all people, not to turn my family history against me. Clearly, I was wrong." He stalked toward his house.

Tom grabbed his arm and swung him around. "Oh, no. You're not getting out of this discussion by playing the sympathy card. What are you covering up?"

If the incredulous look on Hank's face could be believed, he wasn't behind any cover-up. He shook off Tom's grasp. "After all we've been through together, how could you think I'd do something like that?" Hank's voice thrummed with a pain of betrayal Tom recognized all too well.

Lord, show me what to do. Hank gave me the detective's job, no questions asked, based on the strength of a twenty-year friendship. A friendship I discounted as easily as a phony dollar bill. Tom tempered his tone. "You've got to admit that you took an unusual interest in the Leacock case."

"The case was the town's first suspicious death

since I became chief. Of course I took an interest."

When Tom offered no response, Hank added. "I have nothing to hide. I can take you to my dad's right now, to his work too, anywhere you want to search. No warrant needed. I don't want you to have any doubts."

"I paid Herbs Are Us a visit. Your dad was a little unnerved by my interest in the flowers he had ready for a shipment. Why would that be, do you think?"

"How should I know? I thought the place only sold herbs."

"Apparently not."

"Get to the point. Do you want me to take you to my dad's or not?"

Tom blew out a stream of air. Despite their friendship, he had a job to do.

A doe and her fawn ambled across the corner of the clearing and stopped to nibble the grass. The sun, already below the tree line, sliced through what had been a dense stand of trees as if . . . only a narrow strip remained.

"You clear-cut your woods behind the house?"

"What?" Hank followed Tom's line of sight. "No, I just cleared a section for sweet corn."

Corn, a favorite crop for opportunists to hide their marijuana plants among. And not only opportunists. When the police spotted the pot gardens from the air, they rarely suspected the culprit was the farmer, much less the chief of police.

"The corn goes in this week."

Tom nodded, betraying no interest in Hank's admission. He'd give the crop a month to grow. Then he'd take Hank up on the offer to search *anywhere*. About the time the corn topped a foot, the marijuana growers typically replaced a section with their seedlings—neatly hidden by the growing corn.

"It's getting dark, Tom. What's it going to be? Do I take you to my dad's?"

"That won't be necessary," Tom said. As much as he wanted to take Hank up on his offer, to accept would rip the last thread binding their tattered friendship. "I just had to make sure. I'm sorry."

20

At 5:58 the next morning, Keith coasted to the curb in front of Kate's in a nondescript gray sedan. The vehicle suited her plan perfectly. Between the persistent drizzle and lingering fog, the sedan would scarcely be noticed.

Kate darted from the porch and slid into the passenger side before Keith could shift into park. "We have to hurry."

"Good morning to you too. Where to?"

Kate peeled off her rain slicker and tossed it into the backseat. "A Cup or Two."

"It doesn't open for another hour. How about Mike's Truck Stop?"

"We're not going for the coffee. I want to follow Darryl Kish."

Keith pulled a U-turn and headed downtown. "Whaddya got?"

"Darryl's wife thinks he's putting in long hours at the research station, but if anything, for the past month or so he's been putting in shorter days."

"Working a second job to make a little extra cash, perhaps."

"Their shop is always busy. I don't think they have money problems."

"You'd be surprised." Keith's tone suggested he knew more than he planned to divulge. "Appearances aren't always what they seem."

"Well, I'd be thrilled to discover that's all he's doing, because I hate suspecting my friends and colleagues. But Beth told me that Darryl took the bean pods from her castor tree, and castor beans contain a virtually untraceable poison—ricin."

Keith peered through the thickening fog. "You think that's what killed Daisy?"

"The coroner's report won't stop bugging me. It noted hemorrhaging. Thiophene doesn't cause internal bleeding, but ricin does."

"So Darryl's got the means, and working

together gave him opportunity. What about motive?"

Kate turned up the car's heater to chase the chill from her bones. "My theory is that Daisy found out Darryl was up to something, and he silenced her rather than deal with the fallout of being caught."

"You mean like an affair?"

Kate flinched at the suggestion. She couldn't imagine Darryl cheating on Beth. Although until last night she couldn't have imagined him killing Daisy either. "I don't know."

Keith drove slowly past A Cup or Two and parked a couple of building lengths farther down the street. He sunk low in his seat, and Kate imitated him.

"How are we going to see when he leaves?"

"He won't go anywhere in this weather without his car." Keith's gaze was fixed on the rearview mirror. "Hybrid Fusion, right?"

"How'd you know?"

"Darryl has been on our radar for a while."

"Oh." Kate shivered, but not so much from the damp chill as the memory of Tom's recovery effort when she'd gone to the Kishes' apartment. Tom had made his suspicion of Darryl clear then, but she'd been too focused on Edward to pay much attention.

The pitter of rain on the car roof filled the silence. Five minutes passed. Ten.

Keith perked up, squinted at the rearview mirror, then the side mirror.

She glanced in her side mirror and saw nothing but water. She had no idea how he saw a thing in this drizzle.

"We've got movement," he announced.

Headlights beamed through the rear window before they streaked past into the gloom ahead.

Kate sat up and grabbed the dash. "Aren't you going to go? We'll lose him."

He turned his key in the ignition and hitched a brief, wry smile. "There isn't another soul on the street. If we follow too close, he might get suspicious."

Keith shifted the car into gear and eased into the street.

His turtle-like pace stretched Kate's nerves thin. She clenched her jaw and burrowed her fists under her thighs, resisting the temptation to urge him to go faster.

He laid his hand on her arm. "Stop fidgeting. I won't lose him. Trust me."

The red twin streaks of Darryl's taillights vanished around a corner. Keith and Kate made the turn in time to see the flash of color disappear onto another side street.

She clutched the door handle. "Stay on him."

"Stop worrying. He's not going anywhere. We're on the only street out of the cul de sac he turned into."

Kate's grip tightened. This was it. They were about to uncover Darryl's dirty little secret.

Keith killed his lights and idled ten feet from the turn onto the dead end. He extracted a pair of humongous binoculars from under the seat.

Darryl pulled into a driveway at the top of the circle, belonging to a small brick bungalow. A silver car—a Saturn, maybe; hard to tell with the fog—sat under the carport. The curtains were drawn at the big bay window and the two smaller windows on the other side of the front door, but lights were on inside. Darryl made a dash for the carport and entered through a side door.

"Notice anything interesting about that silver car?" Keith passed her the binoculars.

She scanned the vehicle from hood to tires but couldn't see what he saw. He pulled out a cell phone and punched in a number.

"What am I supposed to see?" Kate asked.

"Rear window, center." Keith held up a finger and turned his attention to the phone. "Allison, hi. It's Keith. Have a favor to ask. Can you run a plate for me?"

Kate focused the binoculars on the Saturn's license plate as Keith recited it from memory. Shifting her focus to the rear window, she spotted the university decal Keith had referred to. A student's house? Or a professor's, maybe?

"Thanks, I owe you one," Keith said into his

phone, then snapped it closed. "Care to hazard a guess at who that car belongs to?"

"Haven't got a clue."

"Gordon Laslo."

Kate gasped. "Darryl lied to me. He claimed he didn't know anything about Gord. What do you think they're doing in there?"

Keith withdrew a video camera from behind his seat and slowly panned the house. "Don't assume Gord's in there just because his car is in the driveway."

"Where else would he—" Kate choked on the question. Gulped. Gulped again. "Do you think Darryl killed Gord too?"

"No." Keith leaned over and showed her the viewing screen on his camera. The image was gray and black, with bright white splotches here and there, like around Darryl's tires and the hood of his car. "This is an infrared camera. Shows heat. Look at the bay window."

A pair of ghostly figures stood within the dark gray frame. "Two people are in that room."

"Yes, so the odds are that the second person is Gordon."

"They can't be up to any good or Darryl wouldn't have pretended not to know where Gord was."

"We're likely looking at a meth lab here. Could explain some of the materials missing from the research station, but I suggest we let the police figure that out. We can call in an anonymous tip, and Darryl need never know who fingered him."

"No, we can't. If we're wrong and Darryl is caught up in a police raid, Beth could lose her baby from the stress."

"She's pregnant? You never told me that."

"I promised I wouldn't breathe a word until she passed her first trimester."

"We can't wait till she has the baby to arrest this guy." Keith abruptly dropped the camera into his lap. "Let me handle this."

"What are you talk—?"

A tap sounded on Kate's window and she jerked sideways.

Keith hit a switch and the window slipped open. Rain spit at Kate's face as their visitor, a woman in a bright yellow rain slicker, leaned down. Deep wrinkles carved permanent smile lines into her cheeks and at the edges of her eyes. Kate estimated she was in her eighties.

"Are you with the police?" the woman asked.

"Why would you ask that?"

"I saw you spying on the house up there."

"Do you know anything about the occupants?" Keith asked.

"A young lad rents it. Quiet. Hardly ever see him. The other fellow drops by most mornings and evenings. Never stays more than a couple of hours."

"Anyone else ever visit?"

Kate leaned back, slack-jawed at how deftly Keith drew information from the woman. If this were a meth lab as Keith supposed, someone had to sell the goods, and if Gord rarely went out, that left Darryl or whoever else came to the house.

"Last week an older gentleman in a rental car was there. Didn't stay long."

"Can you describe him?"

"Smartly dressed in a dark gray suit and purple shirt. I remember because I happened to be walking the circle when he climbed out and I thought he looked so dashing in that purple shirt and silver tie."

Keith let her drone on and on for another three minutes until Kate shot him a get-rid-of-her-now glare.

Keith smiled at the woman. Not a polite, plastic smile either. A genuine, I-enjoyed-listening-to-your-story smile.

Kate intensified her glare in case he'd mis-understood her the first time.

"I'm partial to purple myself, but being on the portly side, I'm afraid it makes me look like Barney," Keith interjected when the woman took a second to breathe.

"Oh." The woman looked him up and down, apparently familiar with the giant purple dinosaur from a popular children's show. "Do you really think so?"

Kate squirmed and couldn't hold her tongue a second longer. "Um, we don't want to keep you. This damp weather isn't fit to be out in."

"Aren't you a dear?"

"Ma'am," Keith said, "please don't tell anyone we chatted."

She touched her thumb to her forefinger and twisted them in front of her lips. "You can count on me, Officer." The woman scurried toward a house two doors down from Darryl's mystery place.

"If I were a betting woman, I'd wager a month's salary that she'll spill the story to her husband before her rain slicker hits the coat hook."

"You're probably right."

"Why'd you let her think we were the police?"

"Cover stories were never my strength. I can't bring myself to lie when the truth works just as well."

The side door of the house opened and Darryl appeared. He turned up his collar against the rain but made no move to dash to his car.

Kate grabbed her jacket. "Stay here. I have an idea." Before Keith could stop her, she jumped out of the car and sprinted for the carport.

Keith coasted beside her in the car, leaned over the passenger seat, and pitched his voice through the open window. "Get in."

She kept walking. "I'm just going to talk to him."

"Over my dead body."

The fierceness in his voice punched the breath clean out of her lungs, and in the time she took to recover, Darryl made it to his car.

His gaze collided with hers. "Kate?" The shock on his face morphed into anger. "What are you doing here?"

"I need to talk to you." She reached into her jacket pocket, clawed her keys between her fingers, and prayed that she wasn't about to make the biggest mistake of her life. She shot Keith an apologetic shrug, then jogged up the driveway and ducked under the carport, keeping Gordon's Saturn between her and Darryl. "I know everything. And see the man in that car?" She pointed to Keith, who had a phone pressed to his ear. "He's got the police on the phone as we speak." She hoped the last part wasn't true and wouldn't be necessary.

Darryl's face paled.

"I know this is Laslo's car. I know he's been hiding out here. I know the two of you pilfered supplies from the research station for your"—she motioned toward the house—"little science experiments."

With each statement Darryl looked more peaked.

But knowing she was right didn't feel good in the least. "Daisy found out, didn't she? Threatened to expose your side business. Threatened to expose you." Kate's heart hammered her ribs. "And you killed her, didn't you?"

Darryl's face turned from white to red in a flash. "I never touched Daisy. You're crazy."

"Who do you think the police will believe when they see what's going on here? You? Or me?"

"There's nothing illegal going on here."

"If it's not illegal, why did you tell Beth that you're working late at the research station when you're skulking around here?"

"Because I don't want her to worry. The fertility treatments wiped us out financially. A company invited me to do some extra research for them. The money sounded good. I took the job. End of story."

"I don't believe you. You kept this a secret from more people than Beth. Gord broke off contact with all of his friends."

Like a panther stalking its prey, Darryl edged around the car, his eyes blazing.

Kate drew back her elbow, her keys poised to do damage. "Think about what you're doing here, Darryl. If you hurt me, the police won't even need a warrant to swarm in and search this place."

Keith nosed his car into the driveway, wearing a scowl that would strip paint off a bus.

Darryl threw Keith a wary glance, raised his hands, and backed up a step. "You've got it all wrong. I hired Gordon to help me with the research, and since he wasn't at liberty to discuss the work with his friends, he opted to lie low for a while."

Lie low. She really didn't like the sound of that. "Have you forgotten the nondisclosure agreement you signed when you joined the research station?"

"I'm not selling secrets. This research has nothing to do with my day job."

"You stole our supplies and you expect me to believe you're not selling our secrets?"

He heaved a sigh. "That was a mistake. I've since returned the items I borrowed. You have to believe me. If the police make more out of this than there is, the stress will upset Beth and jeopardize the baby."

The strain in Darryl's voice chipped at her certainty. She searched his eyes for the truth but didn't trust her judgment. "I need more than your word. Let me and my bodyguard see inside the house."

Relief softened the tension creasing Darryl's face. "Okay."

Kate waved Keith over. A moment later her cell phone rang.

"What's going on?" Keith barked.

"Darryl has agreed to let us see the house."

"Can you spell ambush?" Keith's windshield wipers flicked across the windshield. His accompanying glare said if Darryl didn't kill her, Keith might.

"Darryl knows you have the police on standby. Tell them if we don't contact them in five minutes, the SWAT team should be deployed," she said loud enough for Darryl to hear.

"I hope you know what you're doing." Keith hung up but didn't immediately join them, and she wondered if he was calling Tom to make good on her bluff.

Darryl shifted from foot to foot, glancing from Kate to Keith and back again.

She almost felt sorry for him. Almost.

Keith stalked up the driveway, keeping a wary eye on the front windows. "I want the drapes opened and your guy on the inside in plain sight, hands in the air."

Darryl reached for the knob on the door behind him.

"Not so fast," Keith bellowed. "We don't go in until you call your partner and tell him to get those drapes open."

"My phone's in the car."

Keith turned to Kate. "Give him yours."

Kate slid her phone across the trunk of Gord's car.

When Keith made a show of consulting his watch, beads of sweat popped out on Darryl's upper lip.

The living room drapes opened, followed by the blinds in the next two rooms.

"Check the back," Keith said to Kate.

She moved to the end of the carport and looked around the corner. "Everything's open."

Again Darryl reached for the doorknob.

"Not yet. Wait here." Keith pressed his back to the wall and moved cautiously along the front of the house until he reached the first window. He peered over the lip and quickly scanned the room.

He moved to the next window the same way, and Kate's legs turned to Jell-O. She'd never forgive herself if he got shot.

Keith circled the house, checking each window. He even knelt in the wet grass and shone a flashlight into the basement windows. "Okay, we'll go through the front," he said when he'd finished. His tone left no room for negotiation.

Gord stood in the middle of a furnished living room with his hands in the air. The chocolate brown sofa had seen better days and the rug was threadbare, but the forty-two-inch high-definition TV in the corner was state-of-the-art.

"What are you doing here?" Kate asked Gord.

"Research."

"What kind?"

"I already told you," Darryl cut in, "we can't discuss the nature of our research."

"Is Darryl paying you?" Kate asked, letting the earlier question pass unanswered.

"The company is. Plus room and board."

"You expect us to believe that a legitimate company set up a lab in a house?"

"I don't care what you believe. I get paid to do what I'm told."

Kate glanced at Keith to see if he bought the story.

He just shrugged.

They found a sophisticated lab in the back bedroom and a mushroom-growing operation in the basement.

When they returned to the living room, Keith said, "Looks to me like you're farming a new breed of hallucinogenic designer drugs."

"Is that what you think too, Kate?" Darryl said with a note of apology in his voice.

"They're working on a cure for depression," she said without emotion. No wonder he hadn't wanted to tell her.

Keith scratched his ear. "How do you figure?"

"A company out of Switzerland did some promising preliminary research involving mushrooms, but a few days before they were scheduled to release their findings, the research facility exploded. The researchers and all their documen-tation were lost in the fire."

"You mean to tell me this lab is a bomb waiting to explode?"

"No, a gas leak caused that explosion. Some say the lab was sabotaged. Could be Darryl's client didn't want a recurrence. Everything looks legit." Even if Darryl smelled as rotten as the manure feeding his mushrooms. "Nothing here contravenes the terms of his contract at the research station," she said in his defense, but that didn't stop his betrayal from swallowing her from the inside out. "Let's go."

"I'm not convinced he didn't murder Daisy to ensure his secret stayed secret."

"I am. Daisy never would have betrayed his secret."

21

Kate shuffled into the library and slumped onto the foam floor cushion at the edge of the preschool story time group. Enraptured children sat on bright blue and red and yellow spongy mats, listening to Julie read *The Paper Bag Princess*.

Julie gave Kate a curious look, and Kate sank lower on her cushion. She should have gone straight to work after Keith dropped her at home, but Darryl would be there soon and the thought of facing him again made her want to heave.

Julie showed the children a picture of the finely dressed prince scrunching his nose at the sooty princess who wore a paper bag because she'd just rescued him from a dragon. Then, in her best princess imitation, Julie pointed out that he might look like a prince, but he was a bum.

"Isn't that the truth?" Kate mumbled.

A couple of mothers shushed her, and Kate feigned a sudden fascination with the waffle pattern on the spongy mats. For more than a week she'd dug up dirt on all her suspects, people she never would have suspected capable of murder, only to end up back where she'd started—proving nothing but that people aren't what they seem. A lesson Tom had happily dispensed from day one.

Julie asked the children for ideas of how else the princess might have overcome the dragon that had stolen her prince, and a lively discussion ensued. When the suggestions deteriorated into downright silly, Julie ended the class and gave the children free rein of the picture book section.

She pulled up a foam cushion and joined Kate on the floor. "I take it your surveillance didn't pan out the way you'd hoped."

"Oh, Julie, I don't know what to do. Not a single trick I've tried on my 'dragon' has worked."

"Do you want me to ask the children for ideas?"

"Thanks, I'll pass."

"Maybe you're fighting the wrong dragon."

Kate picked at the foam. "Tell me about it. Three times over. First I was sure it was Brewster, only to find the 'key' piece of evidence to convince me it was Edward instead."

"You were right about him being rotten. He conned Daisy."

"True. But then I made the mistake of trusting Tom, only to have him turn on me."

"That was pretty bad." Julie pried Kate's fingers away from the foam. "What about Darryl?"

Kate buried her hands under her legs. "Darryl is moonlighting for some unknown company. And get this—he's developing a product that will compete with mine."

"How can he do that?"

"It's all legal. As far as I can tell, everything I saw was unrelated, technically, to the work he does at the station."

"Just because it's legal doesn't make it ethical."

Her leg began to bob. "Tell me about it. I was so crushed I got out of there faster than ants in a rainstorm."

"You're positive Darryl didn't kill Daisy?"

"As positive as I can be. I should be happy. The last thing I wanted to do was upset Beth, but . . ."

"It's a mixed blessing."

"Yeah. I hate mixtures." Kate shimmied higher and planted her feet to stop her runaway leg. "I forgot to tell you that I found Gord. He's working with Darryl."

"That's great news."

"How do you figure?"

"Look how many people you've crossed off

your suspect list—Gord and Darryl and Edward, whom, by the way, I still don't trust."

"So I'm back to where I started—suspecting the chief of police and his father without a speck of proof."

"Something will turn up. God has a way of bringing us to the end of ourselves so we'll finally be ready to see what's been there all along. Kind of like how the paper bag princess discovered the prince wasn't who she'd wanted to marry after all."

"Huh?"

"You were talking about the story, so I thought I'd extend the metaphor, and . . . Oh, never mind. My break is in a few minutes. Do you want to go for a cup of tea?"

The preschoolers, trailed by their mothers, poured out the doors ahead of Kate and Julie and raced to the adjoining park. The sun had burned off the early morning fog, and the colors of the grass and trees looked richer for their morning misting.

"Hey." Julie pointed to Cal's garage across the street. "Did you see that? Al Brewster just went in carrying a couple of brown paper bags."

"So? Maybe he's eating while his truck gets fixed."

"His pickup is parked outside the hardware store." Julie motioned to a twenty-year-old Ford that had orange Bondo patches covering two-thirds of its body.

"He could be visiting his brother."

Al exited via the big bay door carrying only one bag.

"Mighty short visit," Julie said. "Let's follow him."

"What for?"

Julie looked at her as if she were a few plants short of a flat. "To get your proof."

Kate's confusion must've been splattered across her face because Julie started talking very slowly. "Cal's garage. The 'go-to' place. To give *more* than your car *a boost*. Looks to me like Al's a supplier." Julie started across the street.

Comprehension finally shook Kate's brain into action. She grabbed Julie's arm and yanked her back to the curb. "You can't be so obvious." She steered her toward the discount store's sidewalk display and pulled a T-shirt off the rack. "We need to wait to see where Al heads and then pretend we're going that way too."

Al glanced their way.

"Act casual." Kate raised the T-shirt to eye level and pointed out the unique stitching to Julie, who feigned unusual interest.

A moment later, Al slipped into A Cup or Two, and Kate returned the shirt to the rack. "Shall we have that cup of tea now?"

"Sounds good to me," Julie said, this time sweeping her arm for Kate to lead.

They waited for a delivery truck to lumber by,

then hurried across the street and into the shop. The door swung out of Kate's grasp, and Molly barreled into her before Kate could get out of the way. A round of apologies that drew far too much attention to their arrival followed, and the door shut behind them with an extra loud jangle. So much for being discreet.

Brewster, paper bag in hand, stood at the cash register watching Beth answer the phone. Beth pressed the receiver to her chest and caught Kate's attention. "Can you try to catch Molly? Her dad's on the phone."

Kate rushed outside, but Molly had already pulled away from the curb in Beth's red LeSabre. "Wait," Kate shouted, jogging after her, waving.

Molly drove off, leaving a trail of blue smoke in her wake.

Julie held the door open for Kate and relayed the news to Beth, who relayed it to Molly's father.

"Did you know that your car is burning oil?" Kate added.

"Yeah, Molly's running it to the garage for me. I feel bad that she missed her call because of me, though."

A call from her father? Edward claimed Molly and her father weren't talking, that he didn't know she was in Port Aster. Although now that Kate thought about it, she'd heard Molly on her cell phone with him too.

Beth took the paper sack from Al and handed him a twenty. "Thank your mom again. This stuff works great."

"Will do." Al stuffed the bill in the front pocket of his plaid jacket and left.

Julie and Kate exchanged a look and beelined toward Beth. "What are you buying from Grandma Brewster?"

Beth's cheeks flushed. "You saw that, huh? It's kind of embarrassing. Here I run a specialty tea shop and I'm buying a mixture of herbs from Grandma Brewster to cure my"—she glanced at Julie and lowered her voice—"morning sickness. I don't know what she puts in there, but it works."

Julie's eyebrows disappeared into her bangs. "You're pregnant? Oh, wow! Congratulations."

"Shh," Kate whispered. "Beth doesn't want anyone to know yet." Kate peeked into the bag from Al. The dried leaves were crushed beyond recognition, but she could identify a few familiar aromas. "Have you asked Mrs. Brewster what her secret ingredient is?"

"Every chance I get. If I could replicate this stuff, I'd make a fortune. But she just smiles and says, 'Don't worry, I make for you.'" Beth mimicked Mrs. Brewster's thick German accent. "She learned her remedies in the old country and probably uses stuff that doesn't grow around here, except in her garden."

"Well, I'm so happy her remedy is working for you. You look better every time I see you. If you don't mind parting with a handful of the mixture, I could run some tests and probably figure out what's in it."

"Oh, I'd feel terrible sneaking behind her back to figure it out, but thanks for the offer."

Kate rolled the top of the bag closed and returned it to Beth. "Does Al usually deliver stuff for his mom?"

"Yeah, I'm told that he's been her courier since he was old enough to ride a bicycle."

Julie's shoulders drooped. "I'm sorry, Kate. I really thought we were onto something."

"Onto what?" Beth asked, her eyes bright with interest.

"Nothing. Forget it." Kate quickly scooped together a blend of tea and handed Beth the money. "Um, Beth, why did you tell me Molly had no one when I first asked you about her?"

"She doesn't. Not here. Of course, we've become good friends. And, well, I didn't know about Edward."

"Hmm." Kate carried her tea to the table near the fireplace.

Julie hurried after her. "What was that about? Why didn't you tell Beth about your grow-op theory?"

"There was nothing to tell." Kate pried her suspect list out of her back pocket, smoothed it flat on the table, and jotted down the new information she'd learned.

"I'm sorry," Julie commiserated. "It looks like you've hit the final dead end."

"No, I don't think so." Kate went over the clues, her mind whirling with new possibilities.

"What'd I miss?"

"Edward told me Molly wasn't talking to her father."

Julie jabbed her finger onto the table. "I told you I didn't trust him."

"But you didn't see his face when he told me that Molly left her folks to be with him. He was over the moon. I can't believe he was lying."

Julie sipped her tea and the silence stretched between them. Then suddenly she set down her cup. "Maybe he wasn't lying. Maybe that's what Molly told him. Maybe she exaggerated the rift to win him back, to convince him that he was more important to her than her father's money." Julie straightened her teacup on its saucer. "Not that I'm defending him. He had the most to gain from Daisy's death and the most to lose if Daisy took what she knew about him to the police. Not to mention he had plenty of opportunity to slip poison into her tea."

"I agree."

"You agree?" Julie repeated, looking a little stunned. "So you do think he did it?"

"I haven't ruled out the possibility." Kate's heart

twisted. She didn't want to believe he'd played her.

"Are you kidding me? You accepted a ride with a man you think could be a murderer and then defended him from the guy who showed up to save you. Are you sure *you* haven't been drinking tainted tea? 'Cause I think you might be delusional."

"Thanks for the vote of confidence." Kate took a deep breath to try to dislodge the weight that had settled on her chest. "Okay, let's look at who we've got: Darryl and Gord and their clandestine drug research. The chief who doesn't want me to investigate—maybe because of pressure from the mayor, or maybe to conceal his dad's crimes."

"Alleged crimes. We have no proof."

"Okay, alleged crimes. And then we have Edward and his girlfriend who just confuse me."

"That's because you're too trusting."

Kate looked helplessly at her list. "You're right. I could keep digging until the cows come home in the hope of finding a piece of evidence that will convict Daisy's killer. It's time to take drastic measures. Are you with me?"

Julie leaned back and raised her palms between them. "Oh no. You're not drawing me into one of your crazy schemes."

"It's not crazy. I saw it in a movie. We get all our suspects in the same room, here even, along with lots of witnesses so the killer can't try anything.

And then we flush him out. You'll be perfectly safe."

Julie hesitated so long Kate wondered if she was mentally cataloging friends to find a substitute who would fit into the maid of honor gown if Kate went down in a hail of bullets.

Julie blew out a resigned sigh. "How are we going to get everyone here?"

"That's the easy part." Before Julie could back out, Kate drew her cell phone from her purse and dialed the research station.

Marjorie answered.

"Hey Marge, it's Kate. Listen. Come by A Cup or Two after work tomorrow afternoon and tell all your frien—"

Julie grabbed Kate's arm, pulling the cell phone away from her mouth. "Are you nuts? We don't even have a plan."

Marjorie's voice chirped through the air.

Kate pulled back her phone. "Yes, Marjorie. I'm planning to make a big announcement."

"Oh my, that sounds exciting. Leave it to me. I'll pack the place." Marjorie, all atwitter with her newest scoop, clicked off without saying good-bye.

Julie glared.

"Come on, Jules. You want this to be over as much as I do. We have twenty-four hours to come up with a plan. Keith will help."

"I could ask Ryan if we can borrow surveillance equipment from his dad's hardware store."

"That's a great idea." Kate studied her list of suspects, wracking her brain for a clever way to prod the killer into revealing himself. She picked up her teacup and took a sip. A few drops dribbled from the bottom of the cup onto her paper. As she dabbed the paper with her napkin, her gaze fell to an item she'd scrawled in the margin.

Her breath caught.

People's actions, snippets of dialogue, seemingly unrelated goings-on suddenly made perfect sense.

22

Tom took a seat in the back corner of A Cup or Two and waited for his dad. The place was surprisingly busy for midafternoon. He recognized most of the patrons as locals, but the table by the door boasted a group of bell-bottomed drifters with psychedelic orange-and-green tie-dyed T-shirts straight out of the seventies.

He stretched his neck left and then right in a vain attempt to work out the kinks. Without an active case to justify the use of surveillance teams, he'd handled the last two nights on his own. But no matter how many angles he looked at Daisy's case from, he had nothing. Not on

Brewster, not on Darryl, not on Edward. Nothing that would stand up in court anyway. And no leads on who'd posed as Gordon Laslo.

If Daisy's killer hired a drifter to play the part of Laslo, Tom might never track him down, unless they got lucky with the fingerprints they lifted from his affidavit.

No, he needed more than luck. He needed divine intervention. Kate needed his protection more than ever, but she was still too furious at him for dragging her in for questioning to realize that the guy who tried to frame her for Daisy's murder might try something worse.

At least she'd agreed to let Dad stay on as her bodyguard.

Hank sprawled into the seat opposite Tom and set down a frothy mug of some sort of specialty coffee.

"Since when do you drink froufrou drinks?" Tom quipped to cover his surprise that Hank had stopped the cold-shoulder treatment. The iceberg between them had gotten so frigid, Tom had debated wearing a hat and mittens to the office.

Hank took a sip of his drink, then circled his tongue over his lips, collecting the froth left behind. "Mmm, mmm. Carla got me hooked on this stuff. It's really good." He jutted his chin toward the counter laden with teas. "Better than tea that tastes like weeds."

Tom chuckled and at the same time caught

sight of Kate sitting with Julie at a table in the center of the shop. Kate's gaze slid from Hank's face to his coffee before veering back to Tom. She nodded when their eyes met, but her tight smile suggested she didn't approve of the company he kept.

Not that he should be surprised. She'd already pegged him as Hank's coconspirator once. The softening he'd seen in her attitude toward him, after his desperate search for a bomb in her car, had apparently been short-lived.

Hank must've sensed the direction of his thoughts. "Have you talked to her since you brought her in?"

Tom swallowed the last of his coffee and slapped the mug onto the table. "Yeah."

"I take it she's still mad?"

"I don't want to talk about it." Tom clenched his jaw and fought the urge to lash out at Hank.

"Hey, if you like her that much, I'll have a talk with her. Let her know I—"

"No." Tom lowered his voice. "Thanks. You've done enough."

Hank let out a snort and dropped his gaze to the mug he was twisting in his hands. "I owe you an apology. Two, actually. First for messing with your, uh, love life. Carla overheard what I said about your last girlfriend."

"Zoe wasn't *my* girlfriend."

"It doesn't matter. The point is, Carla reminded

me of all the times you stood by me in high school when . . . well, you know."

"What's the second apology for?"

"The night before last. I know you were trying to do right by me. I gotta admit that after Adams found the marijuana leaf, I scoured the woods around Dad's place too. But it was clean. What I'm trying to say is, I didn't act like much of a friend and I'm sorry. I know you're true blue."

Tom's jaw slackened as he stared at Hank. Hank, his high school chum. Hank, his boss. Hank, the man he suspected of covering up his dad's illegal activities. Was the admission a ploy to throw Tom off the scent? An appeal to his loyalty? Or a genuine gesture?

Questioning his friend's motives left a bitter taste in his mouth. "That's okay."

Hank half smiled, a look Tom recalled from their teen years—whenever Hank thought he'd gotten away with something. For now, that was probably a good place for Hank to be.

Tom's dad straddled the chair between Hank and Tom. "Can you believe how packed it is in here today?"

Tom winced at the sight of how many more people had poured in without him noticing. This business with Kate was making him sloppy. A detective couldn't afford to let his personal life interfere with his job. Maybe Hank had done him a favor.

Kate's gaze drifted to his table again, and the kick in his heart said he didn't want Hank doing him any favors. Too bad she didn't have a tea to cure stupidity. He could have used some of that. Tom followed the direction of her gaze as it tracked across the shop. Behind the counter, Darryl and his wife were engaged in a heated discussion. Dark circles shadowed Beth's eyes, and she appeared to have lost some weight. Apparently, her claim that she'd been sick the night he'd spotted her following Kate hadn't been entirely a lie.

Hank's dad approached the two and made a T sign with his hands.

As Beth reached for the brown paper bag in Al's hand, Tom gauged Hank's reaction.

If he was wary of his dad's actions, Hank didn't show it. He downed the last of his coffee and wiped his mouth with the back of his hand. "I gotta go. Dad and I are going fishing. Nice to see you again, Keith."

"You too," Dad nodded. "You should buy a box of Beth's donuts to take with you."

"Good idea." Hank shifted his attention to Tom. "You on the night shift?"

"Yeah."

"I'll bring you in a fresh grilled perch." He winked. "See ya later."

Dad hitched a thumb toward Hank's departing back. "You two seem to be getting along again. Have you written him off as a suspect?"

"Nope."

Edward stood at the counter chatting with Molly, who glowed under his attention. For her sake, Tom hoped Edward had been straight with him.

Hank interrupted the lovebirds' tête à tête, apparently asking for donuts as Dad had suggested, because Molly folded a piece of cardboard into a box and picked up the tongs. Al Brewster joined Hank and pointed to the tray of jelly-filled donuts.

"Well . . ." Dad drummed the tabletop, a satisfied lilt in his voice. "Looks like all our suspects are here."

Tom snorted, remembering Kate's suggestion that they stage a sting. His gaze skittered past Al, Darryl, and Edward. "Only person missing is Gord."

"You don't seriously consider him a suspect in Daisy's murder?"

"I have as much reason to suspect him as anyone else."

"Then why haven't you brought him in for the thefts at the research station?"

"Let's just say I'm keeping my options open."

Dad tipped his chin down, his gaze on Kate.

Julie's fiancé, Ryan, now shared Julie and Kate's table, and the volume of their discussion rose by the second. Julie's face flushed as nearby patrons started to take notice. Kate, her red hair tied in a ponytail that bobbed with her animated gestures, seemed oblivious to the audience they'd attracted. She slapped her hands on the table. "I'm telling you, Daisy was murdered."

The entire room hushed, and like one person everybody turned to look at Kate.

She surged to her feet, her attention fixed on Ryan. "And I know who did it. Do you hear me?"

Tom choked on his coffee. What was she doing?

At the counter, Darryl, Edward, and Al gaped at the spectacle. Not one of them looked uneasy about her declaration. But Hank . . .

Hank stormed toward her, his face streaked with rage.

Kate suddenly clutched her throat. Her mouth opened and closed in frantic, jerky movements. But no sound came out.

23

Tom's throat constricted at the sight of Kate's glassy, too-large eyes. He rushed past Hank, circled his arms around Kate's waist, and dug his fist under her rib cage, thrusting hard to dislodge the blockage to her airway.

"Epi," she squeezed from her throat, then slumped in his arms.

Tom's muscles quivered uncontrollably as he eased her onto a chair and helped her hunch over the café table in her fight to pull in a breath. "Someone call an ambulance."

Julie ripped an epinephrine pen from Kate's purse and thrust it into the air. "I found it." She scrambled around the table and rammed the injector into Kate's thigh.

Tom's heart stopped for a long, painful moment, then careened against his ribs like a runaway car when she gasped. He smoothed the hair away from her ashen face. Dark shadows rimmed her closed eyes. Her breaths came in shallow gasps.

Rubbing her back, he struggled to keep his voice calm. "You'll be okay. Breathe nice and easy. The ambulance will be here in a few minutes."

Hank met Tom's words with a frown. He snapped shut his cell phone and in a low growl said, "Both ambulances are tied up on other calls."

"We have to get her to the hospital now," Julie said with an urgency that had Hank scooping Kate into his arms before Tom could object.

"We'll take her in my Jeep. You can ride with her in the back."

The crowd parted, making a path to the door. Tom reached for Kate, but his dad laid hold of his arm. "Let Hank and Julie take her. You need to figure out if this was deliberate."

Tom jerked back, but Dad tightened his grip.

"What if Hank's behind this?" Tom hissed through clenched teeth. "What if he—?" The thought of Kate at Hank's mercy snatched Tom's breath.

Julie grabbed Kate's purse and told Ryan to follow in his van.

"I'll go with Ryan and keep an eye on Hank. You do your job." Dad's stern tone slammed the brakes on Tom's racing heart. If this wasn't an accident, someone had to stay behind and analyze the crime scene. And with Kate's life in the balance, he couldn't think of anyone he'd trust to do the job.

His gaze shot to the front window. Outside, Hank set Kate into the back of his Jeep. Julie climbed in on the other side. Hank wouldn't do anything to Kate with Julie in the car and Ryan on his tail.

Tom dragged in a breath. "Okay, go."

Dad squeezed his shoulder. "She'll be okay. You focus on figuring out who wants to shut her up." He strode out the door and the crowd burst into chatter.

Tom raised his hand. "May I have your attention, please? Before anyone leaves, I'd like to talk with each one of you and find out what you saw." Hopeful no one would balk at the request that he had no legal authority to enforce, he turned toward Kate's table to first secure the evidence.

Darryl righted the chair Kate had toppled when she collapsed. Molly had collected the abandoned mugs onto a tray and was wiping off the flowered tablecloth.

"Leave those." Tom tempered the harsh command with a quieter, "Thank you."

Molly's hand stopped midwipe. She shot a questioning look to Darryl, who motioned toward the counter.

"That's okay, Molly. You can go back to the till." Darryl turned to Tom with a mixture of chagrin and alarm. "Sorry. I suggested she clear the table. Do you think this was deliberate?"

"That's what I plan to find out."

"I sent my wife upstairs." Darryl's thumbnail carved a groove into the top of the wooden chair. "She's pregnant, and it's high-risk. She shouldn't have been down here in the first place. I'd been trying to convince her to go upstairs and lie down when Kate cried out. This upset could jeopardize the baby."

"Why are you telling me this?"

His thumb abruptly stopped its fidgeting. "Because you told everyone to wait here."

"Okay, that's fine." Tom didn't like the idea of letting Beth out of his sight, especially when Darryl's cooperative attitude tasted a little too syrupy, but he could hardly justify having the woman dragged back to the shop. "Any idea what Kate might have ingested that had hazelnuts in it?"

"No, our beverages don't have nuts in them. I don't think any of the baked items do either." Darryl swiped at the already spotless counter, clearly anxious to avoid making eye contact. "I can ask Beth to pull out the ingredient lists if you want."

Molly walked to a rack that displayed an assortment of bagged teas. "We have a vanilla hazelnut dessert tea." She picked up a box and showed it to Tom.

"Kate wouldn't have used that tea," Edward cut in. "She always makes her own blend from the loose stuff."

"I'm just saying we have something here with hazelnut in it. Residue could have been left on a spoon or cup or something. I had a guy in my college class who was so allergic to peanuts that if another student had peanut butter for breakfast and breathed in his face, he'd have a reaction."

Darryl took the box and put it back on the rack. "All our mugs and cutlery go through an industrial dishwasher. A residue wouldn't get left behind." His look—defensive, defiant, adamant—suggested that visions of lawsuits and public health inquiries paraded through his mind.

"Who else knew about Kate's allergy?" Tom asked the group in general.

Molly slid a tray of dirty mugs through the kitchen's pass-through window. "Kate wears a

356

medic alert bracelet. Everyone who knows her has probably asked what it's for."

"Really?" Edward poured himself another cup of coffee. "I never noticed she wore a bracelet."

Edward's apparent lack of concern for Kate's recovery coupled with this denial reinforced Tom's suspicions. "But you knew she had the allergy?"

"Sure, Daisy probably told me. I don't remember."

"We don't even know if her reaction was to hazelnut," Darryl countered. "For all we know, she may have reacted to something that's never bothered her before."

Tom pulled out his notepad and pencil. "Molly, do you know what herbs she had in her tea today?"

"Not a clue, sorry. She makes a different blend almost every time she comes in here. But she'll tell you exactly what she put in. She's very careful and insists that everyone should know what they're drinking."

"Apparently not careful enough," Al Brewster muttered from where he'd tucked into his box of donuts at a nearby table.

Tom ground his teeth so hard his jaw ached. How could the man be so callous? Hearing Kate fight for air had shaken him, and he wouldn't relax until he knew she was out of danger. The only way to make that happen was to figure out who wanted her dead.

He never should have allowed her to investigate Daisy's death. The moment he'd realized she was onto something, he should have . . . His pencil snapped under the pressure of his grip.

He yanked the phone from his belt and thumbed in his dad's number. Voice mail picked up on the first ring. He punched in the number for the hospital next, and reception connected him to the ER nurse.

"Hello, this is Detective Parker of the Port Aster police detachment. I need a status report on the condition of Kate Adams."

"I'm sorry, sir. Privacy regulations forbid us from giving out that information over the phone."

"I'm a police officer."

"I'm sorry. I still can't help you."

"Is Chief Brewster there?"

"Yes, if you'll hold a moment, I'll get him for you."

Tom interrogated Hank's dad as he waited for the chief to pick up.

"Brewster here."

"How's Kate? Does she know what triggered the reaction? Who does she think did this?"

"As far as the doctor is concerned, she shows no lingering symptoms of an allergic reaction. But she hasn't regained consciousness."

"What? Why?" The steady beep of a heart rate monitor sounded in the background.

"They've run blood tests, but the results will

take some time. If she doesn't come around, they'll admit her for observation."

"I want her under around-the-clock protection."

"Protection? She reacted to something she ate."

Everyone in the café had their eyes fixed on Tom, searching his face for some indication of what had happened. He turned his back to them and pitched his voice low and urgent. "Someone tried to kill her. Do you want a second homicide in this town in as many weeks?"

"Is that what people are saying?"

"Saying? We all saw it!"

"Tom, you're too emotionally involved here. I don't want you speaking with anyone else. I'll be right over."

"I want Kate under guard."

"Your dad is here. That'll have to be enough."

Tom snapped shut his phone. Drew in a breath.

The room fell silent. All eyes on him. Their anxiety, a thick blanket of smoke, stinging his eyes and choking off his air.

"She's stable," he announced and everyone burst into applause.

Having heard what they'd been waiting for, people soon grew restless.

Tom visualized where his suspects had been in the moments leading up to Kate's attack. She'd already been at her table when Hank's dad arrived. Edward and Molly had been busy mooning over each other, but Kate would have gone between them to pay for her drink just as Hank had when he'd ordered donuts. Edward easily could have slipped a pinch of crushed hazelnut into Kate's tea while Molly kept her distracted.

Tom raised a hand to gain everyone's attention. "We still don't know what triggered Miss Adams's attack. So I'd like to get everyone's name in case we have questions later. And if you noticed or heard anything that you think is significant, please stay behind."

Three blue-haired ladies bustled toward him, all talking at once.

Darryl brushed by him and said, "I'll take down the names of those who want to leave."

As Tom recorded the ladies' accounts, his attention strayed to Darryl, who was assuring people that the shop had stellar health and safety standards. From the expressions on the patrons' faces, more than a few weren't convinced.

Tom might have felt sorry for him if his very presence weren't suspect. By his own admission, Darryl routinely tinkered in his second lab until well past six o'clock.

Hank stepped into the shop and scanned the dwindling crowd. His eyes narrowed when they zeroed in on Tom taking down Mrs. McGuire's statement.

Too bad. Tom wasn't going to sacrifice Kate's safety to pander to Hank's PR concerns. Mrs. McGuire might have seen something significant.

Or perhaps that was exactly what Hank was afraid of.

Hank's dad, seemingly uninterested in the hoopla, sat alone at a back table. Powdered sugar from a jelly-filled donut dusted his beard. He popped a last morsel into his mouth and dug into his box for another.

If he'd slipped something into Kate's tea, he didn't appear worried about being found out.

Hank strode Tom's way, and Tom quickly thanked Mrs. McGuire for speaking with him.

"What are all these people still doing here?"

"Waiting to be interviewed."

"This was not a deliberate attack against Kate." Hank raised his hands. "Folks, you may all go home. Miss Adams is fine. She had an allergic reaction to something she ate."

The scrape of a chair broke the responding silence. Mrs. C pressed her fingers into the table as she stood and drilled her gaze into Hank. "Who killed Daisy Leacock?"

Red splotches crept up Hank's neck. "Miss Leacock's death was self-inflicted. At best, an unfortunate accident. Her friend is simply having a hard time accepting that fact."

"Seems to me we're having too many unfortunate accidents in this town. Seems to me someone wanted to shut Kate up because she'd gotten too close to the truth. Seems to me—"

Hank lifted his hand traffic cop style. "Miss

Adams collapsed mere seconds after claiming she knew who killed Daisy. Hardly enough time for a supposed murderer to act, wouldn't you agree?"

"I want to know who she thinks killed Daisy."

"Yes. Who?" The question buzzed through the crowd.

"Rest assured we will investigate Miss Adams's allegations, but we won't slander anyone's good name by repeating unsubstantiated rumors."

Tom surreptitiously watched Edward's and Darryl's reactions to Hank's announcement, but their expressions betrayed no signs of guilt, only concern. Tom's attention snapped to the table where he'd last seen Al Brewster.

The man was gone.

Tom panned the windows, his pulse racing. Al's rusty pickup was nowhere to be seen. He dialed his cell phone to alert his dad to Al's disappearance. *Come on, Dad, pick up.*

"As for what happened here today," Hank continued, "as I said before, Miss Adams simply had an allergic reaction to something she ate."

"A little too coincidental, don't you think, Chief?" Mrs. C challenged.

Hank's mustache twitched. "If you think you saw something suspicious," Hank said to the crowd in general, "you are welcome to give Detective Parker your statement. Otherwise, you are all free to go." He must've heard Tom's quick inhalation and sensed his intention to intervene, because Hank cut him off with a pointed glare.

For a moment or two, no one moved, as though no one wanted to be the first to leave. Then, to Tom's surprise, Mrs. C let out a loud harrumph and stomped toward the door. He'd thought she'd stick around so as not to miss anything. The others, whispering feverishly, took their cue from Mrs. C and followed her out.

Al Brewster, fishing hat askew and still zipping his pants, ambled out of the bathroom. "Where'd everybody go?"

"Home." The tightness in Tom's neck and shoulders eased fractionally. With his prime suspects all still here, he could delay his visit to the hospital a few moments longer.

"Our fishing trip's off." Hank shoved a chair under one of the tables. "Thanks to Adams's theatrics, I'll be spending the rest of the afternoon doing damage control before the entire town starts ranting that we have a killer on the loose."

Darryl handed Molly an empty tray and motioned to the tables littered with mugs and napkins. "Do you think there's anything to Kate's allegations, Chief?"

"No."

Tom's anger flared, and apparently Hank's brusque response raised more than just Tom's ire.

Edward slammed his mug onto the counter. "How can you say that when you stood there and promised those people you'd investigate? My aunt did not kill herself, and she wasn't careless enough to make tea from toxic plants. If you'd stop worrying about public opinion for half a minute, you might actually get some real police work done and solve a case."

Whoa. Tom hadn't expected a spurt of righteous indignation from a man whose character was weaker than herbal tea.

Molly rushed to Edward's side. "It's okay, Edward. You need to let this go. The police know what they're doing." The pleading note in her voice suggested that she feared Edward would be fingered if the police reopened the case—a possibility that seemed to have slipped Edward's mind.

Edward brushed off Molly's attempts to calm him. "Who does Kate think killed my aunt?"

"She hasn't regained consciousness long enough to share her suspicions. But I have no reason to suspect foul play in the death of Miss Leacock, or in Miss Adams's health crisis." Hank twisted the tip of his mustache between his fingers. "The doctor suspects she is simply over-wrought from the death of her friend."

"That's crazy. Her roommate had to give her an epi injection."

When Hank just shrugged, Tom pulled him aside. "What if we were wrong? What if Leacock was murdered?"

"The case is closed," Hank said with finality.

"After Kate's pronouncement, do you really think the town will accept that answer?"

"The town has no choice. The case is closed. Find out who Miss Adams suspects and put her theory to rest. The mayor wants these wild rumors snuffed out before the weekly paper goes to print."

Tom slammed shut his car door and trudged to the front of the hospital. A frosty north wind bit at his skin, much like the worry gnawing at his insides over how to keep Kate safe.

Whether or not her allergic reaction was from a deliberate attempt on her life made little difference. If Leacock's killer believed Kate knew who he was, chances were he wouldn't hesitate to get rid of her.

Bile scorched Tom's throat. Had his lapse of support, however short-lived, pushed her to the edge of reason? If she'd been thinking at all, she would have known that declaring she knew who killed Daisy was tantamount to saying, "Come and get me."

He yanked open the door of the building. A kind of constrained chaos reigned. Impatient-looking visitors crowded around the elevator doors, their gazes fixed on the numbers above—none of which were changing. Tom bypassed the bank of elevators and pushed through the door to the east stairwell. A bare bulb lit the windowless cavern.

Paint peeled from the ceiling. His shoes squeaked on the worn marble stairs, the sound echoing off the cement walls.

This old hospital had too many entrances and too many blind corners where someone could lurk unnoticed, waiting for an opportune moment to act.

He needed more than his dad standing guard if he wanted Kate protected.

As Tom reached the third floor, he spotted Julie and Ryan arguing outside Kate's room.

When Julie saw Tom, her tense stance relaxed. "Detective, I'm so glad you're here. I didn't know what to do."

He rushed toward her. "What's happened? Is Kate—?"

Julie laid a hand on his arm. "She's still unconscious and I don't want to leave her, but Ryan and I are supposed to be at our last premarital counseling session with the pastor, and we've already rescheduled it three times."

Tom expelled a relieved sigh that Kate's condition hadn't taken a turn for the worse. "You go. My dad and I will make sure she's safe."

"Do you think she's in danger?" Ryan interjected. "That this wasn't an accident?"

"I think it's a possibility."

"Then Julie shouldn't be here at all."

Julie clutched her fiancé's arm. "She's my friend. I can't abandon her."

Tom scanned the empty hallway and lowered his voice. "Has Kate shared any of her suspicions with you?"

"There was Darryl, of course. At first she thought the police chief was involved, then Edward." Julie twisted a tissue in her hands. "But if she still thought it was him, why didn't she let you arrest him? It makes no sense."

"She never mentioned anyone else?"

Julie shook her head, tears pooling in her eyes.

Ryan pulled her into his arms. "Kate will be okay. Parker won't let anything happen to her."

"Ryan's right. You two go on. My dad and I will stay with her."

Tom stepped inside the darkened room. Fingers of light pried past the edge of the drawn curtains, sketching eerie shadows on the wall behind Kate's bed.

Her face lay turned toward the window, her hair spilled across the pillow. An IV bag hung from a pole and dripped clear fluid into her arm. She seemed so vulnerable.

Tom's chest ached just to look at her.

"The doctor said she'll be fine."

Tom startled even though he'd been aware of his dad's presence. He moved closer to the bed. "Has she shown signs of waking?"

Dad rose and pushed a chair toward Tom. "Not yet."

Tom stroked his thumb across Kate's knuckles.

His emotions had been in a whirlwind ever since she'd stormed into the police station. Her spirited, never-say-die attitude had triggered more adrenaline rushes in two weeks than he'd had in two years with the FBI.

"Any of your suspects act nervous or suspicious after we took Kate away?"

"Hank seemed more nervous than anyone, but that likely had more to do with his leadership being questioned by a few of the more vocal patrons."

"What about his dad?"

"We only talked for a minute. He acted clueless about who Kate and Daisy even were until I mentioned the intern. Then he went on and on about how lazy the kid was. Al's either a first-class liar or he had nothing to do with Daisy's murder."

"What about Edward and that other fellow?"

"I'm not ready to rule anyone out."

Dad nudged aside the curtain and peered at the street below. "I take it you couldn't convince Hank to post a guard outside her room?"

"No, but I'm not sure I'd trust whoever he chose anyway. Protecting his image is more important to him than protecting Kate."

"But you don't think he's covering for his dad?"

"I don't know what to think. I've done nothing but chase hunches this entire investigation."

"Sometimes hunches are all a detective has to go on."

The uncharacteristic mollycoddling verged on patronizing, and Tom fought the sudden urge to stuff a rolled bandage into his dad's mouth. "At this rate the only way we'll nab Daisy's killer is if he comes after Kate and we catch him in the act."

"So that's what we'll do."

Tom's foot kicked out, jolting the bed. "No, we won't. This is Kate we're talking about. I won't let her be bait to catch some lunatic because I messed up my job."

"I won't let anything happen to her."

"Dad, you can't stay awake twenty-four hours a day. She should be in a safe house."

"She'll never agree to that. She's supposed to be Julie's maid of honor in another week and a half."

"She will if I tell her how much danger she's in."

"Do you think she would have tried to hunt down the killer in the first place if she was worried about herself?"

Taking a deep breath to keep from saying something he'd regret, Tom stroked a strand of hair from Kate's face. So soft, his heart stuttered. Her eyes were scrunched closed as if she was in pain. He gently brushed his fingers across her cheek. "Kate, can you hear me?"

Her breathing rate sped up, and his heart

crunched against his ribs. Had he destroyed her trust so much that the sound of his voice now frightened her?

Tom folded himself into the chair next to her bed and clasped her hand between his. "I want you to know how sorry I am that I doubted you."

Her hand remained unresponsive to his touch.

Overwhelmed by the need to explain, he said, "I want you to understand that my doubt wasn't personal. It's just that when I was with the FBI . . ." He paused, feeling foolish telling her the story when she was unconscious, but an inner compulsion pushed him to continue. "I learned the hard way that you can't always trust the people you think you can. You see, my partner fell in love with a woman who turned out to be a spy.

"I tried to warn him, to give him a way out, to convince him to have nothing more to do with her. He'd saved my sorry hide more than once. I owed him that much. He agreed to stop seeing her, but a few days later I spotted them talking in a mall parking lot. At first I thought maybe he was trying to catch her in her lies and bring her in. But when I confronted him, he told me I didn't know what I was talking about."

Tom closed his eyes, and everything about that moment flooded his senses. Once again he stood on the sun-baked tarmac, sweat dripping down the back of his neck, the screech of seagulls piercing the air as they swooped between cars scavenging for food. And the icy look in Ian's eyes froze the blood in his veins.

"I tried to reason with him, but he walked away."

Kate's eyes scrunched tighter, and Tom's insides clenched with them.

"I don't know why I'm telling you this now. I guess I want you to understand why I can't risk letting you stay here. If I'd reported my partner's liaison like I should have, he might still be alive.

"But I didn't, and my partner died in a car explosion from a bomb planted by the woman he'd trusted more than . . ."

The blast echoed in Tom's ears. The ghostly force knocked the wind from him the same way it had that day when it threw him off his feet and debris showered down in a fifty-foot radius around Ian's car. His partner hadn't had a chance.

But Kate did.

And Tom wouldn't use her as bait to lure the killer into striking again.

Tom motioned to his dad to follow him out of the room. "I want you to stay here and keep her safe until I get back. I'm going to find her doctor and see how soon we can move her."

"Okay, but she won't be happy."

"I'm more concerned about her being alive than happy."

"I'm sorry about your partner, son. With losing

371

your mom, well . . . I didn't realize there were other reasons you'd come home."

"That's okay, Dad. It's not something I had wanted to talk about. I'm not sure why I felt compelled to tell Kate. Except I don't want anything to happen to her."

Dad squeezed Tom's shoulder. "I understand. You go do what you have to do."

The nurse on duty suggested Tom ask for the doctor at the ER.

As Tom stepped off the elevator on the main floor, Beth ambled toward him, carrying a potted plant. "Detective, hello. Have you been in to see Kate? How is she?" Beth's voice wobbled, and worry laced her swollen red eyes.

"She's sleeping."

Beth stepped back at the gruff edge in his voice. "But she's okay? I mean, they wouldn't let me go up to see her if she wasn't. Right?"

Tom looked from the plant in Beth's hand to the other hand resting on the bulge at her midriff—not the hand of a killer. "I'm sure Kate will be happy to see you." He hurried toward the ER, intent on getting permission to move her before anyone else decided to pay her a visit.

24

Nausea whirled in the pit of Kate's stomach. She flung off the hospital blankets. "I can't do this."

"What do you mean?" Keith cranked up the head of her bed as if her state was as fragile as they'd let Tom believe.

The dreary room intensified the illusion, fooling even her. Scarred walls closed in on her. Antiseptic odors bit at her nostrils, but worse than those, the memory of the anguish in Tom's voice stung her eyes.

"Did you know about Tom's partner? He trusts me, and I'm betraying him. Just like his partner did."

"We're protecting his job. It's not the same thing at all." Keith caught and held her gaze. "This way Hank can't accuse Tom of setting this up. Besides, you heard him. Tom never would have agreed to your plan. Frankly, I'm surprised he risked leaving your side at all. That pained look you faked really got to him."

Kate rolled onto her side and drew her knees to her chest. "I wasn't faking. I feel sick about deceiving him."

"Trust me. He'll understand."

The phone rang once—the signal from the station nurse that someone was coming.

Keith stuck his head into the hallway. "It's Beth. Pull up those sheets." He met Beth at the door.

"Oh," she exclaimed. "I didn't expect to see anyone else here. How is Kate?"

"She hasn't come around yet." Keith swept his arm toward Kate's bed. "Come in."

Through lowered lashes, Kate watched Beth tiptoe into the room as if fearful of making a loud noise.

She placed a potted yellow dahlia on the bedside table. "How are you feeling?" she said in that overly cheerful tone people use around little kids and sick people.

Kate groaned. She felt like she was the one battling morning sickness, sick over deceiving her friends like this. What would they think of her when they learned the truth?

"Kate?" Worry pinched Beth's voice.

Kate swung her head from side to side against the pillow as if fighting off the grip of sleep. At least she hoped that was what it looked like, because if she didn't release her pent-up frustration somehow, the truth was going to spew out of her mouth in all its ugliness.

"The doctor gave her a sedative," Keith said by way of explanation.

"Does he think she's been poisoned? From how Detective Parker took charge, my husband said the detective thought someone had deliberately laced Kate's tea, but the chief said no."

A new dread squeezed Kate's throat. If people thought Beth's tea caused the reaction, her business could suffer. Kate would never forgive herself if their scheme ruined Beth's business.

"It's unclear what caused the reaction," Keith said evasively.

Beth stroked Kate's arm. "Well, thankfully, the chief appeased my customers' concerns. The hint of notoriety might even improve business." Beth chuckled, but the brightness in her voice sounded forced.

Kate hazarded another peek at her friend.

"I brought you a potted dahlia," Beth said, smoothing Kate's blanket.

Her heart lurched. She was certain Beth must've seen her peeking.

"Darryl said they were your favorite," Beth continued in the nervous chatter of someone uncomfortable with silence, and Kate barely restrained the breath from whooshing out of her chest. "He wanted to come by, but he had to run back to the lab to do something. I'll be so happy when he's finished whatever project is monopolizing his time lately. He's running himself ragged."

"Perhaps you should hire more help," Keith suggested.

"Oh, Molly has been a huge help in the shop

and the apartment. A godsend. We can't afford anyone else. My husband doesn't think I know, but I've seen the accounts. If I can't carry this baby to term, we won't be able to afford to try again." Beth swayed.

Keith reached out a hand and steadied her. "Are you okay?"

She braced herself against the bedrail. "Yes, I'm sorry. My husband keeps warning me not to overdo things. I'd better not stay any longer."

"Of course. I'll let Kate know you stopped by."

As Beth's footsteps faded from the room, Kate curled onto her side and let out a moan. Beth was her friend, and here Kate was about to turn her world upside down.

"You okay?" Keith asked. Concern lined his brow.

"I wish I hadn't thought up this idea. It could ruin Beth's business. What if I'm wrong? What if Daisy did kill herself?"

"You don't believe that." Keith sunk into the chair next to the bed, his chest deflating like a pricked balloon.

"I don't want to believe it." Kate fisted the bedsheets in her hands. "Daisy was the one who showed me who God is. If she took her own life, where does that leave God?"

"Is your faith in who God is, or who you thought Daisy was?"

Sunlight edged its way past the curtains. Kate

longed to feel its warmth. She didn't doubt God. Did she?

Julie had accused her of pushing for this investigation because she couldn't accept the police department's findings. Wouldn't accept them.

Because if she had, that meant Daisy *had* taken her life into her own hands . . . on purpose.

"I don't know anymore."

Keith patted her arm. "We all face doubts from time to time, but that's when more than ever we need to go to the source."

"You must've questioned where God was when your wife died."

Keith's Adam's apple bobbed. He closed his eyes and nodded. "I ranted at God, yes, because I knew he had the power to keep my wife alive, and he didn't."

Keith smoothed Kate's sheets and swallowed repeatedly before meeting her gaze again, his eyes red. "I knew Daisy for a good many years longer than you, and I don't believe she poisoned herself. That's why I'm here. But even if she did, that wouldn't change who God is."

"I know that in my head."

"But knowing it in your heart is harder. I know." Keith paced the room. "I figured out a few things this past week. When I was busy feeling sorry for myself, God felt far away, but once I started helping Tom with your case, I started to care about someone besides myself, and I realized God hadn't moved. I had."

Keith stopped pacing and faced Kate again. "Don't get me wrong. I still miss my wife as much as ever, but . . ." Keith plowed his fingers through his hair and looked away. "I don't know. Maybe this is something you have to figure out for yourself."

"No. Tell me what you were going to say."

"Sooner or later just about everyone comes up against a side of God that's hard for them to accept, like I faced when my Norma died. Some wrestle it out with him like Jacob did in the Bible, while others walk away. You have to decide. Are you gonna trust God no matter how the situation looks? Or not?"

"Yes, I am." Kate laid her hand on Keith's arm. "Before I met Daisy, I saw God the way most people see marigolds—something pretty to admire now and again, unaware that one variety offers healing while the rest are counterfeits. Now that I know the truth, I won't settle for a counterfeit."

With the doctor's permission to move Kate secured, Tom strode to his car, intent on arranging a safe house and private nurse before nightfall.

A car roared away—license plate T42. Beth's. Except Beth wasn't at the wheel. The driver looked like Darryl.

When Tom ran into Beth in the lobby, she'd been alone. If Darryl came with his wife, why didn't he visit Kate too?

The image of the potted plant Beth had been carrying flashed through Tom's mind. It was just like the ones he'd seen at Brewster's greenhouse. The ones Brewster hadn't been willing to sell. But . . . something had been off about this pot.

Tom closed his eyes and pictured the gift. Yellow flowers in a green plastic pot, and . . . a fertilizer stick! A fertilizer stick had been stuck in the pot.

A specialist like Darryl would know better than to give Kate a plant like that.

So maybe it wasn't a fertilizer stick. Kate had said that Darryl was delayed at the airport recently because traces of nitrates were found on his computer keyboard. What if those nitrates *were* from explosives?

Tom sprinted back across the parking lot. His terrorist theory had been right all along. A flower shipment would be the perfect cover for smuggling explosives. Bury the explosives in the bottom of the pots, or in plain view disguised as fertilizer sticks. If search dogs alerted to the scent, the border guards would write off the reaction as a response to the nitrates in the fertilizers.

If Leacock figured out Darryl's scheme, he might have rationalized it was her life or his.

Terrorists weren't the type to let their supply line be compromised. And with a wife in the herbal tea business, Darryl had access to every imaginable brew he'd care to concoct to dispose of a nosy subordinate.

No one would suspect Darryl's pregnant wife of delivering a bomb to Kate's room. Just like no one suspected her of poisoning her customer's tea. Tom yanked open the hospital door and charged up the stairs two at a time.

He wove around a lady in a wheelchair and practically took out an old man shuffling along behind her. He skidded to a stop outside Kate's door, and his gaze immediately fell to the potted plant on the bedside table. Not only did it hold a stick of C-4 disguised as a fertilizer stick, but it had an electronic detonator disguised as a moisture meter. The kind of device the Laslo kid liked to make.

"Pull out that fertilizer stick too," Kate called from the bathroom. "Darryl does that to bug me."

"No! Don't touch the stick." Tom veered around his dad and scooped up the plant. Running out the door, he yelled, "Dad, don't let Kate out of your sight."

Tom tore down the back staircase, his heart ready to explode right along with the plant. How could he protect Kate from a friend who hand delivered bombs? Not even Dad had suspected death by dahlias.

Painfully aware that the thing could go off any second, Tom hit the door to the back parking lot at a run, mentally analyzing options.

A Honda Accord rounded the corner of the building and squealed its brakes. "Watch where you're going," the driver yelled, adding a couple of colorful descriptors.

If you only knew, buddy. Racing for the emptiest corner of the parking lot, Tom dodged a cement barrier.

A teen on a skateboard appeared out of nowhere and headed straight for him.

Tom darted to the left.

So did the kid. At the last second, his skateboard swerved right, but not soon enough. He wiped out, ramming hard into Tom's legs.

The impact sent the potted plant sailing through the air.

Tom dove on top of the teen and covered him with his body.

The pot crashed to the ground. Dirt flew everywhere. The plastic shattered.

Tom tucked his chin to his chest, bracing for the explosion.

The six-foot, 170-pound male beneath him shoved him off. "What is your problem?" Without waiting for a response, the teen snatched up his skateboard and glided off across the parking lot.

Tom's breath came in gasps as he stared at the crushed dahlia, the scattering of dirt, the innocuous fertilizer stick—no wires attached. The bomb would've been ingenious—if it had been a bomb.

Tom pushed his hands through his hair and laughed, his relief making it sound a little on the hysterical side.

In the late afternoon sunshine, with lilacs scenting the air and the sound of children's laughter mingling with the twitter of robins and orioles, the idea that a rogue terrorist or drug lord roamed the streets ready to pop off anyone who got in their way was pretty unbelievable.

Unbelievable, if Tom hadn't seen worse.

Much worse.

A black SUV came around the cement barrier. Hospital security.

Great. Tom brushed the dirt off his pants. He probably looked like a psychiatric ward escapee.

The driver pulled alongside Tom and rolled down his window. "What's going on? We just got a call that some crazy guy was stealing plants from patients' rooms." The driver looked pointedly at the dahlia splatted on the cement. "You wouldn't happen to know anything about that, would you?"

Tom cringed at the thought of how distraught Kate would be after the way he'd hijacked her flower. Then jolted at the realization that she'd been awake.

The slam of a car door cut through Tom's rambling thoughts. "Well? What's this about?"

Tom pulled out his identification. "I'm Detective Parker. False alarm."

The security officer looked over the ID and returned it to Tom. "Anything I should know?"

"Yeah, one of the patients on the third floor may be in danger. We're taking steps to relocate her ASAP. In the meantime, you can closely monitor all entrances."

"Who are we looking for?"

"We don't know." Tom handed him a business card with his cell phone number scribbled on the back. "Call me if you notice anyone acting suspiciously."

"You want me to send a guy to the third floor to keep an eye on things?"

Tom glanced at the five-story brick building with more exits than security cameras. "That would be great. Room 308. Thanks. I need all the help I can get."

25

Tom trudged up the stairs to Kate's hospital room. Before he arranged for a safe house, he needed to allay the fears his mad dash out of the hospital had inevitably sparked.

The door to Kate's room opened and his dad

stepped into the hall. "I had a hard time convincing her to stay put. What happened?"

"False alarm." Tom entered the room ahead of his dad.

Kate sat in bed with her legs curled under her. Tenderness washed through him at the sight. "You're awake! How are you feeling?"

"You ran out of here with my plant like it was about to explode. How do you think I feel?"

Her feisty comeback after all she'd been through today brought a smile to Tom's face despite the embarrassing mistake. "Sorry about that. I saw Beth arrive alone, so when Darryl picked her up outside the hospital, I thought it was strange that he hadn't come in to see you too. Then I remembered what you'd said about airport security stopping Darryl on suspicion of smuggling explosives, and . . . well, I thought the plant was a bomb."

Dad chuckled. "Tom worked in Washington too long. Sometimes people really do bring plants to their friends."

"Yeah, Dad, thanks for pointing that out." Tom moved to Kate's bedside. "It's good to see you awake, and already on your feet here earlier. You must be feeling better."

Kate blushed in a most becoming way. "Much."

"Are you sure? You gave us quite a scare."

She ducked her head and her gaze darted to Dad's. "Sorry about that."

Tom took her hand in his and fingered the silver medic alert bracelet on her wrist. "It's not your fault. Do you know what caused the reaction?"

"Um, I can't say for sure."

"Well, now that you're awake, you can tell me who you think is behind all this."

She squirmed, her gaze landing on his nose, then his forehead, then his chin, everywhere but his eyes. "I'm . . . uh . . . not sure."

"You sounded adamantly sure a couple of hours ago. The town is in an uproar and Hank wants your allegations that Daisy was murdered put to rest—one way or the other. Who do you think did it?"

Kate shrank deeper into the pillow.

Fighting exasperation, Tom gentled his voice. "Kate, I want to help you."

Again her gaze darted to Dad's. The side of her neck visibly pulsed.

The sense that she couldn't trust him left Tom feeling bruised. He hunkered down in front of her.

A pained look puckered the tender skin around her eyes. Eyes that refused to meet his own.

After a long moment, she drew in a deep breath and hesitantly lifted her gaze to his. "My allergic reaction was a ruse to draw out the killer."

"A ruse? But a doctor admitted you."

The doctor's words whispered through Tom's thoughts. *We get our share of attention seekers, but we have to believe the symptoms are real until we can prove otherwise.* "A ruse?" Tom repeated the word barely loud enough for her to hear.

He must have misunderstood. Kate wasn't an attention seeker. Maybe the Benadryl the doctor put in her IV had muddied her thinking.

"I couldn't think of any other way to expose the killer. I yelled out that I knew who killed Daisy because I wanted to see who would react."

"After I told you how dangerous a sting would be?" Tom wrestled down the anger mounting in his chest. "Look what happened. You almost died."

"No. I was faking," she whispered.

"What?" He shook his head. "But they stuck an IV in your arm. How—?"

"I called in a couple of favors," Dad spoke up.

"We had to. Don't you see?" Kate pleaded. "So the person who killed Daisy would come after me. I knew with so many people hearing what I said, seeing what happened, that the uproar would provoke demands for the case to be reopened. The killer has to be feeling the heat. By making myself appear vulnerable, I've given the person a false sense of power."

A soul-numbing feeling of betrayal seeped through Tom's body. Not only had Kate not heeded his warning, but she hadn't trusted him enough to tell him her intentions.

She'd used him.

Deceived him.

He'd trusted her, and this was how she repaid him.

"What if the ruse had worked?" He pushed to his feet, dragging the bed cover half off with his fisted hand. He unclenched his fingers, releasing his hold, and turned on his dad. "And you were in on this?"

"I thought her plan was pretty clever."

"Clever? Are you nuts? What if someone really had come after her?"

Dad nodded toward the TV mounted in the corner of the room. A webcam was attached to the edge of its screen, its wire disappearing through a hole in the ceiling.

"What? You plan on capturing Kate's murder on video? A lot of help that will do her."

Kate gasped as if the idea that the maniac might succeed had never occurred to her, but Dad didn't so much as flinch. "Kate believes she can provoke the killer to reveal his plot."

"Well, isn't that optimistic of her? Did you happen to tell her that a statement against interest will only stand up in court if she's alive to repeat what she heard? Unless you have a third person in this room so our murderer doesn't have a reasonable expectation of privacy, anything you record would be considered eavesdropping and inadmissible in court."

Dad strode to the door and pushed it closed. "I have been practicing law enforcement since before you were in diapers, so save the lecture. I know what I'm doing."

Kate sat up and reached for Tom's arm with no sign of weakness whatsoever. How had he allowed himself to be so easily duped?

"Tom, please, help us. I think this will work."

He jerked his arm from her grasp. "Who do you think is going to come after you? Because, aside from Daisy's non-nephew, who you're convinced didn't do it, the last time I checked, I was out of suspects."

"If I tell you, you won't believe me." She wrung her hands and shot him a pleading look. "I need you to trust me."

"Trust you? You lured me into your little sting with your lies, and now you expect me to trust you? The killer, if there is a killer, has evaded detection this long. Do you really think he's stupid enough to confess to you? Unless he's certain you're dead."

"That's enough," Dad cut in. "After you told her about your partner, she wanted to tell you the truth, but I stopped her. We needed you to behave like the worried friend and professional you are."

Blind fury blazed through Tom's veins. "You were awake when I came here the first time?" She'd let him believe she was on death's doorstep while he bared his heart. "You heard what I said?"

The same pain-filled expression he'd seen on

her face when he'd revealed his partner's betrayal returned. "I'm sorry. I wanted to tell you." She ran into the bathroom and slammed the door.

The muffled sound of crying reached through the walls and clutched Tom's heart, but he steeled himself against its grip.

"She wanted to tell you," his dad repeated. He adjusted the webcam so it would presumably capture every corner of the room. "She hated lying to you, but I told her Hank would likely fire you if he found out you were in on her plan."

"I told her I would find Daisy's killer. You should have talked her out of this crazy scheme."

"You know how much Daisy's friendship meant to her. You shouldn't be surprised she'd do whatever it takes to clear her name."

Tom paced the room, clenching and unclenching his hands, fighting to shut out the sound of Kate falling apart. He flung open the curtains. Light flooded the room, and with it, the truth. "No, I'm not surprised. What bothers me is that she considered my friendship of far less importance." He never should have allowed his heart to become involved. "I have to put an end to this charade now, before it's too late."

"How does that proverb go? Faithful are the wounds of a friend. If Kate hurt you, it wasn't meant to harm. Can you say the same if you walk out on her now? She needs you on her side. If you go out there and spin her story in an attempt to keep the killer at bay, we may never get the proof to lock them away."

Tom stared at the bathroom door. The thought of Kate huddled inside, distraught and alone, shattered the last of his resolve to disarm the trap she'd laid.

"What's the plan?" he asked noncommittally.

"Julie has alerted our suspects to Kate's fragile state and suggested visitors would be a welcome distraction."

"Why?"

"To give them the impression she might be suicidal."

"Suicidal?"

"Sure. Grief stricken. After all, the killer wanted Daisy's death to appear self-inflicted."

Tom sniffed the water in the glass beside Kate's hospital bed. "And if he wants to get rid of Kate, he would likely choose a similar means."

"Yes, which means we're not likely to catch them with a smoking gun. So Kate will attempt to lure a confession out of them while we listen in from the next room through the webcam feed."

Tom stopped pacing. "Them who?"

The phone rang. Tom picked up the receiver, but the line went dead.

Dad tapped on the bathroom door. "They're on their way. You have to get back in bed."

"Who?" Tom returned the receiver to its cradle. "What's going on?"

"I'll explain later." Dad beckoned him toward the door. "We have to get out of here."

Kate stepped out of the bathroom, dragging her IV stand. Dried tears stained her cheeks. Her hair was mussed and her eyes swollen. "How do I look?"

"Perfect," Dad said, pushing Tom out the room.

Kate's broken expression tore at his heart. He turned to say . . . something. He couldn't leave her like this.

"Later." Dad shoved Tom into the next room and closed the door.

A laptop sat on the bedside table. An image of Kate's hospital room filled the screen. Kate climbed into bed, straightened her IV, and pulled the covers to her chest. A moment later, Edward and his fiancée walked into the room.

Tom slapped his fist into his palm. "If Kate thought Edward killed Daisy, why did she stop me from arresting him?"

"We're about to find out."

Molly held up a steaming cup. "I made a special blend of tea to soothe your nerves."

Kate wrestled herself to a sitting position and reached for the offered cup. "Thank you." She pried back a section of the plastic lid and sniffed. "No hazelnut, I trust?"

Molly looked mortified. "Of course not."

Kate brought the cup to her lips.

Tom's heart jolted. "What's she—?" He reached

for the doorknob, but Dad grabbed his arm.

"She knows what she's doing. You have to trust her."

Tom squinted at the screen. Kate's Adam's apple bobbed as though she'd swallowed the sip, and his heart misfired a second time. "Are you sure?"

"Yes," his dad whispered, but the assurance scarcely registered over the roar of blood pulsing past Tom's ears.

Molly smiled. "Do you like it?"

"Mmm-hmm." Kate brought the cup to her lips again. "The ginger gives it a nice bite."

"How does she know the tea has ginger in it if she didn't drink any?" Tom demanded, straining to keep his voice low.

"She has a nose."

Tom picked up the phone next to his dad's laptop and punched in the extension for Kate's room. She answered on the second ring. "Kate, don't drink the tea."

"Oh, hi, Tom. Nice of you to call."

Her sing-song voice made him growl. "The drink could be poisoned. Do you understand?"

"Yes, I'm feeling a little better. Can I call you back later? I have company right now."

"Kate, don't drink the tea."

"I won't forget."

Edward scowled. "Sounds like you two made up."

"Spare me. If I want him to help us figure out

who killed Daisy, I need to stay on his good side."

Tom winced. Acting, he told himself, but that didn't stop the way his chest deflated.

Edward dragged a chair to the side of her bed. "Molly and I hoped to convince you to let the investigation drop."

"Daisy was your aunt. Well, okay, she wasn't your aunt, but she was your friend. Don't you want to see her murderer brought to justice?"

"Not if you're going to get hurt in the process." Edward scrubbed his index finger under his nose.

"He's lying." Tom jabbed his dad's arm and pointed to the screen. "Look at the way he's leaning toward her and scratching his nose. The classic signs."

Kate set her cup on the bedside table. "I won't give up."

"But aren't you afraid her murderer might come after you?" Molly asked, her voice high and tight like that of a frightened mouse. She wrapped her arms around herself and shivered. "Detective Parker seemed to think the murderer caused your allergic reaction."

Kate glanced at the webcam. "Well, he knows better now."

Edward threw Molly a worried glance. "Kate, I've got to be honest with you. If the truth about my past comes out, I'm afraid of what might happen to"—he waved his finger between himself and Molly—"us. I could lose my job, possibly be arrested for assuming Edward's identity, or worse." Molly moved to his side, and he squeezed her hand. "We finally have a chance to be happy, and I guess we're asking you to give us that chance. What do you say?"

"Doesn't it bother you that Daisy's murderer would never pay for her crime?"

"Her?" Edward asked. "You think a woman killed Daisy?"

"She thinks a woman did it?" Tom hissed to his dad.

"Shh, listen."

"Statistically, men are more likely to use violent means to get rid of a person," Kate said with an authoritative tone that convinced even Tom. "Whereas women tend to choose methods like poison. Wouldn't you agree, Molly?"

"Me? How would I know?" Molly's gaze flitted around the room seemingly in search of a place to land. "I mean, I suppose it makes sense. But serving tea made from the wrong kind of marigold—is that really poisoning? Maybe it was just a mistake."

Once again Kate brought the cup to her lips and pretended to swallow.

At least, Tom prayed she was pretending.

"Mmm, this almost seems to have a coffee flavor. What all did you put in it?"

"Oh, you know." Molly fluttered her hand.

"Ginger, chamomile, all the herbs that have a calming effect."

"Castor bean too, I think."

Even on the small screen of the laptop, Tom could see Molly's face blanch. "Do you see that?" he said to his dad. "What's castor bean?"

Dad's eyes stayed glued to the image on the screen. "Comes from the castor-oil plant. It has palmlike leaves and a prickly fruit with seeds poking out of it. People grow them as ornamentals."

Tom drew in a quick breath. He'd seen a plant like that. He pressed his fingertips to his forehead, trying to squeeze the memory to the surface. The air he'd gulped must have gotten hijacked somewhere between his mouth and his brain, because he suddenly felt as woozy as Molly looked. "Is it toxic?"

"Deadly. Didn't they teach you this stuff in the FBI? The beanlike seeds contain ricin."

Edward helped Molly into a chair. "Are you okay? You look ill."

Slack-jawed, Tom stared at the screen. *Molly?* "What possible motive would Molly have had for killing Daisy?"

"If you shut up and listen, we might find out," Dad mumbled and pushed up the volume.

Tom snapped his fingers. "Now I remember. I saw a plant like that in Darryl and Beth's apartment. Kate has the wrong person."

Molly pressed her finger under her nose. "It's these hospital smells. They make me nauseous. Always have."

"Let me get you a bottle of water. I'll be right back." Edward disappeared from the view of the camera.

Kate wriggled herself a little higher in the bed. "You ground castor beans into Daisy's tea, didn't you?"

"No." Molly bolted to her feet. "I don't even know what castor beans are."

Dad chuckled. "For someone who doesn't know what they are, she's acting mighty offended."

Kate smoothed her blanket and continued speaking in the same tone she might use to chat about the weather. "Daisy doctored her tea with so much honey she never would have noticed the taste."

Molly's fingertips danced over her lips as if to keep the truth from escaping. She walked around the bed and snatched up Kate's cup.

"Why are you taking my drink away?"

Molly glanced at the half-open lid. "I thought you were done."

"But as you can see, I haven't begun."

Tom planted his fingers on the table and squinted at the screen. "What's Kate playing at? She's never going to get a confession out of anyone this way. Besides, Daisy didn't die from ricin."

Dad snorted. "How do you know? The coroner found the marigold toxin in Daisy's bloodstream, but that doesn't mean it killed her. You have to trust Kate. She knows what she's doing."

"Trust her? The woman has a death wish. If I don't stop her, she's going to end up like my partner." Tom jolted at the comparison.

"You must love Edward very much," Kate said softly.

"Yes?" Molly fussed with her engagement ring. "I mean yes. I do. No one else has ever really cared about *me*."

Tom's attention snapped back to the monitor.

Kate mirrored Molly's posture and movements —a strategy Tom often used himself to gain a suspect's trust. "Edward told me that your parents threatened to disown you if you married him, but I'm surprised you didn't turn against him after he accepted your parents' bribe."

"Oh, that's what they wanted. I knew he loved me, but he's so weak. Dad knew it too. I think he set Jim up as Edward Smythe here in Port Aster, certain he wouldn't be able to resist the con."

"Why did you follow him here if he's so weak?"

"I was mad. I wanted to teach him a lesson. He plays with people's lives all the time. He can't do that." Molly straightened the water pitcher and glass on the night table. "I told Daisy that Edward was conning her, but she wouldn't bring charges.

If she'd just reported him, he would have smartened up."

"You're saying Edward poisoned Daisy?"

"No. Stop twisting my words. Why can't you just let us be happy?"

"I'm trying to understand. You said you wanted to teach Edward a lesson. What do you mean by that?"

"Nothing." Molly's finger nervously skimmed the plastic lid of the teacup. "Like I said, I was sort of mad at him for leaving, that's all."

"You told Daisy about Edward so he would have to face the consequences of his lying?"

"Yes. That's all I wanted."

"But he told me you moved into the tiny apartment and took the waitress job to prove that you loved him more than your father's money."

"Yes. That's right. That's why I moved to Port Aster."

"Not to teach Edward a lesson?"

"Yes. That too. Both. I wanted both. Once I saw him again, I couldn't stay mad, especially after the way he clung to me following Daisy's death. He needs me."

"Did you think Edward's inheritance from Daisy would change your parents' minds about him? I imagine you overheard Daisy in the tea shop talking about changing her will."

"You can't be serious." Molly stretched out her arm, revealing a jewel-studded watch.

"Whoa!" Tom turned to his dad. "Just how rich are Molly's parents?"

Dad snorted. "Stinking rich."

"My watch is worth more than Daisy's entire estate," Molly said. "Why should I care if Edward gets her inheritance?"

"But you left your family and its money behind to prove to Edward that he's all you need." Kate smoothed her bedsheets, letting the contradiction sink in.

Tom grinned. *Oh, she's good.*

"Right?" Kate needled and looked Molly square in the eyes. "You've broken off all ties to your father? That's what Edward believes. So why is your father contacting you?"

"You don't know what you're talking about." Molly disappeared into the bathroom.

Kate glanced at the camera and lifted an eyebrow, as if to ask Tom and Keith how they thought she was doing.

The faint sound of the toilet flushing came through the microphone. A moment later, Molly reappeared minus the cup. She blew a wisp of hair from her eyes.

"Molly, I care about you." The anguish on Kate's face betrayed how torn she felt. "I understand how much you long to be loved. But are you sure Edward loves you for you? He's a con artist. Convincing women he loves them is what he does for a living."

A strange little smirk flitted across Molly's lips a second before Edward stepped into view of the camera.

He slapped a bottle of water onto the bedside table. "How dare you suggest I only love Molly for her money!"

Kate shrugged. "Isn't that what you do? Charm wealthy women out of their wealth?"

"I befriend them. I don't coerce them into sharing their wealth or adding me to their wills. And I certainly never killed anyone. Never."

In the adjoining room, Tom paced to the window and back. "We're getting nowhere. If she thinks Daisy died from ricin, we should be going after Darryl, not these two."

"Molly was in and out of the Kish apartment all the time," Dad said. "She could have easily helped herself to a few castor beans. Or given them to Edward."

"So you befriended Molly's aunt because she was already dying?" Kate grilled Edward. "Except you didn't know that she had no money of her own, right?"

Edward reached for Molly's hand. "Come on. Let's go."

Molly shied away from his grasp.

"Whoa." Tom pointed to the screen. "What was that in her hand? Did you see that? She shoved something into her jacket pocket."

Dad squinted at the image. "The cup, maybe."

"No, it looked like something long. Like a . . . syringe!" Tom raced for the door.

"Molly, what are you doing?" Edward's panicked shout shredded what little was left of Tom's self-control.

He skidded into the room just as Molly plunged the needle toward Kate's IV.

Kate ripped the tube from her arm as Edward dove for Molly's wrist.

She sidestepped and Edward careened into the wall. Whirling around to face Tom, Molly jabbed the still-full hypodermic toward him.

Patting the air with his hands, Tom slowly moved toward her. "Put down the needle. You don't want to do this." Behind him, he heard his dad tell someone to call the police.

"Stay back!" Molly shouted and stabbed at the air. "Or I swear I'll use it."

Hands still raised, Tom froze. "Stay calm. We don't want anyone to get hurt. What's in the needle?"

She smirked. "Ladder-to-heaven."

From the doorway, a nurse gasped. Kate backed herself against the headrest, her eyes fixed on the needle.

On the far side of the bed, Edward clambered to his feet. "Molly, what are you doing?"

"Protecting our future."

"Future? What kind of future will we have if you're in jail?"

"She'll ruin everything." Molly turned to face him fully. "She knows."

Edward's gaze flicked to Tom and back to the needle in his deranged fiancée's hand. The needle she now held dangerously close to Edward's chest. "Knows what, Molly?"

Tom signaled to Kate to get out, but she didn't see him.

Molly cupped Edward's cheek with her free hand. "Don't you know how much I love you? I'd do anything so we could be together."

Tom slipped closer to the bed and tugged at Kate's foot.

"I can't let her take you away from me." Molly lifted her hand and whirled toward Kate.

26

Images of her childhood, her first kiss, her friends, her family—her life—trounced across Kate's vision in silent cinematic Technicolor, ending with Tom's face telegraphing an urgent message. A message her fuzzy brain couldn't decipher.

Then suddenly the sound reel kicked in.

"Move!" Tom yelled.

Kate dove off the side of the hospital bed and

scrambled to her hands and knees. The IV pole toppled after her.

Keith scooped an arm around her waist and scuttled her toward the door.

Tom lunged for the syringe lodged in the mattress.

Edward grabbed Molly by the forearms and shook her mercilessly. "You? You killed Daisy?"

She struggled against his hold, her fiery gaze burning into Tom as he secured the evidence that would convict her.

Tom slapped a handcuff onto one of Molly's wrists, then pried her arms free from Edward's grip. "You're under arrest for the murder of Daisy Leacock and the attempted murder of Kate Adams."

Edward looked like he might be sick. "Why, Molly? You said you didn't care if I had money."

"I don't." She twisted and squirmed in the handcuffs. "This isn't what it looks like. You don't know my father."

Tom shoved her out the door. "Let's go."

Kate clutched a blanket over her hospital gown and, avoiding Molly's smug gaze, met Tom's eyes. "Thank you," she whispered.

Everyone from patients in hospital gowns to nurses in uniforms to visitors in street clothes crowded the hallway.

"Step aside, please," Tom shouted over the hullabaloo.

The crowd parted and Hank and a slew of uniformed officers raced up the hall toward them.

Tom handed Molly over to the chief. "Here's your murderer."

Molly wore her waitress uniform, and Hank skeptically looked her up and down. "The coffee girl?"

Molly lifted her chin. "The daughter of Jeremiah Gilmore." She paused long enough for the realization to sink in that she was the heiress to a diamond empire.

Tom's jaw dropped in sync with Hank's and the collective gasp of the gathered crowd.

Molly sniffed in that snooty way the very rich seem to master soon after birth. "There's not a judge in the country who'll believe I killed an old woman for money."

A chill shivered down Kate's spine. A chill that had nothing to do with her bare feet on the cold marble floor. With the money Molly had behind her, she'd make bail by morning. Then what might she do?

A head bobbed at the fringe of the crowd, a Jimmy Stewart–like mug Kate recognized from the features page of the *Port Aster Press*. He snapped a couple of photos of Molly with his cell phone and then pushed past the people lining the hall and shoved a digital voice recorder into Tom's face. "Sir, can you tell us how you solved the murder?"

"No comment." Tom clamped his jaw shut and marched Edward out of the hospital room and handed him over to Hank. "You'll want to question him too." Tom shot a sideways glance at the reporter and lowered his voice. "I'll fill you in at the station. My dad's getting the rest of the evidence."

Keith emerged from the adjacent room with the laptop and syringe.

The reporter jockeyed past Tom and Edward to get to Keith. "Sir, can you tell us what proof you have that Miss Gilmore committed mur—?"

An alarm sounded at the nurses' station. The crowd in the hall pressed their backs to the wall as nurses and doctors rushed past pushing portable machines. In the confusion, three officers hustled Molly, Edward, and Keith out of the building, away from the reporter's clutches. A fourth officer cordoned off Kate's room with crime scene tape.

As Kate looked at the yellow plastic tape crisscrossing the door—the same way Daisy's house had been cordoned off—the reality of how close she'd come to losing her life sunk in hard and fast. Her entire body shivered uncontrollably.

The spectators soon dispersed. But not the reporter. He hovered, a vulture scouting for its next prey.

"We'll need Miss Adams to come in too," the chief said to Tom. "As soon as the hospital okays her release."

That was all it took for Mr. Reporter to zero in on her. He snapped her photo with his cell phone and then swooped in front of her, voice recorder in hand.

Great. Just great. Not only had she become the number one enemy of the wealthiest family in the country, but thanks to Mr. Reporter and the inevitable media circus he'd stir up, the most unbecoming photo of her was about to be plastered across the evening news of every major city in North America.

Tom, her hero for the third time today, motioned to hospital security who quickly intercepted the vulture—definitely a vulture—and asked him to leave the premises.

She should have told them to confiscate his cell phone too.

A nurse brought Kate the clothes she'd arrived in and directed her to an empty room across the hall.

Concern blazed in Tom's eyes. A concern she'd have to decide how to respond to—sooner or later. Preferably later.

Kate pulled the blanket tighter around her shoulders. "I'll just get changed." She slipped into the hospital room and closed the door. The movement of her reflection in the bathroom mirror as she passed by made her jump. Scolding herself, she scrutinized her reflection.

No wonder Tom had looked so worried. Even

her lips were white. She looked like the blood had been sucked from her body and replaced with milk of magnesia.

She tugged on the string of her hospital gown, but the thing wouldn't untie. Her hands shook so badly she couldn't make her fingers work.

A tap sounded at the door. "Kate? You all right?"

"Yes." Her voice squeaked. She cleared her throat. "I'll just be another minute."

She yanked her pants on underneath her gown and then tried to shimmy the gown over her head, but the opening was too small. She twisted it around so she could see the knot in the mirror.

"Kate?" Tom called again, his tone more anxious than before.

"Almost done." She pried at the knot for another minute and steeled herself against the urge to believe his concern went deeper than that of a cop's for a victim.

For crying out loud, she was still working on forgiving him for arresting her. What was she doing letting a little chivalrous behavior get her all muddleheaded?

She gave the string one hard yank, ripping it from the gown, and quickly finished dressing. Her confidence had long ago leached away, but when she opened the door, she managed to lift her chin and say in a voice that warbled only a fraction. "I need to grab my purse and then—"

She made the mistake of meeting Tom's gaze.

The worry radiating from his red-streaked eyes unraveled what little grasp she had left on her emotions.

"It's okay." He gathered her into his arms. "You're okay. You did good."

The gentleness of his touch and tenderness in his voice unleashed the emotions she'd tried so hard to dam.

Beneath her cheek, his shirt grew damp. His heart ker-thumped a little too loud and a little too fast.

After a long while, he pulled back and cradled her face in his hands. "If you ever pull another stunt like that, I'll slap the handcuffs on you and haul you into jail so fast your head will spin."

She planted her hands on her hips. "On what charge?"

"Trying to kill *me!*"

Tom's cell phone rang, breaking the sudden silence in the hospital hallway.

"Son, you better get down here."

"On my way." Tom hurried Kate out of the hospital and to his car, trying to ignore the way her scent clung to his shirt. When she'd let him gather her into his arms, emotions overwhelmed him—anger and horror at how close her crazy plan had come to costing her life, and relief that she was safe.

Her surrender to his touch gave him hope that

they might find a way back to the friendship they'd started, but he knew better than to take advantage of her vulnerable state. He just wished he hadn't resorted to humor to end their embrace. He didn't know what to make of her stunned silence afterward.

He'd take up the crazy plan part with her later. Tom shifted the car into gear and headed for the station. Glancing at Kate, he noticed her smile. "What's up?"

"The sky seems brighter somehow. Don't you think?" she said, her gaze on the passing scenery. "Look at those tulips. Have you ever seen such vibrant colors?"

He chuckled. He'd experienced the exact same hyperawareness the first time he'd looked death square in the eyes and lived to tell about it. Unfortunately, he needed to cut in on her reverie and get some answers before he faced Molly's high-priced lawyers.

"Do you know what Molly had in that syringe?"

"Ladder-to-heaven is another name for lily of the valley."

"Is it as lethal as it sounds?"

"Its bulbs are very toxic when ingested. Experts claim that even water holding the cut flowers becomes toxic. Maybe that's what she loaded in the needle, but I doubt it."

"Why?"

"She didn't try that hard to conceal what she

was doing, which tells me that she expected the poison to act instantly."

At her detached tone, as if they weren't talking about her life, he ached to pull her back into his arms. Instead, he tried to match it. "She must've been counting on Edward not turning her in."

"That too," Kate said softly.

"The lab will tell us what's in the needle. The fact she brought it with her proves premeditation."

"My guess is potassium. If she'd managed to push it into my IV, it would've stopped my heart instantly."

Tom's heart lurched at the thought. "How would she have known that, let alone gotten ahold of some? More likely she was counting on her lily of the valley water being more potent than it is, especially if injected directly into the bloodstream."

"Maybe, but she was a pharmacology student before she quit to nurse her dying aunt."

"Is that what made you suspect her?"

Kate shifted her gaze to the road ahead. "At Sumpner's Falls, Edward told me that Molly's dad bribed Edward to disappear, and that Molly defied her parents to fight for their love. But I'd overheard her talking to her dad on her cell phone the day after her engagement. She'd said something like, 'Everything is going perfectly.' If she were at odds with her parents, she wouldn't talk to them that way."

Tom took the highway to expedite the return trip to Port Aster. "So why didn't you let me arrest Edward at Sumpner's Falls?"

"I didn't remember the phone conversation at the time. It wasn't until yesterday that I realized Edward's story didn't add up. Then I had to devise a way to figure out if Molly and Edward were in on the murder together."

"Whoa. Back up. What made you think Molly was behind the murder?"

"Her dad called her on the tea shop phone."

Tom's face must've registered his confusion because Kate looked at him as if he were thicker than a tree.

"A call on the shop phone instead of her cell phone meant her dad knew she was in Port Aster. If he'd bribed Edward to stay away from his daughter and then found out she'd run off to the same town, I figured they wouldn't have cheery conversations about how perfect everything was going unless he knew why Molly was really here."

Tom scrunched his face, trying to make sense of what Kate was saying. He shook his head. "I'm not following you. Edward lied about why he was here, but you still suspected Molly?"

"No, he didn't lie. Weren't you listening? She came here for revenge. That's why her dad didn't stop her. And what better way to make Edward pay for hurting her than to make him go to jail for a murder he didn't commit?"

Tom slanted a glance her way. "I think all that adrenaline shooting through your brain is misfiring a few cells. The woman almost killed you to keep *you* from sending Edward to jail."

"Sure, because after Daisy died Edward turned to Molly for comfort and she realized how much she still loved him. When the police declared Daisy's death a suicide, everything turned out hunky-dory for them until I came along and messed up their happily ever after."

"So when the journal surfaced and we figured out Edward was an alias, she hired a kid to impersonate Gord to implicate *you* in the murder, instead of Edward."

"Yeah, but I can't figure out how Molly knew about Gord."

"That's my fault. The night I was at the Pizza Shack, she heard me mention I was looking for him."

"And she probably asked Edward who he was."

Tom exited the highway and took the mountain access road south. He drummed his thumbs on the steering wheel. "How can we be sure they didn't plan the murder together? If Gilmore cut Molly off, her expensive baubles would last only so long and then they'd need money. Daisy's money."

"You saw Edward tackle Molly in the hospital room. He was horrified by her admission."

"Or he's a good actor." Tom rounded the police

station and parked in the back lot. "Don't worry, we'll figure this out. I need to take over Molly's interrogation, so another officer will take your statement. Just tell her everything you told me."

Keith met them in the hall. "We reviewed the video from Kate's hospital room. Molly didn't actually confess to Daisy's murder. She told Edward that she'd do anything so they could be together. She now claims that she was talking about stopping Kate from exposing Edward's past."

Kate took a step back, her hand reaching blindly for the wall. "But she said I'd ruin everything because of what I knew."

Tom squeezed Kate's arm. "Don't worry. We've got her. We'll hold her on the attempted murder charge while we piece together a case against her for Daisy's murder."

Tom left Kate with Dad and joined Hank in the room adjoining the interrogation room. On the other side of the two-way mirror, Molly sat next to a smug-faced lawyer who by the look of his Armani suit raked in a grand an hour. Tom shot Hank a questioning look. No way was Molly's lawyer gonna let her talk.

"They're up to something," Hank said, watching Molly through the glass.

Tom leaned against the back wall, crossed one leg over the other, and folded his arms over his chest.

"My client wishes to make a statement," the lawyer said in a blue-blood accent straight out of Boston.

"This ought to be good," Hank grunted.

"Go ahead, Miss Gilmore," the detective inside the interrogation room said.

Molly conferred with her lawyer in a whisper, then cleared her throat. "I'm sorry for threatening Miss Adams. I didn't want her to get my fiancé in trouble. I wouldn't have really hurt her. I just wanted to scare her into backing down."

"So you're saying your fiancé, Edward Smythe, also known as Jim Crump, killed Miss Leacock?"

She glanced at her lawyer.

"My client has nothing further to say." The man picked up his notebook and pushed to his feet.

"Wait," Molly cried out. "I put the bad marigolds in Daisy's tea. She called an order in to the shop and I mixed a few of the wrong type in."

"That's enough," the lawyer ordered.

Molly ignored him. "I didn't mean for her to die." A smirk teased the corners of her lips. "*If* that's what she died from. I just wanted her to get sick so she'd realize I was telling her the truth about Edward."

Tom uncrossed his legs and kicked a foot back against the wall. "She's confessing to manslaughter so we'll drop murder one."

"At least you've got a confession," Hank said.

"You saw her smirk when she added '*if* that's what she died from.'" Tom flicked his hand toward the two-way mirror. "Kate's been telling us for more than a week that tagete wouldn't kill anyone. And she's the expert. Her lawyer will have a cakewalk convincing the jury that there's no proof. Or he'll argue that she lied in a desperate attempt to protect Edward."

"So we hammer hard on the attempted murder charge. We have a roomful of witnesses and a syringe with her fingerprints on it. One way or the other she'll do her time."

"I want a search warrant on her apartment before her slimy lawyers have a chance to clear out any evidence. Or plant it."

Tom took a deep breath, pasted on what he hoped would pass for a smile, and opened the door to the hallway.

Dad and Kate looked at him expectantly.

"We have our confession."

Kate lifted her arms in a V and let out a whoop.

Tom averted his gaze, not wanting Kate to see his doubts that they'd see justice served.

"What aren't you telling us?" Dad asked.

Tom's jaw clenched. He shot his dad a glare. "She claims she only wanted to make Daisy sick."

"A jury won't buy that," Kate exclaimed confidently. "Ricin's too deadly."

Tom steered them toward a quiet corner. "She

didn't admit to giving Daisy ricin, only tagete."

"But you saw how she reacted when I accused her of lacing the tea with ricin."

"Yeah, but we don't have proof, and she knows it." Tom let out a heavy sigh. "With no criminal record and a father who has money to burn, she'll likely get off pretty light." He squeezed Kate's shoulder. "But you accomplished what you set out to prove—your friend didn't kill herself."

Kate shrank from his touch, tears springing to her eyes. "It's not enough."

Epilogue

Kate drove slowly along the curving roadways through the cemetery. The grass was a lush green, the sky a brilliant blue—a perfect day for planting flowers. After she finished here, she'd get started on the memorial garden in front of the research station. Kate smiled. Daisy would have gotten a kick out of all the different varieties of marigolds Kate intended to plant in her memory.

The song on the car radio cut out. "Lawyers for Molly Gilmore, only daughter of diamond tycoon Jeremiah Gilmore, today demanded attempted murder charges against their client be dropped after key evidence in the case went missing," the newscaster said. "The judge denied the request, citing sufficient eyewitness testimony to proceed. The police continue to withhold the name of the victim, but CZN news has learned that she is Kate Adams, an associate of Daisy Leacock, the research scientist whose suspicious death remains under investigation. In other news, GPC Pharmaceuticals has—"

Kate snapped off the radio. She should've known her anonymity wouldn't last. Now the media would be hounding her *and* Edward. Kate reached the end of the roadway and touched the brakes. *Which way?*

She backtracked twice, trying to find the side drive that passed by Daisy's grave. Finally she located the place, grabbed her trowel and tray of flowers from the trunk, and set to work. As she planted, she talked. "I wish you could hear me, Daisy. I saw Edward today. What you did for him—putting his real name in your will—made a big impression, but after Molly's betrayal I'm not sure how he'll be. He really loved her."

Molly must have loved him too, or she would have stuck to her original plan of revenge and twisted her testimony to make him look guilty.

Kate shook away the thought. Molly didn't deserve her pity.

Kate reflected on her earlier conversation with Edward as he'd helped move her boxes into Daisy's house, her house now. She didn't feel right about accepting the house when Daisy had left it to him, but Edward had insisted. That alone convinced Kate he'd changed. If he hadn't wanted to stick around town, he could have sold the house and pocketed the proceeds. But he'd refused to consider the possibility.

"I reminded him what you wrote in your journal, that you wanted to show him God's love in a tangible way," Kate said aloud. "That even though he lied, you wanted to prove you loved and accepted the person he really was.

"He seemed skeptical, but at least he kept your Bible. That's a start. I wonder if he'll ever come back. He said he had to get away for a while. The news teams have been relentless."

Kate pried a bright orange marigold from the flat and set it in place in front of the stone. "Everything that's been going on got me thinking about Dad. How all these years I've been afraid to find out what really happened. I know. I know. After Mom died, you told me the time had come, that the truth would set me free, but I wasn't ready."

Unfortunately, now that the media had figured out she was Molly's intended victim, it was only a matter of time before they ferreted out the family dirt, especially with GPC Pharmaceuticals moving to the area. What a nightmare.

If she hoped to neutralize the collateral damage, she needed to be armed with the truth, whether she was ready to hear it or not. *Hear* it. The thought twigged a memory. The creepy phone message from weeks ago replayed in her mind. *Kate Baxter . . . I think you'll want to talk to me.*

Shivers tingled down her spine. Thankfully, the caller with the horror-flick voice hadn't bothered her again. But she would investigate.

Of course, she could start by asking Tom. After finding out about her name change, he'd probably scoured the public records to puzzle out her secret.

Except . . . she wasn't ready to face him again. Not just yet. Between Julie's wedding and the move, brushing off Tom's attempts to see her hadn't been difficult.

Kate sat back on her heels and kneaded the warm earth between her fingers. "I miss you, Daisy. I miss you so very much. I wish you could have met Tom. Well, I guess you knew him since he grew up here. I couldn't have caught Molly without him and his dad."

"Nice to be appreciated."

Kate toppled onto her backside at the deep masculine voice and sent her trowel flying.

Tom chuckled.

"Don't scare me like that. Especially in a cemetery."

He picked up the trowel and offered her a hand. "I'm sorry. I was visiting my mom's grave and noticed your car. How are you doing?"

She brushed the dirt from her pants. "Okay, considering."

"You heard the noon news, I take it?"

"Yeah, my five seconds of fame. Yee haw."

"We can hope that's all it lasts."

"Are you *trying* to cheer me up? 'Cause you're not very good at it."

"How about giving me a chance to practice? Say, dinner tonight?"

"Dinner?" She squatted in front of the flowers she'd planted and smoothed the dirt around them. "Um, sure. Dinner sounds good."

She might even scrounge up the courage to ask about her dad's arrest.

What Is Calendula?

Calendula officinalis, commonly known as pot marigold, is an easy-to-grow perennial flower (annual in colder climates). Since the time of the ancient Egyptians, it has been used for everything from medicinal purposes to an inexpensive substitute for saffron to flavor stews. Tea lovers must be careful not to confuse calendula marigolds with the common tagete variety often sold in garden centers. Some varieties of tagete are toxic and all are inedible.

Although calendula is popular with herbal medicine practitioners, as with many natural remedies, little scientific evidence exists to substantiate the benefits offered by calendula tea. However, the friend who passed on this recipe to me (the inspiration for *Deadly Devotion* when I learned not all marigolds are created equal) acquired the recipe from her grandmother in Germany and has drunk the tea for years. She enjoys the taste and has experienced a number of the benefits often attributed to its use.

Benefits of calendula tea include: contains vitamins A and C; helps prevent infection and inflammation (thanks to flavonoids); promotes healthier skin; relieves sore throats; reduces fevers; detoxifies, prevents, or relieves stomach problems; eases menstrual cramps and menopausal hot flashes.

How to dry the petals: Always choose organically grown plants when collecting petals, and wait until the blossoms are fully open. The blossoms may be left whole, but for faster drying, pry apart the petals and spread them on a cookie sheet. Place in a warm, dry area, out of direct sunlight, with good air circulation. Allow several days to dry, turning the petals several times a day. When completely dry, a folded petal will break rather than bend. Dried petals should be stored in an airtight glass jar in a cool, dry place.

Recipe for Calendula Tea

2 teaspoons dried calendula flower petals
1 cup of boiling water

Place calendula petals in an infuser and pour 1 cup of boiled water over the petals. Allow the calendula to steep for 10–15 minutes. Then enjoy.

Calendula petals picked later in the year may be bitter; if so, sweeten with honey. Calendula can be infused with other herbs for added benefits.

About the Author

Sandra Orchard is an award-winning Canadian author of inspirational romantic suspense whose novels include *Deep Cover*, *Shades of Truth*, and *Critical Condition*. She enjoys doing research for her books, such as attending the Writers' Police Academy for hands-on training and simulations at a police training facility, almost as much as she enjoys writing them. When not playing cops and robbers, she lives with her husband of more than twenty-five years in Niagara, Ontario, Canada, where their favorite pastime is playing with their first grandchild. Learn more and find special bonus features for her books, such as deleted scenes and location pictures, at

www.SandraOrchard.com,
or connect with Sandra at
www.facebook.com/SandraOrchard.

Center Point Large Print
600 Brooks Road / PO Box 1
Thorndike ME 04986-0001 USA

(207) 568-3717

US & Canada:
1 800 929-9108
www.centerpointlargeprint.com